Wars of the Roses

MARGARET OF ANJOU

ALSO BY CONN IGGULDEN

THE WARS OF THE ROSES SERIES
Stormbird

THE EMPEROR SERIES
The Gates of Rome
The Death of Kings
The Field of Swords
The Gods of War
The Blood of Gods

THE CONQUEROR SERIES
Wolf of the Plains
Lords of the Bow
Bones of the Hills
Empire of Silver
Conqueror

Blackwater
Quantum of Tweed

BY CONN IGGULDEN AND HAL IGGULDEN
The Dangerous Book for Boys
The Pocket Dangerous Book for Boys: Things to Do
The Pocket Dangerous Book for Boys: Things to Know
The Dangerous Book for Boys Yearbook

BY CONN IGGULDEN AND DAVID IGGULDEN
The Dangerous Book of Heroes

BY CONN IGGULDEN AND
ILLUSTRATED BY LIZZY DUNCAN
Tollins: Explosive Tales for Children
Tollins 2: Dynamite Tales

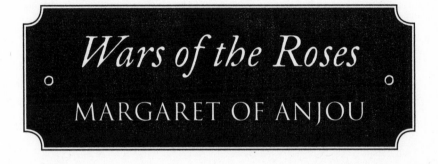

Wars of the Roses
MARGARET OF ANJOU

Conn Iggulden

G. P. PUTNAM'S SONS
New York

PUTNAM

G. P. Putnam's Sons
Publishers Since 1838
An imprint of Penguin Random House LLC
375 Hudson Street
New York, New York 10014

Originally published in the United Kingdom by Michael Joseph, Penguin Group UK,
A Penguin Random House Company.

ISBN 978-0-399-16537-5

Printed in the United States of America
1   3   5   7   9   10   8   6   4   2

Book design by Gretchen Achilles

Endpaper map and battle plan copyright © Andrew Farmer, 2014

To Victoria Hobbs, who tilts at windmills—
and knocks them down

Acknowledgments

I am intensely grateful to the staff at Penguin Random House for producing such beautiful books—and then persuading people to "try a bit of medieval." If you have picked this up to read, or, for that matter, downloaded it, I thank you too. Much has changed. Much remains the same. Finally, I must mention my son Cameron, who came up with the title at the eleventh hour.

Maps and Family Trees

Maps

Family Trees

List of Characters

England at the time of the Wars of the Roses

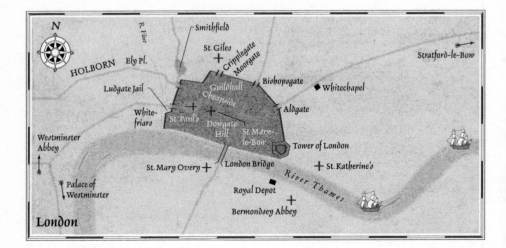

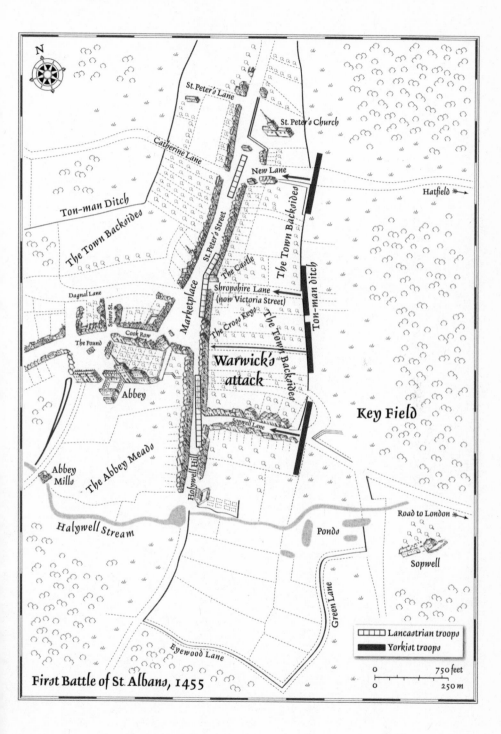

N

St. Peter's Lane

Catherine Lane

St. Peter's Church

New Lane

Hatfield →

Ton-man Ditch

The Town Backsides

The Town Backsides

Ton-man ditch

St. Peter's Street

The Castle

Shropshire Lane
(now Victoria Street)

Dagnal Lane

The Cross Keys

The Town Backsides

Spicer St.

Cook Row

Marketplace

**Warwick's
attack**

The Pound

Key Field

Abbey

Soppwell Lane

The Abbey Meads

Holywell Hill

Abbey
Mills

Road to London →

Halywell Stream

Ponds

Sopwell

Green Lane

Eyewood Lane

First Battle of St. Albans, 1455

⊞⊞⊞ Lancastrian troops
▬ Yorkist troops

0   750 feet
0   250 m

Royal Lines of England

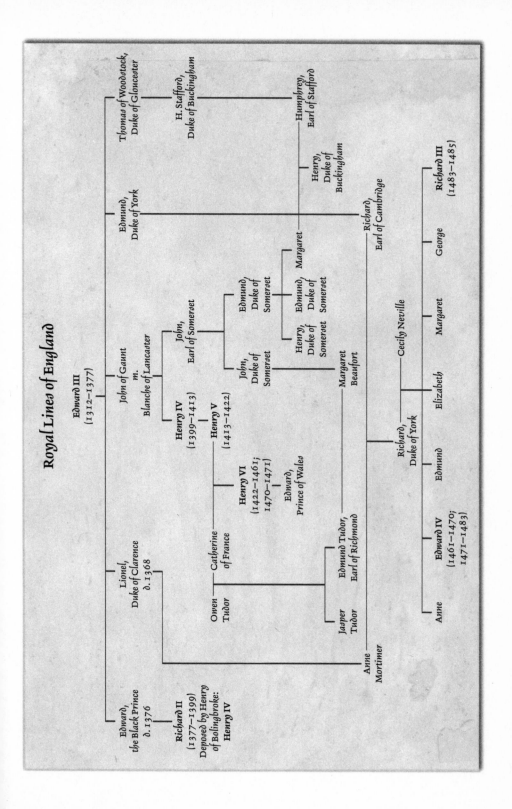

House of Lancaster

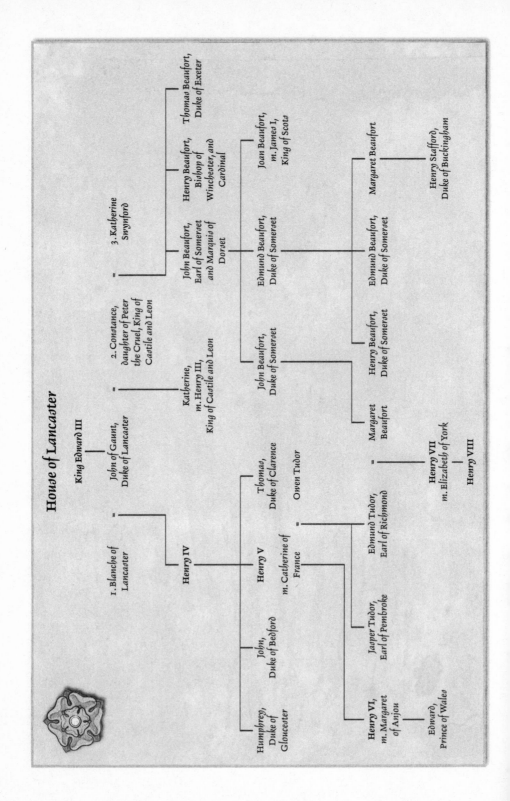

House of York

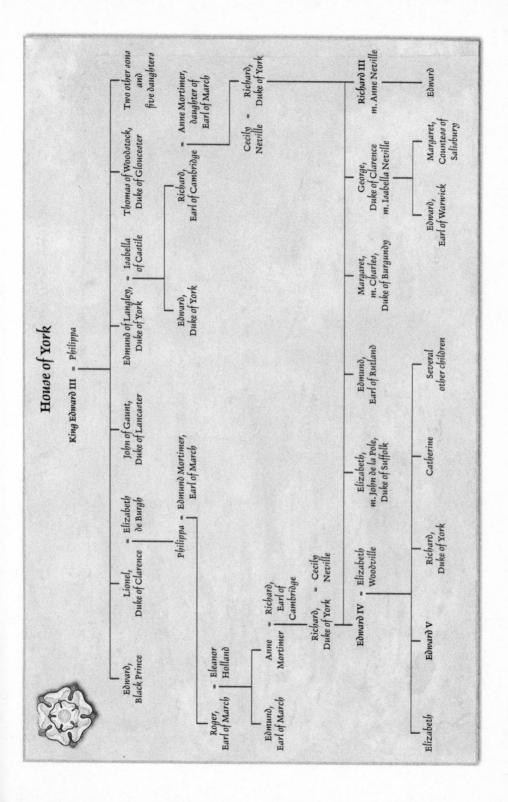

House of Neville

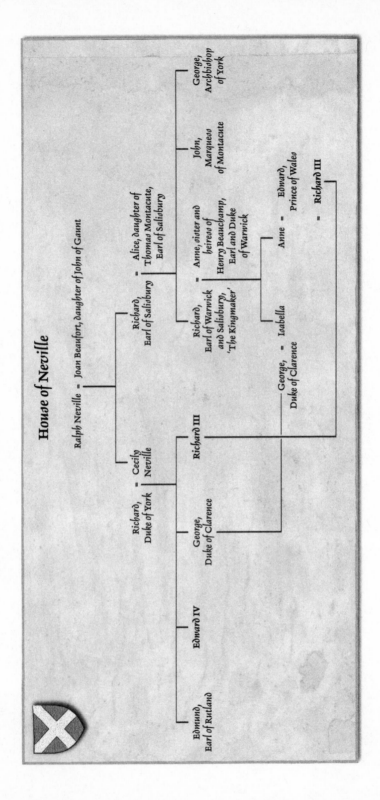

Ralph Neville = Joan Beaufort, daughter of John of Gaunt

Richard, Duke of York = Cecily Neville

Richard, Earl of Salisbury = Alice, daughter of Thomas Montacute, Earl of Salisbury

Edmund, Earl of Rutland

Edward IV

George, Duke of Clarence

Richard III

Richard, Earl of Warwick and Salisbury, 'The Kingmaker' = Anne, sister and heiress of Henry Beauchamp, Earl and Duke of Warwick

John, Marquess of Montacute

George, Archbishop of York

George, Duke of Clarence = Isabella

Anne = Edward, Prince of Wales

= Richard III

House of Percy

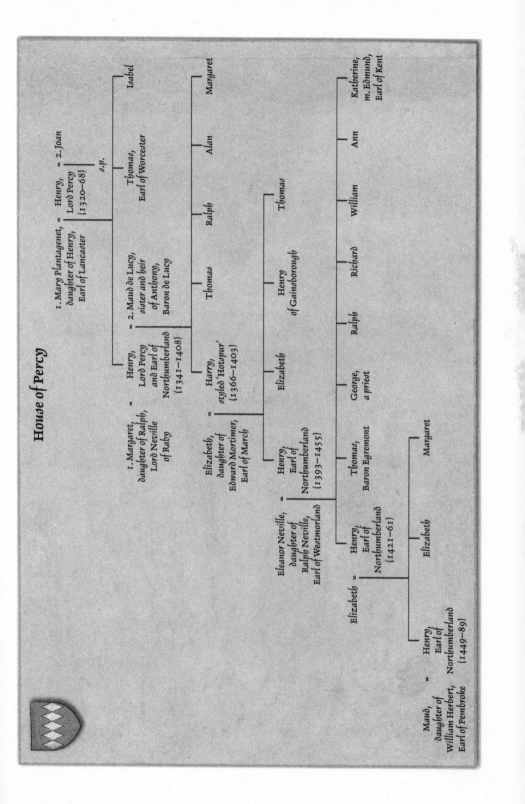

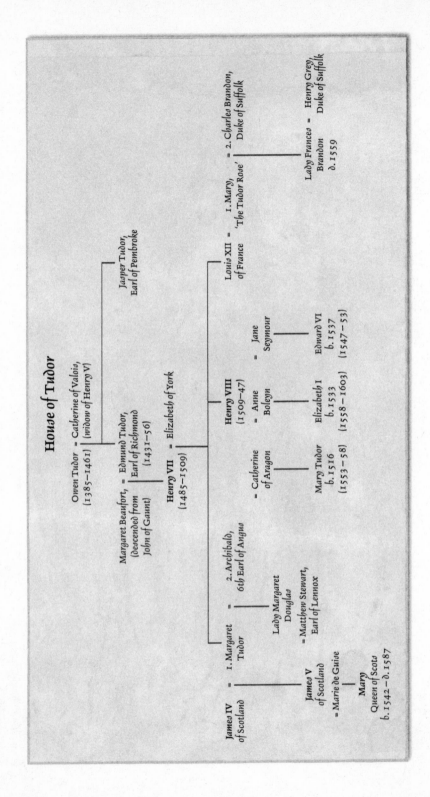

House of Tudor

LIST OF CHARACTERS

MASTER ALLWORTHY Royal physician to Henry VI

ALPHONSE Mute servant to Vicomte Michel Gascault

MARGARET OF ANJOU/QUEEN MARGARET Daughter of René of Anjou, wife of Henry VI

JAMES TUCHET, BARON AUDLEY Veteran soldier and commander of the Queen's Gallants

SAUL BERTLEMAN (BERTLE) Mentor of Derihew Brewer

DERIHEW (DERRY) BREWER Spymaster of Henry VI

HUMPHREY STAFFORD, DUKE OF BUCKINGHAM Supporter of Henry VI

CARTER Horseman in the retinue of Richard Neville, Earl of Salisbury

CHARLES VII King of France, uncle of Henry VI

JOHN CLIFFORD, BARON CLIFFORD Son of Thomas de Clifford

THOMAS DE CLIFFORD, BARON CLIFFORD Supporter of Henry VI

WILLIAM CRIGHTON, LORD CRIGHTON Scottish nobleman who arranged the marriage of James II and Mary of Guelders

RALPH CROMWELL, BARON CROMWELL Chamberlain of the Household to Henry VI

MAUD CROMWELL (NÉE STANHOPE) Niece and heiress of Baron Cromwell

SIR ROBERT DALTON Swordsman and sparring partner of Edward, Earl of March

ANDREW DOUGLAS Scottish laird and ally of Henry VI

THOMAS PERCY, BARON EGREMONT Son of Henry Percy, Earl of
    Northumberland

HENRY HOLLAND, DUKE OF EXETER Son-in-law of Richard, Duke of York

JOHN FAUCEBY Royal physician to Henry VI

WILLIAM NEVILLE, LORD FAUCONBERG Brother of Earl of Salisbury

SIR JOHN FORTESCUE Chief Justice of the King's Bench

FOWLER Soldier at Battle of St. Albans

VICOMTE MICHEL GASCAULT French ambassador to the English court

SIR HOWARD GAVERICK Bondsman knight in the service of Earl of Warwick

SILENT GODWIN Franciscan friar

EDMUND GRAY, BARON GRAY OF RUTHIN Supporter of Henry VI

MARY OF GUELDERS Wife of James II of Scotland

WILLIAM HATCLYF Royal physician to Henry VI

HENRY VI King of England, son of Henry V

HOBBS Sergeant-at-arms, Windsor

SQUIRE JAMES Scout for Henry VI's army at Battle of St. Albans

JAMESON Blacksmith and sparring partner of Edward, Earl of March

EDWARD PLANTAGENET, EARL OF MARCH Son of Richard, Duke of York

SIR JOHN NEVILLE, Son of Earl of Salisbury, brother to Warwick

JOHN DE MOWBRAY, DUKE OF NORFOLK Supporter of Henry VI

HENRY PERCY, EARL OF NORTHUMBERLAND Head of Percy family and
    defender of the border with Scotland

ELEANOR NEVILLE, COUNTESS OF NORTHUMBERLAND Wife of Henry
    Percy, sister of Earl of Salisbury

WILLIAM OLDHALL Chancellor and supporter of Richard, Duke of York

JASPER TUDOR, EARL OF PEMBROKE Half brother of Henry VI

BROTHER PETER Franciscan friar

RANKIN Manservant to Richard Neville, Earl of Salisbury

EDMUND TUDOR, EARL OF RICHMOND Half brother of Henry VI

EDMUND PLANTAGENET, EARL OF RUTLAND Son of Richard, Duke
    of York

RICHARD NEVILLE, EARL OF SALISBURY Head of Neville family, grandson of John of Gaunt

ALICE MONTAGU, COUNTESS OF SALISBURY Wife of Richard Neville, Earl of Salisbury

THOMAS DE SCALES, BARON SCALES Commander of the royal garrison in the Tower of London

MICHAEL SCRUTON Serjeant surgeon to Henry VI

EDMUND BEAUFORT, EARL, THEN DUKE OF SOMERSET Supporter of Henry VI

HENRY BEAUFORT, DUKE OF SOMERSET Son of Edmund Beaufort, supporter of Henry VI

WILLIAM DE LA POLE, DUKE OF SUFFOLK Soldier and courtier who arranged the marriage of Henry VI and Margaret of Anjou

WILFRED TANNER Smuggler and friend of Derry Brewer

SIR WILLIAM TRESHAM Speaker of the House of Commons

ANDREW TROLLOPE Captain of Earl of Warwick's Calais garrison

TRUNNING Swordmaster to Henry Percy, Earl of Northumberland

OWEN TUDOR Second husband of Catherine de Valois (widow of Henry V)

RICHARD NEVILLE, EARL OF WARWICK Son of Earl of Salisbury, later known as the Kingmaker

EDWARD OF WESTMINSTER Prince of Wales, son of Henry VI

RICHARD PLANTAGENET, DUKE OF YORK Head of house of York, great-grandson of Edward III

CECILY NEVILLE, DUCHESS OF YORK Wife of Richard, Duke of York, granddaughter of John of Gaunt

PROLOGUE

Vicomte Michel Gascault was certainly not a spy. He would have scorned the name if he had heard it used of him. Of course it went without saying that the French ambassador to the English court would report anything of interest to his monarch on his return. It was also true that Vicomte Gascault had considerable experience in the royal palaces of Europe as well as the field of war. He knew what King Charles of France might want to know and, with that in mind, Vicomte Gascault took careful note of all that went on around him, little though it was. Spies were grubby, low-born men, given to hiding in doorways and hissing secret passwords at each other. Vicomte Gascault, *d'un autre côté*—"on the other hand," as the English said—was a gentleman of France, as far above such things as the sun above the earth.

Those and similar thoughts were all he had to amuse him in his idle hours. He was certain to mention to King Charles how he had been ignored for three full days, left to kick his heels in a sumptuous chamber in the Palace of Westminster. The servants sent to attend his person were not even well washed, he had noticed, though they came promptly enough. One of them positively reeked of horse and urine, as if he found his usual employment in the royal stables.

Still, it was true Gascault's bodily needs were met, even if his ambassadorial ones were not. Each day began with his own retainers dressing him in the most gorgeous raiments and cloaks he possessed, choosing them from among the garments pressed into the enormous trunks he had brought from France. He had not yet been forced to repeat a combination of colors and if he had overheard one of the English scullions refer to him as the "French Peacock," it bothered him not at all. Bright colors raised his mood and he had precious little else to while away the time. He did not like to think of the food they set out for him. It was clear enough that they had engaged a French cook; equally as clear that the man had no love of his countrymen. Gascault shuddered at the thought of some of the flaccid things that had appeared at his table.

The hours crept by like a funeral and he had long ago read every scrap of his official papers. By the light of a candle-lamp, he turned at last to a dun-colored book in his possession, marked throughout with his notes and comments. *De Sacra Coena* by Berengarius had become a favorite of Gascault's. The treatise on the Last Supper had been banned by the Church, of course. Any argument that strayed into the mysteries of body and blood brought the attention of Papal hounds.

Gascault had long been in the habit of seeking out books destined for the fire, to set his thoughts aflame in turn. He rubbed his hands over the wrappings. The original cover had been stripped and burned to ashes, of course, with those ashes carefully crumbled so that no questing hand could ever guess what they had once been. The rough, stained leather was a sad necessity in an age where men took such delight in denouncing each other to their masters.

The summons, when it came at last, interrupted his reading. Gascault was used to the booming bell that rang each hour and half hour, startling him from sleep and spoiling his digestion at least as much as the poor pigeons that lay so limply on his dinner platter. He had kept no count but still knew it was late when the horse-servant, as he thought of him, came rushing into the rooms.

"Viscount Gas-cart, you are summoned," the boy said.

Gascault gave no sign of irritation at the way he mangled a proud name. The boy was surely a simpleton and the Good Lord expected mercy for those poor fellows, set among their betters to teach compassion, or so Gascault's mother had always said. With care, he laid his book on the arm of the chair and rose. His steward, Alphonse, was only a step behind the lad. Gascault let his eyes drift back to the book, knowing it would be enough of a signal for his servant to keep it from other hands in his absence. Alphonse nodded sharply, bowing low while the horse-boy stared in confusion at the dumb show between the two men.

Vicomte Gascault strapped on his sword and allowed Alphonse to drape his yellow cloak around his shoulders. When his gaze dropped once more to the chair, the book had somehow vanished. Truly, his servant was the soul of discretion and not simply because he lacked a tongue. Gascault inclined his head in thanks and swept out behind the boy, passing through the outer rooms and into the chilly corridor beyond.

A party of five men awaited him there. Four of them were evidently soldiers, wearing a royal tabard over mail. The last wore a cloak and tunic over hose, all as thick and well made as his own.

"Vicomte Michel Gascault?" the man said.

Gascault noted the perfect pronunciation and smiled.

"I have that honor. I am at your service . . . ?"

"Richard Neville, Earl of Salisbury and lord chancellor. I must apologize for the late hour, but you are expected, my lord, in the royal chambers."

Gascault fell easily into step at the man's side, ignoring the soldiers clattering along in their wake. He had known stranger things than a midnight meeting in his career.

"To see the king?" he asked mischievously, watching the earl closely. Salisbury was not a young man, though he seemed wiry and in good health to the Frenchman's eyes. It would not do to reveal how much the court of France knew of King Henry's poor health.

"I am sorry to report that His Royal Highness, King Henry, is suffering with an ague, a temporary illness. I hope you will take no offense, but I am to bring you to the Duke of York this evening."

"My lord Salisbury, I am so *very* sorry to hear such a thing," Gascault replied, letting the words spill out. He saw Salisbury's eyes tighten just a fraction and had to repress a smile. They both knew there were families in the English court with strong ties to France, whether by blood or titles. The idea that the French king would not know every detail of King Henry's collapse was a game to be played between them and nothing more. The English king had been near senseless for months, fallen so deeply into a stupor that he could not be raised to life. It was not for nothing that his lords had appointed one of their number as "Protector and Defender of the Realm." Richard, Duke of York, was king in all but name and, in truth, Vicomte Gascault had no interest in meeting a royal lost in his dreaming. He had been sent to judge the strength of the English court and their willingness to defend their interests. Gascault allowed his pleasure to sparkle in his eyes for just an instant before snuffing the emotion. If he reported that they were weak and lost without King Henry, Gascault's word alone would bring a hundred ships from France, to raid and burn every English port. The English had done the same to

France for long enough, he reminded himself. Perhaps it was time at last that the devil had his due of them as well.

Salisbury led the small group along an endless stretch of corridors, then climbed two flights of stairs to the royal apartments on the floors above. Even at such a late hour, the Palace of Westminster was ablaze with lamps set just a few paces apart. Yet Gascault could smell damp in the air, a reek of ancient mold from having the river so close. As they reached the final, guarded door, he had to control the desire to straighten his cloak and collar one last time. Alphonse would not have let him leave with anything awry.

The soldiers were dismissed and the door opened by guards within. Salisbury extended his hand to allow the ambassador to enter before him.

"After you, Vicomte," he said. His eyes were sharp, Gascault realized, as he bowed and went in. The man missed nothing and he reminded himself to be wary of him. The English were many things: venal, short-tempered, greedy, a whole host of sins. No one had ever called them stupid, however, not in all the history of the world. If God would only make it so! King Charles would have their towns and castles in his grip in just a single generation.

Salisbury closed the door softly at his back and Vicomte Gascault found himself in a smaller room than he had expected. Perhaps it was only right that a "Protector and Defender" would not allow himself the trappings of a royal court, yet the stillness of that room made a shudder pass down Gascault's back. The windows were black with the night outside and the man who rose to greet him was dressed in the same color, almost lost in the shadows of low-burning lamps as he came forward.

Richard, Duke of York, extended his hand, beckoning Gascault further into the room. The Frenchman felt his hackles stand up in superstitious fear, though he showed no sign of his discomfort. As he stepped forward, he glanced behind, seeing nothing stranger than Salisbury watching him steadily.

"Vicomte Gascault, I am York. It is my pleasure to welcome you and a source of great distress that I must send you home so soon."

"*Milord?*" Gascault asked in confusion. He sat where York gestured and gathered his wits as the man took a seat across the wide table. The English duke was clean-shaven, square-jawed, and yet slim enough in his black. As Gascault stared, York pushed loose hair off his forehead with one hand. He tilted his head as he did so, yet his eyes never left Gascault's own.

"I'm afraid I do not understand, my lord York. Forgive me, I have not yet learned the correct term of address for a Protector and Defender." Gascault looked around for some sign of wine, or food, but there was nothing in sight, just the deep golden oak of the table, stretching bare before him.

York regarded him without blinking, his brows lowering.

"I was the king's lieutenant in France, Vicomte Gascault. I am certain you were told as much. I have fought on French soil and I have lost estates and titles to your king. All this you know. I mention it only to remind you that, in turn, I know France. I know your king—and, Gascault, I know you."

"My lord, I can only assume—"

York continued over him as if he had not spoken.

"The King of England sleeps, Vicomte Gascault. Will he wake, at all? Or will he die abed? It is the talk of all the markets here. I do not doubt it is the talk of Paris as well. Is this the chance for which your king has planned and waited for so very long? You, who are not strong enough to take Calais from us, you would dream of England?"

Gascault shook his head, his mouth open to begin a denial. York held up his hand.

"I invite you, Gascault. Throw your dice. Take your chance while King Henry drowses. I would walk again on lands that once were mine. I would march an army on French earth once more, if I had the chance. *Please*, consider my invitation. The Channel is just a thread. The king is just a man. A soldier, well, if he is an English soldier, he is still a man, is he not? He can fail. He can fall. Come against us while our king sleeps, Vicomte Gascault. Climb our walls. Set foot in our ports. I welcome it, as our people will welcome you all. It may be a rough welcome, I grant you. We are rough folk. But we have debts to repay and we are generous with our enemies. For each blow landed on us, we give them three and we do not count the cost. Do you understand me, Vicomte Gascault? Son of Julien and Clémence? Brother to André, Arnaud, and François? Husband to Elodie? Father to two sons and a daughter. Shall I name them, Gascault? Shall I describe your family home, with the red plum trees that bracket the gate?"

"Enough, *monsieur*," Gascault said quietly. "Your meaning is clear enough."

"I wonder," York said. "Or should I send an order to wing faster than you can ride, faster than you can sail, so that you understand my meaning, as well and as fully as I intend it, when you return to your home? I am willing, Gascault."

"Please don't, my lord," Gascault replied.

"Please?" York said. His face was hard, darkened by the dimming lamps as if shadows crept over his jaw. "I will decide, after you are gone. There is a ship waiting for you, Gascault—and men who will take you to the coast. Whatever news you report to your king, I wish you all the fortune you deserve. Good night, Vicomte Gascault. God speed."

Gascault rose on trembling legs and went to the door. Salisbury kept his head down as he opened it for him and the Frenchman took a deep breath in fear as he saw the soldiers gathered beyond. In the gloom, they had a menacing aspect and he almost shrieked as they allowed him out and turned in place to march him away.

Salisbury closed the door softly.

"I do not think they will come—at least, not this year," he said.

York snorted.

"I swear, I am in two minds. We have the ships and the men, if they would follow me. Yet they wait like hounds, to see if Henry will wake."

Salisbury did not reply at first. York saw his hesitation and smiled wearily.

"It is not yet too late, I think. Send for the Spaniard as well. I will speak my lines to him."

PART ONE

LATE SUMMER 1454

○ ○ ○

People crushed by law have no hopes but from power.
If laws are their enemies, they will be enemies to laws.

EDMUND BURKE

CHAPTER 1

With the light still cold and gray, the castle came alive. Horses were brought from their stalls and rubbed down; dogs barked and fought with each other, kicked out of the way by those who found them in their path. Hundreds of young men were busy gathering tack and weapons, rushing around the main yard with armfuls of equipment.

In the great tower, Henry Percy, Earl of Northumberland, stared out of the window to the bustling sward all around his fortress. The castle stones were warm in the August heat, but the old man wore a cloak and mantle of fur around his shoulders even so, clutched tight to his chest. He was still both tall and broad, though age had bowed him down. His sixth decade had brought aches and creaking joints that made all movement painful and his temper short.

The earl glowered through the leaded glass. The town was waking. The world was rising with the sun and he was ready to act, after so long biding his time. He watched as armored knights assembled, their servants passing out shields that had been painted black, or covered in sackcloth bound with twine. The Percy colors of blue and yellow were nowhere in evidence, hidden from view so that the soldiers waiting for his order had a somber look. For a time, they would be gray men, hedge knights without house or family. Men without honor, when honor was a chain to bind them.

The old man sniffed, rubbing hard at his nose. The ruse would fool no one, but when the killing was over, he would still be able to claim no Percy knight or archer had been part of it. Most importantly of all, those who might have cried out against him would be cold in the ground.

As he stood there, deep in thought, he heard his son approach, the young man's spurred heels clicking and rattling on the wooden floor. The earl looked around, feeling his old heart thump with anticipation.

"God give you good day," Thomas Percy said, bowing. He too allowed his gaze to stray through the window, down to the bustle of the castle grounds below. Thomas raised an eyebrow in silent question and his father grunted, irritated at the footsteps of servants all around.

"Come with me." Without waiting for a reply, the earl swept along the corridor, the force of his authority pulling Thomas along behind him. He reached a doorway to his private chambers and almost dragged his son inside, slamming the door behind them. As Thomas stood and watched, the old man strode jerkily through the rooms, banging doors back and forth as he went. His suspicion showed in the deepening purple of his face, the skin made darker still by a stain of broken veins that stretched right across his cheeks and nose. The earl could never be pale, with that marbling. If it had been earned in strong spirits from over the Scottish border, it suited his mood well enough. Age had not mellowed the old man, though it had dried and hardened him.

Satisfied they were alone, the earl came back to his son, still waiting patiently with his back to the door. Thomas Percy, Baron Egremont, stood no taller than his father once had, though without the stoop of age he could see over the old man's head. At thirty-two, Thomas was in the prime of his manhood, his hair black and his forearms thick with sinew and muscle earned over six thousand days of training. As he stood there, he seemed almost to glow with health and strength, his ruddy skin unmarked by scar or disease. Despite the years between them, both men bore the Percy nose, that great wedge that could be seen in dozens of crofts and villages all around Alnwick.

"There, we are private," the earl said at last. "She has her ears everywhere, your mother. I cannot even talk to my own son without her people reporting every word."

"What news, then?" his son replied. "I saw the men, gathering swords and bows. Is it the border?"

"Not today. Those damned Scots are quiet, though I don't doubt the Douglas is forever sniffing round my lands. They'll come in winter when they starve, to try and steal my cows. And we'll send them running when they do."

His son hid his impatience, knowing well that his father could rant about the "cunning Douglas" for an hour if he was given the chance.

"The men though, Father. They have covered the colors. Who threatens us who must be taken by hedge knights?"

His father stood close to him, reaching out and hooking a bony hand over the lip of the leather breastplate to draw him in.

"Your mother's Nevilles, boy, always and *forever* the Nevilles. Wherever I turn in my distress, there they are, in my path!" Earl Percy raised his other hand as he spoke, holding it up with the fingers joined like a beak. He jabbed the air with it, close by his son's face. "Standing in such numbers they can never be counted. Married into every noble line! Into every house! I have the damned Scots clawing away at my flank, raiding England, burning villages in my own land. If I did not stand against them, if I let but one season pass without killing the young men they send to test me, they would come south like a dam bursting. Where would England be then, without Percy arms to serve her? But the Nevilles care nothing for all that. No, they throw their weight and wealth to York, that *pup*. *He* rises, held aloft by Neville hands, while titles and estates of ours are stolen away."

"Warden of the West March," his son muttered wearily. He had heard his father's complaints many times before.

Earl Percy's glare intensified.

"One of many. A title that should have been your brother's, with fifteen hundred pounds a year, until that *Neville*, Salisbury, was given it. I have swallowed that, boy. I have swallowed him being made chancellor while my king dreams and sleeps and France was lost. I have swallowed so much from them that I find I am stuffed full."

The old man had drawn his son so close their faces almost touched. He kissed Thomas briefly on the cheek, letting him go. From long habit, he checked the room around them once more, though they were alone.

"You have good Percy blood in you, Thomas. It will drive your mother's out in time, as I will drive out the Nevilles upon the land. They have been given to me, Thomas, do you understand? By the Grace of God, I have been handed a chance to take back all they have stolen. If I were twenty years younger, I would take Windstrike and ride them down myself, but . . . those days are behind." The old man's eyes were almost feverish as he stared up at his son. "You must be my right arm in this, Thomas. You must be my sword and flail."

"You honor me," Thomas murmured, his voice breaking. As a mere second son, he had grown to his prime with little of the old man's affection. His elder brother, Henry, was away with a thousand men across the border of Scotland, there to raid and burn and weaken the savage clans. Thomas thought of him and knew Henry's absence was the true reason his father had taken him aside. There was no one else to send. Though the knowledge made him bitter, he could not resist the chance to show his worth to the one man he allowed to judge him.

"Henry has the best of our fighting cocks," his father said, echoing his thoughts. "And I must keep some strong hands at Alnwick, in case the cunning Douglas slips your brother and comes south to rape and steal. That little man knows no greater pleasure than in taking what is mine. I swear he—"

"Father, I will not fail," Thomas said. "How many will you send with me?"

His father paused in irritation at being interrupted, his eyes sharp with rebuke. At last, he nodded, letting it go.

"Seven hundred, or thereabouts. Two hundred men-at-arms, though the rest are brickmakers and smiths and common men with bows. You *will* have Trunning and if you have wit, you will let him advise you—and listen well to him. He knows the land around York and he knows the men. Perhaps if you had not spent so much of your youth on drink and whores, I would not doubt you. Whisht! Don't take it hard, boy. There must be a son of mine in this, to give the men heart. But they are *my* men, not yours. Follow Trunning. He will not lead you wrong."

Thomas flushed, his own anger rising. The thought of the two old men planning out some scheme together brought a tension to his frame that his father noted.

"You understand?" Earl Percy snapped. "Heed Trunning. That is my order to you."

"I understand," Thomas said, striving hard to conceal his disappointment. For one moment, he'd thought his father might trust him in command, rather than raising his brother, or some other man, over him. He felt the loss of something he'd never had.

"Will you tell me then where I must ride for you, or should I ask Trunning for that as well?" Thomas said.

His voice was strained, and his father's mouth quirked in response, amused and scornful.

"I said not to take it hard, boy. You've a good right arm and you are my son, but you've not led, not beyond a few skirmishes. The men do not respect you, as they do Trunning. How could they? He's fought for twenty years, in France and England both. He'll see you safe."

The earl waited for some sign that his son had accepted the point, but Thomas glowered, wounded and angry. Earl Percy shook his head, going on.

"There is a Neville marriage tomorrow, Thomas, down at Tattershall. Your mother's clan has reached out to bring yet another into their grasp. That preening cockerel, Salisbury, will be there, to see his son wed. They will be at peace, content to take a new bride back to their holding at the manor of Sheriff Hutton. My man told me all, risking his bones to reach me in time. I paid him well for it, mind. Now listen. They will be on horses and on foot, a merry wedding party traipsing back to feast on a fine summer day. And you will be there, Thomas. You will ride them down, leaving no one alive. That is my order to you. Do you understand it?"

Thomas swallowed hard as his father watched him. Earl Salisbury was his mother's brother, the man's sons his own cousins. Thomas had been thinking he would ride out after some weaker branch of the Neville tree, not the root itself and the head of the clan. If he did as he was told, he would make more blood-enemies in a day than in his entire life to that point. Even so, he nodded, unable to trust his voice. His father's mouth twisted sourly, seeing once again his son's weakness and indecision.

"Salisbury's boy is marrying Maud Cromwell. You know her uncle holds Percy manors, refusing my claim to them. It seems he thinks he can give *my* estates in dowry to the Nevilles, that they are now so strong I will be forced to drop my suits and cases against him. I am sending you to show them justice. To show them the authority Cromwell flouts as he seeks a greater shadow to hide beneath! Listen to me now. Take my seven hundred and kill them all, Thomas. Be sure Cromwell's niece is among the dead, that I may invoke her name when next I meet her weeping uncle in the king's court. Do you understand?"

"Of course I understand!" Thomas said, his voice hardening. He felt his hands tremble as he glared at his father, but he would not suffer the old man's scorn by refusing. He set his jaw, the decision made.

A knock sounded on the door at Thomas's back, making both men start like guilty conspirators. Thomas stood away to let it swing open, blanching at the sight of his mother standing there.

His father drew himself up, his chest puffing out.

"Go now, Thomas. Bring honor to your family and your name."

"*Stay*, Thomas," his mother said quickly, her expression cold.

Thomas hesitated, then dipped his head, slipping past her and striding away. Alone, Countess Eleanor Percy turned sharply to her husband.

"I see your guards and soldiers arming themselves, covering Percy colors. Now my son rushes from me like a whipped cur. Will you have me ask, then? What foul plan have you been whispering into his ears this time, Henry? What have you done?"

Earl Percy took a deep breath, his triumph showing clearly.

"Were you not listening at the door like a maid, then? I am surprised," he said. "What I have *done* is no business of yours." As he spoke, he moved to go past her into the corridor outside. Eleanor stepped into his path to stop him, raising her hand against his chest.

In response, the earl gripped it cruelly, crushing her fingers so that she cried out. He twisted further, controlling her with a hand on her elbow.

"Please, Henry. My arm . . ." she said, gasping.

He twisted harder at that, making her shriek. In the corridor, he caught a glimpse of a servant hurrying closer and kicked savagely at the door so that it slammed shut. As his wife whimpered, the old man bent her forward, almost doubled over, with his grip tight on her hand and arm.

"I have done no more than your Nevilles would do to me, if I were ever at their mercy," he said into her ear. "Did you think I would allow your brother to rise above the Percy name? Chancellor to the Duke of York now, he threatens everything I am, everything I must protect. Do you understand? I took you on to give me sons, a fertile Neville bride. Well, you have done that. Now do not dare ask me the business of my house."

"You are *hurting* me," she said, her face crumpling in anger and pain. "You see enemies where there are none. And if you seek my brother, he will see you dead, Henry. Richard will kill you."

With a grunt of outrage, her husband heaved her across the room, sending her sprawling across the bed. He was on her before she could rise to her feet, tearing her dress and bawling at her in red-faced rage as he wrenched at the cloth and bared her skin. She sobbed and struggled, but he was infernally strong in his anger, ignoring her nails as she left red lines on his face and arms. He held her down with one hand, exposing the long pale line of her back as he drew his belt from his trousers and doubled it over into a short whip.

"You will not speak to *me* in such a *way*, in my own *house*." He landed blow after blow with the snapping sounds as loud as her desperate cries. No one came, though he went on and on until she was still, no longer struggling. Long red welts seeped blood to stain the fine cloth as he gasped and panted, fat beads of sweat dropping from his nose and brow onto her skin. With grim satisfaction, the earl replaced his belt and left his wife to sob into the coverlet.

SERVANTS OPENED THE DOOR to the marshaling yard beyond as Thomas Percy, Baron Egremont, walked out. The noise of hundreds of men crashed over him under the blue sky, making his heart beat faster. With an irritated glance, he saw members of his own staff were already there, suborned by his father and waiting patiently for him. They carried armor and his weapons, while other men worked on Balion, the great black charger he had bought for a ruinous price the previous year. It seemed his father had been in no doubt as to the outcome of their conversation. Thomas frowned as he approached the group within the milling mass of men, taking in the sheer complexity of the scene. Far above them all, he could hear his mother screaming like a butchered sow, no doubt as the old man laid into her yet again. Thomas felt only irritation that she should intrude so on his thoughts. He was forced to look down rather than suffer the unwanted intimacy of other men's eyes. With each new wail, they either grinned or winced, while his anger at her only grew. The rise of the Neville family *ate* at his father, ruining the old man with suspicions and rages when the earl should have been enjoying quiet years and turning over the running of estates to his sons. As the sounds died away at last, Thomas looked up to the window of his father's private rooms. It was typical of the old man to set his plans in motion for days or weeks without even bothering to tell his own son what he intended.

With quick, neat motions, Thomas removed his leather breastplate and cloak, stripping down in the yard to hose and undertunic, already showing patches of dark sweat. There was no modesty there and scores of young men joked and shouted to one another as they hopped with an armored boot, or called for some piece of their equipment that had found its way into someone else's spot. Thomas seated himself on a high stool, sitting patiently while his servants worked to fasten the padded gambeson jerkin and strap him into each plate of his personal armor. It fitted him well, and if the scars and marks were from the training yard rather than a battle, it was still a good set, well worn. As he raised his arms for the breastplate to be strapped on, he glared at the marks of a scourer, the metal dulled by some kitchen girl working it like a pot. The blue and yellow crest had been obliterated and he craned his neck to see his sword where it lay ready to be handed to him. Thomas swore softly then, seeing the fine enamel badge had been chiseled from the guard. It was on his father's orders, of course, but he had carried that sword since his twelfth birthday and it hurt to see it damaged.

Piece by piece, his armor was put on, until he stood, feeling the wonderful sense of strength and invulnerability it brought. Lord Egremont reached for the helmet his steward held out reverently to him. As he rammed it onto his head, Thomas heard the voice of his father's swordmaster echoing across the marshaling yard.

"When the gate opens, we are *gone*," Trunning shouted to the gathered men. "Be ready, for there'll be no riding back like lady's maids after a dropped glove. No personal servants beyond those with mounts who can hold a sword or a bow and keep up. Dried beef and raw oats, a little ale and wine, no more! Provisions for six days, but ride light, or be left behind."

Trunning paused, his gaze sweeping across the knights and men as he readied himself to give another half-dozen instructions. He caught sight of the Percy son and moved on the instant to come to his side. It gave Thomas some small satisfaction to look down on the shorter man.

"What is it, Trunning?" he said, deliberately keeping his voice cold. Trunning didn't reply at first, just stood, looking him over and chewing the white mustache that drooped over his lips. His father's swordmaster had trained both Percy sons in weapons and tactics, beginning so early in their lives that Thomas could not remember a time he had not been there, shouting in anger at some poor stroke, or demanding to know who had taught him to hold a shield "like a Scots maid." With no effort of memory, Thomas could recall five bones broken by the red-faced little man over the years: two in his right hand, two cracked forearms, and a small bone in his foot where Trunning had once stamped down in a tussle. Each one had meant weeks of pain in splints and withering scorn for every groan he made while they were bound. It was not that Thomas hated or even feared his father's man. He knew Trunning was intensely loyal to the house of Percy and Northumberland, like a particularly savage old hound. Yet for all the differences in their station, Thomas, Lord Egremont, could not imagine the man ever accepting him as an equal, never mind his superior. The very fact that his father had placed Trunning in command of the raid was proof of that. The pair of old bastards were cut from the same rough cloth, with not a drop of kindness or mercy in either of them. It was no wonder they got on so well.

"Your father has talked to you, then? Told you the way of it?" Trunning said at last. "Has he said to mark my orders in all things, to bring you safe home with a couple of new scratches on that fine armor of yours?"

Thomas repressed a shudder at the man's voice. Perhaps the result of so many years bawling across fields and streets at those he trained, Trunning was always hoarse, his spoken words mingling with deep, wheezing breaths.

"He has told me you will command, Trunning, yes. To a point." Trunning blinked lazily, weighing him up.

"And what point would that be, my noble lord Egremont?"

To his dismay, Thomas felt his heart hammer in his chest and his own breathing grow tight. He hoped the swordmaster could not sense the strain in him, though it was near certain after knowing him for so long. Nonetheless, he spoke firmly, determined not to let his father's man rule him.

"The point where you and I disagree, Trunning. The honor of the house is mine to guard and protect. You may give orders to march and to attack and so forth, but I will consider the policy, the aims of what we are about."

Trunning stared at him, tilting his head and rubbing at a spot above his right eye.

"If I tell your father you are chafing, he'll make you come along as a pot-boy, if at all," he said, smiling unpleasantly. He was surprised when the young man turned to face him fully, leaning down.

"If you carry tales to the old man, I *will* stay. See how far you get from the gates without a son of the Percy family at the head. And then, Trunning, you'll have made an enemy of Egremont. Now I've told you my terms. You do as you please."

Thomas deliberately turned back to his servants then, beckoning for them to adjust and add a drop of oil to his visor. He felt Trunning's gaze and his heart continued to race, but he was certain of himself, in that one thing. He did not look round when the swordmaster stalked off, not even to see if Trunning would march into the castle and take his complaints to his father. Lord Egremont lowered his visor to conceal his expression. His father and Trunning were both old men and, for all their will and spite, old men fell away in the end. Thomas would take the archers and the swordsmen against his uncle's wedding party, either with Trunning or without him it mattered not at all. He looked again at the small army his father had called to Percy service. Hundreds were no more than town men, summoned by their feudal lord. Yet whether they worked as smith, butcher, or tanner, each of them had trained with ax or bow from their earliest years, developing skills that would make them useful to a man like Earl Percy of Alnwick. Thomas smiled to himself, raising his visor once again.

"Form on the gate!" he roared at them. From the corner of his eye, he saw Trunning's trim shape jerk round, but Thomas ignored him. Old men fell away, he told himself again, with satisfaction. Young men came to rule.

CHAPTER 2

D erry Brewer was in a foul mood. The rain poured down in
sheets, drumming against the bald dome of his head. He
had never realized before how a good head of hair really
soaked up the rain. With his pate so cruelly exposed, the dreadful
pattering made his skull ache and his ears itch. To add to his discomfort, he wore a sodden brown robe that slapped wetly against his bare
shanks, chafing the skin. His head had been shaved by a fairly expert
hand just that morning, so that it still felt new and sore and appall-
ingly exposed to the elements. The friars trudging along with him
were all tonsured, the white circles of scalp gleaming wetly in the
gloom. As far as Derry could tell, none of them had eaten a morsel of
food since dawn, though they had walked and chanted all day.

The great walls of the royal castle lay ahead up Peascod Street as
they rang their bell for alms and prayed aloud, the only ones foolish
enough to stand out in the rain when there was shelter to be had.
Windsor was a wealthy town; the castle it existed to serve was only
twenty miles from London, like half a dozen others around the capital, each a day's march apart. The presence of the king's household

had brought some of the very best goldsmiths, jewelers, vintners, and mercers out of the capital city, eager to sell their wares. With the king himself in residence, more than eight hundred men and women in his service swelled the crowds and raised the prices of everything from bread and wine to a gold bracelet.

In his sour humor, Derry assumed Franciscan friars would be attracted by the flow of coins as well. He was still unsure if his grubby companions were not just rather clever beggars. It was true Brother Peter harangued the crowds for their iniquity and greed, but the rest of the friars all carried knives to sell as well as begging bowls. One wide-shouldered unfortunate seemed resigned to his role among them as the carrier of a large grindstone. Silent Godwin walked with it on his back, tied on with twine and so bowed down that he could hardly look up to see where he was going. The others said he endured the weight as penance for some past sin and Derry had not dared ask what it had been.

At the intervals of abbey services throughout the day, the group would stop and pray, accepting offers of water or home-brewed beer brought out to them as they assembled a treadle and set the stone spinning, sharpening knives and blessing those who passed over a coin, no matter how small. Derry felt a pang of guilt about the tight leather purse he wore snug and close to his groin. He had silver enough in there to feed them all to bursting, but if he brought it out, he suspected Brother Peter would give it away to some undeserving sod and leave the monks to starve. Derry puffed out his cheeks, wiping rain from his eyes. It washed down his face in a constant stream, so that he had to blink through a blur.

It had seemed like a good idea to join them four nights before. As a result of their humble trade, the group of fourteen monks were all armed. They were also used to nights on the road where thieves might try to steal even from those who had nothing. Derry had been lurking in the stables of a cheap tavern when he'd overheard Brother Peter talking about Windsor, where they would pray for the king's recovery. None of them had been surprised another traveler would want to do the same, not with the king's soul in peril and all the country so beset with violent men.

Derry sighed to himself, rubbing hard at his face. He sneezed explosively and caught himself opening his mouth to curse. Brother Peter had taken a stick to a miller just that morning for shouting a blasphemy on the open street. It had been Derry's pleasure to see the meek leader of the group exercise a wrath that would have made him a minor name in the fight rings of London. They'd left the miller in the road, his ears leaking blood from the battering he'd received, his cart overturned and his flour bags all broken. Derry smiled at the memory, glancing over to where Brother Peter walked, sounding his bell every thirteenth step so that it echoed back from the stone walls at the top of the hill.

The castle loomed in the rain, there was no other way to describe it. The massive walls and round baileys had never been breached in the centuries since the first stones had been laid. King Henry's stronghold squatted over Windsor, almost another town within the first, home to hundreds. Derry stared upward, his feet aching on the cobbles.

It was almost time to leave the little group of monks and Derry wondered how best to broach the subject. Brother Peter had been astonished at his request to be tonsured as the other men. Though they accepted it for themselves as a rebuke of vanity, there was no need at all for Derry to adopt the style. It had taken all Derry's persuasive skill before the older man allowed he could do as he pleased with his own head.

The young friar who had taken a razor to Derry's thick hair had managed to cut his scalp twice and scrape away a piece of skin the size of a penny right on the crown. Derry had endured it all with barely a grunt of complaint, finally earning a satisfied pat on the back from Brother Peter.

In the downpour, Derry wondered if it had been worth it. He was thin and worn-down already. In an old robe, he might have passed with his head unshaven, but the stakes were the highest and the men hunting him had already shown their determination and ruthlessness, more than once. With a sigh, he told himself once again that it was a price worth paying, though he could not remember his spirits ever being lower in all his life.

Being the avowed enemy of Richard Plantagenet, Duke of York, was not something he had chosen for himself. When he looked back on his dealings, Derry supposed he could have been more conciliatory. The man who had trained him would have wagged a finger in reproof at the pride he'd shown. Old Bertle would have lectured him for hours, saying that a man's enemies must never see your strength, *never*. Derry could almost hear the old boy's exasperated voice as he trudged up the hill. If they believe you are weak, they don't send hard, killing men from London to track you down. They don't pay silver to every rumormonger for news of your whereabouts. They don't put a price on your head, Derry!

Becoming a Franciscan for a time may have saved his neck, or simply wasted a few days, he'd never know. It was certainly true that Derry had passed groups of hostile-looking men while he'd walked with the monks, men who'd laughed and jeered and turned away as Brother Peter asked them for a coin. Any one of them or a dozen might have been in the pay of York, Derry had no way of knowing. He'd kept his gaze on the ground, trudging along with the others.

The rain ceased for a time, though thunder grumbled nearby and dark clouds still rushed overhead. Brother Peter chose that moment of quiet to place one hand on the clapper of his bell and raise the other to halt the shivering group.

"Brothers, the sun is setting and the ground is too wet to sleep in the open tonight. I know a family on the far side of town, not a mile further, over the crest of Castle Hill. They will allow us to use their barn to sleep and eat, in return for blessings on their house and joining us in prayer."

The monks cheered up visibly at his words. Derry realized he had developed at least a whisper of respect for the odd life they led. With the exception of the bull-like mass of Silent Godwin, none of them looked strong. He suspected one or two saw the mendicant life as better than working, but then they did take their poverty seriously, in an age where every other man was working to get away from that miserable estate. Derry cleared his throat, stifling a cough that he'd developed somewhere in the wet and cold.

"Brother Peter, might I have a word with you?" he said.

The leader of their little group turned back immediately, his expression placid.

"Of course, Derry," he said.

The older man's lips were blue. Derry thought again of the fat purse tucked warm against his testicles.

"I . . . um . . . I won't be going on with you," Derry said, looking down at his feet rather than witness the disappointment he knew would be there in the monk's face. "There's a man I must meet at the castle. I'll be stopping there for a time."

"Ah," Brother Peter replied. "Well, Derry, you'll go with God's blessing at least."

To Derry's surprise, the older man reached out and placed his hand on the sore skin of his crown, bowing his head with gentle pressure. He endured it, strangely moved by the old man's faith as Brother Peter called on Saint Christopher and Saint Francis to guide him in his travels and trials ahead.

"Thank you, Brother Peter. It has been an honor."

The older man smiled at him then, letting his hand fall away.

"I just hope those you seek to avoid have the sun in their eyes, Derry. I will pray that they are as blind as Saul of Tarsus when you pass by."

Derry blinked at him in surprise, making Brother Peter chuckle.

"Not many of those who join us insist on a tonsure after just a day or two on the road, Derry. Still, I dare say it did you no harm, despite Brother John's roughness with the blade."

Derry stared at him, amused despite his discomforts.

"I did wonder, Brother, how it is that some of you have a circle no more than three fingers wide on your pates, while I seem to have been shaved right down to the ears."

Brother Peter's dark eyes glinted then.

"That was my decision, Derry. I thought if a man was so very keen to have a tonsure, we should perhaps indulge his desire to the utmost. Forgive me, my son, if you would."

"Of course, Brother Peter. You have brought me here safe and well."

On impulse, Derry hitched up his robe and reached deeply inside the folds, bringing out his purse. He pressed it into Brother Peter's hands, folding the fingers over the damp leather.

"This is for you. There's enough there to keep you all for a month, or longer."

Brother Peter weighed the purse thoughtfully, then held it out.

"God provides, Derry, always. Take it back, though your kindness is touching."

Derry shook his head, backing away with his hands raised.

"It's yours, Brother Peter, please."

"All right, all right," the older man said, tucking it away. "I'm sure we'll find a use for it, or someone with a greater need than our own.

Go with God, Derry. Who knows, there might come a time when you decide to walk with us for longer than just a couple of days. I will pray for it. Come, brothers, the rain is starting once more."

Each one of the group came to grip Derry's hand and wish him well, even Silent Godwin, who crushed his hand in his big fist and patted Derry on the shoulder, still bowed down by the grindstone on his back.

Derry stood alone in the street at the top of the hill by the castle, watching the group of friars make their slow way down. It was true the rain was falling again and he shivered, turning toward the gatehouse of the royal fortress. He had a strong sense of eyes on him and he moved into a trot, heading into the shelter of the walls and approaching the dark figure of the guard on duty. Derry squinted in the gloom as he drew closer. The man was drenched to the skin just as he was, standing there in all weathers with his poleax and bell to sound an alarm.

"Good evening, my son," Derry said, raising his hand to make the sign of the cross in the air.

The guard looked at him.

"You're not allowed to beg here, Father," the guard said gruffly, adding, "sorry," after a moment's thought.

Derry smiled, his teeth showing white in his sunburned face.

"Send word to your captain. He'll want to come down and see me."

"Not in the rain he won't, Father, and that's the truth," the man replied uncomfortably.

Derry took a quick glance up and down the road. There was no one around and he was weary and starving.

"Tell him 'vineyard' and he will."

The guard looked dubiously at him for some time while Derry waited, trying to show as much confidence as he could muster. After a time, the guard's will faded and he shrugged, giving a sharp whistle.

A door came open in the gatehouse at his back and Derry heard a voice swearing at the rain and cold that blew in.

The man who came out bore a fine set of mustaches, already wilting in the rain. He was in the process of wiping his hands with a cloth, traces of fresh egg unnoticed on his lips. He ignored the friar standing in the rain and addressed himself to the guard.

"What is it?"

"This monk, sir. Asked me to fetch you out."

Derry felt his temper fray as the captain of the guard continued to ignore his presence. He spoke quickly, though his chattering teeth made it hard to form the words.

"I'm cold, wet, and hungry, Hobbs. The word is 'vineyard' and the queen will want to see me. Let me in."

Captain Hobbs was opening his mouth to respond angrily at being addressed in such a tone when he realized his name had been used, as well as the word he'd been told to remember some weeks before. He grew still then, his manner changing on the instant. He peered more closely at the grubby friar standing before him.

"Master Brewer? Good lord, man, what happened to your head?"

"I am in disguise, Hobbs, if you must know. Now will you let me pass? My feet are aching and I'm cold enough to drop dead right here."

"Yes, sir, of course. I'll take you to the queen. Her Highness was asking about you just a few days back."

The rain fell harder, drumming against the miserable guard as they left him behind and went into the warm.

As tired and bedraggled as he was, Derry couldn't help but notice the aura of hush that increased as Hobbs brought him to the king's apartments. Servants walked without any of the usual clatter, speaking in whispers if they spoke at all. By the time Hobbs had brought him to the right door and given another password to the two men guarding it, Derry was certain there had been no improvement in the king's health. Some fourteen months had passed since King Henry had collapsed into a stupor so deep he could not be roused. The year 1454 had aged to the end of summer with no king on the throne in London, only the Duke of York to rule in his stead as "Protector and Defender of the Realm." England had a long history of regents for royal children—Henry himself had needed good men to rule in his stead when he'd inherited the throne as a child. Yet there was no precedent for madness, inherited no doubt from Henry's mother and the taint of her royal French line.

Derry endured a thorough search of his person. When the guards were satisfied he bore no weapon, or at least had found none, they announced him and opened the door to the inner chambers.

He swept through, taking in the sight of the queen at dinner with her husband. At first glance, King Henry looked as if he sat normally, nodding over a bowl of soup. Derry spotted the ropes binding him to his chair so he could not fall, as well as the servant who looked up as he entered, holding a soup spoon to feed his master. As Derry came closer, he saw Henry wore a bib that had collected as much soup as went inside him. Rich broth dribbled down the king's slack lips and as Derry knelt and bowed his head, he could hear soft, choking sounds coming from him.

Captain Hobbs had not stepped beyond the threshold. The door closed at Derry's back and he saw the young queen rise from her seat, an expression of horror on her face.

"Oh your *head*, Derry! What have you done to yourself?"

"Your Highness, I preferred to come to you without my movements being noted and reported at every step. Please, it is nothing. It will surely grow back, or so I am told." He noticed in exasperation that the queen seemed to be struggling with laughter.

"It's like an egg, Derry! They've left you hardly any hair at all."

"Yes, Your Highness, the Franciscan who wielded the razor was unusually thorough." As he rose from kneeling, he felt himself stagger slightly, the combination of the room's warmth and hunger bringing a wave of weakness.

The queen saw his frailty and her smile vanished.

"Humphrey! Help Master Brewer to a seat before he falls down. Quickly now, he is close to fainting."

Derry looked around dazedly for the man whom she addressed, feeling himself taken under the arms and dropped into a wide, wooden chair. He blinked, trying to summon his wits from where they had suddenly scattered. Such weakness was embarrassing, especially considering he knew Brother Peter was still out in the rain, heading for his barn and a place to sleep.

"I'll be all right in a moment, Your Highness," Derry said. "I've been on the road a long time." He did not say that he'd been hunted, stretching his wits and his contacts to their limits just to stay ahead of the men searching for him. He'd been spotted and chased three times in the previous month, twice in the week before he'd joined the monks. He knew there would come a time when his legs failed or he couldn't reach a safe spot to hide. The Duke of York's men were closing a net all around him. He could almost feel the rough twine on his throat.

Derry looked up to thank the man who had helped him, his eyes widening as he recognized the Duke of Buckingham. Humphrey Stafford was red-faced and large, a man of enormous appetites. He'd handled Derry as easily as a child, and the spymaster could only wonder how much weight he'd lost on the road.

The duke leaned in to peer at him, the man's swollen great nose wrinkling in distaste.

"Dead on his feet, almost," Buckingham announced. To Derry's discomfort, the man leaned even closer and sniffed at him. "His breath is sweet, Your Highness, like rot. Whatever he has to say, I'd get him to talk now, before he ups and dies on us."

Derry squinted back at the face looming over him.

"I'll survive, my lord. I usually do."

At no time had any of the three looked directly at King Henry. He sat mute at the table, unseeing and unfeeling. Derry risked a glance from under lowered brows and wished he hadn't. The king was thin and pale, but that was not so strange. The eyes were open and utterly empty. Derry might have believed him a corpse if he hadn't breathed, his head bobbing slightly at every inhalation.

"Hot broth for Master Brewer," Derry heard Queen Margaret say. "And bread, butter, more of the cold beef with garlic, anything you can find." He closed his eyes in thanks, letting the aches and pains become distant as the room's heat settled into his bones. He hadn't been close to a good fire for a long time. Relief and exhaustion stole over him and he was almost asleep by the time plates were placed under his nose. The smell roused him and he fell to with a sudden surge of appetite that brought a sparkle of amusement back to Margaret's eyes. He could feel the hot soup bringing him to life, as if its goodness reached right down his limbs and seeped along the marrow of his bones. Derry smacked his lips and tore at bread so fresh he did not even have to dip it in the soup to soften it.

"I think he'll live," Buckingham said wryly from across the table. "I'd watch the tablecloth, if I were you, Your Highness. He might eat it, the way he's forcing food down his throat."

Derry looked coldly at the man, biting his tongue rather than make another enemy. One duke seeking to bring him down was probably enough, at least for the moment.

He settled back in his chair, knowing the queen indulged him more than most of those who served her. He was grateful for it. Derry used the cloth to mop the corners of his mouth and smiled at Buckingham as he did so.

"Your Highness, thank you for your patience. I am revived enough to report what news I have."

"You have been gone for two months, Derry! What kept you away from the king for such a time?"

Derry sat up straight, pushing aside his plate just in time for it to be whisked away by a servant.

"Your Highness, I have been strengthening the ranks of those reporting to me. I have men and women in every noble house, loyal to King Henry. Some of them have gone, either found and taken, or forced to run. Others have moved to positions of greater authority, which they seem to believe means higher pay from me. I took the time to explain how loyalty to the king cannot be measured in silver, though some would ask thirty pieces at a time."

Queen Margaret was a beautiful young woman, still in her twenties, with clear skin and a slender neck. She narrowed her eyes as Derry spoke, flickering a glance at her husband as if he might respond after all the months of silence. Derry's heart went out to her, wife to a man who knew her not at all.

"What of York, Derry? Tell me of him."

Derry looked up at the ornate ceiling for the length of a breath, deciding how best to describe the Protectorate without dashing her hopes. The simple truth was that York had not botched the work of running the country. Of all the accusations Derry might have leveled at Richard Plantagenet, incompetence was not one. In his heart of hearts, he knew the duke was managing the vast and complex business of state with rather more skill and understanding than King Henry ever had. It was not the sort of thing he could say to the king's young wife, desperate for good news.

"He makes no secret of his support for the Nevilles, Your Highness. Between York and Earl Salisbury, they are gaining estates and manors all over the country. I heard of a dozen cases brought to court, where a Neville seizure of land is at the heart."

Lines appeared on the queen's brow and she waved a hand in a gesture of impatience.

"Tell me of unrest, Derry! Of his failures! Tell me the people of England are withholding their support for this man."

Derry hesitated for a beat, before going on.

"The garrison in Calais has refused orders, Your Highness. That is a thorn in York's side he must overcome. They are the largest army available to the Crown and they claim not to have had any pay since the fall of Maine and Anjou. The last I heard was that they had seized the season's wool and are threatening to sell it for their own coffers."

"Better, Derry, much better. He could send Earl Somerset to treat with them, if he had not lost that good man's support by his attacks on my husband. They would listen to Somerset, I am certain. You know York has reduced the king's own household? His men came with their writs and seals, dismissing loyal staff without even a pension, taking horses from the stables here, to be distributed among their master's supporters. Bloodlines that can never again be collected in one place. All in the name of his mean silver pennies, Derry!"

"I did hear that, Your Highness," Derry said uncomfortably. He wondered when York slept, to have accomplished so many things in a single year. The problems with the Calais garrison were one of only half a dozen minor black marks against the York Protectorate. The country was running well enough and though some spoke out against the reductions in the royal household, York had been ruthless in his collection of state funds, then spent the income wisely to gather even more support. Derry could see a time coming when the country would prefer King Henry never to wake, if things went on as they

were. He and Margaret needed York to suffer a disaster, or the king
to recover his senses. They needed that, most of all, before it was too
late. Derry looked again at the blank-faced monarch nodding in his
chair, feeling a shudder race through him and goose pimples rise on
his arms. For a living man to be reduced to such a state was an evil
thing.

"Has there been no improvement in the king's illness?" he said.

Margaret sat a little straighter, armoring herself against pain as
she replied.

"There are two new doctors to tend him, now that fool Allworthy
is gone. I have endured all manner of pious men come to prod and
poke and pray over my husband. He has suffered much worse, such
sickening practices as I will not describe to you. None of them have
brought his spirit back to the flesh. Buckingham has been a great
comfort to me, but even he despairs at times, don't you, Humphrey?"

The duke made a noncommittal sound, choosing to sup from the
bowl of broth set before him.

"Your son, though, Your Highness?" Derry asked, as gently as he
could. "When you showed him to King Henry, was there no response at all?"

Margaret's mouth tightened.

"You sound like that Abbot Whethamstede, with his probing
questions. Henry looked up when I showed him the babe. He raised
his eyes for a moment and I am *certain* he knew what he was being
told." Her eyes gleamed with tears, daring him to contradict her.

Derry cleared his throat, beginning to wish he had not come.

"The council of lords will meet next month, Your Highness, to
name your son Edward as both royal heir and Prince of Wales. If
York interferes with that, his ambition to rule will be revealed.
Though it would be a cruel blow, I almost hope for it, that others may
know the true face of his Protectorate and what he intends. Those

noblemen who still bluster and refuse to see the truth will not be able to deny it then."

Margaret looked to her husband, anguish written clearly on her face.

"I cannot hope for that, Derry. My son *is* the heir. For little Edward, I suffered the humiliation of York and Salisbury present at the birth, creeping around my bed and peeping under the covers to be sure the babe was my own! Lord Somerset almost came to blows to protect my honor then, Derry. There are times when I wish he *had* put a sword through the Plantagenet then and there, for his impudence and his insults. No, Master Brewer. No! I must not even think of those cowards denying my son his birthright."

Derry flushed at what she had endured, though he had heard the tale before, more than once. A part of him could admire York's twisted mind for even thinking the pregnancy could have been faked and another child brought in. At least that had been laid to rest, though there were still rumors of a different father. Somerset's name was whispered there, dutifully reported back to Derry's twitching ears. Knowing Somerset's prickly honor, Derry doubted it was more than a scurrilous lie, if a clever one.

As he sat and thought, Derry found himself nodding almost in time with the king, exhaustion overwhelming him once again. He could have blessed Margaret when she saw he was flagging and sent him away to be tended and to rest. He knelt to her and bowed to the Duke of Buckingham as he left, looking back once more at the king in his stupor, blind and deaf to all that went on around him. Derry stumbled along behind a servant until he was shown to a room that smelled of damp and dust. Without even bothering to remove his wet robe, he fell full-length onto the bed and slept.

CHAPTER 3

The mood was light as the wedding party awoke. Those with sore heads from the night before stood patiently in line for bowls of beef stew and dumplings, rich and greasy fare that would soak up strong ale and settle uneasy stomachs. As it wasn't a Wednesday, Friday, or Saturday there was no reason not to eat meat, though few among them would usually have filled their stomachs so early in the morning. Yet a wedding was a time for excess, where guests and retainers alike would be able to say they had been feasted until their senses swam and their belts creaked.

As head of the Neville family, Richard, Earl of Salisbury, was in an expansive mood as he emptied his bladder into a bush, watching steam rise with something like contentment. The wedding had gone well, his son John cutting a fine figure and acquitting himself with dignity. Salisbury smiled as he tucked himself away and knotted a drawstring, yawning until his jaw cracked. He'd drunk more than was surely good for a man of his age, so that he sweated even in the dawn cool, but if a father couldn't celebrate his son's wedding, there was something wrong with the world. It didn't hurt that Maud was a rare beauty, wide-hipped and strong, with round crinkled marks on her right cheek that showed she had survived that particular scourge and would not bring the smallpox into his family. The earl had enjoyed himself setting up a marriage tent on the mossy ground, hooting and calling out instructions with the rest as the new couple blushed crimson and the tent shook with amorous struggle and her fit of nervous giggles. His own wife, Alice, had dragged him away in the end, shooing the men clear to give the couple some shred of privacy.

The Neville retainers had gone on drinking after that, emptying skins of ale and white Sherris sack they'd brought on carts for the journey across country. Only a few were awake to cheer the following morning when young John hung out a cloth spotted with virgin's blood. The young man himself had emerged some time later, to walk proudly among the crowd, clapped on the back as he went. His mother had spoiled it slightly by stopping him to wipe smudges from his face in front of them all.

It had been a good day and the weather was holding fine. A smaller party might have spent the night in an inn by the road, but Salisbury had more than two hundred soldiers and archers with him to travel north. Over the previous year, there had been too many men killed all over the country for him to risk his wife and children anywhere without his best guards close to hand.

His manservant had brought him a small wooden stool and shaving table, resting it on the grass with a white cloth, razor, oil bottle, and a bowl of steaming hot water. Salisbury rubbed the bristles on his chin idly, frowning as he considered all the work ahead. It was a joy to take a few days aside from the management of his estates and titles, not least among them lord chancellor to the Protector. For just a short time, he was no more than a proud father like any other, guiding a young couple safely home. The days on the road would be the only break from his duties that year, he was certain. Sheriff Hutton was one of his favorite houses, where he and his wife had spent part of their own honeymoon. He knew Alice would love seeing the old place again, despite not being able to stay long. His son and Maud would enjoy another week or so there, arranging to administer the dowry manors she had brought to the Neville name.

Salisbury smiled easily at that thought, settling himself on a stool and accepting the cloth around his shoulders as his servant brushed warm oil onto his face and stropped the razor. On the borders of Scotland, a place he always pictured frozen or battered by stinging rain, Salisbury knew his old colleague Earl Percy would be spitting mad with rage. The thought brought further balm to an already perfect summer's morning.

His manservant raised the blade and Salisbury held up his hand.

"Let's make it interesting, shall we, Rankin? A stripe on your back for every nick, a half noble if you manage the task without one. How does that appeal to your black gambler's heart?"

"Very well indeed, my lord," Rankin replied.

It was an old game between the two men. Though it was true the servant had been flogged half a dozen times over the years, he'd won enough to give a good dowry to his three daughters, a fact he was sure the earl knew very well. Rankin's hand was steady as he shaved away the bristles from Salisbury's throat. Around master and servant, Neville men-at-arms nudged each other and grinned, making their own quiet bets among themselves as they packed up their camp and made ready to march north.

Alice, Countess Salisbury, emerged from the tent without her shoes on, grasping the turf with bare feet and breathing deeply of the morning air. She saw her husband was being shaved and decided against calling out. She knew Rankin treasured the coins he won far more than his usual salary. For a long moment, Alice stood and watched her husband with visible affection, pleased that he remained so strong and hale despite his years. His fifty-fifth birthday was coming in just a few months, she reminded herself, already thinking of what gift she might have made for him.

Running footsteps made some of the men turn from the scene, though Rankin continued to smooth and scrape, concentrating on his task and its reward. Salisbury looked up slowly and carefully to see one of the young boys who'd accompanied the wedding party. He had a vague memory of the lad from the night before, sucking deeply on a wineskin before being violently sick, to the amusement of the men.

"My lord!" the boy called as he ran in and skidded to a stop. His eyes were wide at the sight of a man being shaved in a field.

"What is it?" Salisbury said calmly, stretching his chin out to give Rankin a clear line for his razor.

"Men coming, my lord. Soldiers and bowmen, all running along here."

Salisbury jerked and then swore as the razor bit his cheek. He stood up abruptly, grabbing the cloth from his neck to wipe the oil and the smear of blood from his face.

"Mount up!" Salisbury roared at the startled men around him.

They darted away, sprinting for their horses and weapons.

"My horse, here! Rankin, you clumsy sod, you've cut me. Horse! Alice! God's bones, will you put your shoes on!"

The drowsy tableau broke apart as men ran in all directions, stumbling and shouting for the captains who commanded them. By the time Salisbury had mounted, there were ranks of horsemen between their master and whoever approached. Those with the sharpest eyes called out "Archers!" over and over, so that shields were thrown up to the horsemen and the Neville bowmen ran forward, stringing their own weapons as they went.

"My lord, your armor!" Rankin said. The man had grabbed an armful of metal, one arm through a circular gorget, hanging half open on its hinge. He ran beside the stirrup as the earl trotted his horse forward. The stewards who would have dressed their lord were nowhere to be seen. Rankin handed up a long sword and almost vanished under the hooves as he stumbled.

"No time, Rankin. That gorget though, I'll take that. And fetch me a shield, would you? There's one hanging there, on that tree, can you see it?" He reached out as Rankin tossed the collar up to him, snatching it out of the air and snapping it shut around his throat. Ahead, a hundred and fifty foot soldiers and sixty archers waited patiently for him to join them. Salisbury looked behind him to see that his wife and son had been found horses. The new bride was there as well, her hands twisting whitely before her. An expression of worry came over the earl's face at the sight of that vulnerable little group. He turned back and his son looked up at the sound of hooves.

"What is it, sir? Who's coming?"

"I don't know yet," Salisbury said. "I'll just have to leave a couple alive to ask them, won't I? Your task is to get your mother and Maud to safety. This is not your concern, John, not today." He did not say aloud that if the young couple were killed, there was a chance those valuable dowry manors could revert to Lord Cromwell or even fall into Percy hands once again, exactly the sort of dispute that kept the judges of the King's Bench busy for months or years. It was not the sort of thing to say in front of a new bride, though Salisbury was pleased to see Maud leap into a saddle, as nimble as any farm girl of good stock. Her long skirts rode high up her legs and, in the presence of his wife, Salisbury looked away. His son blushed and dismounted to tug the layers down.

"Let it be, John. I've seen a girl's legs before. Alice? Heed your son in this. I'll want you safe. Stay well clear of any fighting, unless the day is lost. Then you'll run south, back to Tattershall."

"Sheriff Hutton is closer—and ours," his wife said, wasting no words with her husband twitching to be away.

"We don't know what lies ahead, Alice, just behind. Follow John. The south is clear and Cromwell will surely keep you safe until one of the family comes for vengeance. That's if I fall. These are my best men, Alice. I'd risk my last coin on them."

"You want us to ride now?" his wife said.

He loved her then, for the serious look and the complete lack of any fear in her. Salisbury could see Maud watching the older woman and learning just a little about being a Neville that day.

"Not until you hear I have fallen, or the day is lost. You'll be safer here, with my men in reach, than riding out." He stopped, realizing that an enemy could well have circled around in the night, ready to catch anyone escaping to the south.

"Carter! Come here, would you?" he called to a heavyset horse-man passing them.

The man jerked in the saddle, craning around to see who spoke his name, then turning his horse in place with great skill.

"Good man, Carter," the earl said as he came close. "I need some fellows to scout to the south, to check the line of retreat. Take four and report back here to the countess."

"Yes, my lord," the man replied, raising his visor and whistling sharply to catch the attention of a group of riders belting past.

"Good enough," Salisbury said. He smiled at his wife and son. "I'm needed now. God's blessing be on you all. Ladies, John. Good luck."

Salisbury dropped his visor and dug in his heels, missing the spurred boots that would have had his horse leaping forward regardless of who or what lay in front. Yet he had a sword in his right hand, a shield in his left and good iron around his throat. It would have to do.

He cantered up to the ranks of mounted Neville men, then through them as they pulled aside to let him come to the front. Salisbury could see a large number of soldiers riding and marching without haste toward his position. He squinted into the distance, wishing he had the sharp eyes of the young lad who'd spotted them first. Whoever they were, they wore no colors, carried no banners ahead of them. He swallowed dryly at the numbers, more than three times the size of his own force.

"My wife said I'd not need so many of you, not for a wedding walk," he said to the man next to him, making him grin. "If any of us live through this, be so kind as to tell her she was wrong, would you? She'd be grateful for the knowledge, I'm sure."

Those around him chuckled and Salisbury was pleased at their confidence. Every man there had fought against hordes of savage Scots up on the borders when he'd last been warden for the king. They knew their trade and they were well armored in steel ring mail or plate, backed by sixty good archers who could take a bird in flight if there was a flagon of beer for the shot.

"Skirmishers! Seek 'em out!" Salisbury roared, sending his archers loping into the long grasses ahead. He could see the approaching force bleeding its front edge as they did the same, dark trails of bowmen trotting away from the main force to wreak havoc and destruction. They would meet each other in the sun-dried meadows between, slotting arrows down the throats of those they faced. Numbers would tell there and he strained his eyes to see how many came against him. His charger snorted, chafing at the bit and the delay, so that he reached down and patted its neck.

"Easy there, boy. Let the archers clear the way."

Both sides had drawn to a halt by then, while loping bowmen darted through the trees and long grasses between them, raising dust and butterflies in their wake. It was a golden morning and, though he was outnumbered, Salisbury gripped his sword, hearing the leather saddle creak as he leaned forward. He had a dozen enemies, more, but only one who might have risked such a force and had the funds and men to send it against him.

"*Percy,*" Salisbury muttered to himself. He only hoped the old man was there in person, so that he could see him cut down. It was too late to curse himself for not expecting the attack. Salisbury had brought a larger force to his son's wedding than anyone had thought necessary, but still, there was a veritable army riding against them. He told himself he should have guessed the Percy lord would not sit quiet in Alnwick while he lost manors. Salisbury knew every detail of the Cromwell dowry estates. It was one reason he had been so happy to receive them, to spite the bitter old man who ruled the north.

He shook his head, clearing away regrets and doubt. His men were well trained and fanatically loyal. They would serve.

THOMAS, LORD EGREMONT, watched the neat files of archers trotting away. Over the long summer, the grasses had been baked almost to white, yet grown so tall that a man only had to drop to one knee to vanish. He'd had the very devil of a time even finding the Neville party in lands he did not know well. Trunning had sent scouts ranging out in all directions the night before, casting his net wider and wider until one of them came bolting back in, red in the face and yelling his news. The Percy swordmaster had the men up and ready to march while Thomas had still been yawning and staring around him.

He and Trunning had said little to each other since the lines had been drawn in the yard at Alnwick. Thomas had told himself he didn't need the sour little strip of gristle, but the truth was, Trunning knew how to campaign. Old soldiers and townsmen looked to Trunning for orders, because he was always there to give them. It was no great skill, as far as Thomas could see. All it required was an eye for small things and a blistering temper. Thomas wondered if he imagined the man's disdain whenever their eyes locked. It didn't matter, even so. They had found the Neville wedding party and though there were far more soldiers than either of them had expected, they still had the numbers to slaughter them all.

Thomas drew up at the center of a line of horsemen, forming the right wing to five hundred ax and sword men, already bright with sweat from the hard march through the predawn. As the archers went in ahead, it was a chance for those men to catch their breath. At least the day's heat was still no more than a threat. It would be a misery later on, with the weight of armor and weapons and the sapping exhaustion of using them. Lord Egremont grinned at the thought, an expression that faded slightly as he saw Trunning bring his mount up close and insert the animal into the waiting line. The man was never still, and Thomas could hear his hoarse voice yelling threats at some unfortunate who had wandered out of position.

Ahead of them, six score archers disappeared into the brush, each man on his own as they advanced and sought out targets. Thomas had no idea if the Nevilles had brought archers with them. If they had not, his hundred and twenty would begin the butchery with shafts, cutting them to pieces without the loss of a single one of his small army.

Thomas jerked his head up as he heard someone scream, a distant figure lurching out from where he had been hiding himself. More yells sounded and across the mile of open ground, Thomas could see scurrying men who stopped and seemed to twitch and then moved on, sending arrows ahead of them. He shuddered, imagining the panting archers trying to look in all directions, waiting always for the sudden agony as they were seen and spitted through with a shaft. It was ugly work and it was clear by then that the Nevilles had their own lads out with bows to meet them.

Thomas took a breath, looking stonily ahead rather than at Trunning for his approval.

"Close up on them! With me, in good order!" he shouted along the line.

The men-at-arms took a firmer grip on their swords and axes and the horsemen clicked tongues in their cheeks, urging their mounts into a slow walk forward. The archers would be reaching the Neville lines, in range to bring them crashing down.

Ahead of him, Thomas saw two burly men stand up suddenly, appearing out of the gorse and bushes. He saw them bend longbows and jerked his shield up, rocked back an instant later as a shaft struck it with a loud crack. The other disappeared past him, causing someone to cry out in pain or shock behind. Trunning was bellowing an order, but the line was already moving. Archers had to be charged and the line of horsemen surged ahead of those on foot, shields held high and visors down, swords ready to strike. Thomas felt excitement swell as he used his spurs to send his huge black horse into a plunging canter.

The two archers tried to dodge, throwing themselves to the ground as the first horsemen closed the distance. Thomas saw them in a cloud of dust, scrabbling desperately to fend off hooves and a sword-blow as a knight galloped over them. Then they were behind, left for the axemen to cut as they raced up.

He was riding hard by then, the line of armored knights growing ragged as they encountered the natural obstacles of the land. Thomas felt his mount bunch and guided it over a thornbush, clipping it with its hooves so that the thing quivered in his wake. He adjusted his shield and leaned back, slowing the pace so that he would not get too far ahead. The Nevilles were there, just eight hundred yards or so away, looking small and weak against the pounding line of horses.

"Lord Egremont! Slow down, you stupid . . ."

Thomas looked around in fury as Trunning's horse cut across him. The man had the impertinence to take hold of his reins and yank on them.

"Take your hands off!" Thomas snarled at him. He looked around then and saw that he had left his main force far behind.

Trunning removed his grip, raising his visor and mastering his anger with some difficulty.

"My lord, you'll have them all blown, trying to keep you in sight. Half a mile is too far to run in mail. Where are your wits! Did those archers break your courage? Whisht, man, there aren't so many now."

Thomas felt an almost overpowering desire to cut Trunning from his saddle. If he'd thought his father's man could have been surprised he might have risked it, but Trunning was a veteran, always ready to leap away or attack. Even the swordmaster's horse seemed to skitter in small steps from side to side, the old bag of bones as used to the clash of arms as its master. Thomas knew by then that Trunning was right to have halted him, but the words still stung and he could hardly see for rage.

"See to the men, Trunning. Shout and order them as you please, but I'll have your head on a *pike* if you dare touch my reins again."

To his disgust, Trunning merely grinned and pointed at the Neville force.

"The enemy lies over there, Lord Egremont, if you are uncertain. Not here."

"I sometimes wonder, you pompous little whoreson," Thomas snapped. At least he'd scored a point with his father's man. Trunning's face darkened and he opened his mouth to reply, then ducked suddenly from some instinct as arrows flew around them, sent from both sides. Thomas swore, seeing two archers in jerkins of silver and red fall with arrows through their chests. He raised a hand in thanks to the pair of his men who had brought them down. They touched their forelocks to him, loping on.

"Close up!" Trunning roared. "Close on Egremont! Here!"

The lines re-formed around Thomas as he sat his saddle and fumed. He could hear the rasping breath of the men-at-arms as they reached him. They were panting hard in the thick morning warmth and it galled to know Trunning had been right, as always.

"Stand here and rest," Thomas called to them, seeing relief flood their faces. "Take water and wait. We are three times their number, can you see?"

When they had settled, he walked them all forward, his mount stepping gingerly over the bodies of dead archers as they came across them, each one lying alone with arrows standing like bristles in his flesh. Thomas could still hear the clatter of bows across the shrinking strip between the two forces, but he thought there were more bodies in Neville colors than his own gray men.

All the time he had been racing about in the meadows with the horsemen and Trunning, the Nevilles had stood still, waiting for him. As his men settled down to a slow walk, he saw their line suddenly leap forward, coming in a rush. Thomas blinked. The Nevilles were so badly outnumbered, it was suicide to come out to where he could surround and destroy them. He had assumed Salisbury would dig in and defend his camp for as long as he could, perhaps while the man sent riders to summon aid. For them to attack made no sense at all.

"Archers! Sight on the front ranks!" he heard Trunning yell. It made Thomas's spirits soar to see a dozen hidden men lurch up from the long grass, abandoning the savage game with the Neville bowmen to respond to Trunning's order. As soon as they left cover, Neville archers leaped up in turn and arrows flew once more: short, chopping blows that snatched them from their feet. The toll was appalling on both sides, but Thomas could see six or eight of his bowmen survived to take aim at the Neville line. It was too late for them to run, and they shot volley after volley until they were engulfed.

With a great roar, Salisbury's knights rode over those who stung them, horses and men crashing down together, falling behind. Not two hundred yards separated the forces then and Thomas felt his mouth dry and his bladder swell. They moved well, those Neville horsemen. Thomas swallowed nervously, understanding at last that he faced Salisbury's own guard. A quick glance to the left and right reassured him. He had the width of the line. He had the numbers. Thomas Percy, Baron Egremont, raised his arm for one glorious moment and then Trunning gave the order to charge before he could, the treacherous little bastard.

CHAPTER 4

Richard of York was in a fine, expansive mood. The day was hot, with an odor of plaster and stone dust in the dry air. The Painted Chamber in the Palace of Westminster was centuries old, with a dark red ceiling that was cracked right along its length and almost always damp. For once, it had dried, and the smell was quite pleasant.

York sat back as a piece of parchment as long as his arm was passed around the long table. Each of the seated men paused reverently as he received it, reading again the words that would make Edward of Westminster both the Prince of Wales and the heir to the English throne. More than one of the gathered lords sneaked glances from under lowered brows at York, trying to discern his deeper game. Edmund Beaufort, Earl of Somerset, made them all wait as he read the formal declaration from the beginning once again, searching for something he had missed.

The silence grew strained as they all waited for Somerset to take up the quill and sign his name. Nearby, the Westminster bell was struck for noon, the notes booming through the corridors. York cleared his throat, making Somerset look up sharply.

"You were present as this was written, my lord," York said. "Are you unhappy as to its purpose? Its effect?"

Somerset pushed his tongue between his top lip and his teeth, his mouth twisting. There was no subtle clause he could see, no clever wording to deny King Henry's son his rights of blood and inheritance. Yet he could not escape the suspicion that he had missed something. York surely gained nothing by allowing the line of Lancaster to go on for another generation. If there was ever a time to declare for the throne, Somerset was certain it was that very moment. King Henry was still senseless, witless, drowned in fog. York had ruled in the king's name for more than a year with neither disasters nor invasion from France, beyond the usual raids on shipping and the coastal towns. Somerset was only too aware that York's popularity was growing. Yet there it was, on papers Parliament had witnessed and passed on for the Lords and of course York himself to sign, seal, and make law. The men in that room would confirm a baby boy as the future King of England. Somerset shook his head irritably as two more barons cleared their throats, wanting to move on to lunch and the afternoon.

"This has been four months in the making," Somerset said without looking up. "You'll wait a moment more while I read it through again."

York sighed audibly, settling back in his chair and staring up at the ceiling high above. He could see the mud nest of a swallow in the rafters, some valiant or perhaps foolish little bird who had chosen that room to raise its young. York thought he could see a flicker of movement at the entrance hole and fixed his gaze on it, content to wait.

"The boy Edward will be invested in Windsor," Somerset said aloud. "There is no mention here of regents while he grows."

York smiled.

"His father is still king, Edmund. Appointing a regent would be an error twice over. I have agreed to protect and defend the kingdom for the duration of King Henry's illness. Would you have me appoint a third man, or a fourth? Perhaps you would have us all ruling England by the time you are done."

Chuckles echoed his words around the table, while Somerset glowered.

"King Henry will wake from whatever presses him down," he replied. "Where will you be then, my lord York?"

"I pray for it," York said, his eyes showing only amusement. "I have services said every day that I may lay down the terrible burden of my authority. My father's line may come from King Edward, but the sons of John of Gaunt stand before mine. I have not desired the throne, Edmund. All I have done is to keep England safe and whole, that small thing, while her king dreams. *I* am not the father to this child, only his Protector."

There was a subtle emphasis in his final words and though Somerset knew York sought to goad him, he bristled even so, his right fist clenching on the table. He had heard the rumors drifting through the Lords and the Commons. Such whispers were beneath contempt, sprung from the wicked desire to ruin Queen Margaret and deny her son his rightful place. With a muttered curse, Somerset snatched up a quill and signed his name with a flourish, allowing the scribes in attendance to take the scroll from him and sand the ink before passing it at last to York.

Perhaps to infuriate the older man, York let his own gaze pass slowly over the words in turn. It was not a moment to rush and he scratched his neck as he read, sensing the amusement in the other men and the simmering anger in the duke across from him. In truth, York had considered delaying the passage of the discussions in Parliament even further. If King Henry passed from the world before it was signed and sealed, York was at that moment the royal heir. He had been made so by statute four years before, when it had seemed the queen was barren, or the king unable to perform his duties.

The thought was a pinch in his mind, even then, that only his own signature lay between himself and the Crown. Yet Salisbury had persuaded him. The head of the Neville family knew better than anyone how to manage power and secure it for those of his own blood. It was most gratifying to see all that Neville intellect and cunning employed to his advantage, York mused as he read. When he had married Cecily Neville, the house of York had gained the strength of a clan and bloodline so wide and varied that they would surely come to rule, regardless of the married names or the particular coat of arms. He was only grateful that they had decided upon York as their champion. A man standing with Nevilles could rise far, it seemed. Standing against them, poor devils like Somerset could not rise at all.

York nodded at last, satisfied. He took up his own quill and dipped it, adding his name to the end of the list and continuing on in decorative swirls, showing his pleasure.

It was too early to declare for the throne, Salisbury had convinced him of that. Too many of the king's noblemen would take up arms without a second thought, the moment a usurper made himself known. Step by step, the path lay ahead of him, if he chose to walk it. The life of a newborn was a delicate thing. York had lost five of his own to distempers and chills.

He smiled at the scribe setting lead weights on the corners of the scroll. As Protector, the Great Seal of the throne of England was his to use, the final stage. Four common men had stood by for the entire discussion, heads bowed and waiting for the part they had to play.

When York nodded to them, they approached the table, laying out the two halves of the silver Seal and collecting a bowl of wax from where it had been warmed to liquid over a tiny brazier. All the men there watched as the Royal Seal clicked together and the image of King Henry on his throne was covered over in blue wax. One of the men, the Chaff-wax, used a small knife to trim the disk as it formed and began to cool, while another laid lengths of ribbon on the document itself. It was the work of skilled craftsmen and those present watched with interest as the warm disk was upturned and pressed onto the parchment, staining the page with oil. The halves were lifted away and a thin four-inch medal of wax remained, pressed down onto the ribbons until it could not be removed without ripping the paper or breaking the seal itself.

It was done. The bearers of the Seal busied themselves clearing away the tools of their trade, placing the silver halves back into silk bags and then a locked box of the same polished metal. After bowing to the Protector, they trooped out in silence, their part finished.

York rose, clapping his hands together. "There is a child made Prince of Wales, heir to the throne. My lords, I am proud of England today, as proud as a father of his own son."

He looked to Somerset, his eyes bright. Even then, Somerset might have ignored it if one of the others hadn't laughed aloud. Stung, the earl dropped his hand to his sword's hilt, facing York across the table.

"Explain your meaning, Richard. If you have the courage to accuse a man of dishonor and treason, do so clearly, without French games."

York smiled more widely, shaking his head.

"You mistake me, Edmund. Let your choler bleed away! This is a day of joy, with King Henry's line secured."

"No," Somerset replied, his voice deepening and growing hoarse.

He was forty-eight years old, but he had not grown weak or stooped as his hair grayed. He rose slowly from his chair with his shoulders squared, his anger pushing him on. "I believe I will have satisfaction, Richard. If you would speak false rumors, you must also defend them. God and my right arm shall surely decide the outcome. Now apologize and beg my forgiveness, or I will see you tomorrow dawn, in the yard outside."

If not for the table between them, he might have drawn and struck at York then and there. Others in the room touched their own hilts nervously, ready to act. York kept his own hands away from his sword, knowing he was in reach of a sudden lunge and that Somerset was damnably quick. Carefully, he too came to his feet.

"You threaten the Protector and Defender of the Realm," York replied. His voice had grown soft in warning, though he still smiled, unable to hide his delight at this course of events. "Take your hand off your sword."

"I have said I will have satisfaction," Somerset grated in reply, his face flushing.

York chuckled, though the tension in the room made it sound false.

"You are mistaken, but your threat is a crime I cannot forgive. Guards!" He raised his voice at the end, startling those around him. Two heavyset men entered on the instant, drawing blades as soon as they saw the rigid scene before them. York addressed the parliamentary soldiers without looking away from Somerset for an instant.

"Arrest Lord Somerset. He has threatened the person of the Protector. I'm sure investigation will reveal some deeper plot against the throne and those who serve it."

Somerset moved at last, drawing his sword in one smooth motion and lunging over the width of the table with it. His reach was extraordinary and York threw himself back, crashing into the wall behind him so that dry plaster rained down in spirals from the ceiling. In wonder, he raised a hand to his face and looked at the fingers, half expecting to see blood. Yet the guards had lurched for Somerset even as he moved, grappling him and spoiling his blow. As he struggled, they took his sword and jerked his arm behind his back, making him growl in pain.

"You fool, Edmund," York said, his own anger swelling. "You will be taken from here along the Thames to the Tower. I do not think I shall see you again, while charges are prepared. I will send news of your arrest to the queen, in Windsor. I do not doubt she will be distraught to lose one so *very* well loved."

Somerset was dragged away, still roaring and struggling. York wiped sweat from his forehead. He waved a hand at the parchment on the table.

"Have that taken to Windsor, to be read and given to King Henry. God knows, he will not hear the words, but it must be done, even so."

York gathered himself then, raising his head and striding out into the warm air of Westminster Palace. The other lords traipsed out behind him without a word.

BARON EGREMONT RODE HARD at the Neville center. He knew only too well that he was utterly committed to destroying the wedding party. Even with the Percy arms scrubbed out or covered, his archers had drawn first blood and gone on to kill half a dozen of the Neville knights and men-at-arms. No quiet withdrawal would be allowed after that, no second chance. He could see Earl Salisbury's fury written on his face as Egremont cantered in. The Neville earl was surrounded by his best warriors, swinging his sword left and right as he pointed with it and yelled to alter the formation. Thomas guided his horse straight at the older man, his shield and sword feeling light in his hands. He had trained for this. He had brought seven hundred against less than a third as many. He would have them down before the sun reached noon.

All along the line, Percy and Neville horsemen crashed against each other and through, whipping past in thumping blows that left one or both reeling and dazed. It was a frightening moment for the Percy knights, as they struck and were carried on by their own speed, shoved away from those who rode with them. Horses slowed against the solid mass of Neville men and suddenly Percy warriors were at a standstill, hacking and blocking, their mounts kicking out at anyone milling around their legs.

Thomas slashed wildly at the first Neville knight he faced. The man dodged so sharply that his sword glanced across a plate, scoring a spiral shaving of bright metal. Thomas yelped as his left leg was struck with a clang, instantly numb as he slid past the man he was trying to kill. He heard the knight's growled curse, but neither of them could turn back. Two more faced Thomas and, beyond them, he could see Richard Neville, Earl of Salisbury.

"Balion, strike afore!" Thomas roared, feeling his huge horse bunch under him as it responded. It had taken him almost a year to train the animal not to rear to its full height, as it might have done against another stallion. Instead, Balion rose and lunged almost in the same moment, barely leaving the ground before its front hooves punched out against the horses ahead.

God knew, Balion would have led any herd in the wild. The massive destrier needed no urging and the danger was only in losing control when it began to buck and smash. Thomas saw movement behind him and roared "Strike back!" as he parried a blow with his shield. He heard a shriek cut short as Balion hammered a rear foot against some unseen assailant. Thomas found himself laughing in his helmet, exulting in the damage he could do with just a word.

"And *steady!*" he called to the excited stallion, though Balion still pranced and skittered, snorting and wanting to rear once more. As the huge beast settled, Thomas took a heavy impact on his backplate. He rose in his stirrups to give him height as he swung with all his might in reply. Thomas shouted in triumph as his heavy sword cut a great gash in a knight's side, sending blood spraying over lips of torn metal. It was not a mortal wound, but the Neville man fell sideways, losing his grip on the saddle. One leg flailed and kicked upside down, while the other was held by a twisted stirrup. Lord Egremont watched in delight as a man who had faced him in battle was dragged from the field by his bolting mount.

Something crashed against his helmet then. Thomas grunted in pain, cutting back automatically as his vision blurred. He could hear the tumult all along the line and, with a touch of guilt, he hoped Trunning was out there, keeping a cool head. There was no chance to oversee the fighting, not from the thick of it. Those around him pressed with savage vigor, denting and scarring his armor, aiming to break the metal joints or stab and slash at Balion so that the animal's fall would bring him down.

For a time, it felt as if they could not touch him. His armor was good, thicker and harder than the wrought-iron pieces worn by poorer knights. God knew, it hurt to be struck, but Thomas was encased, protected, while others fell to his swinging sword. Salisbury seemed to have vanished in the press, but Thomas saw him again and dug razor spurs into the gashes on Balion's flanks, making fresh blood flow. The stallion leaped forward, crashing over two axemen who had come creeping through the ranks of horse. They hardly had time to raise their weapons before they were kicked down and trampled. Thomas had eyes only for his uncle then, his expression wild inside the visor. His head still rang from a blow and he could taste blood in his mouth, but his father would hear if Thomas took the head of the

Neville clan himself. The Percy family might not be able to trumpet a victory of hedge knights, but his father would know he had sent the right son.

"Salisbury!" Thomas shouted, seeing the older man twist in his saddle to see who called his name. The Neville wore no chestplate or armor beyond an iron gorget. His shield was unmarked still, as no one had reached him through his guards. Perhaps because their master was so ill equipped, those men clustered close around him, losing half a dozen from the fray to protect the earl they served. It was all to the good. Thomas could see the numbers were beginning to tell. Trunning's terrible hoarse voice could be heard somewhere on his right, ordering men against the flanks. It would not be too long, Thomas realized, before he was master of the field, the victor for his house.

"Percy!" Salisbury spat back in his direction. Thomas almost yanked on his reins in shock, a momentary hesitation that had Richard Neville showing his teeth. "Of course, a Percy son! Who else would ride without colors and attack a wedding? Which of you honorless whelps is it? Henry? Thomas? Raise your visor, man, that I may put my sword through that ugly Percy beak."

With a wild shout, Thomas dug in his spurs once more and Balion lunged in. He could hear the Neville lord laughing as his way was blocked. For the first time, Thomas found himself matched by men as skilled as he was. No, he realized, overmatched by their sword arms. He could not force his way through and, all the time, the old bastard hooted, for all the world an echo of his father's derision that made his sight turn red and his ears rush with blood until it felt like sea-waves breaking. Thomas blinked against blood running from some gash high on his head. The helmet was well padded, but a blow from a heavy mace had dented in a sharp edge that ground against his skull like he was being trepanned. His breath labored hot against the breathing holes and still he swung and snapped at Balion to strike, though the beast was flinging froth from its bit and losing strength from blood sheeting down its ribs.

In among the feet of the struggling knights, gray axemen had reached the fighting. The wounds they caused were horrific, striking at the legs of horses to send men tumbling with their screaming animals. On the ground, armored knights were dazed and vulnerable until they could stand once more. The fight had become a savage mêlée, neither side giving way. Percy soldiers still swarmed in greater numbers, but Thomas saw too many of them cut down by Salisbury's men. The Neville's personal guard were both burly and quick, oath-sworn to protect their master and armored as well as Thomas himself. When those men came against ax-wielding smiths and butchers, they went through them in quick, chopping blows.

The fighting coalesced around the raging center—those who were bred and trained for such work, who had built their wind and muscle to fight all day. Armor was vital to withstand the crushing blows that came from all sides as men fought and tore sinews, wrenching limbs and joints to hammer the enemy in a frenzy. Those who had no such protection fell like wheat to the scythe, the white grasses rolled flat by dying men. All the time, the sun continued to rise above them, bringing heat that had knights gasping like birds, their mouths open in their helmets, so that their teeth clashed and broke against the iron when they were struck.

After less than an hour, the fighting lost its manic, jerking pace. Stamina alone began to decide who would live or die as each pair or three met and fought and staggered on. Most of the Percy townsmen had been killed by then, or bore such savage wounds that they could only limp and wander back, holding arms and stomachs that were bloody ruin. The Neville guards had been reduced to no more than eighty men, surrounded by twice as many in good armor.

Thomas could barely raise his head as he sat Balion some way back, taking stock of the progress and scowling at the seemingly inexhaustible energy of Trunning. He could see the swordmaster riding up and down the Percy line, exhorting fading men to greater efforts. Thomas tried to clench his right hand in a gauntlet that dripped blood from some unseen wound. The first sharp agony of his gouged scalp had faded to a dull throbbing. Even Balion's great armored head was dipping toward the long grasses and, as far as Thomas could tell, Salisbury still lived. Thomas clenched his jaw in frustration. He hadn't seen the man's son, the groom, at any stage of the fighting. The dead lay all around that field, but those who had fallen were all retainers of the houses, with not a single name between them.

Thomas tried to summon the energy to go in again, needing only to imagine his father's scorn to prick his spirits from their drowsy stupor. He could see Trunning gesturing at him out of the corner of his eye and it was the implication that he hung back from fear that truly gave him the will to attack once more. Calling him in, like a reluctant schoolboy! Thomas only wished some Neville would cut Trunning's foul head from his shoulders. *There* was a name he would like to leave on the field, even if it was the only one.

As he trotted back to the fighting, Thomas felt Balion stumble, recovering too slowly so that the horse almost went down. He made a quick decision, seeing how few of the Nevilles were still on horseback. Raising his visor, he whistled to a pair of wounded men watching the killing struggle, checking first that they wore no colors. They took his reins and helped him to dismount, his legs feeling oddly weak as they touched the ground and let him know how they had been battered. Thomas swayed slightly, but beyond bruises and a little blood, he was still strong, still fast enough, he was certain. He patted Balion's neck, pleased that the valiant destrier would not be killed for its exhaustion.

"Find him water, if you can. I'll expect him to be brushed and his scratches covered in goose fat by the time I come for him."

The men were pleased enough to leave the bloody meadow. They touched their foreheads, dipping low for Lord Egremont as they led his warhorse away.

Thomas turned, raising his head into the breeze. God, it was a relief to feel the air move on his face after so long confined. He stalked forward, passing a spray of yellow blossoms standing out among the white grasses. His armor creaked and grated, the oil rubbed away from the joints. He swung his sword as he went, loosening the pauldron plates across his shoulders and chest as well as the blackening muscles beneath them.

"Egremont!" Thomas called as he closed on the fighting, letting his men know who and where he was. He swore and dropped his visor down a moment later, shocked to see Salisbury moving backward through his men, beginning to disengage. They were moving away with their master and Thomas suddenly wished he'd kept Balion. Those still horsed were harrying the Neville line, but there was no doubt they were retreating.

"No!" Thomas bawled at them. "Stand and face us!" He could see the drooping black shape of Balion growing smaller behind him and he began to jog forward, not knowing what else he could do.

A Neville knight stood with his arms waving over his head, perhaps hoping to call his own people back. With savage strength, Thomas hacked at the man's neck as he passed, sending him broken to the grass. He ran on, puffing so hard he had to raise his visor once more. Trunning rode up then, the swordmaster's face only slightly redder than usual as he chewed his drooping mustache and peered down at Thomas Percy.

"Trunning!" Thomas gasped in relief. "Give me your horse. We have to catch them, ride them down. Balion is done, exhausted. Quick, man, dismount."

"That would be a battle order, my lord Egremont. Not the policy and purposes of your father's house, but a simple matter of which of us gets to ride—and which of us walks. I'm afraid I choose to ride, my lord."

"You disloyal . . ." Thomas gasped at him. He reached for the man's reins, but Trunning's old nag danced away from his grasp. "I'll watch you swing for disobeying me."

"Do you think so, my lord? It's my feeling your father will be more concerned with how many of his men you've lost today, without a single Neville head to bring him in exchange. Or did you find one, Baron Egremont? Did you find a good Neville head to tie to your saddle by the hair? I didn't see one."

Thomas stayed silent, refusing to answer the man's barbs with another word. Neither he nor his father could have known Salisbury would bring so many of his best swordsmen with him. Thomas blew air from his puffed cheeks. They had fought well, his mother's people. All the Nevilles had needed to do was survive his attack, and they had managed that. Thomas knew he and his men must have butchered over a hundred of Salisbury's best, but as he watched, the armored core of them moved further and further away, pulling back in good order. A few dozen archers might have stung them then, if he'd kept a reserve. Thomas could only watch glumly as his uncle escaped the trap he'd laid. He swore, panting. He wanted to remove his helmet, but the blood would have stuck it to his hair and scalp in a sodden mass and the thought stayed his hand. Trunning was still there, watching him and munching at his mustache as if it was a feast for a starving man.

"You can tell your father you fought well, my lord. I won't give you the lie on that. You nearly reached the old devil himself. I saw."

Thomas looked up in surprise, half wondering if this was some subtle taunt. He saw no mockery in Trunning's expression and shrugged.

"Not enough though, was it?"

"Not today," Trunning replied. "Men trip and fall on their face, that's the way of things. It doesn't matter. Who stands at the end, that's what matters."

Thomas felt his brow crease as he stood there, amazed that Trunning didn't seem to hold the lack of a victory against him. He shook his head, making the little man smile.

"I'll fetch your horse, my lord," Trunning said. "I told you when you bought him that he was too big, but he has heart, that one. Blown or not, he'll carry you home."

The breeze strengthened as Trunning trotted away. Thomas felt a dozen sharp pains spread in him as his flesh understood it would not fight again and could begin to ache and heal. He had not won, but he had tested himself. To his surprise, he was not ashamed. He raised his hand to anyone who could see, cutting an arc in the air that pointed back the way he had come, a morning and an age before.

CHAPTER 5

Thomas could see Alnwick Castle growing steadily ahead of him, the vast yellow fortress dominating the landscape. The sight did not cheer him. After three days on the road, he was both sore and dirty, reeking with old sweat and dried blood. His helmet had come away at last with oil and hot water, but he had a hot, stitched line the length of a finger across his crown and he had only stared when he saw the dent that had caused it. Thomas could feel his spirits sink lower with every step of Balion under him. He had a thousand childhood memories of those pale gold walls, but first and foremost, Alnwick meant the old man. It meant meeting his father.

Heading away from the battlefield, the mood among his men had been almost joyous at first. It was true Salisbury had escaped them, but that was the Percy son's concern. For the rest, by God, they were survivors, giddy with it. They had come through the terror of the crush, each man there with a dozen stories of personal combat or a crippling gash barely escaped. The first night on the road had been raucous, with great bearded soldiers laughing and miming a cut they'd relished or ducked. One of them had a reed whistle, with holes he'd carved himself. The fellow could coax a lively tune from it and some of the men leaped and danced as if they were drunk. Thomas had considered ordering silence as the sun set. For all they knew, the Nevilles were out hunting them. It had seemed madness to shout their position to the night sky.

Perhaps Trunning had guessed his thoughts from his dark expression. The little man had strutted over, leading Thomas away to have a quiet word.

"They'll settle, my lord," Trunning had said softly, staring out over the setting sun. His hoarse voice had been almost a purr then, making Thomas's skin crawl. "I have scouts out to watch for anyone a-creeping up on us. We won't be surprised, I promise you. The lads are just . . . happy to be alive, my lord, with all fingers counted. Let 'em sing a bit, if you would. The shine in the blood dulls again, soon enough. They'll wake a little grimmer, a little surly maybe, but they'll be right as rain in the morning."

Thomas had only been able to stare. There had been a gentleness in Trunning's red and mottled face then. To say Thomas had found such an observation surprising hardly did the word justice. If the sun had appeared once more above the horizon, he might have had an equal sense of wrongness in the world. Yet there it was, a glimmer of affection for the red-faced soldiers bawling out some maudlin tune, men who would snap the spine of the first one to suggest there was anything in them but Alnwick stone, blood, bone, and their oaths. Thomas had nodded sharply to Trunning and his father's swordmaster had walked away. Not once had Trunning looked directly at him. The entire speech had been delivered to the air, as if they stood side by side at the same pissing trough.

Those who had been wounded stayed away from the firelight. As they'd left the battlefield, Trunning had "found" a few carts in the first village along their path, though nowhere near enough for the sixty or so men who needed them. The Percy swordmaster had made them all line up for inspection, checking each wound with rough hands and saying "Cart" or "Walker" before moving on to the next. One or two were dying as they stood there, their wounds draining them white and small. Trunning had paused before each of those, his eyes dark as he shook his head. They knew, just as he did. He still let them on the carts, to die in peace.

That first evening could easily have become a feast, if there had been something to eat beyond dried strips of meat in their pouches. As the moon rose, Trunning had decided it was time to call a halt to the chatter, appearing from darkness and snapping at laughing men to get their heads down and save some strength for the morrow. Thomas had wondered then if daylight would bring Neville trackers heaving into view. In the darkness, all his worst fears seemed possible. There was a chance Salisbury would arm for war as soon as he reached a stronghold. Only time would reveal how many soldiers the earl had within reach. The simple truth was that Thomas had thrown a spear at a savage old boar and damn well missed with it.

No Neville soldiers had appeared on their backtrail the next morning, or the one after that. Trunning set guards and checked every watch, seeming to need no more than short naps himself before he was up and away again, marching around the boundary of their little camps. They had been seven hundred, just a week before. Including the wounded, two hundred and forty men remained to walk or ride back into Alnwick.

It was an odd feeling to approach the fortress on the third day, without drummer boys or banners held proudly ahead of them. The townspeople heard them passing, of course, coming out of their homes. Women gathered up skirts to run out to the main road, squinting into the setting sun to see if their men had returned. Thomas set his mouth tight, clenching his jaw as he rode past them. He could not close his ears to the calls back and forth as wives asked desperately about their husbands, and children began to wail for lost fathers. The sight of the men in the carts caused a great keening to go up from the townspeople. By then the wounded were a pitiful collection, hot with fevers, some dead for two days and swollen with wind and rot.

Staring neither left nor right, Thomas rode Balion in, shuddering slightly as he passed the archers' steps above his head. There were builders working there that evening, perched precariously as they slathered mortar and eased new stones into place.

Thomas saw Trunning's skinny horse edging ahead of him and added a slight pressure at his heels, so that Balion pushed on in a trot. He didn't look back as Trunning grunted something under his breath. He was a Percy son and he was Egremont. He would be damned if he'd let anyone else come home to Alnwick before him. No doubt his father was watching from the high windows. Thomas held his chin up, feeling the swollen stripe throb on his scalp as he left the sound of weeping crowds behind and entered the main keep.

Servants rushed to take the reins of his warhorse, transforming the silent yard with their clatter and noise. The returning men were somber in their replies, shaking their heads again and again in response to questions. Thomas felt his heart thump as he looked up at the tower and saw the old crow wrapped in his furs, staring down.

"See to the men, Trunning," Thomas called. "I'll take the news to my father."

SALISBURY RODE with his hands gripping the reins so tightly it spread a dull ache up his arms to add to his bruises. To be forced to run from a Percy enemy was a humiliation that burned so bright it was hard to think at all. A week before, Baron Cromwell had gathered the townsfolk at Tattershall to wave and cheer as his niece Maud left with a new husband and two hundred soldiers. Six days later, they came limping back, fewer than half of those who had left, with too many wounds bound in rough cloth. It was Salisbury's duty to explain what had happened and to assure the man his niece was unhurt. As Salisbury imagined Cromwell's reaction, he growled softly, shaking his head like a series of twitches, each one a bitter child of the shame spilling through him.

He could feel the eyes of his wife and son on his back as he led the battered soldiers south toward Tattershall Castle. Local boys raced ahead of him, carrying the news of his return. There was nothing he could do about that and he only glowered, his head low and his breathing harsh. Salisbury knew he brooded when events turned against him. His father had been a man to shrug off the worst setback and go on, waking fresh and able to laugh at his own dark moods. Richard, Earl of Salisbury, had been cut from more sullen cloth. He had known great joys in his life, but even at his moments of triumph there were always deeper threads shifting beneath, twisting his muscles and thoughts in the blackness.

The town lay to the north of the brick castle, standing like a red spear on a hill that had been cut square to hold it. Salisbury looked past the shocked faces of merchants and townsfolk, all coming out to stand and whisper, shaking their heads and crossing themselves. There was work to be done, work he told himself he did not welcome but was vital nonetheless. He had not been able to collect the Neville dead, in the field. To save himself and his remaining men, Salisbury had ordered a withdrawal. Some of the wounded had cried out in disbelief when they saw him go. They'd held up their arms, as if seeing them would bring him back, as if they had only to beckon for Salisbury to return. It all burned in him, an acid that swelled and choked his chest until he thought it must spill from his mouth and burn holes in the bloody gambeson he wore.

Rage. He had not felt the pleasure of the real thing for years, the clean, hot burn that strengthened the arm and built a man's confidence to a dangerous level. As he rode, he struggled for the calm he would need to plan and prepare, but could not find it. Rage filled him like water into a jug. He would gather his men. He would gather an army—and he would see the Percy strongholds in ashes. Salisbury made his oaths as Tattershall grew before him.

He was not surprised to see riders come out of the main gate before he reached the hill, cantering down the steep slope that separated the castle grounds from the town. Cromwell had trusted his niece's safety to the head of the Nevilles. The man would be expecting the worst possible news.

Salisbury raised his hand, halting his followers as the first three horsemen drew up and faced him. Ralph Cromwell was not a well man, his face swollen around his collar and too darkly red, though Salisbury knew the surgeons bled him regularly. At sixty, the man's hair was bone-white and wispy as a babe's, whipping back and forth over his bald crown in the breeze. The man had ridden out without banners, still wearing a tunic spotted with juices from whatever he had been eating before.

"My lord Salisbury," Cromwell called, though his gaze slid over Richard Neville and searched the others. When the old man's wet eyes stopped on his niece, Salisbury saw him sag in the saddle, relief in every line of him. He knew then that Cromwell had not been part of the plot. Though the baron was childless, it was well known he doted on his sister's daughter as if she were his own. Salisbury had been almost certain the man would never have placed her in danger. Yet "almost" had brought him close to striking Cromwell dead. Not many had known Richard Neville had been present at Tattershall. For Salisbury, it was an effort to unclamp his hand from his sword hilt, so hard had he been holding it.

Cromwell's gaze snapped back, perhaps sensing some of the threat in the dark expressions of the battered group. Salisbury inclined his head in sour greeting.

"Maud lives, Lord Cromwell. As do my wife and son. As do I. The Percy brigands failed, though they brought three for every one of mine."

He watched as Cromwell understood, stiffening slightly while his hair waved in the wind like a white flag.

"Percy?"

Salisbury watched the man's mouth tighten.

"It was the dowry manors, then. My lord, I knew their spite, but nothing of their intentions. I swear it on the honor of my house and name."

"I hold you innocent, my lord. If I did not, I would not have returned to Tattershall."

The baron lost some of the tension in his face. Richard Neville was not a man to cross, not with the ear of the Protector. Cromwell wiped his forehead, where it had begun to glisten.

"For now though," Salisbury went on, "I must ask that my men are tended in your care, while I send word."

"Send word, my lord?" Cromwell asked. His oyster-eyes were always wet, it seemed, red-rimmed and shining as they darted back and forth among those watching him.

"To Richard of York, Baron. The king's Protector. To my son, Earl Warwick." Despite his struggle for calm, Salisbury heard his own voice growing loud and harsh. "To every man-at-arms in Neville service in England, to every house bound to us, by blood or marriage. I will call them all, Baron. I will cut out the Percy family, root and branch, to be thrown on the fire!"

It would have been courtesy to allow Cromwell to lead them back to his castle, but Salisbury was his superior in rank and, in that moment, beyond such niceties. He dug in his heels and his horse jerked into a trot past the astonished baron, followed on the instant by eighty scarred and scowling men. His son John went with him, staying at his father's side. Only Maud and Salisbury's wife, Alice, hung back, the older woman putting her hand out to prevent Maud trotting dutifully after her husband.

"Baron Cromwell," she called, "Richard would want me to thank you for allowing us to lodge at Tattershall once more." She could not apologize for her husband's rudeness, so sought words to smooth the older man's ruffled feathers. "You may be sure that your name will be spoken in London as a man we trust and honor."

Cromwell dipped his head, still bristling as he glared at the rear of the men riding into his home.

"I'm sure Maud would appreciate your counsel, Baron," Alice went on. "I'll leave her with you, in your care, where she was always well kept—"

"Enough, Alice," Cromwell said in grim amusement. "Your husband charges into my keep without waiting on my permission, but who could blame him after what he has seen? If I were younger, I would be blowing the horns myself after what he has endured. It is forgotten, though you have my thanks for your grace."

Alice nodded, smiling at a man she liked very much. It was only a shame that Cromwell's wife had died before producing sons, leaving him to rattle around Tattershall on his own. She dug in her heels and rode after her husband, leaving uncle and niece alone.

"Your mother-in-law is a fine woman," Cromwell said, looking after her. "I thank God you came through safely, Maud. If I had known—if I'd heard even a breath of a threat to you . . ."

"I know, Uncle, you would not have sent me out, even with two hundred Neville guards. Be at peace, I saw very little of the killing.

John and Countess Alice took me away before the battle was truly joined." As she spoke, the young woman shuddered, goose pimples rising along her arms to give the lie to her words.

"I gave you to be a Neville, Maud," Cromwell said, looking after the soldiers as they rode into his home. "Salisbury spoke of houses allied to his and he was not boasting. They run through every line, every house that matters, at least now that mine is joined to them." He smiled at his own conceit and was rewarded by dimples appearing in her cheeks before his mood turned serious once more. "If there is to be a war, Maud, we have chosen our side by your marriage. I do not envy those who stand against that man, not with Richard Plantagenet on one hand and Earl Warwick on the other. Those three together could break the country in two, were they so minded."

"Perhaps it will not come to that, uncle. You told me once that gold begins and ends wars. Perhaps Earl Percy will make recompense for the wounds he has caused."

Her uncle shook his head.

"I do not think there is gold enough in the world to prevent the struggle now. I will pray for peace, Maud, but there are times when there is a boil to be pierced, when foul matter must be pressed out to clean the wound. My dear, this may be such a time."

THOMAS PERCY STRODE alone through the corridors of Alnwick Castle. Perhaps the servants avoided the old man when there was bad news on the wind, he did not know. Whatever the reason, the castle seemed empty as he walked, his blood-smeared spurs jingling. He had let his bladder go during the battle, not from fear but simply the impossibility of finding a quiet place to remove his armor while the forces clashed. Four times since then, he'd let hot urine dribble down his leg and out of the open boot-tips as he rode. The inner padding of his armor was drenched with it, chafing the skin on his thighs until it was raw. He could smell the taint strongly on him, though he thanked God his bowels seemed to have blocked. There had been battles where entire troops of mounted knights had come back with brown stains down the flanks of their horses. For all it was a necessary evil, men still bent their wit to sharp comments when they saw such a thing. He would be spared that, at least, when he met his father.

From the marshaling yard, he'd seen Earl Percy standing at the window of the tower library. Thomas climbed the stairs there without seeing a single soul. His mother's absence was strangest of all and he wondered if his father had sent her away to another of the Percy holdings so she could not witness his return, or demand to know what had happened.

He reached the door and found it slightly ajar, pushing it open with his mailed glove. His father was inside, still standing by the window, staring out. Thomas cleared his throat, feeling a sudden rush of anger that he had to come before the old man in such a way, as if he were a boy sent to be punished after stealing. There had been many such whippings in his childhood, when the man at the window had been younger. Thomas found his heart was thumping in his chest and he imagined how good it would feel to push his father through the leaded glass and watch him break on the ground below. The thought of Trunning's expression at seeing that almost made him smile as his father turned to him.

"I sent you out with seven hundred," Earl Percy said. The old man's face was subtly swollen, the web of veins across his cheeks and nose seeming almost black against the brick-red skin. His eyes were sharp as he gathered his furs around his shoulders. "I'm surprised you even dared to come home, with so few left at your back. I see from your frightened glances that you have brought me no victory. The men in the yard hang their heads, as they should, if seven hundred cannot butcher a young groom and his servants. Well? Give me the truth of it, boy. I am weary of waiting."

"Salisbury had his own guard with him. Two hundred or more of his best men, sixty archers among them. We killed and cut two-thirds of them, more, but Neville escaped, with his son and the Cromwell bride."

The old man crossed the room in jerky steps, standing to look up at his son in grim appraisal.

"You come back to Alnwick with nothing? If I had sent your brother Henry, do you think he would be standing there with the same sulky looks, telling me he failed?"

"I don't know," Thomas snapped, his voice hoarse with rising anger. "Salisbury had his best men. They gave a good account of themselves and still we murdered more than half of them before they could get away. I don't think Henry could have done any more than that!"

His voice had grown louder as he replied and the old man reached out suddenly and smacked him hard across the face. For just a heart-beat, Thomas flinched, the instincts and memories of childhood ruling him. In another moment, he felt rage and shame at his own reaction. He dropped his hand to his sword, suddenly determined to draw and cut his father in two.

Earl Percy's hand gripped his, a claw that held him still.

"Oh *rule* thyself!" Percy snapped. "Control thy choler, you impudent boy! You failed, though you might have *won*. I knew the risk when I sent you out. The Neville is cunning and I did not think he would die easily. Yet it was worth the lives you lost to try, do you understand? It was worth the chance I took, with my men and my son, for the gains you might have had."

Thomas tensed his arm to draw once again. He felt the old man's strength waver and knew he was stronger, that he could draw and cut if he wanted and there was nothing his father could do to stop it. The knowledge was so surprising, he let his hand fall away.

His father grunted in satisfaction.

"Master that temper, Thomas, before it masters you. It was ever a Percy failing, though we can bind it well enough."

Thomas saw a glint of metal among his father's cloaks. His eyes widened at the thought that there had been a dagger there, hidden so quickly he would never be certain. He stepped back and Earl Percy tilted his head, watching him with amusement.

"I cannot take a step back, Thomas. Not one. You failed, because the Neville is suspicious and wary—and right to be! It doesn't matter. I planned for this, as well. Your mother is in a convent, bound to holy orders. I asked the abbess to impose a vow of silence on her, but the old bitch said it was not their way. She will come to regret that, I think!"

To Thomas's surprise, the old man chuckled and shook his head.

"Still, it is well that she is away from me, before I killed her, or she took a dagger to me while I slept. Fire and oil, boy, your mother and me, each made worse by the other." He saw the confusion in his son and clapped him on the shoulder. "Now open your ears. You struck and you missed the heart of the Neville clan. They'll be coming for us, this year or next spring. Everything I have made, everything I have gathered to the Percy name is in danger now. Yet I would rather go to my grave knowing I had thrown and failed than not dared to throw, do you understand? We will go to war with the Nevilles, with York if we have to, that Plantagenet snake curled up so tight around the king and his son! No Percy weighs the odds, or counts the numbers when we raise banners. I welcome it, Thomas. I welcome the chance to take the field one last time. What good are these old joints to me if I cannot ride against my enemies? When they come, we'll meet them in King Henry's name. We'll stand with a dozen earls and dukes more loyal to King Henry than his damned York Protector, married to a Neville. Do you understand? I gambled to finish it in a day, but one poor throw does not mean the end, Thomas. It means the beginning!"

CHAPTER 6

C old days dropped hard on the country that year. December opened with bitter frosts that froze town and monastery stew ponds, covering fat carp as they lay beneath in darkness, barely moving their fins.

The town of Windsor was luckier than most, with many households able to afford coal, or enough wood to line a wall and keep the families warm. Work went on even in the coldest months though, as the frost deepened, there were soon starving men begging for Christmas alms on every street. With the autumn crops gathered and stored, there were still odd jobs repairing shutters and wooden shingles for those with the skill. Hundreds more drifted in for the royal feasts that would mark the birth of Christ, fourteen hundred and fifty-four years before. In the castle, banquets of two dozen courses were prepared in the knowledge that some of it would be handed out to the poor. It was a tradition around the royal residences, and the best spots on the streets close to the royal kitchens were all taken, though a bad night could reveal one or two frozen bodies in the gutter the following morning.

The gong-farmers, or cesspit men, took on a few laborers in search of work, preferring to dig out the shafts in the wealthier houses while the contents were firm with cold. Those men at least were warm as they descended with shovels, and rags wrapped around their faces, into the bowels of the earth. Some were always overcome with fumes and had to be pulled out on a rope. It was hard work, but a good pit man could earn a laborer's weekly wage in a single day, and they guarded the right to the best streets from all those who might try to undercut them.

As Christmas came closer, the roads around the castle filled with those the royal family had invited for the twelve days of peace and celebration. It seemed Queen Margaret was determined not to let her husband's illness spoil the festivities. Jugglers, magicians, and singers competed for coins in the inns, while every room in town had been booked long in advance, until even the stables were filled with snoring families. Acting troupes arrived with raucous fanfares from their own servants, coming into town in elaborate processions, all hoping to perform for the queen. Eclipsing even Easter and Whitsun, Christmas was the greatest festival of the year and Windsor's busiest time.

With King Henry still lost in his dreaming, there was no public healing planned that Christmas, where those with illnesses would be allowed to come forward and touch his hand. The most desperate sufferers came even so, with nowhere else to turn. Lepers and cripples rang bells on the streets, gathering together for protection as one or two alone could be set upon and beaten by local men.

Those of noble blood rode past the shops and mummers performing for coins, heading for the comforts available in the castle itself. The Duke of York may have been ruling the country in London, yet he could not draw the king's earls and dukes and barons to a Christmas celebration. The choice of guests in Windsor was the sole province of Queen Margaret and it was no accident that the invitations to forty-four noble houses omitted York, Salisbury, and half a dozen others linked to the Neville family. Margaret had considered sending one to Earl Warwick, the younger Richard Neville. She had met him during the siege of London, when Jack Cade brought an army into the city. Warwick had impressed her then, but York's chancellor was his father and, with regret, she decided that his loyalties were beyond her influence.

One or two guests had sent their regrets, if they were too old or ill to make the journey. Yet over three days, thirty-eight lords and their retinues had come to Windsor, a show of enduring respect for the king that gave Margaret enormous satisfaction. She made a point of coming out to greet those whose support she needed most, honoring them publicly. It was no small thing that she did not make them come to her, and their pleasure showed in flushed cheeks and the proud smiles of their wives.

Derry Brewer made himself invaluable as each household arrived. He wore a simple dark tunic and hose, standing unremarked among the royal staff. He smiled vaguely at everything he saw, but his eyes were sharp and he missed nothing.

From just after dawn, servants in the colors of great houses would come running along the road, announcing their masters and mistresses long before they were in sight. Some would send stewards to prepare the way still further. By the time the heads of noble houses actually rode through the great gates, Derry had delivered a stream of whispered information to the queen's ear. He carried no ledger, merely tapping his head when Margaret expressed surprise or even blushed at what he knew.

Baron Gray was one she would remember. He had sent no one ahead, arriving up from the town with his rather thin wife on horseback beside him and two fresh-faced lads struggling along in matched tunics, carrying a heavy box. Margaret warmed to the man instinctively, her expression freezing as Derry whispered, "Sodomite and pederast, like the Greeks. Fond of his wife, but I'm told he preys on poor lads. Discreet enough. Proud as the devil and about as cruel." Margaret glanced at her spymaster as Baron Gray approached. Derry had described a number of peculiarities in the noble guests, from suspicions of an old theft to a broken marriage promise and a ruined girl paid to keep silence. She had heard a tinge of humor in his voice more than once, but no sense of judgment, just a dry recital of old sins and weaknesses. Yet there was something unpleasant in Derry's eyes as Lord Gray approached. Margaret caught a glimpse of it before it was shuttered away, something dull and flat and murderous.

Baron Gray bowed deeply to her. His eyes suited his name, rather small and hard in a fleshy, pink face. His wife curtseyed deeply, her entire head hidden by an elaborate bonnet. Words failed Margaret and she only stared, extending her hand to the man. Before that day, she could not honestly have said she knew what a pederast actually was. Derry's brief description had filled her mind with unpleasant images that made it very hard not to shudder as Gray touched the back of her hand with moist lips. The moment passed and the baron moved on, his wife looking back with thin-lipped pride as they were ushered away. Margaret forced herself to breathe, focusing on Derry saying something about tin mines and an elderly baron bowing like a dancing master, though he was twice her age.

By nightfall, Margaret retired at last, her feet sore from standing. She had rested for brief periods during the day, called away from food or a welcome chair to greet another arrival. She had seen their pleasure that she had done so and, though she was weary, she did not regret the time lost. For the twelve nights following, she would know every man and woman in the castle.

With Derry's aid, she had been able to place old enemies far apart. She had even ensured the prickly sensibilities of one senior countess were not inflamed by the view of a pretty young cousin as she rose each morning. On Derry's suggestion, Margaret had made a great fuss of Baron Audley, a white-bearded old soldier who flushed delightedly at her attention. Yet when Baron Clifford arrived, her spymaster grew stern as he leaned close, facing Margaret so that his back was to the man coming toward them both.

"Give him an inch and he will take it as weakness, my lady," Derry muttered. "Lord Clifford sees either wolves or deer—nothing in between. Needless to say, he does not respect the deer."

Margaret had raised her head at that, determined not to wilt. Her expression had been chilly as she welcomed Baron Clifford. The man matched her for stiffness, following the servants to rooms far from the main halls.

The absence of one name was a source of enduring bitterness. Margaret counted Somerset as a friend and she hated to think of him being held prisoner. The earl's rank allowed him some freedoms in the Tower, even as he was held for trial. Yet York had refused to allow the man his parole for the season, replying to Margaret's request with a pompous letter about high crimes against officers of the state. York had sent his spidery script enclosed with her husband's own Seal. She knew she must not dwell on his pleasure in doing so. If she let herself think of York too long or too often, she would discover she had wound loops of her hair around her fingers until they had gone purple. She had already mourned for Somerset, his loss one more thorned branch on the fire within, a constant burn that she struggled to keep hidden.

Windsor Castle was busier than it had been all year. Huge and elaborate hunts kept the guests entertained, as well as plays, magicians, and music in the evenings. The mood was light among them, despite the presence of so many armed retainers and servants, a symptom of the age. Even in the royal castle, there was fear amidst the revelry.

As Christmas morning dawned, Margaret returned to her private

rooms in time to watch her son feed from his wet nurse, sucking bus-
ily at the pink teat until he could be belched and put to rest for a short
time. Young Edward was a year old and had discovered crawling, so
that he could no longer be left with any expectation that he might
remain in the same place, or even the same room. The nurse wiped
away a little milky vomit and placed a cloth on Margaret's shoulder
before handing over the child. Margaret felt the warmth of him as he
clucked and shifted, screwing up his tiny face in irritation at something. She smiled and the nurse responded to her unguarded expression, before dipping into a deep curtsey and leaving the room.

For a brief time, Margaret was alone. She found herself yawning
and shook her head in amusement, thinking of all the things that still
had to be done before the great feast later on. There would be a service in the chapel to attend, and as they all prayed for the health
of the king, the kitchens would be as busy as a battlefield. The staff
would already be decorating and impaling carcasses, spicing and
seething dishes to impress her husband's nobles—all men and women
who employed their own cooks. Margaret had insisted on a French
flavor to all of it, knowing that the dishes of Anjou would be mostly
unknown to her guests. There were geese, of course, roasted by the
dozen, but there would also be woodcock, partridge, and pigeon;
delicate sugar tarts and pastries; savory jellies cast in huge copper
molds; and soups, stuffed prunes, cakes, eels in brine, a hundred different dishes for the Christmas Day feast.

She began to sing softly to the child on her shoulder, feeling him
shuffle and peer around before he laid his head back down. Her
breasts had ached terribly for a time after he was born, but the custom
of a wet nurse was one she was happy to continue among the English.

Margaret looked up from the fussing child at a clatter of boots
nearby. Someone was calling for her, asking loudly where she was to
be found. She tutted to herself, looking down at the Prince of Wales

as he sucked his thumb and opened his eyes for a moment. They were very blue. Whatever he saw seemed to satisfy him and he closed them again, but the shouting had not ceased. Margaret frowned. The moments alone with her son were precious and too rare. She only hoped no one had been injured out in the vast hunting park. One of the Duke of Buckingham's servants had broken his ankle the previous day and she did not want the nobles to remember a spate of bad luck during the season.

The nurse came back in, her face unaccountably flushed. From instinct, the young woman reached for the sleeping child and Margaret handed him over, feeling a deep pang in her womb as the weight left her shoulder.

"My lady . . ." the nurse began, so nervous that she could hardly speak. Her movements were all unthinking as she settled Prince Edward once again in the crook of her arm. Of course he chose that moment to begin bawling, shaking tiny fists at the world in paroxysms of rage.

"What is it, Katie? Did I not say to give me an hour? A single hour in the day, is it too much to ask?"

"M-my lady, Your Highness . . ." the voices and steps were still clattering closer. Margaret felt a sudden spasm of fear, imagining assassins or murder.

"Out with it! What has you in such a flutter, Katie?"

"Your husband, the king, my lady. They are saying he has woken."

Margaret took a step back, so hard did the words strike her. Her eyes widened and she gathered her skirts, rushing to the door. By the time she reached it, the king's chamber servants were already coming through, panting from running.

"The king, Your Highness!" one of them exclaimed. His presence across her path checked her in body and mind, allowing a moment of stillness.

"Wait," Margaret retorted. She raised her hand as if to push the man out. He backed hurriedly away until she closed the door on his astonished face. She turned to the nurse and her son, both staring at her.

Margaret had cultivated dignity in her manner ever since arriving at the English court aged just fifteen. For Henry's honor she had tried to become a queen in her bearing, a noble swan in manner as well as the symbol of her house. She had learned all she could, but being his wife was about far more than simply knowing the names of houses and estates. It was more than the laws of England and the peculiar little traditions that seemed so entwined about them. Above all else, being queen to a helpless king meant Margaret had to think before she rushed in. It meant she had to taste before she ate, and sip before she drank.

Henry had been weak and in danger for over a year. She ached to run to him, her skirts gathered up at her thighs, pelting down the corridors like a market urchin. Instead, she thought, and thought, finally nodding to herself and opening the door. Then she walked.

The news was everything she had hoped for, everything she had wished a thousand times, but the reality brought its own fears. There were many who would rejoice at Henry's waking, while others would rage and flap and curse. She did not doubt some of his lords had expected him to die—and planned for that end. Margaret came up short at the entrance to Henry's rooms. She sent the door crashing back, stinging the hands of those fumbling to open it.

The sun was rising behind her husband. Margaret raised a hand to her heart, unable to speak as she saw he was standing—*standing*, by God—looking back at her. King Henry was thin, his skin stretched over his bones. He wore a long white shift that reached to his ankles, one hand resting on the bedpost. Two men fussed around him as he looked at her, touching the king's wrists with their fingers and leaning across his view. Doctors John Fauceby and William Hatclyf were the royal physicians, with three yeomen assistants and Michael Scruton, the serjeant surgeon for the king's person. Bowls of urine and blood steamed on tables by the bed, with two of the men peering into them and calling out their observations on clarity and sediment for the recording scribe. As Margaret stared, Hatclyf dipped his fingers and tasted the urine, noting to the scribe that it was too sweet and recommending bitter green plants be added to the king's meals. His colleague sniffed at the king's blood and he too touched the liquid in the bowl, rubbing his fingers together to check its grease before his pink tongue darted out. Their voices clashed and called over one another, each man struggling to be heard and to have his observations written down first.

It was a bustling scene, but at the center of it, the king was there, awake, very still and very pale. His eyes were clear and Margaret felt her own fill with tears as she went to him. To her astonishment, he held up a hand to halt her.

"Margaret? I am surrounded by *strangers*. These men are telling me I have a son. Is it true? God's wounds, how long have I been lying here?"

Margaret opened her mouth, shocked to hear her husband use an oath for the first time she could ever recall. She had known him as a drowned man, pushed under by agues and dreams until he was completely lost. The man staring at her neither blinked nor looked away. She swallowed, nervously.

"You do have a son. Edward is just over a year old. I showed him to you when you were taken by illness. Have you no memory of him?"

"Not that, nor anything else, no . . . moments, instants, nothing I can . . . a son, Margaret!" His eyes narrowed suddenly, an expression of dark suspicion. "When was he born, this Prince of Lancaster?"

Margaret flushed, but then raised her head, suddenly angry.

"The thirteenth day of October, the year of Our Lord 1453. *Six* months after you fell ill."

Henry stood for a moment, rubbing the fingers of his right hand against each other as he thought. Margaret could only wait, overwhelmed as he nodded and seemed satisfied.

"And yet you stand there still! Bring him to me, Margaret. I would see my heir. No, by God, send someone else. I must hear everything that has happened. I can hardly believe I have lost so much time. It is as if a year was stolen from me, torn out of my life."

Margaret gestured to one of the chamber servants, sending the young woman running back to fetch the Prince of Wales.

"Longer, Henry. You have been . . . absent, no, ill for over eighteen months. I prayed and I had services said every day. I . . . you don't know what it means to see you awake." Her lip quivered suddenly and tears spilled down her cheeks, wiped quickly away. She watched as her husband's gaze turned inward, a frown creasing his forehead.

"How fares my England, Margaret? The last I remember . . . no, it does not matter. Everything I remember is so long ago. Tell me quickly. I have lost so much!"

"Richard of York was made Protector, Henry, a regent to rule the country while you were . . . unable." She watched in wonder as her husband's fists clenched, almost in a spasm. Not once had he given thanks to God for his deliverance, this man who had prayed for hours every day in all the time she had known him.

"York? How very pleased he must have been to have my crown dropped into his lap." The king twisted a ring on his finger almost viciously, as if he wanted to take it off. "Which of my lords forgot their honor to such a degree? Surely not Percy? Surely not Buckingham?"

"No, Henry. They stayed away from the vote with many others. Somerset too, though he was put in the Tower for his refusal to accept York's authority."

King Henry's face darkened, the flush of blood to his cheeks standing out like a banner against the white skin.

"That much I can change today. Where is my Seal, that I may sign an order for his release?"

The king's steward chose that moment to speak, his own eyes still bright with moisture from being witness to the king's waking.

"Your Grace, the Duke of York has the Royal Seal, in London."

Henry staggered slightly, stretching out his hand to the bedpost. His arm was too weak to hold him and gave way, so that he sat hard on the bed. His doctors reacted with febrile excitement, murmuring all the time on his color and his disposition, the sound like a drone of bees around the king. Doctor Fauceby reached once more for the king's neck to check the strength of his heart's spasms, only to have Henry slap his hand away.

"By Christ, I am as weak as a *child*," Henry snapped, his color deepening in embarrassment and anger. "Very well. I will see my son and the servants will dress me. Then I will ride to London to put York out of my place. Now help me up again, one of you. I want to be standing when I see my son for the first time."

"Your Highness, this is the crisis," Hatclyf said as firmly as he could. "I must recommend you rest."

The physician was trembling, Margaret realized. For more than a year, Henry had been little more than a pale body to be washed and clothed, tapped and measured like a blind calf. The men around King Henry were intimately familiar with his flesh, but they knew the man not at all. She wondered if she did herself.

Margaret watched as Fauceby exchanged a glance with Hatclyf. Both doctors had a monkish air, all thin fingers and sunken cheeks. Yet Fauceby was the more senior, and when he spoke his voice was firm and low.

"Your Highness, my colleague is correct. You have been very ill for a long time. You are sweating, a sign that your liver and tripes are still weak. If you excite yourself, you risk collapse, a return of the sickness. You should rest now, Your Highness, in normal sleep. Hatclyf and I will prepare a broth of dark cabbage, sowbread, and wormwood for when you wake again, with your permission. It will purge and restore your humors, so that your recovery will be more lasting."

Henry considered, looking aside as he judged his own strength. He was appalled at the weakness that beset him, but if he had judged the lost time correctly, he was thirty-three years old. The realization that he was the same age as Christ at his crucifixion hardened his will. He had woken on Christmas Day, at the age of Christ at his death. It was a sign, he was certain. He would not wilt, or spend one more moment in his sickbed, no matter what it cost him.

"No," he said. "You two there. Help me stand."

The two yeomen servants responded instantly. They took Henry under his outstretched arms and lifted him to his feet once more, shuffling back with bowed heads as Henry found his balance on trembling legs. They could all hear footsteps coming closer and the wet nurse entered the room at that moment, struggling to curtsey and hold up the baby prince at the same time. She did not let her eyes settle on King Henry while he still stood in his nightclothes.

"Bring him here," the king said, his smile unforced. He took the child and held him up, though his arms shuddered with the effort.

Margaret put a hand over her mouth, trying not to sob in relief and joy.

"You," Henry said to the tiny boy looking down at him. "By God, I see you, my own son. My *son*."

CHAPTER 7

King Henry felt himself shivering as he reached the sweeping curve of the River Thames. Though he could see the Palace of Westminster, he was still half a mile west of the city of London. It was said the two parts crept closer each year as merchants built workshops and storehouses on cheap land within range of the London markets—and the city grew beyond its Roman walls.

The darkness only increased the horrible, biting cold. The wind brought a spatter of frozen hail as the sun set, but the weakness the king felt was all his own. Henry was appalled at how feeble he had become, so wasted of limb that barely twenty miles on horseback had reduced him to a gasping mass of aches, with sweat pouring from him under his armor. He thought at times that only the iron kept him from falling.

He had not intended to ride to the Palace of Westminster in procession, but there had been almost forty loyal lords in attendance in Windsor. As word spread that the king had risen from his bed and intended to ride to London, they'd begun to cheer and stamp, the noise growing and swelling throughout the castle until it reached the town outside and was doubled and redoubled on a thousand throats, until it became a great bellow to match the winter gales.

Before he'd left, King Henry had endured the Christmas service in St. George's chapel, sitting pale and still as all those present gave thanks to God for his deliverance. The great feast waiting for them had been pillaged by passing men, excitedly summoning horses and servants to join the king as he set forth. The winter sun had already been sitting low in a red sky by the time Henry took to the road with more than a hundred men, all armed and armored, with the royal lion banners fluttering on the freezing wind.

The Palace of Westminster had been built upstream of the city, away from the foul miasmas that brought disease each summer. Henry took the road that followed the banks of the river, with Buckingham on one side, Earl Percy on the other, and Derry Brewer following with the rest in serried ranks behind. By then, the king was walking his horse to eke out his strength. It had already taken five hours or more to ride the miles from Windsor, and Henry was worried his will had taken him beyond the strength of his body. He knew if he fainted and fell, it would be a blow to his standing from which he might never recover. Yet Somerset was still imprisoned by York's order. Henry knew that if he tarried too long, the earl might be made to vanish. Even without that concern, he wanted his Royal Seal from York. He had no choice but to push on and ignore the fluttering heart in his chest as well as the pain in every joint and sinew. He could not recall such physical exhaustion before, but he reminded himself over and over that Christ had fallen three times on his way to Calvary. He would not fall, he told himself, or if he did, he would rise and mount and go on.

With Westminster in sight, Henry could feel the expectations of those riding at his back, the weight of faith from all those who had been shoved aside by York's favorites over the previous year. Their complaints against the Nevilles had gone unheard, their cases in law dismissed by judges in the pay of the Protector. Yet the king had woken and they were jubilant, almost drunk on it. It helped that villages around London emptied out onto the road to see Henry pass. They left their Christmas meals and services to stand and cheer, recognizing the banners and understanding the king had returned at last to the world. Hundreds ran alongside where there was room, trying to keep the monarch in sight, while Henry only wanted to rest. His legs were shaking inside the armor and more than once he reached up to wipe itching sweat from his eyes only to have the gauntlet scrape noisily against the iron.

He had thought at first that he would enter the city and cross to the Tower to free Somerset from his imprisonment. Shuddering pain made him reconsider, so that the Palace of Westminster became the only place he could reach that night. He prayed to God as he went that he would be able to recover there, at least for a time.

Henry rode in, between the royal palace and Westminster Abbey, bringing his horse around in a tight circle to dismount. Buckingham sensed his king was close to collapse and jumped down from his own saddle to stand by Henry, shielding him from staring eyes as best he could. Henry leaned forward and struggled to the ground, standing for a moment with his gauntlets still on the saddle-horn until he was sure his legs would take his weight. Royal heralds blew long notes across the yard, though there were already men running to carry the news of the king's arrival, shouting it as they went.

Henry stood upright, feeling he had the strength. He reached out and rested his hand on Buckingham's shoulder for just a heartbeat.

"Thank you, Humphrey. If you lead me in, I would have my Seal brought to my hand."

Buckingham's chest swelled, making his armor creak. On impulse, he knelt. Earl Percy was in the process of dismounting, tossing the reins to one of the men he had brought with him. Though the wind was bitter and the old man's knees protested, he too sank slowly to the cobbles, clasping his furs around his shoulders. All around them, the noblemen and knights did the same until only Henry remained standing. He took a sharp breath, looking over their heads to the great door into the Palace of Westminster.

It had been too long.

"Rise, gentlemen. It's too cold to stand here in the dark. Lead me in, Buckingham. Lead me in."

Buckingham rose with joy written on his face, striding forward. The rest followed Henry like a regiment in his wake, ready for anything.

Henry could have blessed his armor as he walked down the long central corridor of the Palace of Westminster. The weight surely sapped his strength, but it gave him bulk, making him appear the man he might have been. The palace staff were red-eyed with weeping at his recovery, striding ahead to lead the king's party to the royal apartments, where York was in residence. At least the Protector had not been off somewhere in the north, though that would have made some aspects of the day easier. The Seal was no more than two pieces of silver in a bag and a chest, but no royal proclamation or new law could be made without it. For all it was a mere symbol, whoever held the Seal held some semblance of power in the land.

It was a little warmer out of the wind, though the Palace of Westminster was a cold, damp place at the best of times. Henry was still sweating from his ride, walking bareheaded in clanking plate down the long route to his rooms overlooking the river. As he went, he struggled to find the right words to say to the Protector and Defender of his realm. He knew by then that Richard Plantagenet had not ruined the kingdom, that he had not beggared her with a war. From the comments of his lords, it seemed York had not suffered rebellions or riots, or much of anything, while Henry drowsed and dreamed in Windsor. It was difficult to explain why such news had kindled anger in the king, but that emotion too had its uses, whatever the cause. He would not allow himself to falter until he had dismissed the man who ruled in his name.

After climbing a long flight of stairs, Henry was forced to stop and pant, waiting for his shaking muscles to recover. In part to conceal his need to rest, he gave orders for Buckingham to have fast riders ready to take an order for Somerset's release to the Tower, the moment the Seal was in his hands. Instructions to fetch the keepers of the Seal from their rooms were passed back down the crowd of men accompanying their king.

Henry's mouth was dry. He touched his throat and coughed, then accepted a flask from Derry Brewer as the spymaster held it out without a word. The king turned red and choked as he discovered it was whisky. Derry tilted his head in amusement, smiling wryly.

"Better than water. It will give you strength, Your Highness," he said.

King Henry almost snapped an angry reply at him, then decided it was having an effect, so took another swig before passing it back. The "water of life," they called it in some places. He could feel its warmth spreading.

Another long set of steps brought him onto the floor of his own rooms. Henry picked up the pace then as servants opened doors ahead. He could remember the trial of poor Suffolk in that place, William de la Pole, who had been condemned to banishment and then murdered at sea as he left England. Such events were glimpsed through gauze in his mind, the memories of a different man almost, one who was drowning even then. As he went through, Henry realized his mind was clear, as if the smothering cloth had been ripped into tatters. The thought of losing himself once more was a dull and chilling horror, as a sailor who had been cast out of the sea might look back at dark waves still tugging at his feet.

"God grant me the will," Henry muttered as he entered the room, his gaze falling on the two men who were already standing to greet him.

Richard of York had grown a little heavier in the time since King Henry had last seen him, losing the last traces of the lithe young man he had once been. He was clean-shaven and black-haired, his strength showing in wide shoulders and a thick-muscled waist. Richard, Earl of Salisbury, was older than York by a generation, though he remained wiry, a Borders man, with a healthy bloom of color in his cheeks. Henry saw Salisbury's expression darken as he caught sight of Earl Percy, but then both York and Salisbury dropped to one knee, their heads bowed.

"Your Highness, I am overjoyed to see you well," York said as Henry gestured for them to rise. "I have prayed for this day and I will give thanks in all the churches on my lands."

The king glared at him, realizing that part of his anger was that the man had been too skilled at the position he had won for himself. It was surely beneath him to find fault with either York or his chancellor, but then Henry recalled Somerset, held for trial and execution on York's orders. His will firmed. Spite of any kind was unfamiliar to him but, for just a moment, he reveled in the advantage of his position.

"Richard, Duke of York, I have ordered the Royal Seal brought to this room," Henry said. "You will pass it into my hands. When you have done so, you are dismissed as Protector and Defender of the Realm. Your chancellor, Richard, Earl Salisbury, is dismissed from that post. By my order, those you have bound will be freed. Those you have freed will be bound!"

York went pale as he felt the lash of the king's anger.

"Your Highness, I have acted only in the interest of the country, while you . . ." He chose his words carefully, to remove all insult. "While you were ill. Your Majesty, my loyalty, my faith is absolute." He looked up from under lowered brows, trying to judge the differences in the man who stared so coldly around him. The Henry he had known had been weak in thought and body, a man with no desires of his own beyond a love of prayer and silence. Yet the king standing before him seemed stronger in will, though he was white as candlewax.

However Henry might have responded, the men in the room all turned to the door as the four Seal carriers entered behind the king, bearing the silver box that was their charge. All of them were panting from a long run through the royal palace with it, the hands of the Chaff-wax shaking as he placed it on the table.

"Open it, Richard," Henry ordered. "Hand me my own image, my Seal."

York took a deep breath, doing as he was told, though he could hardly believe it was the same man, giving commands so clearly. Where had the beardless boy gone, to have come back so hardened and angry? York opened the box to reveal the silk bag, with its chinking halves of silver within. He tugged at the drawstring and removed the metal pieces, passing them to the king's hand.

"You have my thanks, Richard Plantagenet, Duke of York. Now, you are dismissed from my presence until I call you again. Both of you. Leave me to rest. And if you would pray, pray that Lord Somerset is still hale and whole, in the Tower."

York and Salisbury bowed deeply, side by side, holding themselves with whatever stiff dignity they could muster as they left the room. Earl Percy watched them go with enormous satisfaction written on his face.

"This is a day I'll long remember, Your Highness," Percy said. "The day you came home to rule, casting out snakes and villains."

CHAPTER 8

Margaret could hear the Westminster bell struck seven
times as she approached the royal palace. The dawn sun
was hidden somewhere behind a great bank of dark
clouds across the city, barely more than a dim brightening. She had
sat through nightfall in Windsor, in a castle suddenly emptied of all
its life and Christmas bustle. Midnight had come and gone while she
waited for news and then decided she would not wait any longer. Her
husband had gone to London with his most loyal lords, but it was too
easy to imagine Henry pushing himself too hard, collapsing or fainting or losing himself once again, while she sat safe by a warm fire,
forcing the night to run through her fingers. Though she knew there
was no sense in thinking it, it felt like a betrayal that Derry Brewer
had gone with her husband. His place was at Henry's side, she knew
it, yet she had grown used to his companionship. Without his presence, she spun alone, in tightening loops.

She'd roused the servants from their beds to attend her, not just
the ones who remained awake at night or walked the walls of the
castle. The twelve days of Christmas were traditionally a time of

truce. She had no regrets in stripping the castle further, taking two dozen guards to keep her safe from brigands on the road. The three men who had overseen Henry's care in his illness were not slow in asking to accompany her. Without the king to tend, his doctors had nothing to occupy them and she could see Hatclyf, Fauceby, and Scruton were delighted at the chance to observe Henry's recovery more closely.

Her son, Edward, would be safe enough with the wet nurse in the warm, she told herself yet again. They had not spent a night apart since his birth and it was painful to think of him snuffling and looking around for his mother, then crying when she was not there. She thinned her lips against the stinging cold and the decision, wrapping a huge hooded cloak even more closely around herself, the folds long enough to drape the haunches of her horse.

The road had been too dark to ride hard and fast, but even a walking pace had eaten the miles, while her face had grown completely numb, her eyebrows bright with tiny crystals of snow or ice. She had ridden toward the dawn and yet she felt no weariness, not with the prospect of seeing Henry once again. That joy had not begun to pale. It filled her with every breath, an inner warmth to defeat the winter cold.

She felt resentment as well, much as she tried to deny it. For all the time her husband had been helpless, she had worked to keep his authority alive, yet the moment he woke, he was off with men like Buckingham and Percy, leaving her behind. It was a bruise in her mind, a painful spot she could not help prodding, returning to it over and over without relief.

The great hall of the Palace of Westminster resembled a barracks at her arrival, with horses brought inside to stand and whicker, where only lawyers and Parliament men walked by day. Lamps had been lit, so that she could see the gleam from outside. Margaret dismounted there and followed her guards as they led her horse into the vaulted building, with sparrows looping far above in the gloom. Her face felt like a board, as if it might crack apart if she smiled. Away from the wind, she took a moment to rub her cheeks with gloved hands, bringing a little color and life back to the frozen flesh. The hall was quiet, but as well as the horses ambling or tied, dozens of men slept wherever they'd been able to find a spot, regardless of their rank. One of King Henry's stewards saw her come in and rushed over, dropping awkwardly to one knee on the straw.

"Where is my husband?" Margaret whispered.

"He sleeps, Your Highness. In the royal rooms. Please, follow me."

Without a word, the two royal physicians and the serjeant surgeon fell in behind her, carrying their black leather bags. Margaret felt like a ghost as she stepped around the sleeping men as quietly as she could, smiling as they grumbled and twitched in their sleep. Those men had come to that place for King Henry and she felt affection for them all.

She knew the way well enough, but her husband's steward seemed pleased to lead her little group through the corridors and up two flights of stairs to the king's rooms. The men there were more alert, including two guards at the doors who stood ready with drawn swords at the approaching footsteps until they recognized the young queen.

Margaret could hear a muted conversation as she entered the outer drawing room, breaking off as the door opened. Buckingham and Earl Percy both rose in silence, then bowed deeply. Margaret saw Henry Percy's face was mottled with broken veins and he seemed irritated at the interruption, saying nothing as Buckingham came forward to her.

"Your Highness, I did not expect to see you today. You must have ridden all night, and in this cold! Earl Percy and I were considering a cup of hot mead to take the chill from our old bones. Will you join us?" Buckingham ignored the doctors at her back. For their part, they stood with their heads bowed.

Margaret shook her head, sensing that she was an interloper in that room and resenting Earl Percy's sullen expression as he regarded her.

"Where is my husband, Humphrey?" she said, touching him on the arm.

"Asleep beyond that door, but sleeping well, Your Highness. Sheer will kept him in the saddle and he is exhausted." His tone eased slightly, becoming gentler. "If it is your wish, I shall have him woken, but Margaret, I think the king needs to rest. Can these men not wait to bleed and poke at him?"

Margaret turned to the doctors, still standing with their bags clutched in front of them and their heads dipped like children being punished.

"Wait outside, gentlemen. I will have you called when the king wakes."

They trooped out, closing the door behind them without a sound and leaving Margaret alone with the two older men. With studied dignity, she took a seat on a padded chair, settling her skirts and showing no sign of the aches in her legs, still sore from riding.

"Sit, please, both of you. If Henry is asleep, there is no urgency. Is Master Brewer abed?"

"He was worn out, my lady," Buckingham replied. "He's been like a dog with two tails ever since your husband dismissed York and Salisbury. He'll be somewhere close by, if you'd like me to have him brought to you."

Margaret opened her mouth to agree, then changed her mind, determined not to show the two men any trace of weakness.

"No, I don't think so. Let him sleep. You can tell me all that has happened—then perhaps we can consider our choices."

Buckingham smiled to himself as he took a seat on an ornate oak bench along the side of the room. Earl Percy remained on his feet, his overlarge eyebrows and great blade of a nose seeming to make a glower his permanent expression. Under Buckingham's quizzical stare, the earl made a sound deep in his throat and lowered himself into a chair across from them both, three points of a triangle with the crackling fire behind Margaret.

Buckingham repeated the king's actions since his arrival at Westminster the night before, a short list of orders given, though Margaret made him repeat every detail of York's dismissal along with Salisbury's. Earl Percy shifted in his seat while Buckingham spoke, failing to hide his impatience. Under such provocation, Margaret was tempted to have Humphrey go through it all again, not least for the joy of hearing her husband's firm orders. Yet she allowed the duke to fall silent. Buckingham leaned over his knees and stared amiably into the fire as she considered his words.

"I have waited so very long to hear such things," Margaret said softly. "To know that York and Salisbury were forced to leave and lick their wounds, far from here. To know my husband's spirit has returned to him. I pray that Earl Somerset can be brought safely out of the Tower, that he has not been broken by his confinement. His loyalty has been a touchstone, where others fell away. I trust him, Humphrey. I do not doubt Somerset will play a part in what must come."

"In what must come, Your Highness?" Buckingham said softly.

"It is not enough for Henry to change his rooms! What does the country know of my husband's return to health, beyond those few who saw him ride here? No, he must be seen! In London of course, but right across the country as well. They must see the king and his noblemen, to know that York has power no longer, that the true

Protector and Defender of the Realm is once again King Henry of Lancaster."

Buckingham would have replied, but Earl Percy spoke first, his voice the high wheeze of an old man, a sound that made Margaret's skin creep.

"King Henry has the noble heads of families to advise him when he wakes, Your Highness. The manner and detail of his return to public life is better left till then. You must not fear for your husband. His Highness has loyal Englishmen all around, with no love of York, or the Neville, Salisbury. We will walk the path that needs to be walked. We will cut the bad crop, if that is to be the way of it."

Margaret felt color come to her cheeks. For a year and a half, she had been isolated, forgotten in Windsor with her dreaming husband. Earl Percy had not visited her once in that time. His meaning was clear enough, but in the firelight, she felt a vast resentment toward the crow in his hunched furs, willing enough to fly back to her husband's side now there was flesh on his bones. She closed her mouth on her first response, then spoke slowly, measuring every word.

"I have been my husband's voice when he had none, my lord. This loyalty you mention—it is a thing men love, is it not? I have heard them use the word many times since Henry was struck down by his illness. Perhaps they prefer it more in the ideal than the reality, when it calls for hard work and pain."

Earl Percy scratched the side of his nose as he looked back at her.

"I see I have somehow given offense, Your Highness. I meant none. King Henry—"

"Must be seen, Earl Percy," Margaret interrupted. She was rewarded by a deepening flush beneath the purple web of veins across his cheeks and nose. "How fortunate that some of us have planned what must be done when Henry returned. I did not doubt, Earl Percy. I had faith and my prayers have been answered, every one."

"As you say, Your Highness," Earl Percy replied, his mouth puckering.

Margaret nodded briskly.

"When the king rises, I will begin arrangements for a Judicial Progress. I passed through Westminster Hall an hour ago, my lord. I saw half the lawyers' stalls under dusty cloth, unused for too long. It is over a year since the judges of the King's Bench traveled the country, hearing cases in law and making judgments. What better way to be seen, than by dispensing justice to the people of England? To hear their complaints and let them see justice done—and criminals punished? A great Royal Progress, with two dozen judges, the county sheriffs, a thousand men-at-arms, all the noble houses in attendance on the king! From the highest to the lowest, they will know Lancaster has returned to rule. A house with an heir and the support of the king's most powerful lords. *That* is the path my husband must walk now, no other."

Earl Percy turned his head to look at the dawn light, gleaming beyond the windows. Buckingham watched him in a sideways glance that contained more than a little amusement. In his months at Windsor, Buckingham had grown used to Margaret's French accent, a delight to the ear that could only be a contrast to the force of her words. Earl Percy was discovering the young queen's determination all at once, a meal perhaps too finely spiced for him to enjoy.

"Your Highness seeks to bring peace by royal command," Earl Percy said at last. His knuckles paled as he tightened his hands in his furs, despite the warmth of the fire. "Does Your Highness believe a man like York will come meekly to heel? A man like Salisbury? Will Your Highness have them follow behind the king in measured pace?"

The old man hesitated as a thought struck him, looking more closely at the dark-haired young woman sitting so neatly in her chair, her head cocked to listen. "Or is it that Your Highness does not believe they will answer that call, making them oath-breakers who could then be taken as traitors? That . . . would be a path I'd walk, my lady."

Margaret regarded him in turn, feeling again an instinctive dislike of the old man before her. His eyes were cruel, she thought, but he was on her husband's side, regardless of his reasons. That was what mattered most.

"If my husband called those lords and they did not come, it would mean a war to tear England apart. No, I do not believe these wounds can be bound and forgotten. If we misstep, they will rot and spoil all the good flesh." She spoke with calm certainty, the words spilling out of her to hold the two men still. "My lords, I had no intention of inviting York, or Salisbury or Warwick to accompany my husband. Let those men bite their nails and worry, while the King of England gathers his most ardent supporters around him. Let York see the strength that would be arrayed against him if he dares to raise a single banner." Margaret leaned forward, her eyes unblinking. "I do not doubt York remains a threat, my lord. Such men who have tasted power will always long for it again. I saw it in my own father and all the crowns he claimed and failed to win. Yet my husband is but a day from waking. He must show his strength and ride under the three lions. He must be seen, well and vital, before we turn our hands to the threat of York and Salisbury. Warwick may yet be saved, I do not know. Do you comprehend? Do you follow me, my lord?"

The double meaning of the last was not lost on the old man. His mouth moved as if he was trying to dislodge a pip from a back tooth. In the silence, he bowed his head, looking up from under his brows.

"Of course, Your Highness. I believe we wish for the same things.

The king strong. The destruction of the Neville taint in all those who nurture treason in their breasts. King Henry has my support, on my honor and the honor of my house."

Margaret sat back. The man might as well have dismissed her. He would follow Henry, not the wishes of his French queen. She inclined her head as if in acceptance of his words, though she seethed inwardly.

Buckingham gave a yawn, wide and long, until Margaret had to smother her own.

"It's my feeling the king will rise late today," Buckingham said, standing. "I'm for a nap, to restore my strength before it fails me."

Earl Percy rose in turn, both men bowing and excusing themselves from Margaret's presence. She watched them leave, suspecting that they would continue their conversation somewhere else in the palace, where she could not listen and interfere. Her hands gripped each other as she looked into the fire. She needed Earl Somerset. She needed Derry Brewer. Most of all, she needed her husband and her husband's lords to listen to her. It was clear enough that they wished to bargain and maneuver without her voice. It was infuriating, but she would not step back. Henry was her husband. She was his wife. They would find her in their path, whichever path they took.

Left alone, Margaret rose and passed through the inner doors to her husband's bedchamber. She found him there, snoring softly under thick blankets, his long dark hair unbound and tousled on the bolster. He looked at peace, with a good color in his cheeks. Margaret felt the weariness of her long night steal upon her and she unpinned her cloak and lay by him, tugging a single cover over herself and turning her body so that she could feel his warmth. Henry murmured something at her touch, though he did not wake, and she was soon asleep at his side.

CHAPTER 9

York rested his hands on a wooden railing, his pride showing as he watched the boy take his position. His eldest son Edward, Earl of March, was thirteen, though taller and far stronger than town lads with three years or more on him. He raised his sword to his father before using the hilt to knock down the visor of his helmet.

"Watch this," York said under his breath.

Salisbury smiled, leaning one shoulder against a stone pillar. He and York had spent the best part of a month in Ludlow Castle, making their plans and adjusting to the sudden reverse in their fortunes. From that massive stone fortress, the two men had sent out riders to all their separate holdings, ordering their captains and best men in until the village and fields around it resembled a military camp. There was little chance of raids from Wales that year, once word had spread across the border to the west. Ludlow had become the largest armed gathering in the country, and still they came in. It gave Salisbury some pleasure to take a step back from the complex business of supplying so many with food, ale, and equipment, just to watch a favored boy fight.

Two men faced Edward on the training yard, overlooked on all sides by cloisters in gray stone. In fine armor, they too raised swords to York, bowing their heads. Jameson was a massive figure, a blacksmith by trade. He stood a head taller than the boy and was about twice as broad and deep in the chest. In deliberate contrast, Sir Robert Dalton was slim and moved with grace and perfect balance, his feet always steady on the ground.

York held up his hand and a drummer boy in the corner of the yard began to tap out a martial rhythm, making the hearts beat faster of anyone who had known that sound on the field of battle.

All three carried shields bound to their left arms and gripped inside the curve. The boy moved lightly with his, though Salisbury saw it was a little too large for him. Earl Edward took slow steps to his right, keeping the shield up and spoiling the chance of both men attacking him at once. His sword was held out straight, an adder's tongue, waiting.

The larger man moved first. Jameson gave out a great roar that echoed back on all sides, meant to startle and frighten his young opponent. The blacksmith's sword came swinging fast from Edward's left, crashing against the shield he held away from his body to soak up the blow. Man and boy produced a storm of cuts and strikes, hammering each other, hitting back at the slightest gap in the defenses. It lasted no more than a dozen heartbeats and both painted shields were battered and scratched as the big man backed off.

"More, Jameson!" came a taunt from within the boy's helmet. "Has your wind gone already?"

Before the big man could reply, his companion slid in on quick, darting steps. Sir Robert relied on speed and skill far more than the blacksmith. He feinted and turned, his feet always moving to find the best spot to lunge, then ducking away or batting aside a blade with his own when it came too close. This bout was more like a dance, but the watching lords winced as Earl Edward took a hilt into his gut, making him stagger. Sir Robert followed up immediately, pressing Edward and forcing him back, hitting faster and faster until the hand holding the shield would have been numb to the shoulder. With Edward's father watching coldly, Sir Robert was battering the boy to the ground, his eye on the shield, with his right leg outstretched before him. Almost from a crouch, the boy lashed out at the leg, landing a low blow just above the ankle. Sir Robert shouted in pain. He was fast enough to catch himself before he fell, but still limped as he backed away.

Edward of March rose to his full height, half blinded by stinging sweat, but as angry by then as only a thirteen-year-old boy can get. With a yell, it was his turn to leap forward, forcing the slim knight to bring his own shield back into play. Edward raised his sword to smash a blow against it and then suddenly darted aside, lunging at the big blacksmith as the man circled around him. The move caught both the older men by surprise and Edward's sword hammered against the neck joint of Jameson's armor, stunning him. If he had been full-grown, it would have been a killing blow.

In the moment of shock, the still-limping Sir Robert Dalton took a step forward, resting his own sword on the boy's neck.

"Dead," he said loudly and clearly.

All three reached to pull their visors up, though the young earl's had been buckled in the first flurry and he struggled with it. The blacksmith rolled his neck uncomfortably as he came forward and gripped the edge, heaving until it creaked open.

"What was that, then?" Jameson said, his voice a deep bass. "Going for my neck with a man right in front of you?"

The young earl shrugged, delighted with himself for all to see.

"I had you cold and you know it, Jameson. And I'll have men with me to watch my back when I take the field. You, maybe, if you're not too old by then. You'd have broken Sir Robert's head for him if I'd given him an opening like that—while I took down another."

The blacksmith chuckled, his smile creasing his wide, square face.

"I would, yes. I've spent long enough training you. I won't let someone else make a fool of me, not after all the batterings I've taken." It was clear enough that he was unharmed by the display, though he made a point of stretching his bruised neck back and forth.

"Well done!" York called from the side of the yard. "Heed your masters, Edward. You grow stronger and faster every time I see you."

The swordsmen both bowed deeply at hearing York speak, while Edward flushed with pleasure at his father's approval, holding up his sword in pride.

"He is a cool thinker," Salisbury said, his own spirits raised at seeing the childlike pleasure in his friend. "Good balance, the first signs of speed. He has been well trained."

York tried to shrug it off, but the joy of seeing his eldest son fight well came off him like heat.

"Edward has courage—and Jameson and Sir Robert know how to bring it out. He won't meet many as strong as the blacksmith, and Sir Robert was trained first in France, then England. I have seen few better men with a blade. In just a few years, the boy will be one to watch, I think."

Both men turned as steps approached from the far end of the cloister. Salisbury saw it was his sister, Duchess Cecily, wife to York and mother to the excited young man now cutting through a host of imaginary opponents in the training yard. It made Salisbury feel old to see such a young life, with its true battles still far ahead.

"We have been watching Edward practice, Cecily," Salisbury called to his sister as she walked closer. "He shows great promise—

though with his blood, how could he not? I wonder if his namesake, King Edward, was so tall at such an age? The boy grows like wheat, an inch more whenever I look away. He'll be taller than your husband, I don't doubt it." Salisbury saw his sister clutched her youngest to her chest, resting in an embroidered cloth sling that she had tied over her shoulder. The child was crying with astonishing volume, a raging, high-pitched sound that was already painful from just a few feet away. Salisbury sensed York's mood darkening as she came up to him.

"And how is my nephew?" Salisbury asked, forcing cheerfulness into his voice.

"He suffers still. I found the doctor trying to stretch him out, but he screamed so terribly I could not let it go on. Was that at your order?" Her sharp gaze pinned her husband, so that York looked away rather than face her.

"I suggested he try it, Cecily, that is all. The man seemed to think some sort of wooden brace might help his growth, just for a few years. I have artificers who could design such a thing, if you agreed." As the squalling noise rose to new levels, York winced and put a finger in his ear. "Good God, listen to him now! The child never sleeps, for crying! I thought if his back could be pulled straight, it might grant him ease."

"Or be broken, so that he died!" Cecily snapped. "I'll have no more talk of braces. You'll leave Richard's care to me, from now on. I won't have him tortured by fools who would wring him like a cloth."

Faced with the discomfort of witnessing such anger between husband and wife, Salisbury moved away to watch the instruction in the yard, deliberately taking a few steps around a pillar to give them some semblance of privacy. He bit the inside of his lip when York spoke again, mortified to overhear a married couple too angry to care.

"Cecily," York said loudly, to be heard over the child's yelling, "if you would have him shown mercy, you'd put him out on a winter's night and let the cold take him. He's two years old and he still screams all night and day! I tell you the Spartans had the right of it. My doctor says his spine is bending, that it will only get worse. He won't live without pain, and he won't thank you for sparing him if he grows to be a cripple. Would you shame my house, with a twisted son? Will he be driven mad by it, left in some lonely house to be tended by servants like a mad dog or a simpleton? There is no sin in letting him go, just putting him into the cold. Father Samuel has assured me of that."

When Cecily replied, her voice was little more than a hiss, making her brother cringe for his friend.

"You will not touch a *hair* of his head, Richard Plantagenet. Do you understand me? I have lost five children for your house and name. I have borne six alive and I am pregnant once again. I believe I have given enough to York. So if I choose to keep this one safe, if he never walks even, it is not your concern. I have done enough, borne enough. This child needs me more than all the rest, and I will tend him alone if I must. Say you will not whisper to the doctors, Richard. Tell me I do not have to watch to be sure they do not slip him some foul dose."

"Of course you don't," he growled at her. "I swear this child has unhinged your mind, Cecily. Children die, it's the natural way of things. Some live to grow strong—and some poor souls suffer like this one, caught between life and death. I wish now I had not given him my own name. If I'd known he'd be this little screaming scrap of—"

"Don't," Cecily replied, her eyes bright with tears.

Her husband took a slow breath.

"When you're with child, you are a different woman, Cecily. I don't understand you at all. Go on. Do as you please with him. I have other sons." He turned away then, glaring out at the training yard where his eldest was attacking a wooden post wrapped in cloth and leather, battering the thing in great gashes. York could feel his wife's furious gaze on him for what seemed an age. He refused to look round at her and, after a time, she walked stiffly away.

Coming back to stand at York's shoulder, Salisbury let his friend recover his peace, both men staring out into the yard as young Edward hacked the striking post in two, shouting in triumph as it fell. The contrast between the sons could not have been greater at that moment.

"He will be a terror on the battlefield," Salisbury said, hoping to see just a little of the pride and pleasure return.

Instead, York frowned across the yard, his gaze focused much further away.

"Perhaps he won't have to be," he said, his voice raw. "If I can yet make peace with Henry. You saw him, Richard, standing like the man he was *meant* to be, at last. He reminded me of his father for the first time. It was perhaps the strangest moment of my life. The king sent me from his presence like a beaten hound, yet in response, my heart swelled to see such strength in him!" York shook his head in wonder at the memory. "If I can make Henry understand I'm no threat to him, my son may not have to fight in his lifetime. My house and name are my concern, no other—my duty lies in keeping my titles and lands safe for Edward to inherit."

"Seeing you reconciled would give me joy," Salisbury replied, hiding his dismay. "Yet you've said yourself the king has too many men with no love of York whispering in his ears—and his French queen too, who is no friend of yours. I take it, then, that you have not yet been called for his grand Council, this Progress?"

"Have you?" York asked. "I've heard nothing. Dukes and earls and lowly barons will ride with the king, but not you and not me. Men I have known for years no longer answer my letters. What about your son, Warwick?"

Salisbury shook his head.

"He too has fallen out of favor, it seems. My brother William has been called to London. Earl Percy has a Neville *wife*, yet he too stands at the king's side. What does it mean, do you think?"

Some of the angry exchange with Cecily still colored York's tone as he replied.

"It means King Henry's ears are filled by poison, that is what it means. All this talk of 'securing the realm against those who would threaten peace'—who else could they mean but York and Salisbury? Aye, and Warwick too if he stands with us. It seems like petty spite to darken my name, after everything I have done for the Lancaster throne. You and I made his son the Prince of Wales, by God! While the king slept, we protected England from all those who eyed her. Perhaps I should have let the French control the Channel and raid our coasts, or ignored the bribery and corruption of venal lords when I was called to rule on their conduct. God's *wounds*, I have enemies, too many to count. One by one, all those I called friends have fallen away, taken under the wing of Queen Margaret. I wrote to Exeter, Richard. Despite our differences, the man married my eldest daughter. I thought if it came to a choice, he and I . . . well, it does not matter. I have not had a reply from him. My own daughter's household has gone dark to me."

"You cannot have expected more. He was made to abide in Pontefract at your order, Richard. Exeter will not forgive that, not easily. No, Exeter stands with the Percys—and they stand in the gutter. Yet you do have allies," Salisbury replied. "I have promised my support. My name is linked to yours in all ways, so we rise or fall together. My son Warwick still comes to Ludlow, with more than a thousand men-at-arms from his estates." Even in the stone heart of the fortress, Salisbury dropped his voice to little more than a murmur then. "We'll have enough to take arms against them, if they make traitors of us."

"By God, *no*, that's not what I want," York said. "You told me on my wedding day to Cecily that the Nevilles were with me, do you remember? You have kept your word when it mattered and I am grateful." His hands tightened on the railing, the knuckles showing white. "My father was executed for treason, Richard. Can you understand I will not lightly walk his path? If the throne falls to me, I won't refuse it, of course not! Yet I lived my entire childhood as a ward, with that stain on the honor of my house. Would you have the name of York burned black?" He leaned close, his voice a harsh whisper. "I tell you, I will not take up arms against him. I *cannot*, not as he is now. When Henry was ill and men said he would die, it was different. Now he has woken—and he is not the man he was. You were there, you saw him! Perhaps his spirit drank itself full while he slept, I don't know. Perhaps God restored his wits to him in His infinite mercy. *Everything* has changed now the lamb has woken fully, now that he has returned as a man. Everything is new."

On the yard, Edward of March was gathering his equipment to leave. He had removed his helmet and his hair was black and wet with sweat. Salisbury saw the boy look to the cloisters for his father's approval, but York did not see him.

"If I could have just an hour with the king," York went on in a rush, his hands twisting the railing as if he wanted to break it in two. "If I could be sure he read my letters, or if I could snatch away those whispering men, I could yet lance this boil. Somerset! Did you hear he has been made a duke now? And Captain of Calais? *My* title, gone! The man I imprisoned declared a "true and faithful subject" on every street corner of London, making mockery of me in turn. Somerset, Percy, Exeter, Buckingham, and Derry Brewer. While those men live and thrive like weeds, my king's chance to live is stolen away. I tell you, he will drown again, with those men about him."

Salisbury felt only irritation as York spoke. The man had been a rock to anchor Neville ambitions to before. One meeting with the woken king and the York stone seemed to have cracked to the heart. Salisbury allowed no sign of his disappointment to show as he replied.

"Whatever is said against us, no king can rule without his three strongest lords. Henry will see that in time, I am certain. But my friend, you know we cannot go before him without armed men, or we would be bound, caught like fish in a withy trap. With your soldiers and mine to guarantee our safety, King Henry will have to listen to our just complaints. I will not sit and wait for men like Earl Percy to have me declared an enemy of the Crown! Nor should you. We must act with resolution and force to make our case. By summer, this will be behind us and peace will be restored. Why not? Nothing has been done that cannot be undone. Not yet." Salisbury felt his words were flung against a wall. York was not listening to him, hard and cold as he stood there, still angry with his wife.

"I am sorry to learn your son is . . . poorly formed," Salisbury said.

York shrugged, shaking his head.

"I have buried children before. I will again. It doesn't matter what happens to one sickly boy, though I fear for the strain on his mother." He looked directly at his friend, pain written deep in his eyes. "Cecily has become obsessed with him. There are times when I just wish the little thing would . . . It doesn't matter. Come, you must be hungry. Let my cook prepare something to please you. She can do wonders with a bit of poached fish."

York clapped his friend on the shoulder and they moved off toward the banqueting hall, some of the strain easing in both men at the thought of a good meal.

CHAPTER 10

After the first cruel frosts, the winter had been almost mild that year. The royal apartments in the Tower were still heated by fires in every hearth, sometimes on both sides of the same room, all struggling to warm the ancient fortress against the chill and damp of the river running close by the walls.

Derry Brewer had replaced some of the flesh he'd lost. His hair had grown out and been trimmed by the king's own barber and his skin had lost the waxy, sallow quality of too little food and too many worries. On the orders of doctors Hatclyf and Fauceby, he had filled his belly to bursting with bowls of beef broth and dark cabbage each morning, followed by three pints of small beer—almost the same diet as the king endured to restore his blood. Derry had grown heartily sick of cabbage, a vegetable which seemed to follow him like a ghost, even though he cleaned his mouth with French brandy from a flask. It pleased him to feel his strength coming back, like Samson when his hair grew.

The king too had a little color in his cheeks, Derry noted. Henry sat quietly enough, but his eyes were alert, his face no longer a slack mask. That simple interest was astonishing to those who had known him before the collapse. Sitting just a few feet across from the king, Derry had to struggle not to stare. The man he had known was just a shadow of the one who had come back, there was no other way to describe it. He knew Margaret felt there was a fragility in him still, as if Henry was a pot that could shatter at the lightest blow. Yet the great sleep had somehow restored the king, healing his broken will, for all the cracks that might have remained beneath the surface.

Henry sensed Derry's silent scrutiny and looked up in question, just as his spymaster dropped his gaze to his boots. Derry had seen madness before, in many forms, brought on by rage or grief, or drink, or just come from nowhere on the summer wind. He knew the mind was its own world, all the stars and planets no more complicated than a man's thoughts. Whatever devil or infirmity had sucked the king's will and made him a child, it was gone from him. The man beneath could speak at last.

Derry breathed out, feeling his eyes spring with tears, surprising himself. With his head down, he wiped them away before anyone else could see, thinking instead of his work, with all its petty irritations. He had already been forced to quash rumors that the king's spirit had been tainted in some other place. Londoners had a talent for whispers, he sometimes thought. Given the slightest opportunity, they would hide their mouths behind hands and hiss about devils or bastards or secret Jews in high office. He had begun a few lies of that sort himself and it was much harder to deflect them. Sometimes, Derry thought idly, people needed either a good shepherd or a good kick up the backside.

As Derry sat with his head hanging low, Somerset paced up and down the room, his nervous energy some consequence of his captivity. Edmund Beaufort had spent many months as a prisoner in the Tower, though his rank meant he'd been confined to two large rooms, with a soft bed, a writing desk, and servants to attend him. Derry looked up to observe the man's twitching tension with some interest, seeing how the calm center of Somerset had vanished despite all the comforts of his imprisonment. At least the man's enmity toward York was certain. It gave Derry some pleasure to hear that name blackened and maligned without fear of reprisal. Somerset had been given a dukedom for his support and loyalty, a sign of the king's support that would not be lost on those who favored York and Salisbury. Derry smiled to himself at the thought.

"Your Highness," Somerset said, "I have judges and their staffs filling the rooms of every tavern in the city. The Tower itself is stuffed full of men-at-arms, the best guardsmen to accompany Your Highness north. We are waiting now for just a handful of names—Henry Holland, Duke of Exeter, the most prominent among them."

"Cousin Exeter had four hundred men, before," King Henry said softly. "Before" had come to mean the period before he had fallen into a dreaming state. "A firebrand, I remember, young Holland. He has received my messenger?"

"Of a certainty, Your Highness," Somerset replied. "The scroll was placed into his hand. I believe he was much weakened during his imprisonment in Wales, but he gives his oath he will come. He has no love of York."

"He is married to York's daughter, even so," Margaret said. She sat at her husband's side, claiming him with her closeness. Derry looked up as she spoke. "That alliance may yet pull him apart."

"No," Henry replied. "York punished him for siding with the Percys. Exeter's loyalty is set. Everything he is comes from my hand. I will not doubt the man for his Plantagenet wife, any more than I doubt Earl Percy for his Neville one. Yet I will not wait for him. What else?"

Somerset turned to track another line along the rug before the fire. Given the chance, Derry chose to answer the king's question.

"Your Highness, it worries me still that we have made no approach to York or Salisbury. Somerset and I may have our grievances against those men, but if they are not brought into London to give an oath of fealty, I fear their armies. With young Warwick, they have more land and men than any other faction beyond the royal house itself. York on his own is the richest lord in England, Your Highness. Can such a man be ignored?"

In previous years, Derry knew the king would have been nodding by the end of his words, saying, "As you say, Derry," almost before he could finish speaking. It was oddly discomforting to see the man weigh a contribution instead of blurting out his agreement. Yet it was Margaret who spoke first, before her husband.

"We are private here, Master Brewer, are we not?"

"Of course, Your Highness. I have my most trusted men around this room. No one can overhear a single word."

"Then I will say aloud what has long been in my thoughts. There will be no peace while York lives. He covets my husband's throne and he will take it, if we give him any chance at all. We have called this great gathering a Judicial Progress, and so it is, but it is also a show of strength. The lords who go north with their king will see how many others stand in support of the house of Lancaster. They will see the king is restored to rule, made whole by the Grace of God. If York and Salisbury challenge us then, they will be met by armies, by thousands, who will stand in their way. At least then the issue will be settled."

Derry frowned as he listened.

"My lady, if York and Salisbury turn traitor, if they raise banners against the King of England, I do not believe the outcome is certain—with stakes too high to miss a step. York and Salisbury have their enemies, of course, but there are too many others who whisper that they have been poorly served for their loyalty. I cannot know the secret hearts of all the lords, Your Highness, only that some of them still feel sympathy for those two men. I do know there are some who would rather they were cosseted and brought back, even rewarded for their good service."

He lowered his head once more as Margaret's gaze sharpened, looking away from her into the fire.

"My lady, I would be content to hear our intention is to strike against Ludlow, to lay siege to it and starve York out or break down his walls. This other business, this Royal Progress north is merely a distraction, with no good outcome assured. York is a subtle man, Your Highness, a subtle, vengeful man with both wealth and soldiers at his call. I would rather see him broken than ignored."

"I know him rather better than you, Master Brewer," King Henry said from his musings. "Though I cannot know his 'secret heart,' Richard of York cannot be restored to favor with gifts and promises—as you say, he can hardly be raised further, with all his titles and his wealth. If I summoned him, it would be to hold a viper to my breast, with soft entreaties that he not sink his teeth into me. No, my wife has the right of it, Master Brewer. A loyal army fills London and I will ride north to Leicester with them. If York can blacken his soul beyond redemption, if he can break oath and accept certain damnation, I will answer him . . ." The king's words drifted away and he stared into nothingness while the others waited, growing anxious. At last Henry shook his head, looking confused as a deep flush spread across his face. "What was I saying?"

"York, Your Highness," Somerset said uncomfortably. The duke had paled, his expression reflected in both the queen and Derry

Brewer as they feared for Henry's burdened spirit. Derry repressed a shudder at the thought of the king's weakness returning, still curled like a dark vine in the young man he followed.

"York . . . yes," Henry went on. "If he brings his followers against me, the country will rise at his treachery. Every one of my companion earls, every duke, every baron, every knight and man-at-arms will take up swords and bows and lances against him. Every village, every town, every city! The king may not be touched, Somerset. The king is inviolate, anointed by God. Any man who stands against me shall burn in hellfire. That is the answer to men like York and Salisbury. I shall go north in peace, but I shall answer him with war if he stirs one step from his fortresses." King Henry stopped to knuckle pain from his temples, closing his eyes. "Margaret, would you be so good as to summon Hatclyf? He makes an excellent draft for pain, and my head is split apart."

"Of course," Margaret said, rising. Derry stood with her and she chivvied the men from the room to tend her husband, calling beyond the open door for the doctor's presence. A servant rushed away to fetch him.

As the door closed at his back, Derry found himself in a much colder corridor, glancing briefly at Somerset and seeing his own worry reflected in the man's face. Neither of them would mention the king's sudden lapse, he was certain. The thought that Henry might have only a brief time before he was pulled back into his dreaming madness was too awful to contemplate, a horror that made Derry shudder and feel ill. To put words to that fear was to make it real. With silence, they could both tell themselves they had imagined it.

"Can we avoid a war, Brewer?" Somerset said suddenly.

"Of course, my lord. The question is, *should* we avoid it? I'm half convinced our angry young queen is right. Perhaps we should tear down the false garments of this Judicial Progress and march the king's armies against York. Part of any victory is choosing the moment to attack. I do not want to miss the best chance we might ever see."

Somerset was watching him closely as Derry spoke.

"But . . ." he prompted.

Derry's mouth quirked.

"But—oh, there are a hundred 'buts', my lord. 'But' Queen Margaret is right that the king needs to be seen after so long absent from the realm. 'But' York is not yet a traitor, for all the queen detests him. God knows I am no friend of his, but he made Margaret's son the Prince of Wales and ruled with diplomacy and skill while he had the right. I would not trust Salisbury within a hundred miles of Earl Percy, mind you. They hate each other. York though? I cannot see him laying a hand on the throne. For all I dislike the man, he is yet too full of his own prickly honor. And if it does come to swords and bows and axes, we could still lose, my lord, with no second chance to come back to this day and choose a better path."

"Queen Margaret sees York as a threat to her husband and son," Somerset said. "I do not think she will be satisfied with any solution that does not mean his head on a spike."

"And she has the king's ear," Derry said, looking away in thought. "Men like me—men like you or Earl Percy—can shout and argue from dawn till dusk, and she will still be there that night to murmur to him." Derry sighed aloud. "If we could put a wedge between York and Salisbury, or Salisbury and his son, we might lose only one and keep two, restored to the king's good graces. I know Queen Margaret admires young Warwick and would not willingly see him brought down with his father. I could write to him, my lord, if I could find the right words. The right words are always there, if a man's sharp enough to see them."

"Earl Percy was saying we should consider York's son, Edward of March," Somerset said softly. "He wonders aloud whether York's death from illness or misadventure might bring an end to all these threats."

Derry looked into the other man's eyes, seeing the tension.

"And how did you answer him, my lord?"

"Why, I told him to go to the devil, Brewer. I hope you would say the same, if he mentioned such a foul thing to you."

Derry felt some part of him unclench in relief. He liked Somerset, a man who saw no shades of gray at all in his judgments. He inclined his head.

Master Hatclyf came rushing along the corridor then, pink and perspiring from running the length of the Tower grounds.

"Excuse me, my lord, Master Brewer," he said. "The king has called for my presence."

Both men stepped aside and the doctor bustled in, closing the door firmly behind him.

Derry turned back to Somerset when the man had gone.

"York writes letters, my lord. I have seen some of them, copied out for me by those who distrust him."

"Treason?" the duke demanded, his eyes brightening.

"Not at all. He honors the king in every word, but complains bitterly about you and Percy and the other lords around the king. He does not know this Henry. I think, in part, he still sees the king as he was: the lamb, the beardless boy. God knows, I want York to fall, my lord. I desire nothing more than to stand over his cold body on a cold field. While he lives, he threatens my king, simply by his strength and the support of the Nevilles—whether he ever dares reach for the throne or not."

In frustration and weariness, Derry scuffed his foot at a small stone on the flagged floor, sending it skittering away.

"I think I spoke the truth before. If swords are drawn, I cannot be certain of the victor. There must be another way, a solution to the problem of York. Between us, we'll find it. Until the trumpets are blown, my lord. Until that moment, there is still a chance to bring York to heel. If they sound, we will have failed to find it."

"And if they do sound?" Somerset asked, though both men knew the answer.

"Then you and I will work to destroy York and anyone who stands with him. We will give our lives to take his, if it comes to it. If diplomacy fails, my lord Somerset, war must follow—and if it does, I will not see York triumph while I live." He smiled bitterly then. "After all, he would not let either of us remain alive for long."

Somerset nodded thoughtfully.

"You know, Derry, when I was a boy, I stole out one summer to visit a country fair, to chase the local girls and drink and have my fortune told. My father never even knew I had slipped away from my room. You must have done the same sort of thing."

Derry grinned widely at that, shaking his head.

"I suspect my childhood was a little less . . . noble, my lord, but go on."

"I drank too much mead and ale, of course, and I recall fumbling with some lass who insisted on being paid first before she let me lay her down. The night is a blur for the most part, but I remember a gypsy woman with her patterned tent. She read my palm in the darkness, while her tent swayed around me and it was all I could do to keep from vomiting."

His eyes glazed in memory, and Derry folded his arms.

"And you were robbed? Or was she the girl in the long grass?" he prompted.

"Good lord, I wasn't *that* drunk. No, she told me Somerset would die at the castle, not on the battlefield, not from a chill or an illness. I hadn't told her my father's name, Derry, though she knew it anyway."

Derry glanced at the signet ring that adorned the duke's hand, carrying the crest of his family.

"It is their craft to look for signs, my lord. I'm sure she took your coins for her promises and said much the same thing to the next man."

"You don't believe in such things? I have fought in a dozen campaigns since that day and never taken a wound, Derry. Not a scratch. I have never been ill even, while I know a dozen men who died before their time, no, two dozen, sweating out their lives to some scourge of the flesh. Do you comprehend? I have led a charmed life, when others died all around me. And do you know why?" Somerset leaned very close then, his eyes bright as he took Derry into his confidence. "I have never traveled to Windsor, not once in thirty years. It is the king's own residence, the largest in the country. What other castle could be 'the' castle, do you see?"

Derry laughed suddenly, barking out the sound so that the duke twitched in surprise.

"I'm sorry, my lord," Derry said, making a wheezing sound in his amusement. "You are a man I respect and you have chosen to share this private thing with me. I should not—" He broke off again, unable to control his amusement.

Somerset looked offended and his wounded expression left Derry gasping for breath and leaning against a wall for support.

"I was going to say that York will not be the end of me, for all his dislike," Somerset went on stiffly. "I feared for a time while I was in the Tower. Predictions can be vague things and I thought that could have been the place I would die, but then I was delivered, sent forth once more to serve my king. Nothing else will make me afraid again, not York or Salisbury or . . . anything."

"I am sorry, my lord. I should not have laughed," Derry said, wiping his eyes and mastering himself. "I wish I had some magical talisman, or beggar-woman's promise to aid me beyond my own wits, I really do.

I wish I could know for certain whether the threat was York, or Salisbury, or some other devil I have not yet even noticed, hiding in a dark place."

Somerset was far from appeased, the muscles on his jaw standing out.

"There are some with real powers, Derry, whether they come from devils or angels, whether you choose to believe in them or not. I meant to bring you some small reassurance, not to make myself the target of your mockery. I will bid you good night." The duke inclined his head and set off, leaving Derry to stare in amusement after him.

CHAPTER 11

Richard of Warwick reached Ludlow Castle in late April, bringing his brother John and just over twelve hundred men to add to the forces arrayed around that fortress. Six hundred of those with him were prime archers, who knew their worth and walked the streets with cocky self-assurance. In a short time, they had set up archery butts around the castle grounds, practicing their skill for all the hours of daylight. The rest were ax and bill men, levied and armed from the incomes of Warwick's midland and northern estates, called to his service as their feudal lord. To the amusement of York and his father, Warwick had dressed every man in bright red tunics over their mail shirts, dyed the color of blood with the madder root. As their commanding officer, he wore the color himself, inlaid with a white stripe.

York's mood had improved on seeing so many added to the forces at Ludlow. He had fretted over weeks of inaction, writing letters and sending messengers, trying to gather supporters while the king regained his strength and prepared for his Great Progress from London. York insisted on celebrating the arrival of Salisbury's sons with a feast that first night, emptying the fortress cellars of ancient French barrels to make sure every man had a full cup to toast their leaders.

The following morning, York was to be found snoring in his rooms. Warwick and his brother were less affected, both young men rising at dawn to hunt with their father. They rode out through a vast array of tents and soldiers breaking their fast over small fires. The men stood respectfully in the presence of nobles before settling back down to eat, polish, mend, and sharpen. Despite the splitting heads that morning, Warwick's arrival had increased the tension in the camp. Armies were not gathered in such numbers to sit around in the spring sunshine.

"They make a pretty company, your red men," Salisbury called to his son as they rode along a farm track. "I think in the field, our enemies will fall back from their glory alone."

Warwick rolled his eyes for the benefit of his brother John. Both of Salisbury's sons were enjoying being out that morning. The sun was up and they were in good health, with an army at their beck and call.

"I want them to feel they are one band, one battle of men, Father. The tunics will mean they can see each other on the field, know friend from enemy with just a glance. You'll see, if it comes to it."

Salisbury gave a derisive sniff, though his pride in his son was obvious to both of them.

"I imagine an archer would enjoy such gaudy targets as well," Salisbury said.

"My bowmen wear the same red," Warwick replied. "They'll answer any mockery with shafts of their own. It cost me a fortune in dyes and broadcloth, but they walk taller in the one color, Father, I swear it."

The three Neville men rode beyond the sentries and scouts around York's castle, though not so far that they could not have raced back if they were spotted and hailed by some enemy. The roads around Ludlow were empty of thieves and brigands that year, moved on to towns that did not have a host of armed men camped on their doorsteps. Yet there were always threats. London was more than a hundred miles away—another country almost, for its distance from Ludlow. Yet two of the Nevilles had been present for the Percy attack on John's wedding, and only a fool would have ridden without care and caution.

Salisbury reined in at a small wooden bridge across a stream, beckoning to Richard and John so that they came close enough for him to speak quietly. The day was growing warm, and red and green dragonflies darted above the water, drawing the eye as they snapped insects out of the air.

"We are alone here," Salisbury said, looking around him, "and there may not be another time to talk as one family."

His two sons glanced at each other, pleased to be included in their father's plans.

"Our friend York no longer champs at the bit. I think he can be brought close to King Henry with his men, but he still hopes for some resolution without a drop of blood being shed."

"And you, Father?" John asked. At twenty-four, he was the shortest of them, dark-haired and slim at the waist, though his shoulders were wide. At home, his wife, Maud, was heavy with their first child. John had come to Ludlow for one reason and his cold tone made it clear he did not enjoy hearing of any softening of intent.

"Be at peace, John. You know better than to doubt me. Was I not there? I know what we owe the Percy family. The old man will be at the king's side and at least one of his sons with him. I expect he has left his eldest boy at Alnwick. Egremont will surely ride with his father—the man we want most of all, though I do not doubt Earl Percy gave the order."

"What if York is intent on peace though?" John said. "I have come a long way from home, father. I've left my family and estates for this and I've sworn to see the Percy dogs cut down. I won't sit still while York and Lancaster are reconciled, with new oaths and toasts drunk to their health."

"Be careful, John," Warwick said softly. His brother was a mere knight and had brought no more than six retainers with him. The armies of his elder brother and father gave him more authority than he could claim on his own, though his grievance was greater. Perhaps because of that, John Neville shot his brother a look of anger before their father spoke again.

"We have two thousand Neville men to York's one. It is my intention to make an example of the enemies of our house and I will not be put off that path by anyone. Is that clear enough for you, John? Let York worry about the Duke of Somerset whispering in the king's ear. Our concern is with the Percy lords. If they ride north with the king, they'll not survive our meeting. My oath on that."

Salisbury held out his hand and both his sons gripped it in turn, sealing the agreement between them.

"We three are Neville men," Salisbury said proudly. "There are some who have yet to learn what it means to cross that name, but they will, I promise you both. They'll learn, even if King Henry himself stands in our way."

He clapped first Richard, then John on the shoulders, reaching out to them while their horses stamped and nipped at one another.

"Now beat the bushes and find some game for your old father to stick a spear through. We should bring something back to Ludlow.

It'll be good practice for you both. If we are to flush out the Percys, we'll need to march soon, to await the king on his path north."

MARGARET STOOD before her husband, wiping an oily cloth over his shoulder pauldrons so that they would shine in the spring sunlight. They were alone, though armed men and horses were all around the Palace of Westminster, gathering in hundreds of small groups. King Henry's half brother, Jasper Tudor, had come in the week before, bringing news of an army encamped in the northwest, around the castle of Ludlow. That new information had lent an urgency to the proceedings that had been missing before. There were still many senior men who refused to believe York or Salisbury would raise banners against the king, but the procession had begun to resemble an army making ready to move, with more and more lords choosing their best men to stand with them.

"You will keep our son safe in Windsor, Margaret," Henry said, looking down at her, "no matter what lies ahead."

"I would prefer you to wait another month, two. You grow stronger every day that passes, and there is still the garrison at Calais. If you called them back, they would surely draw the teeth from the Plantagenet, whatever he plans."

Henry chuckled, shaking his head.

"And leave the Calais gates open? I have lost enough of France without stripping my last fortress there. I have two thousand men, Margaret—and I am the King of England, protected by God and the law. Please, we have talked and talked. I will take the Great North Road to Leicester. I will ride and be seen—and those lords of mine who still waver will be abashed. The Duke of Norfolk has not responded to me. Exeter is still claiming illness. God's *wounds*, I need to be seen, Margaret, just as you've said so many times. When I have revealed the shining ranks of all those who stand with me, then I will declare York and Salisbury traitors. I will put the mark of Cain on their heads and they will find what support remains to them vanishing like frost in summer."

Margaret touched the cloth to his brow, wiping away a smudge.

"I do not like to hear you curse, Henry. You did not before, that I remember."

"I was a different man," Henry said, his voice suddenly hoarse.

She looked up into his eyes and saw the fear there, almost hidden.

"I was *drowned*, Margaret, fat with water and unable to cry out. I would not wish such a fate on any man, no matter what his sins."

"You are stronger now," Margaret said. "You must not talk of it."

"I am frightened to," he murmured. "I feel it in me, this *weakness*, as if I have been allowed to stand in the sun for just a time, knowing I must go back. It is like fighting the sea, Margaret, too vast and green and cold. I build . . . walls and still it rushes in, clutching at me."

Sweat had broken out on his forehead, and Margaret wiped his skin dry. Her husband shuddered, opening his eyes once more and forcing a smile.

"But I will not let it through, I promise you. I will build a fortress to hold it back. Now, if you have finished polishing me like a trumpet, I should go and mount. I have a long road ahead before I rest tonight." He reached down suddenly and kissed her, feeling her lips cold under his. "There! That will keep me warm," he said, smiling. "Make little Edward safe, Margaret. England will be his to rule when I am gone. But she is *mine* today."

York led the column from Ludlow, riding with his son Edward at the head of a procession of trudging men who talked and laughed as they took minor paths and then reached the great Roman road of Ermine Street, still laid with flat stones as it ran north and south, almost the length of the country. On such a surface, they could match the pace of the old legions, making twenty miles a day with ease. Three thousand men ate far more than they could find at roadside inns, though they stripped those bare to the walls as they reached them. York had spent fortunes from his treasury on the supply train following behind the marching men and horses, so that whenever they stopped, a host of retainers would light fires and set stews and salted meat to bubbling for the appetites of weary men.

They reached Royston first, then Ware the following day, where York halted the column to rest. Salisbury and his sons rode into the village to find rooms, while York stayed for a time to oversee the camp, giving praise to his captains and observing their spirits.

The three Neville men made a tight group as they gave their horses to a stable lad and headed inside to the only tavern.

"How soon before we reach the king's Progress?" John Neville asked his father. "Do we even know the route they will take?"

"We're not out hunting pheasant," Salisbury replied. "When he leaves London, the king will come up the Great North Road, with all his lords and judges. He will not be hard to find. The only question is what York will do when he has no other choice but to bear arms against the king."

"You think it is so certain?" Warwick asked. The taproom of the tavern was empty, but he still kept his voice low.

"I do not think those around the king will ever let York or me come back into the fold. They fear him—and they fear us. The Percys will not allow peace, lad. The old man is scenting the wind at this very moment, straining for his last chance to break the Nevilles. And I welcome it. Peace is nothing in the face of that."

"I do not think my lord York is ready for battle," Warwick said. "He seems in earnest, to me, with all his talk of healing wounds."

Salisbury shook his head, sipping a tankard of ale and smacking his lips in appreciation.

"Nonetheless," he said, softly.

THE GREEN FIELDS AND FARMS of Kilburn stretched all around the royal camp. Beyond the city of London, King Henry had ordered a halt and courts to be set up for three hours across noon. His two dozen judges had heard a number of cases in that time, freeing six men who had languished in prison for months, fining more than thirty, and ordering the execution of eleven more. Justice might have taken an age to reach the town of Kilburn, but once it had arrived, it was swift and sure. King Henry left scaffolds being erected behind him, passing cheering crowds come out to catch a glimpse of the royal party dispensing justice.

The mood among the two thousand was that of a celebration, with feats of arms and riding performed for the king's pleasure by those who hoped for some recognition. Thomas, Lord Egremont, was the victor of two demonstration bouts, giving such buffets to those who stood against him that they had to be tied to their horses later on, or fall. While the trials went on, the local towns provided ale, bread, and meat, for which they were paid in silver.

The first day of the Progress had gone well and King Henry's mood was light as he ordered his heralds to turn off the road and seek lodgings around the town of Watford for the night. By the time darkness fell, he was settled in a local manor house, enjoying the company of his half brother Jasper Tudor as well as Earl Percy and Egremont. Henry found he had drunk a little too much of good local mead and, though his doctors hovered within call, he felt strong, pleased enough at the prospect of another dozen days like the first before he reached Leicester.

He retired late, knowing he would feel it the following morning, as the Royal Progress moved on to St. Albans. He would pause and pray in the abbey there, at the oldest Christian shrine in the country. He had been told Abbot Whethamstede had been one of those who came to Windsor to poke and prod him while he had been senseless. It gave Henry some small pleasure to consider greeting the abbot on his feet, a man who had known him only on his back. Before he slept, he imagined taking the abbot's hand in a strong grip and seeing him kneel to the King of England and his most loyal lords.

AFTER THE KING and most of his guests had retired to their beds, Earl Percy remained, with his son Thomas and the younger Tudor still at table. It was oddly difficult to find a private place for a quiet conversation and the earl hoped the king's Welsh half brother would leave. Jasper Tudor, Earl of Pembroke, was dulled with drink, but in that state where an hour can pass almost unnoticed. Earl Percy had to stifle yawns every few moments, too aware that at sixty-three he could not rise restored after just a few hours of sleep. He toyed with his cup of wine at the long table, watching the earl throwing grapes into the air and catching them in his mouth. The young Welshman was tilting his head up to the point where he was in some danger of falling back off his chair.

"I knew your mother well, Pembroke," Earl Percy said suddenly. "She was a great lady and a fine wife to old King Henry. I was her steward at her coronation, did you know that?"

Jasper Tudor righted his chair with elaborate care before replying.

"I did, my lord. Though I was just a child when she passed. I cannot say I knew her, though I wish I could."

Earl Percy grunted.

"Your father, though, I don't know him at all. A Welsh soldier is all I ever heard of Owen Tudor, though he married a queen and has two earls for his sons! Rising like bread, in just a generation."

Jasper Tudor was short, with thick black curls that he had allowed to grow long. The Welshman sat straighter as Earl Percy addressed him, sensing something hostile in the old man's talk, so that he played with his knife, scoring the wood.

"He lives still, a fine man," he said, closing one eye as he squinted up the table.

"And a lucky one, for a Welshman," Earl Percy said, emptying his cup. "Now here you are, his son, in the presence of the King of England and his court."

"My brother called and I came, to represent my branch," Jasper replied warily. "And I brought a hundred of those Welsh archers that have made such a place for themselves in England these last years." He held up a hand as if to forestall an interruption. "Please, my lord, no thanks are necessary. Though I see too few bowmen in this grand Progress. I know my lads will make their mark if they are called upon."

"I just hope you have them on a tight rein," Earl Percy said lightly, staring up at the rafters. "I have known some men of Wales to be little more than savages. It is a dark country and there are some shameless fellows who call them thieves, though I would never count myself among that number."

"I am relieved to hear that, my lord," Jasper said. For those who knew him, his voice had grown dangerously soft, a murmur before a storm. "We say the same thing about the English in the north."

"Well, you would, wouldn't you?" Earl Percy said. "Still, I am glad to have such as you close to the king. Who knows what baubles might yet drop into your hands from his? There is no meanness in this King Henry. It has long been a generous line."

Jasper Tudor rose suddenly, swaying as he glared blearily down the length of the table.

"I think I've had enough for one sitting. I will find my bed. Good night, my lord Northumberland, Baron Egremont." He stumbled out of the room to the stairs, where he could be heard crashing about for some time.

Earl Percy smiled to himself, looking over to his son, almost as stupefied by drink as the young Welshman.

"I hope the servants count the spoons tomorrow," he said. "The Welsh are like jackdaws, you know, every one of them."

Thomas smiled at that, his eyes half closed and his head drooping.

"You should seek out your own bed, Thomas. This whole procession is too much like a spring fair. You young men should be sharp, with Nevilles armed for war. Do you understand? God, lad, how much have you drunk tonight?"

"I understand," Thomas complained without opening his eyes.

"I wonder. I do not trust a Neville when I can see him, never mind when he is off somewhere else, doing God knows what. Go on, sleep it off and rise sharp to protect your king—and your father. Good night. Trunning will be up at dawn, I guarantee you that. I'll have him throw a bucket over you if you sleep in. Go. God be with you."

With a groan, Thomas rose to his feet, gripping the table to steady himself.

"G'night," he said, staggering as he left the table's support behind.

Alone, Earl Percy used his knife to cut slivers of cheese from a square wooden platter. With no one left to observe him, his features settled into their habitual frown. The king's Great Progress had started well enough, but he could not enjoy Henry's return to health while Salisbury and his sons were out there in the wilds with York. The king's recovery had been the answer to prayers for the Percy family. The Nevilles had lost the foundations of their strength, but Earl Percy knew they would be all the more dangerous for that. With a grimace, he forced himself to drink another cup of wine, feeling his senses swim. Without it, sleep would never come.

CHAPTER 12

There were more than a few sore heads and white faces in the king's column the next morning. The day dawned clear and cold and the mood was light across the great camp. Half of those present were mounted, so that horses whinnied and snorted in huge herds, tossing their heads at the first touch of jingling bridle and reins. Senior judges who had found no place to sleep in town rose stiffly from their tents, yawning and scratching under their robes as they were tended by their servants.

Each of the lords traveling with King Henry had chosen their own spot around the town of Watford, marked by the banners of their houses, so that hundreds of brightly colored pennants fluttered in the morning breeze. Such a seemingly chaotic assembly was well ordered by name, status, and loyalties, in family groups. The cooking fires made a fog that hung over the fields like a cloud bank drifting down. By eight o'clock, they had packed up the baggage train and saddled the mounts. The Percy ranks were closest to the line of march, more than six hundred knights and axemen, by far the largest single contingent. No one challenged the earl's right to lead. Both

Somerset and Buckingham outranked him, but they had barely two hundred veteran soldiers between them, a massive force and investment that was nonetheless lost in the king's host. Other noblemen jostled for position, with the places closest to the king often gambled at dice, or sold. The column took form and scouts swept out ahead, searching the land all around for any threat, their movements made visible by the rooks and crows they startled from distant trees.

King Henry had donned a full set of armor in the manor house, rising before the sun and visiting a local chapel. He shone as he rode along the flank of the column, his great destrier cantering easily. The helmet he wore had a barbed golden circlet set into the brow, as much a part of the steel as royalty was part of the man. He came surrounded by knights and heralds holding three-lion banners as he guided his horse onto the great slabs of stone that made up the road north.

Henry felt alert and vital, lifted by the sight of so many craning to watch him pass. They cheered the sight of the king, the sound drawn out of them by a sudden rush of pride and pleasure. It was unplanned and discordant, but it delighted Henry for all that. He reached the head of the column and took his spot behind the first three ranks, where Lords Percy and Buckingham rode.

"God's blessing on you all," Henry said.

Both men smiled and dipped as low as they could in the saddle, sensing the king's mood and feeling it lift all those around them.

Henry settled, touching various spots on his armor and saddlebags as he took note of his equipment. In truth, it was just a show, his mind subtly distracted as he patted his horse's great neck and rubbed at its ears. He did not yet trust his recovery and it had become his habit to take any private moment to breathe long and slowly, testing his joints and his mind, searching for broken parts. There were certainly aches in his bones and muscles, still weak after so long abed.

Yet his thoughts were clear as he took a good grip on the reins. He was satisfied. He looked back along the column, seeing the eyes of waiting soldiers on him as his gaze swept over them. For many, it would be a moment to tell their children, when the King of England had looked directly at them and smiled. Henry nodded to them all, then turned back to look ahead. The sun was up and he was ready. He only wished Margaret could have been there to see him whole.

"My lords, gentlemen," he said loudly. "Onward."

The lines of knights and axemen moved off in step, the rank too wide for the Roman road so that it stretched and plunged over fields on both sides. It was an idle thought, but Henry knew his father would have ridden with as many when he broke the French at Agincourt. His heart swelled at that image of a man he had never known, feeling closer to him at that moment than he ever had before. He closed his eyes, trying to sense his father's spirit. The battle king would surely see his son, if he could. It may have been a mere Judicial Progress, with judges, scribes, and pinch-faced lawyers at the rear, but it was also an army in the field and Henry felt the joy and rightness of it.

Without the pressure of advancing through hostile territory, the men in ranks called and chatted to each other as they marched or rode, carrying on conversations as varied as any group of washerwomen. The first six miles passed under the rising sun, lending a spring warmth to a day that remained clear.

Behind the wall of Percy knights, King Henry was not immediately aware of the scout racing back toward the column, waving his free arm as he forced his mount over broken ground and risked both their necks. The man was one of Henry's own household, so that he ignored the questions called out by other men, shoving angrily through them as they clutched at his jerkin and cloak. Earl Percy exchanged a glance with his son and both he and Egremont reined in and halted to let the marching ranks pass them, drifting back to the royal presence.

"Squire James! Come closer," Henry called as he recognized the young man. He beckoned him in and the scout bowed low in the saddle, taking gulping breaths before he could speak.

"Your Highness, there is an army by St. Albans. I saw the white rose of York, the eagle of Salisbury, and Warwick's bear and white staff on red. They are camped to the east of the town and I could see no sign of them within the streets themselves."

Earl Percy had brought his horse close enough to hear every word, the old man seeming to swell with indignation on behalf of his king.

"May I question him, Your Highness?" Percy said, dipping his head.

Henry nodded, willing to let the men speak while he thought.

"How many?" Earl Percy barked at the scout. "What numbers do they have? You've shown your eye is keen enough."

"They were hard-packed, my lord. Standing close, like reeds. I would say more than we have here, but I cannot be certain, for a column stretches and they merely stood."

"In what formation?" Percy snapped at him.

The young man began to stammer, aware that his words could mean they rode to battle. He was barely sixteen years old and he did not have the experience to answer well.

"I . . . no, my lord . . . I . . ."

"Spit it out, boy! Have they come to fight or not? Did you see pikes held ready or still stacked to the sky, ready to be snatched up? Were the horses saddled? Were there fires lit, or damped down?"

As the young scout opened his mouth, Thomas, Lord Egremont, added his own questions.

"Where was the baggage? Sent to the rear? Which of the noble banners lay closest to the town?"

"I . . . believe they did have pikes to hand, my lords. I do not recall fires, or whether the horses were all saddled. No, wait, yes I saw some knights at the fore who were armored and in stirrups. Not all, my lords."

"Enough, my lord Percy, Thomas," King Henry said to father and son. "Let the boy alone. We will see soon enough. What is it now— two, three miles to the town? We'll know it all in an hour or so."

Earl Percy scowled at the king's response, smoothing his face with his hand before he answered.

"Your Highness, we should halt and consider our own formation. If we are to ride to battle, I would place the men in a wider line, with horse on each flank. I'd bring Tudor's Welsh archers up to the front and—"

"I said *enough*," Henry interrupted. His voice was firm and clear, silencing the earl as if he had been struck. Henry could feel the ears twitching of every man around him and he drummed his fingers on his saddle horn.

"If the rose, the eagle, and the bear are in the field for war, my lord Percy, be certain I will not disappoint them. There's time enough to array for battle when we can see what lies ahead. I won't have our horses blown to exhaustion in the mud while there is a fine road into the town ahead of us."

His gaze fell on the scout, who was watching and listening with his mouth hanging open like a village idiot.

"Pass the word down the line, Squire James. Let the men know what we are about, what we may face this morning. And find Derry Brewer, wherever he is skulking. I'll want to know his thoughts. Bring him up to me and then take those sharp eyes of yours out once again. You have my thanks and my blessing for your service."

The scout went scarlet with mingling pleasure and embarrassment, almost falling out of the saddle as he bowed for his king. Not trusting himself to speak, he took his horse out of the column and dug in his heels, galloping away to the rear.

Richard of York rode along the edge of a plowed field, avoiding the deep-laid furrows as he surveyed the town with its abbey tower visible over all. On his right shoulder, three thousand men filled Key Field from one side to the other, waiting for orders. He looked over their heads as he cantered along the town's eastern boundary, keeping his worries hidden as best he could. He did not yet know what the day would bring, whether his fortunes would be restored or utterly broken. Salisbury and Warwick had fallen back a way as he increased his pace, though his son Edward remained at his side, looking to his father in uncomplicated joy, just to be present. The four of them rode along the rear walls of timber-framed houses, glimpsing staring faces at the open windows.

It was galling to York that neither Salisbury nor Warwick seemed to share his concerns. The king was coming north with a large body of men. York knew it was the most dangerous provocation just to assemble an army in Henry's path. Yet he'd been forced to accept Salisbury's advice, given over and over during the previous months. They could not approach the king without an armed presence. York had his own spies in Westminster and, to a man, they reported only growing hostility to his name and cause. Salisbury's informers had claimed even more—that men like the Duke of Somerset and the queen were arguing openly for his destruction. He shook his head like a twitch. If he and the Nevilles rode in alone, they could be captured and brought to trial on the spot. The king had his judges and his Seal with him, as well as peers of the realm. He needed nothing else.

York fretted as he halted his horse, looking over the entrances to the town from the east. Three paths lay ahead, as clear as the three entrances to St. Albans. One choice was already made, as he had decided not to remain at Ludlow with his head down. York had been the king's lieutenant in France and Ireland and he could not sit back and wait for his fate to be decided by others. He knew if he had taken that coward's course, the king would have reached Leicester in peace—and would have immediately named York and Salisbury as traitors. Salisbury's men in particular had been certain of that. Whatever else, York could not allow that declaration to be made.

York removed his gauntlet, laying it over the saddle horn as he wiped sweat from his face, looking south to the stone road stretching away across the hills. He had the forces to attack, a choice with no certain outcome, a choice that would mean he was indeed a traitor to the Crown. He would be oathsworn and damned in front of his eldest son, a thought that sickened him. Such an act would raise the country in righteous rage against a kingslayer. He would never know peace again and he would not sleep for fear of men sent to kill him in the night. York shuddered, rolling his shoulders in the armor. Such men existed, he knew very well. Two centuries before, King Edward I had been cut by some dark-skinned maniac, fighting him off with a chair in his own rooms. That was no kind of fate to choose.

He could not run and he dared not fight. The choice he had made was the weakest of them all, though perhaps a fraction less likely to end in complete disaster. York turned his horse to face Salisbury and Warwick, meeting the older man's eyes as they bored into him, watching and judging his every change of expression.

"When the king arrives," York said, "there will be no sudden movement among our people, is that understood? My orders are to stand, to hold. The royal ranks will come with hackles raised at the sight of so many arrayed against them. One fool then among us—just *one* calling an insult at the wrong time—and all we have planned and prayed for will fall apart."

Though there were four of them, the conversation was between the two fathers in that group. York and Salisbury faced each other on the dark earth, while their sons looked on and said nothing.

"I have agreed all that, Richard," Salisbury replied. "You want your chance to lance the boil. I understand. My men will obey me well enough, you have my word. Send your herald to the king, make the demands we discussed. I think the words will not reach Henry, or if they do, that he will not listen, but I've made my objections before. It's your tune to play, Richard. My men won't start a fight unless they are attacked. I can't answer for the peace then."

York screwed his face up on one side, reaching up to scratch and rub the roughened skin. He was very aware of his son listening to every word and, for the first time, wished he had not brought him from Ludlow. Edward's height and breadth made him look like a young knight, especially with his visor down. Yet he was thirteen. The boy still believed his father could not be in the wrong, while York saw only closed paths ahead. Irritated with himself, York swallowed spit and replaced his gauntlet, tugging at it until his fingers reached the end, then clenching the hand into a fist until it shook.

"King Henry will hear me," he said, as confidently as he could. "If he allows a parlay or a truce, I'll walk into his presence before noon today. I'll kneel and take any oath of fealty he would have of me, as my rightful king. That is how I would have this end, my lord Salisbury. In peace and with our offices restored, with you as chancellor once again, your son as Captain of Calais."

"And for you?" Salisbury asked. "What title would you have of the king?"

York shrugged carelessly.

"First Counselor perhaps, or Chief Constable of England— whatever name that means I stand once more at his right hand. It is no more than I am owed for my service."

York looked to the south, straining his eyes for the first sign of the king's army. The wind was getting stronger, stealing some of the warmth from the air. He did not see Salisbury and Warwick glance at each other, both men looking quickly away.

"He *will* hear me," York said again.

DERRY BREWER JOGGED along the column, urged on by the young scout who could not understand why he had refused a horse. Rather than take the time to explain that he had no idea how to stay on one, if he could even have mounted at all, Derry had decided to run to the king. He hadn't counted on the fact that the column kept moving, turning his mile from the rear into at least twice that distance. By the time he reached the front ranks, he was blowing hard and pouring with perspiration, barely able to speak.

Edmund, Duke of Somerset, looked down at the scarlet spymaster with an expression of amusement. Even the dour Earl Percy lost his frown at the sight.

Derry was gasping so hard, he had to reach out and lay a hand on the king's stirrup to stay abreast of him, rather than fall behind.

"Your Highness, I have come," he panted.

"Half dead and half late," Buckingham muttered, over on his right, earning himself a glare.

"I wanted your advice some time ago, Master Brewer," King Henry said stiffly. "Learn to ride, on my order. Borrow a spare mount and have one of the scouts show you how it is done."

"Yes, Your Highness. I'm sorry," Derry replied through wheezing breaths. He was furious with himself, all too aware that he could once have run three times as far and still arrived ready to fight or run again.

"York and Salisbury lie ahead of us, Master Brewer, with Warwick.

My scout reports an army at least the equal of this column. I must know their intentions, Brewer, before I march the men into the town."

Derry had heard the news called a dozen times as he trotted up the line. He'd had time to think, though it could never be enough with so little information to aid him.

"Your Highness, it is impossible to know York's mind at this moment. I did not believe he would leave Ludlow, but as he has, the threat cannot be ignored. He has complained about the influence of Somerset and Percy on your royal person. It may be he will take a chance to argue his case, if you grant him safe passage under truce. But I would not trust the man, Your Highness. More, I would send Earl Percy to the rear."

"*What?*" Percy snapped immediately. "*You'll* send me *nowhere*, you impudent whoreson! How dare you advise the king in such a way? I'll have you stripped and flogged, you—"

"I called Master Brewer for his counsel," King Henry said, speaking over the old man's anger. "I'll thank you to remain still while he speaks. *I'll* judge the worth of what he says."

Earl Percy subsided with bad grace, his eyes promising terrible retribution as he continued to glare at the unfortunate spymaster.

Derry's breathing began to ease.

"There's no secret to the feud between Percy and the Nevilles, Your Highness. Whatever York intends, the men-at-arms they command should not be allowed to come close to each other. Dogs will fight, Your Highness. Loyalty to their masters could begin the bloodshed, where the patrons want only peace."

"You think York has brought an army just to be heard, then?" the king said, staring ahead up the road. The first houses of the town were coming into view, less than a mile away, forcing his hand.

"I think he would have met us on open ground if his intention was to fight," Derry replied. "Battles are not fought in towns, Your

Highness—at least, not well. I was in London when Jack Cade came in and I remember the chaos of that night. Young Warwick was there and his memories are no sweeter than mine. There were no tactics then, no maneuvers of the field—just running and panic and bloody murder in the alleyways. If York intends to attack, he will not allow this column to enter St. Albans."

"Thank you, Master Brewer," King Henry replied. A memory surfaced and he smiled slightly as he went on. "Though you have no beer, you do have my trust."

Derry blinked at the echo of a different time, a half-forgotten shadow. The king he faced showed little sign of that drowned man in his clear gaze.

"Thank you, Your Majesty," he said. "You honor me." Derry looked up at the still-glaring Earl Percy then, hoping the old man had noted his standing with the king. He had enough enemies.

"The town lies yonder and there is no sign of York's ranks marching out to meet us," Henry said. He clenched his right fist on the reins and Derry saw anger swell, mottling the king's face. "Yet there is an army in my path, a stone in my way. It will not be borne, my lords. Not by me. We will not go on from St. Albans until I am satisfied—and if they are traitors and damned men, I will line the road back to London with their heads, every mother's son of those who wait for us. Every one!"

"Shall I retire to the rear, Your Highness?" Earl Percy said to the king, his gaze still fixed malevolently on Derry Brewer.

"No," Henry replied without hesitation. "Lead the way into the town, Earl Percy. Have the trumpets sound and the banners held high. Let those ahead know I am here and I am not abashed by their presence. Let them fear damnation and death if they lay a hand on a blade against their rightful king."

CHAPTER 13

The bells of St. Alban's Abbey tolled ten times as the king's column entered the town. The clock there was said to be a wonder of the age, capable of predicting eclipses as well as striking the hours, with the hands of monks employed only to lift its slow-falling weights and rewind the mechanism.

The echoing notes sounded over deserted streets, though every window was packed full of nervous faces. No one living within the bounds of the town had left their homes that day, to work or buy food. The stalls and shops were either empty or still in piles of canvas and lumber, their owners fled.

Marching in from the open road, King Henry's men fell silent almost rank by rank, intimidated by the houses on either side as they went further and further into the town. On their right shoulder, beyond the rows of tall houses, they all knew a massive force stood in Key Field, waiting. There was fear in all of them, but also determination. They rode or walked uphill with the king and he could be seen at the head of the column, his banners gold, red, and white. Fortunes were made and lost in battle when a king was present. Every man of lower rank considered, at least for a moment of private reflection, that he might be blessed that day, perhaps knighted for some act of valor, or even made noble by the king's hand. For some, such a prospect would be their only chance to gain both wealth and power for their names.

In the center of the town, an open marketplace stood, a long triangle surrounded on all sides by the homes of wealthy merchants and St. Peter's Church at one corner. The front ranks reached it before the abbey clock tolled again and the king reined in. More and more of his lords and their men filled the space until soldiers had to be halted further back. As soon as they dismounted and touched the cobbled street, Somerset and Percy sent men out to observe the enemy positions. Senior captains went to kick in the doors of pubs along the route, to guard the ale from those of their men who might prefer to vanish into the cellars for the day. Others forced the entrances of private homes against the terrified cries of the owners, while many more simply picked a clean spot on the open street, calling up the baggage carts and borrowing dried fuel and pots to prepare a midday meal. Without the presence of the Yorkist army outside the town, it might have been a cheerful morning, but the threat of violence made men grim as they went about their business.

Around the king's position on the hill, cobbles were levered up and stakes hammered into the ground to anchor a great awning for Henry to rest and be private. The king dismounted, waiting patiently while benches and a table were brought up from carts further down, carried along like turtles through the stream of busy soldiers. In just a short time, Henry and his senior lords had a place to sit and canvas to protect them from the wind and the common gaze.

As his horse was taken away to be brushed and fed, Henry called for Percy, Somerset, Buckingham, and Derry Brewer to attend him. He removed his gauntlets and nodded to the servants who laid a cup

and jug of wine and a platter of cold meats before him. His four summoned men entered to stand in silence, waiting on his command.

King Henry drank deeply of the wine, smacking his lips. He
caught sight of his doctors hanging back beyond the first row of
guards and frowned to himself, performing his internal check once
more. No, he was all right, he reassured himself. He knew there were
moments of vagueness, when he lost the thread of his thoughts, but
they came and went quickly. He did not need to call those old spiders
and endure their prodding and sweet mixtures.

"My lords, Master Brewer, I do not believe we will be hearing
cases today. That ragtag collection of traitors outside the town is our
only concern. What reports do you have? What do you suggest?"

Somerset spoke before anyone else. He'd had his scouts riding
through the town before the king reached the boundary. By his expression, nothing he'd learned had pleased him.

"Your Highness, there are three entrances from the east. Two are
narrow roads, alleys almost. We passed thornbushes outside the town
and, with a little work, those two can be blocked against the most
determined attack. The third is wider and harder to stop up. I'll need
to take tables out of houses, perhaps even beams, or a horse trough."
He did not say he had already given the orders and that forty men
were hard at work securing that side of the town. Some things were
too urgent to be left, and Somerset merely waited for the king to nod.

"You would have me hidden away behind thorns?" Henry asked
softly. "I . . . that does not please me, my lord Somerset. Not thirty
miles from London, the King of England . . ." he broke off, his drumming fingers growing still on the wooden table.

After a beat of awkward silence, Derry swallowed nervously. He
suspected the king was passing through one of his blank moments
and he chose to speak over it, whether Henry heard him or not.

"Your Highness, whatever the slight to your honor, we have three wolves in the field. No one leaves the door of their house open with such hungry eyes looking in." He paused as King Henry blinked, shaking his head like a spasm and looking up in the beginnings of confusion. "Until we know what York and Salisbury and Warwick intend, Your Highness, it is the merest sense to bolt the door against them."

"Yes, yes, of course, Derry," Henry said. "As you say. I trust your judgment."

The king's eyes brightened and he raised his head, finding Earl Percy staring oddly at him.

"Well, Earl Percy? Will you stand there like a post?" Henry demanded, glaring back at the old man. "How many of them are there in Key Field? You can answer your own questions now, for me, as you put them to Squire James before."

Earl Percy pursed his mouth into a thin line. God had placed his most dangerous enemy in opposition to the king, but his confidence fluttered like a candle in a breeze with the younger man's strangeness.

"My men say they have three thousand, Your Highness. They report at least four hundred archers among the Warwick men, all wearing red. Perhaps another two thousand are pike and axemen, with the rest on horseback. No small force, Your Highness—and traitors, as you say. Salisbury is there, with his son, two cunning men who have shown nothing but scorn for your royal authority. It's clear enough to me that their fall from grace has left them wounded and angry still. There can be no other reason for them to stand and threaten the king."

Henry took another draft of the wine, the cup instantly refilled by a servant standing at his shoulder.

"Three thousand?" he repeated. "By God, it's true then. The fortunes of men like York and Salisbury have grown too large if they can afford to arm and feed so many." The king looked sharply at his spymaster. "Brewer. Without the men of my household and the judges, lawyers, pot-boys, heralds, and the like, how many armed men stand with me today?"

It was a question Derry had considered with Somerset, making a close count as they approached the town.

"No more than fifteen hundred, Your Highness, though we could arm a hundred of the serving lads as well, if we had to."

"Those with us are the finest quality of soldiers," Percy added. "The personal guards of your lords, Your Highness. Each of them would be worth two or more of those standing with the Nevilles, no doubt quaking at the thought of besieging their king."

"And *York*, Lord Percy," Somerset said irritably. "You seem to think only of the Neville father and son, while it is York who commands, York who was Protector and Defender. It will be their loyalty to *York* that concerns us, not your petty disputes."

Before Earl Percy could snap a furious reply, Somerset addressed the king once more.

"Your Highness, do I have your permission to block the three roads in? We cannot sally out against so many, but we can leave them to break themselves on thorns, if they attack."

"Yes, give the order," Henry replied, still gloomily considering the numbers against him.

Somerset made a point of summoning one of his men and giving him the instructions. The man knew very well the barricades were already being constructed and Somerset shoved him roughly on his way before his confusion became a question.

By the time Somerset stepped back into the king's presence, Henry had risen from his seat. His cheeks were a little flushed from the wine, but he seemed resolute and aware.

"Put a man in that church tower at the end of the marketplace, ready to ring the bell and call down news of an attack from any other direction. I will not be flanked, now I have reached this place. Pray, gentlemen, that those who have lain in wait for me have not yet considered the true scope and results of their actions. I will not leave here until this threat has been broken or dispersed. Let them come, if they must. We will make this town a fortress for them to dash their heads against. Go about your business. Whatever York and Salisbury intend—"

King Henry broke off at a rising tumult outside the pavilion tent. A herald in black cloth marked with a white rose on his shoulder was trying to come through the crowd of soldiers, though he was buffeted and shoved with every step. There was already a trickle of blood running from some cut on his scalp and he looked wild-eyed and terrified as he called for the king.

"Let him through, there!" Henry snapped, loud enough for the soldiers to fall back instantly. "Stand away!"

A space opened in the heaving ranks. The herald was panting and pale as he knelt on the stones and held out a scroll sealed in white wax with the rose of York. With his free hand, he touched the wound to his head, staring in dismay at the red smear on his fingers.

Though the man appeared to be no threat, it was Somerset who took the scroll and broke the seal, allowing no potential enemy close enough to strike at his king. The dazed herald was led away out of earshot while the duke read quickly, his expression hardening.

"Well?" Henry demanded impatiently.

"York asks for me, Your Highness," Somerset said sourly. "That I be brought out to him, along with Earl Percy. He claims we are an evil influence on Your Majesty and that we have spread lies about his duty, faith, and allegiance. He asks for your mercy and your forgiveness for his presence with men-at-arms, but . . ." he read on, his lips moving, ". . . asks only that it be noted he wants nothing for himself beyond the fair trial of those 'foul whisperers' in your court."

"Am I mentioned?" Derry Brewer asked.

"No," Somerset said without looking up.

"Oh, he can go to the *devil*," Derry said instantly. "I've been a thorn in that man's side for years and he doesn't even put me on his list? It is worse to be overlooked, my lord!"

The spymaster's indignation made Somerset smile tightly as he continued to read. In turn, Derry watched the king, hoping he had headed off an eruption of anger. Henry had grown very still as Somerset read aloud, the blood draining from his face.

"I will not have one of my lords make such demands on me," Henry said, his voice almost a whisper. "Reply to him, Somerset. Have your herald proclaim for all to hear that York and Salisbury and Warwick will be *traitors*, damned and oathsworn if they do not depart immediately from this place, to await my judgment and to pray for my mercy. Tell them that and nothing else. Then we will see."

Earl Percy was beaming, Derry noticed. The blustery spring day could hardly be working out better for him, with the king's anger ringing out against Percy's own enemies. Somerset bowed and left. Derry paused only to gain the king's permission to leave before following him, taking York's still bleeding herald by the arm in a tight grip as the small group headed down to the barricades.

SOMERSET'S MEN had been busy from the first moment of their arrival in town, Derry realized. As well as the thornbushes ripped from the ground, dozens of heavy tables and chairs had been roped together across the three roads in from the east. It was not an impregnable barrier—anything man had made could be torn down by others—yet Jasper Tudor had brought his Welsh archers to those points on his own initiative: small, dark men with long yew bows to defend the barriers and even clamber onto them to give the best field of view. Derry shivered at the thought of assaulting such a position. He did not envy York's forces, if they came against the king.

Somerset helped York's herald climb over the mass of wood and thorn, ignoring all protests as the man's clothes snagged and tore. Even as he was sent on his way, Derry could see the herald taking in every detail of the archers. The man did not look pleased at what he saw.

A stone came from somewhere outside, looping through the air and making an archer swear in Welsh as he had to flinch away or be struck. Derry's mouth tightened in anger.

"My lord Tudor!" he called loudly. "Do your men know King Henry has given orders to stand here and make no attack?" It was not strictly true, but his shout was for the benefit of those who might let anger or sudden pain rule their thinking. The archer who had dodged the stone glared down at him from his position on top of the barrier, but Earl Jasper Tudor nodded, speaking in Welsh and pointing at the man until he dipped his head and turned to stare out once again. Another great piece of flint crashed down against the wood and Derry hissed a curse to himself. Somerset was busy with his own herald, but the problem was that armed men under threat of injury were not reliable at all. He heard one of the Welshmen call out a mocking insult to someone on the other side, lost to view. The man's companions all hooted with laughter, while Derry's spirits sank. The barrier was dry wood for the most part. He saw there were buckets of water ready in case it was fired, but there were different kinds of spark.

Somerset's herald finished nodding through his instructions, helped by the Welshmen to climb the barricade, on the heels of York's man. The herald was pale as he went, not enjoying the prospect of passing through jeering soldiers on the other side of the barrier.

Somerset walked over to where Derry was peering through gaps in the thorns, looking grim.

"If York has sense, he'll pull his men clear before someone gets a shaft down his throat or calls the wrong insult," Somerset said.

"Those are Salisbury's men, my lord. And they look as if they are spoiling for a fight. My lord, if you hear Earl Percy is intending to come down here, you might want to dissuade him. There are scores to settle between Percy and Neville and I don't want them settled today, if you take my meaning."

As Derry spoke, another flight of stones came over, knocking one of the archers back so that he fell screeching into the thorns, slipping down between two great oak tables. Those close to him shouted in anger and Derry saw one of them bending his bow with his teeth bared, blood running down his face. Jasper Tudor was bellowing an order, but the archer loosed his shaft and then howled in triumph. Half a dozen more took it as a signal to attack, and Tudor's orders were lost in a roar from both sides.

Derry heard a scream of pain sound above the noise and then almost lost his footing as the entire barricade lurched, rocking back and forth. He could feel axes chopping into wood and he drew his seax knife from the sheath on his hip.

"Christ!" he muttered. "My lord Somerset, we need more men here!"

In answer to his prayers, a troop of soldiers were already running toward the blocked road, swords bared and ready. Somerset ordered them into ranks and Derry stepped back to observe the defenses. The barrier was a brutal obstacle, whether those beyond it were just a small group of angry men or the first ranks of a full assault by Salisbury's forces. It would hold for a time, with Tudor's archers shooting in volleys, yelling a count to each other as they picked targets at close range. To Derry's astonishment, one of them was declaiming in verse, call and answer, with all the Welsh archers joining in.

Somerset saw Derry almost dancing from foot to foot in indecision.

"I have it here, Brewer," he said. "Go!"

Derry ran, cutting around the timbered home of some wealthy merchant and along to the second and third barriers. They were even tighter than the first, smaller alleys blocked to the height of two men and swarming with soldiers who clambered up the beams of the houses on either side to get a look at the enemy.

"Hold this position!" Derry shouted as he reached them, careless of his own right to give orders. "They don't get past!" The barricades were solid enough, he realized, sprinting back up the hill to the marketplace, where the king and the bulk of the royal column were still crammed in. At every step, Derry passed men jumping up from their meals and resting places, streaming down against his course toward the sounds of fighting. It was chaos, with no obvious figure in charge of any of it. Derry cursed York and Salisbury under his breath as he pounded up the hill until his breath felt like flame in his lungs.

YORK CLENCHED HIS FISTS tight behind his back as he faced Somerset's herald. The man had sunk to both knees in the presence of a duke and Earl Salisbury, but the fact that he was in Somerset's livery rather than the king's meant York knew what he would say before the herald opened his mouth. York's expression darkened further as the nervous man stammered through the message he had been given. Words that had been spoken by King Henry while surrounded by his loyal lords sounded much harder in York's own tent.

". . . you must then, d-depart from this place to await the king's judgment and . . ." The herald cleared his throat and rubbed the back of his scalp under York's cold gaze, ". . . and pray for his mercy." He shut his mouth and dipped his head, praying on his own behalf that he would not be beaten or killed for carrying such a message. Back toward the town, some ruckus was beginning, with shouting voices raised in anger. It all seemed far away at that moment and the herald swallowed uncomfortably.

"Damned and oathsworn?" York repeated in wonder, shaking his head. "King Henry offers me nothing but *damnation*?"

"I was told only to repeat the king's words, my lord. I . . . I have no permission to add more."

The shouting had become a roar and York looked up from the hapless subject of his fury.

"Salisbury? Send someone out to see . . . no, I'll go myself."

He strode past the herald without bothering to dismiss him. Salisbury followed on York's heels and the man was left in the empty command tent to wipe sweat from his brow.

York swore as he looked across the field and saw the barricade across New Lane rocking back and forth, cries and shouts sounding across the field. He could see archers scrabbling around on the makeshift construction, taking shots as they fought to keep their footing.

"Have your men brought back out of range," York snapped. "Then summon the captains."

Salisbury inclined his head without a word, careful to show no sign of his own satisfaction. The chance for peace had come and gone in a few rash words from the king. Salisbury could have blessed Henry at that moment.

The sun was still rising as thirty-two men gathered around York. Each was a veteran, well armed and sufficiently experienced to have risen to command for their noble patrons. He saw their grim determination and chose his words to suit.

"I have received King Henry's herald," York began, making his voice ring out with a sizable fraction of the anger and betrayal he felt.

Hundreds of soldiers began to trot closer to that small group of captains as they realized their fate was being decided. The barricades were left behind for the Welsh archers to jeer at the retreating soldiers. A dozen bodies lay at the foot of the thorns and piled wood, already cooling.

"Although it was my aim to settle this dispute without recourse to arms," York went on sternly, "I have been denied. King Henry has evil men around him who think nothing of trampling the names of York and Salisbury under their heels. Aye, and Warwick too." His fury swamped him so that his voice rose to a bellow. "Do not mistake me! My quarrel is not with the king! I am no traitor, though there are some poor fools who call me so—and who would make traitors of every man here. I do not believe my plea for justice reached the king at all, but was instead caught and held by liars and knaves. If the king had heard my suit, he would have granted me a meeting under truce."

He paused to glare round at the assembled men, seeing that his words were reaching a vast audience. His chest swelled, while Salisbury stood in silence, watching his friend's anger take them on, wherever it would lead.

"Instead, I have been scorned! Cast out from the king's grace by lesser men. All those who stand in Key Field will be hunted and hanged as traitors unless we settle this today. That is the choice I have been given. Must I choose to slink away? Must I leave my king in the clutches of whispering traitors, there to wait for a judgment that will mean the end of York?"

It was too much for the men beyond their captains. They cried out in his support, a growl of unformed words. Many of them were Yorkshire born, loyal to his house above all other claims on them. Even among Warwick's red-coated followers, there were fists held high and voices yelling to bring down the king's counselors.

"They have already shed the blood of good men who desired nothing more than peace!" York roared at them, pointing back at the barricades and the littered corpses. "They will have my answer now. They will have an answer that tears down their banks of thorns and frees the king from their grasp."

More and more cheered him, breathing faster as they listened, standing tall on the churned earth.

"King Henry's safety is your charge and mine," York warned them all. "He will not suffer one scratch, on the soul and honor of every one of you. I am no traitor! And I see none *here*."

The noise had grown with every passing moment so that York had to shout at the top of his lungs just to be heard.

"Captains! Return to your men. We will make a breach into the town and rescue King Henry from those who hold him. Go, gentlemen, in your fury. York holds the left, Salisbury the center, Warwick the right. Form ranks for me now. Take this town for me. Save the king. *God* save the king!"

As his final words were echoed in a great hoarse bellow, the captains ran to their positions, followed by hundreds of their men, so that the crowd seemed to explode out from where York was standing. It took only moments for three battle groups of a thousand to grab their weapons and armor and race to stand facing the town.

Salisbury, Warwick, and York's son Edward were waiting quietly together as York turned to them, his face flushed from shouting. Salisbury shook his head in awe.

"Good God, Richard. I saw your great-grandfather in you then. The blood runs true, I think."

"Remember that I wanted peace, first," York said, his gaze falling to his son. He kept his eyes on Edward, wanting him to understand. "I will free King Henry from those who hold him hostage, nothing more. That is my order. They may call me a traitor. I will not *be* one."

Edward swallowed and nodded, his pride showing clearly.

"Stay at my side, lad," York said, gentling his tone. He raised his head to give the formal command. "Earl Salisbury, if you would do me the honor, your position is the center ground. Earl Warwick, yours is the right wing. There are three ways into the town, gentlemen. All guarded and blocked. I'll wager I will climb the hill before you."

They smiled, as he wished them to, just as his own expression became serious.

"Protect the king, gentlemen. Above all else and with your own lives, if you must. Our quarrel is with Somerset and Buckingham and Percy, not Henry of Lancaster. Give me your word."

All three swore an oath on their honor and York nodded, satisfied.

"This morning is already old," he said. "Let's use the light."

CHAPTER 14

J asper Tudor had split his Welsh archers among the three barricades, sending thirty and an experienced captain to each one. He'd known they would be valuable men to bring to the king's Progress, but not that they would be absolutely vital to his defense. The houses that backed onto Key Field had one or two high windows set into the walls that were perfect for the task, so that his Welshmen kept a rain of arrows snapping down on the attacking forces. Tudor felt satisfaction, mingled with awe, as the barricades rocked and shuddered. This was no raid or skirmish, he could tell that much. Three armies had formed out on the rough earth, then come in with a roar and clatter.

The barrier groaned, heaved back and forth. Tudor heard something snap in its midst, a different crack to the thumps of bows sounding on all sides. The Yorkist soldiers were using long pikes to snag the ropes and heave backward. Other men protected the teams with shields, and they would have had the barrier in pieces in no time at all if not for his lads. At a range of just a dozen feet, his archers sent shafts right through the straining warriors, laughing and calling out the count of those they'd snatched from life. One of his captains chanted lines from *Y Gododdin*, the martial poem, raising the spirits of those who knew the language, and irritating the rest.

Tudor saw the Percy son, Lord Egremont, come racing down the hill with a few score of axemen at his heels. Egremont took in the situation at a glance and grinned to Tudor, a mark of appreciation for his efforts, as he arranged his own men to repulse any sudden break-through. Without the archers, the barricade would have fallen before he'd arrived, but they were still taking a terrible toll, emptying quivers until their shoulders trembled with the repeated strain.

Tudor stood back as pieces of mud-brick fell around him. A few of his lads had gone inside the house overlooking the lane and kicked out a hole in the wall of the upper floor. One of them leaned out with his arm gripped by a mate inside, seeking the best vantage spot. Tudor was looking up at him when a shaft came from the field and slotted through the archer's jack vest, tearing him away from the grip of his friend so that he fell, striking the ground headfirst. Tudor heard Egremont swear in shock at the sight, but they'd known there were archers with York. Those men had been brought up and now the work to defend the lane became much harder, a game of quick glances and quicker shots. Tudor's bowmen dared not aim for longer than a heartbeat, not with other archers watching for their heads to appear. Their accuracy suffered as a result, and York's pike teams dragged weak sections of the barricades back and away, cheering every small reduction in the mass of thorns, rope, and wood that blocked their path. On the street side, Tudor saw Egremont's men bringing up more tables and dragging uprooted thorn trees from a great pile to adorn them. The barrier deepened and grew, about as fast as it was ripped out.

Jasper Tudor turned as Egremont approached him. Tudor was an earl faced with a mere baron, so Egremont bowed deeply, to the

Welshman's private delight. Egremont was both taller and broader than he was, with the massive chest and shoulders of a swordsman trained from his earliest years. On the other hand, Jasper Tudor was half brother to the king. He smiled in greeting.

"I've sent a runner up to my father," Egremont said. "We can hold them here, I think. We'll need more men—and to set them to maintaining the barriers." He frowned as he spoke, and Jasper Tudor understood immediately. Men like Egremont were trained for maneuvers in the field of battle, not to defend tables and thorns in a side alley. If the York soldiers broke through, the fighting would be vicious, but until then, it was a grinding, bloody stalemate.

"Have you word of any plan beyond holding the roads?" Tudor asked.

Egremont glowered to himself, shaking his head.

"Nothing yet. God knows, we can't have the king stopped in one town forever. I think I saw messengers riding out to the south, though if it's reinforcements they're after, we'll be here a week, waiting for them."

"And there could be more coming to bolster York's numbers," Tudor said, rubbing his face with his hand.

"My father says all you Welsh are cunning, like the Scots," Egremont said with a half smile. "Can you use those wits to find a way for us to beat them? I have a powerful desire to see Salisbury's head on a pike-pole today, along with his sons. His family will be hard-broken after this treachery. At least there's that, to keep me warm."

"Your father does not like my countrymen, I've noticed," Tudor said warily.

"No, he calls you trolls," Egremont replied lightly, "though he likes your bows well enough. I've yet to make my own judgment."

"On the bows or the men?"

"On the men. I would give a good-sized manor house for more of your archers here. That much I know. They may steal the spoons, but by God, they can make a shot."

Earl Tudor stared closely at the young baron, his eyebrows high in surprise. After a moment, he realized the man was needling him for his own amusement and he chuckled.

"They were telling me they can't get to the spoons. Every time they go into a house, one of your English virgins pulls them into a closet. I think you'll use those spoons to feed a few Welsh bastards next year."

"Yes, he calls you that, as well," Egremont said. He clapped Tudor on the shoulder and both men chuckled, the tension easing. Thomas held out his hand and Jasper Tudor took it briefly, each of them gripping hard enough to crush.

As they shook hands, three hundred men-at-arms came trotting down the hill, wearing Percy blue-and-yellow surcoats and carrying banners. Egremont looked up, pleased to see his father's men.

"We can hold here—all day or all week, if we must. Though it galls me to be unable to strike back, we can take a toll of them from our barriers. Either way, at least the king is safe. For all their God-cursed arrogance, York and the Nevilles have chosen the wrong town to attack—and the wrong way to do it."

FOR A FULL HOUR, Warwick watched coldly as a shield wall and pike-men assaulted a barrier as tall as he was on his horse. He had hidden his anger all morning. Both his father and York had their own reasons for being there, but between them they had hamstrung the captains they commanded. York had wanted to meet under truce with the king, and Warwick's father had wanted only to get in range of the Percy lords. As a result, they'd wasted every chance to use the larger army they'd brought to St. Albans. If Warwick had been able to make the sun rise again, he knew he would have met the king on the road, on open land. King Henry would have been forced to surrender, or they'd have slaughtered his column, overwhelming it with sheer numbers of fighting men and archers. Instead, his father and York had managed to place themselves in a position where three thousand men had to funnel through narrow alleys into the town. The massive advantage of numbers was next to useless, and Warwick could only thank God his archers were there to hamper the shots of Welshmen from the other side. It would have been a slaughter without his redcoats—and yet the barricades remained, with each side picking at them.

Warwick clenched his jaw in frustration. He'd rejected the idea of setting fires as soon as he'd seen the wooden beamed houses on either side. The entire town would become a furnace and then a tomb for the king. York had made it clear enough he would not countenance such an action, which left their soldiers to heave and struggle and die, with no way through.

Digging in his spurs, Warwick rode his mount further out along the line of rear walls. He could see the tower of St. Peter's Church above the town and he sensed he was observed. A sudden tightening of his eyes was the only sign of his interest, invisible to anyone watching. St. Albans was an ancient town, sprawling on past the main streets in all directions. Some of the houses had gardens at the rear and he'd seen a short length of wooden fence alongside one great white home. It looked like open air beyond it, as if the gap ran along the full side of the house.

The king's men had blocked the roads, so of course his father and York had assaulted those barriers. The more Warwick stared, the more he wondered if they had ignored other ways in. He had fought in London when Jack Cade's Kentish men had attacked the city. Perhaps it was that mad rush of side roads and doubling back in darkness that had him looking for another route around the obstacles in his path.

One of his bondsmen knights was in the process of trotting his horse past with a dozen axemen in mail running in his wake. Warwick hailed him.

"Gaverick! Sir Howard!" Warwick called, feeling a shiver of excitement.

As the knight raised his visor and looked round, Warwick gestured him closer. The group halted, relaxing instantly at the slightest opportunity to rest.

"I need . . . three hundred fresh men. A hundred of my redcoat archers and the rest with axes and shields. Fast men, Sir Howard—men who can run and cause havoc if we break through. Have no horns blown. There are sharp eyes at every window in town, ready to run with news to the king's supporters. Gather the men to me and then be ready to follow."

For just an instant, the knight's gaze flickered over to where York and Salisbury were watching the assault on the barricades. Warwick shook his head before Sir Howard could ask his question.

"No. I will not trouble York with this, not until I know where it leads." Warwick was twenty-six years old and had inherited the service of men like Sir Howard just six years before. He spoke with all the confidence he could muster, depending on the man's loyalty to his colors and rank.

"Very well, my lord," Sir Howard said stiffly, bowing from the waist. "You lads, remain here with Lord Warwick. Don't cause trouble."

He said the last while pointing at a surly-looking brute who had already settled down on the dark earth and was rummaging in his pouches for something to eat. The man glared back, tearing off some dried meat with his back teeth. Warwick saw Sir Howard open his mouth to comment and then decide against it, turning his mount and galloping over to the main force.

Warwick watched him go, his eyes narrowing in thought. He turned as the rest of the men sat down where they stood, encouraged by the example of the first. Warwick hesitated, then felt anger at himself as much as them.

"Get up. Go on, up, all of you. I want you ready to march and fight."

None of the men replied, though some leaped to their feet. Others rose more slowly, showing only irritation. Warwick returned their stares until he saw that just the first man remained sitting, looking up with a wry smile on his face.

"What is your name," Warwick asked, "to refuse an order on the field of war?"

The man stood sharply at that, revealing great height and breadth, with a face half hidden in black whiskers.

"Fowler, my lord. I didn't catch the order, my lord. I'll follow, you don't need to worry about me, my lord."

The man spoke with studied insolence, though those around him showed only discomfort. Warwick realized the man was not well liked, perhaps one of those who brought a level of anger to every path they crossed. Yet he needed angry men for what he had in mind.

"You were slow to stand, Fowler. You'll go first, with me, into the town. Hang back and be hanged, or fight well and rise." Warwick shrugged deliberately, as if it mattered not at all. "Make your choice now and I'll watch to see."

For what seemed an age, Fowler held his gaze, revealing some barely banked resentment deep in his dark eyes.

"I'll fight well, my lord. The chance to put good steel in the guts of the king's fancy nobles? I wouldn't miss a chance of that, not for two o' Christmas this year. If you'll lead, that is, my lord."

"Watch me," Warwick replied, irritated with the man. He was saved from the exchange by Sir Howard's return, bringing hundreds of men to surround the young earl on his warhorse.

"With eyes on us, I will not point out the path," Warwick called to them as they settled, waiting for orders. "My aim is to break through the gardens of the houses and make our way up the hill to the king's position. Anyone with hammers come to the front. Knock down anything in our way. I can't see us climbing fences like boys after stolen apples." He paused as the assembled men chuckled. "If there is a way through, we don't stop. If they've made other barriers beyond, we'll turn aside and fall on the defenders at the first line. Those are my orders. The cry is 'Warwick,' but not until we break through. Is that clear?"

Three hundred voices muttered, "Yes, my lord," as Warwick dismounted.

He saw Fowler's eyebrows rise, but the path he hoped to take would only be possible on foot. He would not give up his armor, however, no matter how much speed it stole from him. Once more, Warwick remembered the dark alleys of the Cade rebellion and repressed a shudder. He drew his sword and took down his shield, gripping the straps.

"Follow me. Hammers and axes to the front."

It was not possible to sprint in a full suit of plate armor. Warwick walked as fast as he could, stalking along while three hundred men trotted in his wake. At first, it seemed their intention was to reinforce the shield wall at the barricades, but then he cut right, along the back walls of houses. The noise they made was no pleasant jingling, but the tramp and ring of armed men, ready to slaughter anything in their path.

WARWICK REACHED THE HOUSE he had spotted before, halting his followers with a raised hand. The man Fowler had been true to his word, staying so close to Warwick's shoulder that the young earl wondered if he was a threat. Fowler stood ready, one of his eyebrows fixed high.

"Take hold of my boot and lift me up, Fowler," Warwick ordered him. "I need to see."

The big man gave a grunt and laid his ax by the fence, grabbing hold and shoving the earl so hard he nearly went straight over the top and into the garden.

Warwick breathed in relief as he gripped the fence-beam. Beyond, a tiny alley barely the width of a man's shoulders stretched the length of the house. He could see a gate blocking any further view of the street, but it looked promising.

"Down, Fowler," Warwick said.

The man seemed willing to hold him there all day, but then he let go and Warwick landed with a clatter of metal. He looked up in anger, galled at such close quarters to realize his head only came up to the lowest point of the man's beard. Fowler seemed to realize his greater stature at the same moment, so that a smile spread across his face.

"My thanks," Warwick said, earning a shrug as he turned to the rest of them. "This fence has to come down. After that, we'll head up through the town. If we can reach the main street, our task is to roar 'Warwick' and put the fear of God into the king's men. Most of them are down here to defend the Key Field, but the king will be protected. I'll know more when we reach the top of the hill. I hope you have the lungs and heart for the run."

"If you have, my lord," Fowler muttered.

"Shut up, Fowler," Warwick snapped at him.

The big man seemed to loom over him for the moment that followed, but one of the axemen shoved Fowler from the side in rough warning.

"Aye, shut up, you big sod," another man said. "Or would you have us back there, tugging at those barricades? I'd rather be here."

Warwick saw the speaker was one of his red-coated archers and he smiled to himself, seeing the broadcloth was clean and brushed, a garment worn with pride.

Fowler snorted and lowered his head mulishly, though he could see the mood was against him. Warwick didn't wait beyond that.

"Get the fence down," he shouted. "Axes and hammers."

There wasn't space enough for more than a few men to stand and bring heavy iron against the wood. The fence was an old construction, its main beams made of strong oak. Even so, it was reduced to kindling in moments, and the first rush of men included Warwick and Fowler, still clinging to his shadow.

The weight of mail and weapons alone might have been enough to smash the rickety gate at the other end of the tiny alley. Those in the front rank brought hammers against it and the thing exploded into pieces on the road. On their left, they could hear the tumult by the closest barricade, the roaring and screaming of furious, struggling men. Ahead lay a narrow path between rows of houses, stretching up the hill.

"Keep moving there! No one stops!" Warwick shouted over his shoulder. He caught a glimpse of two soldiers in Percy colors coming to a shocked halt. Both men were knocked down in vicious cuts by axemen before they could cry out, then stabbed and trampled by those behind.

The sun was almost directly overhead and the day was growing warm as Warwick's three hundred raced each other up the hill. None of them knew the town well, but the king would surely take the highest point for himself. As long as they moved up, they'd find him.

Somewhere lower down, Warwick could hear alarm horns sounding, as well as a different note as men yelled news of their breakthrough on both sides. He grinned at the thought of his father and York hearing he was already in the town. Those at the barricades would have to leave their posts to block his progress. The York advantage in numbers would tell then.

To his dismay, Warwick found himself panting wildly, his heart hammering and sweat making his eyes sting with salt. He'd kept his visor up, but running a hill in armor was a brutal exercise and he wondered if he'd reach the top only to burst his heart in the effort.

Women shrieked in fear and warning from high windows as he passed them, yet his three hundred went up the town like a dagger-strike, hardly seeing another armed man. Across their path, Warwick could see a main street running along the crest, with nothing higher. He could hardly believe his luck had held for so long, though he almost fell from exhaustion as he stopped just before the junction, leaning over to brace himself against a wall and wrestling his helmet from his head so that he could breathe. Sir Howard watched for a moment, then singled out the man at Warwick's side.

"Fowler!" he said. "Stick your head out and tell me what you see."

Fowler wrinkled his lip, but he didn't have to look at the men glaring at him to know he couldn't argue. He sidled up to the corner and glanced around it, then paused to stare.

"Well?" Warwick called behind him.

"No one within a hundred yards," Fowler said, turning back. His eyes were wide and he shook his head in awed disbelief. "I saw the king beyond."

"His banners?" Sir Howard demanded, even as he copied the man's furtive action and leaned around the corner to look.

"No, the king himself, sure as I'm standing here. Surrounded by hundreds of men and some sort of tent the size of a house, all stretched."

Warwick was recovering his breath as Sir Howard returned to him for orders. All the men there and down the street were waiting on his word, whatever it would be. Warwick removed a gauntlet to rub sweat from his face. He had no right to the luck he'd been given, but he'd take it just the same. They'd broken right through and it was too late to wish he'd brought a thousand men instead of just three hundred.

"Will you wait, my lord?" Sir Howard said, clearly thinking the same. "I can send a runner back for more."

"No. That back garden can be blocked just as easily as the others," Warwick said. "We were seen and ten men could hold that path until kingdom come. No, Sir Howard, we'll make a noise up here. We'll attack. Those at the barricades will come rushing up the hill to protect the king. They won't have any choice. And then those barriers will be pulled down and we'll have them caught on two sides."

The prospect of taking arms against the king's own household and nobles was a sobering thought for most of them. Archers and axemen exchanged uneasy glances and many crossed themselves, fearful of divine judgment on their actions. Yet no one stepped back and Fowler was beaming like he'd been made mayor for the day.

"Archers across this road," Warwick said, his voice feeling tight in his throat. "As wide a rank as you can make. I won't have you shooting at my back, so you'll get one chance to knock the fight out of them and then we'll go in. You're to hold this spot in case we're faced with too many and have to return here."

"My lord, might I have a word?" Sir Howard said, clearing his throat.

Warwick frowned, but he let the man lead him away from the closest ears.

"What is it?" Warwick demanded. "I won't lose this chance in argument, Sir Howard. Quickly, man."

"If you have your archers shoot down the street, the *king* could be killed, my lord. Have you considered that? An arrow does not know royal blood from common."

Warwick stared. On the death of his wife's father and brother, he had inherited a dozen castles and more than a hundred manors, stretching from Scotland to Devon. With that extraordinary wealth had come more than a thousand soldiers in his service, bequeathed to him as the new Earl of Warwick. Sir Howard was his feudal bondsman and Warwick knew he could order his total obedience. He could see the man shaking slightly as he stood there, fully aware that he risked his oath and honor even by questioning the command. Sir Howard Gaverick was not a fool, but Warwick knew time was too short, the advantage dropped into their laps too fragile to debate the point.

"You may withdraw, Sir Howard, if you do not feel you can stand with me. I have been given this chance and I will take all responsibility for however it turns out. I absolve you from any guilt in this matter. It is on my head. If you choose to leave, I will not harm you or yours after the battle is won. You have my word, but choose to stand or go, quickly."

Warwick left the older man there, his mouth slightly open and his eyes wide. When the young earl looked back, it was to see Sir Howard marching alone back down the hill through the ranks of waiting men.

"Archers!" Warwick called out. "This must be settled today. You all heard my lord York. If we fail here, we'll be hunted down as traitors. Rank or wealth is no protection, not here in this town. It is my order that you send your shafts along this street. Now! Cry out my name and let them know we are here."

Three hundred voices roared "Warwick!" at the top of their lungs, smothering the noise of a hundred archers filing out in ranks with their quivers low-hung on their hips.

A heartbeat passed and then St. Peter's Street filled with rushing shafts. Another heartbeat brought the reply: screams and shouts and panic in the marketplace where the king stood.

CHAPTER 15

Every man in the royal tent froze, the instant they heard "War-wick" roared out. The harsh sound was close enough to terrify and strangle all conversation. The king had only just come back inside and he turned sharply toward the noise. Buckingham drew a breath to shout an order, but it went unheard as arrows came ripping through the group, punching holes in the cloth and sending the king's steward to his knees with an arrow through his chest.

Derry Brewer threw himself flat. Buckingham saw something flash and raised his hand, too slow by far to protect himself. An arrow struck the pauldron of an armored knight and deflected, thumping into Buckingham's face. He made a low, keening sound, raising a hand to the shaft and finding it wedged in bone, having pierced him just above his teeth. Blood poured into his mouth, so that he had to spit and spit again. Unable to speak, Buckingham lurched toward King Henry, knowing that he lived only because the arrow had lost most of its force on the first impact.

The young king stood perfectly still, his face as pale as it had ever been. Through watering eyes, Buckingham saw Henry too had been struck. A shaft had passed right through the metal joint of his neck and shoulder. The arrow still remained, showing a bloody tip on the other side. Buckingham began to pant in shock, his face swelling as he spat another black gobbet of blood onto the ground, and managed to stagger over to stand between the king and the arrows tearing through the tent as whining blurs. Buckingham raised his head, barely able to see as he waited.

Earl Percy had his blue and yellow shield raised in the direction of the attack as he too lunged to protect King Henry. The earl pursed his lips at the sight of Buckingham's blood pouring out onto the ground, then cried out as Henry suddenly staggered and fell. Derry Brewer scrambled over to him, keeping low the whole way, covering the king's body with his own.

"Doctors!" Percy bellowed. The king's surgeon, Scruton, ran in then, braving the shafts that still punched holes in the thick canvas. More shields were raised above the king, forming a shell around him.

"Let me see," Scruton growled at Derry Brewer, who nodded and moved to one side. Protected by the shields, the king's spymaster crouched, panting, his eyes wild as Scruton examined the wound.

Buckingham watched with a sense of sick horror. His mouth felt as if it was being boiled and every movement brought a scraping of bone. He could feel his face swelling all around the wound, his lips already fat, filling with blood from the inside. It was all he could do not to panic and wrench at the thing stuck in him. With a savage twist, he removed a loosened front tooth and began to work the arrow free in grim silence, ignoring the blood that made a slick down the front of his jerkin until a wave of dizziness hit him. Slowly, Buckingham went down on one knee and then rolled onto his back.

While Scruton worked on the king, Master Hatclyf appeared at the duke's side without a word, opening his leather bag for tools.

Hatclyf tugged the duke's hands away, clipped the arrow shaft with small shears and placed one hand on the man's forehead to hold him still while he cut the arrow clear with a razor and iron pincers. The doctor completed the task with a quick jerk that took out another loose tooth and split the roof of Buckingham's mouth all the way to the back of his throat. Buckingham began to choke, drowning. He lurched up and vomited on the ground. There was too much blood to spit, and Hatclyf could only press a wad of cloth against the duke's torn lips as Buckingham passed out.

Only one man in the tent had been killed outright, a stroke of marvelous fortune against the odds. All the rest looked up in fear as they heard running feet coming toward them. Outside the awning, there were many more wounded or lying still. Knights limped to protect the king with shafts still in their armor, or lay slumped, breathing their last. The arrows had stopped, replaced by the call of "Warwick" coming again and growing louder.

"To me, Percys! Protect your king!" Earl Percy roared at the top of his voice.

Bannermen and knights were pouring in from all directions, beginning a surge up from the forces on the hill. The stalemate at the barricades had shattered the moment Henry had been struck, with no man knowing yet if it was a mortal wound or not.

"My lord Percy, someone must send orders to hold the lower town!" Derry Brewer shouted suddenly. "With the king hurt, all our men will come here. York and Salisbury will follow them. Please, my lord! Give the order."

Earl Percy ignored him, as if Derry had not spoken. With a snarled curse, Derry raced away, searching for Somerset. As he went, the tattered awning came down in a crash as some vital pole was kicked out or broken. Great swathes of canvas covered the king and his surgeon as the man worked to snip the shaft and ease it out without tearing the delicate veins so close to the king's throat. There was royal blood all over the surgeon's hands, his grip slipping as he tried to grasp the cut shaft. Henry's hands kept reaching up to the wound and Scruton collared one of the king's chamberlains, ordering him to hold them clear. The man stood in blank shock at the sight of his fallen master and Scruton had to shake him from his stupor before he dared to take hold and let the surgeon work. Around them, knights were cutting or heaving the heavy canvas sheets away, revealing the king to the open air.

Warwick's soldiers raced down St. Peter's Street with swords and shields held high, howling in savage glee at the chaos they had caused. The king's own guards came out against them, forming a shield line to take the first impact. More and more men were flooding back into that spot and the two forces crashed together.

Derry Brewer found himself struggling against a torrent of men as he ran downhill, yelling for them to hold position. God knew, the king's life was in peril, but if they all abandoned the barricades, the day would be lost. As he moved further away from the marketplace, Derry could see a host of soldiers pushing and running to get up. At the bottom of the town, there was a great growling roar as York and Salisbury found the barriers unmanned. The king's forces were retreating before them, leaving the barricades to fall.

Derry Brewer came to a shocked halt in the street, his shoulders thumped by men still trying to get past until he pressed himself against a building and was left alone. No one thought clearly when the monarch was in danger. Loyal soldiers were almost mindless with rage, determined to repel whoever dared threaten the king's person. Derry swallowed, his mouth dry. He'd known he would be little use on the march north. A king's spymaster worked in secret, uncovering traitors or cutting throats in the dark. In the bright morning, on open streets, he was just another body, without even a set of armor to keep him safe.

Derry stared down the hill, seeing the line of York's men already breaking through, shoving thorns and tabletops aside in a frenzy. Some of those rushing away from the barriers were looking back by then, aware of the threat. They chose to keep going to the top of the hill, perhaps hoping to rally there for a fight back through the town. Derry shook his head, sickened. York had a greater army by far, twice the fighting men of those around King Henry. There could only be one outcome, especially now the king had been wounded. God had surely blinked when that single archer sent his shaft, for it to have done so much damage.

Derry forced air into his lungs, feeling his heart pound and his hands shake. He could get out, he was almost certain. He'd considered an escape route when they'd first entered the town, as was his common practice. The abbey loomed over St. Albans and Derry knew he could run to it. It would not be hard to find a monk's robe to throw over himself, either hiding among the brothers in their quarters, or taking a path out west of the town, before York and Salisbury reached the marketplace. If he did that, Derry knew he would live, to take the news to the queen. He told himself that someone had to get out. Someone had to survive the disaster still unfolding, and it might as well be him. He saw a side street across the path of the main road down the hill. He could cross against the tide of men and simply vanish. He'd done it before. York would not leave him alive, that much was sure as sunset. Derry could see the ranks of fresh Yorkist soldiers forcing their way up the hill toward where he stood. The road had cleared between the two armies, with all the marketplace crammed full of the king's men. York and Salisbury were coming with blood in their eyes, and Derry stood alone between them.

"Just run," he muttered to himself. "*Run*, you daft bastard." King Henry could be dead already. Derry could hear the clash of arms in the marketplace, with the tramp of marching feet on stone coming closer until the whole town seemed to shake with it. The Nevilles and the Percys were unleashed to slaughter each other in broad daylight and Derry knew he had no choice at all. He was a king's man. It came down to that and nothing else. With dragging steps, he found himself heading back the way he had come.

YORK HAD BEEN ABLE to watch the thin stream of red-coated soldiers race up the hill toward St. Peter's Street. He couldn't see the marketplace from Key Field, though he thought he had heard the name of Warwick cried out before it was borne away on the wind. The sun was at noon overhead when his men at the barricade began to shout in triumph, heaving great pieces away, faster and faster as the king's troops abandoned them. York didn't understand the reason for the sudden lack of defense, but he took full advantage, throwing everyone he had at the remaining obstacle and ripping it out of position in great blocks. His men scrambled over the scattered mess of broken wood and thorns, pushing on with no resistance to stop them.

The forces of York were faster off the mark than those of Salisbury, so that he reached the streets of the town first, reining in to stare at the mass of running men heading uphill away from him. Once more, York could hear "Warwick" roared up by the marketplace and he only had to point in that direction as his captains ordered the ranks on, giving chase. God had blessed the moment and York was determined not to waste the chance. He saw his son bring his horse through the gap and called the boy to his side.

On his right, Salisbury's men came battering through, causing the men of York to whistle and jeer at them for being late to the fight.

York could not see Salisbury then, but the earl would find his own way to the king. He trotted his mount uphill toward the fighting, rolling his right shoulder and taking a firm grip on his shield as he dropped his visor and peered out at the world through a narrow slit. His banner knights rode on either side of him and his men cried "York!" as they climbed, ready to spend all the frustration of the barriers on those wretches who had abandoned them.

As they drew closer to St. Peter's Street, York could see only chaos. There was fighting on one edge of the marketplace, he could hear it. Ahead of his position, the king's soldiers seemed willing just to fall back and back, with no one to command them. He brought his horse to the front rank of his soldiers, walking in line with them. More than once, he saw individual king's men stop and watch with baleful glares, then turn their backs and hurry further away. Inspiration struck him when one group of three took a position right in his path, carrying axes like they meant to use them.

"By God, get out of my way and guard the king!" York roared at them. He almost smiled in surprise when they too turned and jogged off toward the tumult ahead. York shook his head at the confusion all around. His captains had the men in order, sending them out into side roads so that, in time, they would have the triangular marketplace completely surrounded. As they went, they came across Salisbury's men doing the same thing, bawling the name of their patrons before they could attack each other in error.

On the edge of the market proper, York found his way blocked at last by determined ranks. Worried for his son, he thanked God there didn't seem to be archers among them, one of many strokes of luck in that day of wonders. He eyed the shield wall warily, but his men strode on without hesitation, breaking into a run with each of his captains controlling the mob as best they could. York heard them yell to make a path for him, and he and Edward walked their mounts slowly on, ignoring the struggling, dying men on both sides as they broke the shield wall and opened a narrow track in the press. York saw arrows looping over the crowd then. He dismounted quickly, rather than make himself too obvious a target. Edward of March and his banner knights dropped to the ground at his side, leaving their horses to be swallowed in the crush of struggling men. York's son was staring around him in amazement, holding his sword out before him.

It was as if they walked in a dream. Time and again, soldiers tried to reach York's small group of men only to be snatched away by others wearing his colors, brought down by swearing groups and sheer numbers. In open space on the cobbled road, they walked untouched until, to his astonishment, he reached hillocks of torn canvas and the king himself, laid out on the ground.

York looked around him, understanding at last the confusion and utter panic in the king's followers. He caught a glimpse of Salisbury on his right, still on horseback, making hard work of the fighting against Percy forces. He too was inching his way to the same spot as best he could.

More arrows whirred overhead and York saw one of them crack and shatter into splinters on the stone ground, not far from where the king was being tended. He looked back at Edward in time to see him flinch and duck. York could only admire the courage of the physician coolly wrapping bandages around the king's throat while Henry pawed weakly at him.

Henry looked up as York's shadow fell across his face. His eyes widened and he shook his head, recoiling from the surgeon's touch. Scruton swore softly, seeing the bandages redden again, unaware of the duke or anything else as he fought to save the king's life. Henry's head sagged, his eyes showing white as he lost consciousness. For a long moment York could only stare, standing with his sword drawn and held uselessly. All around them, York sensed the fighting intensify between the soldiers in Percy colors and Salisbury's men, with some of Warwick's redcoats caught up in the fray. York made a decision, turning to his banner knights. Whatever he had expected or hoped for that day, it was not this.

"Take the king to the abbey, to sanctuary. Guard him well on the hallowed ground, in peril of your lives and good names. Edward? You'll go with them."

It was York himself who reached out to touch the surgeon Scruton on the shoulder, interrupting the man at his work.

"Stand back from the king, sir. You may accompany him to the abbey, but he must be moved from this place."

Scruton looked up for the first time and froze in fear at the sight of York in full armor, standing before him. The surgeon had known the day was going badly for the king's forces, but seeing the man responsible for it all standing with a drawn sword at his side reduced him to stammering shock.

"He must not, cannot be . . . my lord, he cannot be moved."

"No. He must be. Stand aside and let my men take him to safety. I will not be denied, sir. I will not see my king trampled by men running berserk in these streets."

Scruton stood, wiping bloody hands on his apron as he gathered tools and strips of linen back into his bag. One of York's knights gripped Henry under the arms and another took his feet, bearing him back from the center of the chaos and shouting all around them. The king groaned, near senseless and too weak to respond. York called two more of his captains and a dozen burly soldiers to accompany the king, giving orders to kill anyone who stood in their way, regardless of colors or loyalties. His orders would prevail over all others, he made sure of it. Most importantly, his son would be kept safe. The king's surgeon found his nerve and fell in behind as the small group took Henry from the fight, heading toward the abbey. York watched his son go until the men were lost behind the still-heaving mass of soldiers.

Salisbury had either dismounted or had his horse killed under him. The earl had fought his way to the same spot of bloody cobbles and torn canvas and was panting hard, flushed and sweating. Sir John Neville stood to guard his father's back, gazing out at anyone who might try to take Salisbury unawares.

"Where is the king?" Salisbury demanded.

York turned to him, raising his visor to reply.

"I had him taken to the abbey. He was sorely wounded, but I have him now, alive." Realization of their victory surged in him, filling his chest. "I will have the horns blown and call a truce. There is nothing to fight for now."

"No!" Salisbury snapped. "You will *not*. There is work for me to finish before I'm done. On our friendship, make a promise to me. You'll not blow your horns, Richard. Percy and Egremont live. My ending lies ahead."

York narrowed his eyes at the aggression in both father and son.

"The battle is over," York said firmly. "Didn't you hear me say we have the king?" As the head of the Neville family gave no reply, York pointed at his chest. "You gave an oath to follow me, Salisbury."

He saw a spasm of strain pass across the older man's face. His son John began to speak, but York glanced coldly at him.

"Close your mouth, boy."

Furious, Sir John Neville looked away.

"My oath holds," Salisbury said stiffly, irritated at his son's humiliation as well as the reminder of his honor. "Give me but an hour. That is all. If I cannot bring the dogs to heel by then, I'll blow the horns myself. My word on it."

"An hour, then. I will tell my heralds," York said, choosing not to press the matter further.

Salisbury turned to watch the course of the fighting going on around the marketplace and York stood still to watch him, seeing further and more clearly than he had before. The fate of the house of York, even the fate of the king, had never been Salisbury's concern. York considered those of his men who waited on his command all around.

"Force a path to the abbey," he told them. "God grant Henry lives yet, that I may speak to my king."

CHAPTER 16

As York left the marketplace, Salisbury took command, bellowing orders to attack the Percy soldiers. Both Earl Percy and Lord Egremont had been forced further down St. Peter's Street in a running action, away from the failed stand at the marketplace. Salisbury could see the banner of Somerset close by the same group, before the man holding it was killed and it vanished underfoot. Soldiers in red coats pressed them cruelly and some steady part of Salisbury's mind noted the usefulness of the colors they wore, when all other banners had been broken or trampled.

With a weary breath, he clapped his son John on the shoulder.

"Stay close to me," he said.

In formation, the Neville soldiers pushed after them. Salisbury could feel his years in every step, but the weakness of his flesh was held at bay by the chance to settle his feud once and for all. York and the king had been taken from the center. The battle then was between Neville and Percy, with the Neville forces two or three times the number of his enemies.

Salisbury and his son marched down St. Peter's Street after them, in time to see Somerset and his guards smash their way into a pub. A hundred yards further on, Warwick was pressing against the Percy faction, giving them no space to breathe or plan. Yet Somerset had trapped himself and Salisbury saw a chance to put York in his debt. He halted in his rush, gathering men around the broken door of the inn and sending more round to the back of the building so there could be no escape. There was darkness and silence inside and no one was in a hurry to rush on to the swords and axes of those waiting for them.

"A pouch of gold to a knight, a knighthood to a common man," Salisbury announced to the ranks of soldiers around him. "Whoever brings down Somerset will choose his own reward."

It was enough to sway the undecided and they rushed the door, four of them pressing through. Salisbury waited as grunting sounds followed, with the clash of metal on armor. More of his men went in and the thumps and cries of pain grew louder, as Salisbury bit his lip in irritation. He wanted to move on, to see the Percy men cut down.

"Quickly, then! More of you!" he snapped.

As he spoke, a figure came out of the door and a hush fell in the street. Somerset's armor was red with blood, running freely from the oiled surfaces so that he dripped as he stood there on the threshold. He was breathing hard, but when he saw Salisbury, he raised a heavy ax in both hands, his eyes lighting up. There was no sign of those who had gone in against him, nor any of his own guards.

Somerset was alone.

"Neville!" Somerset called, taking a step out into the light. He seemed to have no care for the armed men on all sides. "Traitor, Neville!" he roared.

One of Salisbury's knights rushed in and Somerset spun to meet him, chopping the ax into the man's neck with appalling force before he could land a blow.

"Come to me then, Neville!" Somerset yelled, his voice hoarse. "Come, traitor!"

There was something terrible about the bloody duke as he stood there and beckoned them all in. The mob of soldiers stood in superstitious awe, simply staring. Salisbury braced himself to be attacked as Somerset came further out into the street. Another burly yeoman took two quick steps and crashed a sword against Somerset's side, hammering a great dent into the armored plate and making the man gasp. The return blow sank Somerset's ax upward into the man's ribs, cutting his mail so that a dozen rings spilled to the cobbles with a sound like dropped coins. The yeoman soldier collapsed onto his face and Somerset raised his ax again with a huge effort. As he brought it down into the man's back, he clipped the pub's swinging sign. Salisbury saw Somerset look up as he wrestled the ax blade free of bone.

The pub's name was The Castle and a crude picture of a fortress tower had been painted gray on black. All the blood drained from Somerset's face as he saw it and he closed his eyes for an instant, strength and rage vanishing to leave him empty.

Salisbury made a sharp gesture and two knights ran in, smashing their swords against the knee joints of Somerset's armor. He cried out as he dropped, a long sound that was cut off as a third man brought an ax down onto his neck, chopping through metal and flesh beneath.

For an instant, no one moved and half the men there expected Somerset to rise again. They had seen a king's duke killed and the shock of that rippled through them. More than a few crossed themselves, looking to Salisbury for his reaction.

"That one for York," Salisbury said. "Turn now for Percy. Then we are done."

Leaving the body behind, Salisbury and his son John walked on along St. Peter's Street to join Warwick. Salisbury's men followed in silence, each one looking down at the bloody corpse of the king's counselor as they passed.

The dwindling forces with Warwick had harried the enemy every step from the marketplace, struggling against Earl Percy's most determined soldiers as they bore their noble master away. There was no quarter or respite given on either side, but Warwick's numbers were fewer and only the narrowness of the street prevented them being flanked and overwhelmed. By the time his father caught up with him, Warwick had Earl Percy and Baron Egremont backed hard against another inn, the Cross Keys. A side road lay just beyond and Warwick's men fought to reach Percy before the fight could widen and offer him a chance of escape.

Warwick looked back in fear at the sound of marching feet, then breathed in relief as he saw the eagles, crosses, and red diamonds on the shields of his father's knights. He caught sight of his brother John and the younger Neville nodded to him, a moment of private satisfaction in the chaos of the day. They faced the men who had attacked John's wedding and Warwick dipped his head, acknowledging his brother's right.

Salisbury had brought two or three hundred of his best men along the street, leaving the rest of the fighting factions to secure the town on their own. Horns sounded somewhere further away, but Salisbury ignored them, shouting fresh orders as they joined Warwick's redcoats and pressed through them to reach the enemy.

Facing this new rush of soldiers, Henry Percy, Earl of Northumberland, was exhausted. He had been forced to retreat along the main road, attacked again and again. His helmet had been knocked from his head and his white hair swung in rat's tails, wet with perspiration. Gray in the face, he looked as if he could barely lift the sword he held in both hands. He and his son Thomas stood in the second rank of Percy men, resplendent in blue and yellow. The head of the Percy house would have fallen long before if it had not been for a small and wiry man in mail who carried a dagger like a needle point. Trunning allowed no man to close on his master without darting in and stabbing through an eye-slot or a joint with appalling accuracy. He was responsible for half a dozen bodies on the street already, and Warwick would have given his back teeth for just one of the archers he had left behind in his rush to the marketplace.

As the Percy forces retreated once more, the side road opened on their left flank. Warwick heard Earl Percy call to his soldiers that they faced those who had killed the king. He blanched at hearing that. The old man's words gave new strength to those around him, so that they pushed back and won a few yards for themselves. Fresh blood ran from armored knights and spattered onto the cold street.

Warwick could only watch as his father's men shoved pikes past shields, jabbing and piercing until the blades came back red, then plunging in again. He could see Earl Percy arguing with Egremont, the older man pushing his son away and pointing down the open road. Egremont was red in the face, unwilling to leave as his father embraced him and shoved him roughly away.

Salisbury came up, panting hard as he reached his son's shoulder.

"King Henry is only wounded, though he may die yet," he said. "You've done well. It was your breaking through the town that brought this ending here today. No other man."

"Where is York?" Warwick asked, never taking his eyes off Percy and Egremont. The two men seemed almost unaware of the battle around them as Percy pointed once again down the open street. Some of the earl's guards bowed their heads as they were given orders to accompany the Percy son. The boldest of them took Thomas, Lord Egremont, by the arms and walked him backward, though he fought their grip and called to his father. The old man turned his back on his son, once again facing the Neville lines. Warwick cursed softly under his breath. He might have imagined it, but Earl Percy seemed to catch his eye and raise his head as he did so, wearing an expression of bitter pride.

"York has gone to the abbey, no doubt to weep or pray over the king," Salisbury said. "It doesn't matter. Our business is here." He took a massive breath, filling his lungs to blast his orders. "Bring them down! Cry 'Salisbury!' Cry 'Warwick!' Cry 'Neville!' And kill them all."

The fighting intensified, aided by the loss of the Percy soldiers who had gone with Egremont. Warwick saw the small man with the needle dagger dart between two struggling knights, finding a space as if he knew exactly how they would turn. The Percy swordmaster slid between fighting men like a shadow, feinting left and passing a second rank as a soldier swung the wrong way. In just a heartbeat, he was through and facing them. Trunning lunged at Salisbury, but both Warwick and John Neville had seen the threat. They met his strike with outstretched swords and Trunning was pierced through. Even then, he grinned through bloody teeth at them, reaching out to jam his narrow dagger into John Neville's shoulder joint. John cried out in agony as the man worked the blade, laughing as a stream of blood slid out across the polished metal. Warwick withdrew his sword with a jerk and cut into Trunning's neck, letting him fall.

Salisbury howled in triumph as he saw Earl Percy tumble down in a crash of armor. One of the old man's guards stood over his fallen form, using sword and shield with great skill to hold back the Neville soldiers. The nameless knight moved well, his strength seemingly unending. Yet he could not take a step away from his master. Wherever he turned and killed, another would strike until an axeman smashed his knee with a huge swing, so that he too fell to be broken underfoot.

The Percy forces were cut away from the old man, so that Warwick and Salisbury reached him. Earl Percy still lived, though his lips were tinged in blue. With a groan, the old man pushed himself up to a sitting position, braced on his locked elbows.

"John! Here!" Salisbury commanded.

His son's arm had gone limp, the muscle cut through in his shoulder. He had pulled out Trunning's dagger with his left hand. He was white with pain, but his eyes were fierce as he stood before his enemy.

"My dying does not make you less of a traitor," Earl Percy said, wheezing audibly. The words and the old man's gaze were aimed at Salisbury.

John Neville only shook his head. With the dagger still wet with his own blood, he reached out and speared the flesh under the old man's chin. Earl Percy stiffened, giving out a growling, hissing cry of agony. His head was forced up with the blade as it pushed through his mouth. Watery blood spurted as John pulled it out and slashed it across the throat. The three Nevilles watched the earl fall onto his side, his eyes dulling as his mouth still worked to speak with no sound.

"Where is Egremont?" Salisbury said to his sons.

Warwick pointed down the open road where they could see a group of knights moving swiftly away. Horns were blowing again in the distance, and Salisbury's mouth and jaw tightened at the sound. He had given his word to York and in the aftermath of violence he could feel exhaustion creeping over him. Salisbury turned to his son John and rested his hand on the younger man's shoulder.

"This is our victory, John. Egremont can't run so far that we can't catch up with him. It's done. Today is done."

"Let me take a hundred, on his heels," John Neville replied.

For an instant, he thought his father might allow it, but the earl's head was dipping in weariness, not lack of will.

"No. Obey me. You'll have your chance again."

The earl filled his lungs, his gaze still on the body of his oldest enemy.

"Enough!" Salisbury shouted. On his left, some men still fought on both sides and he could hear York's horns blowing a third time in the distance. His hour was up and he had his vengeance. "Blow horns who has them. Enough, I said. Put your swords away. No man need die now, after this. If you would live, put up your swords."

Panting, bloody men heard him and gave in to the desperate hope that it could all stop, that they might survive the day. For as far as Salisbury's voice carried, soldiers stood apart from the fray, and then further, as Neville captains repeated his orders and more horns sounded across the town, until the blare and shouts for peace could be heard in every street and every home.

RICHARD OF YORK WALKED ACROSS wide flagstones to the massive outer doors of the abbey. He could hear the tumult still going on behind him, the crash and shouting of thousands of men struggling to kill each other, yet crammed so tight in the roads they hardly had room to swing a sword. He looked back as a great roar sounded, but he could not guess the cause. Salisbury's words troubled him, casting the previous months in a different light. York's aim had always been to strip the whisperers away from King Henry's side before his house was destroyed by them. He saw that Salisbury's intention had been to break Percy, before all other considerations. It seemed their path had been the same, with both men carried to St. Albans. York shook his head, trying to twitch away worry and indecision. He was tired and hungry, but King Henry lay within the abbey that stood so tall before him. He did not know even if the king lived.

The men he had summoned to bear King Henry away to safety

had remained by the abbey doors, preferring that quiet spot to any thought of heading back into danger. Edward of March stood awkwardly with them, his rank and youth too much of a barrier for him to overcome. The men stood to attention as York trudged toward them, bruised and battered soldiers who had already fought that day, yet still looked shamefaced at having been found away from the struggle. York barely noticed them, his mind on what he would find within the massive stone walls. The abbot was nowhere to be seen, but his abbey was holy ground nonetheless—sanctuary. York shuddered beneath his armor as his men pushed the great doors open and he passed across the threshold. His son took a step toward him then, his expression hopeful. York shook his head. He did not know what he would find in the abbey, nor what he would do.

"No, Edward. Stay here." York crossed the entrance and waited while the doors were pulled shut behind him. He looked up.

A great blaze of color met his eyes on all sides, pressing for his attention in every painted column and wall. A huge image of Christ on the cross summoned his gaze, resplendent in reds and blues and golds so bright they could have been created just days before. Other scenes from the Bible combined to create a vast panoply of vivid hues, stretching away. It was overwhelming and York became aware that he stood in grimy armor, looking down the long nave ahead to the stone rood screen. An altar was before it, where the king lay like a broken doll. There were only two men with Henry, distant figures who turned white faces toward the man coming in like a wolf into the sheep pen.

York paused just beyond the threshold, leaning his shield against a stone column that soared to a ceiling impossibly high above his head. With aching hands, he unstrapped his sword and scabbard, placing the weapon by the shield and straightening. The head of the house of Lancaster lay helpless before him, a cousin descended from the same battle king of England and given the throne by the distance of one son. York raised his head, refusing to be intimidated by scenes of the damned falling into a fiery hell. His armor creaked and his steps sounded loud as he made his way down the length of the church, following the long line of the Latin cross.

He walked a hundred paces to reach the King of England. Henry was alive, his back to the altar as he sat on the cold stone floor with one leg raised and bent. York could see the king watching him approach, the younger man's face so white and drained that his flesh looked like fine linen. Henry's mail collar and shoulder pauldrons had been removed, so that bandages could be seen, tight around his neck and under one armpit. The surgeon, Scruton, stood away as York came close, bowing his head and clasping his hands in prayer.

On the short side of the altar, the Duke of Buckingham rested, close enough to Henry to reach out to him. The duke was breathing in short, hard gasps, in such terrible pain that he could do nothing but endure. York saw the man turn to watch his approach and he felt a shiver run through him at the seeping ruin of his mouth. Buckingham's scorched red eyes still ran with tears and York did not know if the cause was his wound or the lost battle.

York halted, staring down on the men before him. Though he had left his sword behind, he still carried a dagger on his right hip, not quite forgotten. He knew if he made the decision to strike, none of those three could have stopped him.

He looked up for a moment, his attention drawn by some flutter of movement. He saw small birds flying across the vast open space above, the closest representation of the vault of heaven on earth. He crossed himself, reminded once again of the sacred ground on which he stood. He could feel the presence of God in that cold eternity around him, a subtle pressure that made him bow his head once more.

York went down on one knee before the king.

"Your Majesty, I grieve to see you hurt," he said. "I ask your forgiveness for all I have done, your pardon."

Henry struggled to sit straighter, pushing himself upright with his bare hands pressed white against the stone. His eyes seemed to wander in and out of focus, turning his head a fraction back and forth to peer at the man who had brought so much destruction.

"And if I do not grant what you ask?" he whispered.

York closed his eyes for a moment. When they opened again, his expression was stern and hard.

"Then I must demand it. Your free pardon for all that has happened today. For me, and every man with me. I have been called traitor, Your Grace. I will not be called that again."

Henry slumped, his back-plate scratching the stone as he slipped back to where he had lain before. He knew his life hung by the thread of one man's patience and his will faded, a rock swallowed by a rising sea.

"As you say then, Richard. I will not hold you guilty for anything you have done. You are right, of course. As you say."

The king's eyes fluttered closed and York sensed the surgeon edging closer. He held up his hand, staying the man. York reached out and laid his gauntlet against the king's cheek.

Henry's eyes snapped open once more at the touch of cold metal.

"Who is it?" he said. "Richard still? What do you want of me?"

"You are my king," York said softly. "I ask only to stand at your side. You need good counsel, cousin. You need me."

"As you say," Henry replied, his voice little more than a breath as the terrible weariness in him stole away his will.

York nodded, satisfied. He rose to his feet, still unable to drag his gaze from the king.

Buckingham tried to speak then, his words a mush that caused fresh blood to run from his mouth.

"The king is a good man. Too good, Richard. I will call you traitor, if he will not."

York could barely make out the man's speech. He could have ignored the wounded duke, but he shook his head.

"Your words are wind and slush, Buckingham. You will be arrested. I suspect the bond you will pay for your release will cover my costs."

Buckingham flushed around his wound and swollen flesh, struggling to speak clearly.

"What crime can you name for me, one who has served his king?"

"You stood against his loyal lords, Buckingham. You stood against York and against Salisbury, as we tried to save the king from poisonous counselors. You will not speak clearly again, I think. A split tongue is apt enough, but speak too harshly to me and it will not be the end of your suffering today."

Buckingham tried to curse him, but fresh blood spattered from his torn palate and the words were unintelligible.

"The king lives, and will live," York said loudly. "I am loyal to the house of Lancaster."

He favored the spluttering Duke of Buckingham with a brittle smile, then turned on his heel to walk back down the nave, calling for his men.

STANDING AGAINST a pillar of the transept, Derry Brewer stared in grief. He had entered the abbey through a lesser door, slipping into a room where monks' robes hung on pegs and deciding on the instant to fling one over his own clothes. After his experience with the Franciscans, a Benedictine robe held no mysteries.

As he'd turned to leave, he had been pulling up the hood to conceal his face when he heard York's voice, one he knew as well as any other. Derry had watched the entire meeting from his hiding place, his fingers gripping his seax knife where it hung under the robe at his waist. He had thought for a time that he would be witness to Henry's murder. Yet York had stayed his hand and Derry had watched the king's humiliation in sorrow.

When York strode back down the nave, Derry knew at last that it was all in ruins. He'd seen Somerset fall, brought down in blood and violence. Derry had *tried* to stand with the king. He'd struggled to reach him against the tide of men. Seeing Somerset butchered had brought it home. The day was lost. The cause was lost. The king was lost. Blind with tears and mute with grief, Derry had run then for the abbey, thinking only of escape.

He pulled up the hood, his head bowed. York and Salisbury and Warwick had triumphed, gaining everything they wanted.

Derry felt a fresh prickling of his eyes and rubbed at them with the sleeve of the robe, angry at himself for his weakness. He clasped his hands in front of him and adopted the gliding steps of his disguise as he headed away from his fallen king.

CHAPTER 17

L ondon felt like the heart of the world. Those who had died were in the ground, and wounds had become scars for those who lived. The fears and dark memories were already fading, driven out and swept away in the roar of cheering throats.

Huge crowds had gathered from long before dawn for their one chance in a lifetime to see the king and queen of England. None of them had fought on the hill at St. Albans. Though the town was barely twenty miles from the city, the butchers and tanners and aldermen of London had not been there to see Henry fall, nor the barricades torn down. They knew only that the strife between houses was at an end, that peace had returned and King Henry had forgiven his rebellious lords.

The entire city seemed to have turned out along the route of the royal procession through the great, wide road of Cheapside, toward St. Paul's. The mob heaved against lines of soldiers in bright colors, their faces strained with duty and irritation. There were a few scuffles—moments when a purse was cut, or screeching urchins ran wild through the throng—but for most the mood was light.

Rain had fallen the day before, washing much of the city cleaner than usual. That July morning had dawned clear and warm, with hundreds of carts rattling out with the sun to prepare the king's route. From huge sheaves in the open backs, women had scattered clean, dry rushes where Henry and Margaret would walk later on. The wet muck underneath would seep again, but for a time, the road was clean and made new.

The treachery and bloodshed at St. Albans had been deliberately forgotten as the city prepared for the king and queen to walk among the people of the capital. There would be no more talk of traitors and civil war, not after that day. All the crowds saw was the triumphant parade through the heart of the city, led by fine destriers groomed and gleaming in perfect ranks. Banners of a dozen noble houses in support of the king were held high to flutter in the wind, overtopped by those of Lancaster and York, brought together in peace.

Behind six dozen ranks of knights came hundreds of royal retainers in their most colorful garb, throwing flowers or even coins into the crowd from baskets at their sides. Imploring hands reached out to them and the women blew kisses to handsome men. Their passing brought the greatest sound and then, following, each section of the crowd seemed to draw a breath, a long moment of whispering awe, before the applause and cheering crashed out once more, enough to make the houses tremble on either side.

King Henry of England walked alone on white rushes. He wore a cloak, tunic, and hose in darkest blue, almost black, his chest embroidered with three gold lions "passant guardant," lying still but ready. The cloak was held by a silver clasp.

He looked neither left nor right as he walked in the path of hundreds before him, nor took care to step around the steaming heaps of manure left by the warhorses gone ahead. For those who could see through tears of joy, the king was very pale, but his back was straight and his head held up. News of the battle at St. Albans had taken wing around the country. Rumors had flown of Henry's wound, even of his death, as they were built and embroidered into fantastical tales. He needed to be seen alive and strong, at York's order. The king had already opened the Parliament that morning, sitting through fresh oaths of allegiance to him, led by Richard of York as his most ardent supporter. Lords spiritual and temporal had come to kneel and take Henry's hand and swear their lives and honor over to the king. He looked around him with blank eyes, following those ahead.

Behind Henry, Queen Margaret walked with the Duke of York, his chest puffed out with pleasure as he gripped her hand and would not let it go. In his private thoughts, York wished Henry would acknowledge the crowd. There was something discomforting about the white-faced king stiffly following the route they had laid out, as if no mortal spark animated him at all. York and Margaret were three paces back, too far from him to exchange even a word. Instead, York raised his left hand to the passing rows of faces, jammed together and hanging from every high window. He saw flowers trampled into the rushes as the crowds pushed and heaved against the ranks of soldiers. Some of his men joined their staffs across at waist height, making a barrier of them as the Londoners grew frantic to see and hold a memory they could cherish for the rest of their lives.

"See how they love the king," York said, turning to Margaret. She made no response and he leaned closer to her, so that his lips brushed her ear. "They love your husband!" he shouted over the roar.

Margaret looked up at him then, her eyes so cold that he broke the gaze even as it began, looking back to the cheering people. The grand procession through London had been Salisbury's idea, now walking some way behind with his two sons. Perhaps the suggestion had been some recompense for the angry words they had exchanged in the marketplace of St. Albans, York didn't know. The people of London would see the house of York was restored to the very heart of royal favor. There would be no more whispers about his name or line. York felt the queen's hand move in his own, both their palms sweat-slick after so long pressed together. He tightened his grip, fearing she might pull away. He did not see her wince, nor the way she carefully ordered her expression to blankness once more.

This was York's day, Margaret could not doubt it. Her husband walked like a prisoner ahead of his executioners and she ached to go forward and stand with him. She had no choice but to walk behind, staring at Henry's back as if she could reach out and comfort him with her love and thoughts alone.

St. Paul's lay ahead of them, that ancient cathedral where an even larger crowd had gathered from long before dawn to see the king accept his crown from York's hands. No greater symbol of power existed, and York felt his spirits soar higher as the massive building came into view. God and good luck had been with him and with his house. If Henry's wound had been just a fraction closer to his throat, Prince Edward would have become king. As things stood, King Henry lived, but York would rule. He gave thanks to God for that, recalling that he had services being said day and night in gratitude for his good fortune.

Warwick had been given the Captaincy of Calais, that wealthy port, in return for his part in the action to save the king at St. Albans. Salisbury was once more the king's lord chancellor, though his reward was truly in the death of Earl Percy and his triumph in the feud between his family and Northumberland. York had asked for and been given the title of Constable of England, with powers to command in the king's name. Perhaps most importantly of all, Henry had meekly signed the pardons for all men involved in the battle, absolving them of all guilt or stains on their honor. The houses of York and Lancaster were reborn, together, on a summer's day of blue skies.

Margaret looked up at the man she hated hard enough to curdle milk. When the farce was over, with its mummer's games of crowns handed to the king from unworthy hands, she would see who still stood with her and with Henry. When the crowd were back in their homes and there was silence, she would see. She had learned a great deal since coming to England as a girl. She would not move quickly, nor rashly. But when the time came, she *would* move.

York sensed her gaze on him. When he glanced down at the queen walking at his side, he was relieved to see Margaret was smiling.

PART TWO

1459

The realm of England was out of all governance . . . for the king
was simple . . . held no household, maintained no wars.

ANON.
[15TH-CENTURY ENGLISH CHRONICLER]

CHAPTER 18

Derry Brewer stood in sheeting rain and watched the column of armed soldiers ride the great avenue toward the castle of Kenilworth. On the open land, there was no protection from the downpour that hissed over them. They rode with their heads bowed, seven score of men in full plate armor, carrying banners so drenched that they had wrapped around the poles. Even so, they were alert, ready for an attack. Despite four years of peace, the entire country seethed, jangling and clashing like a pot-lid on a fire.

Derry stepped into the path of the men, taking up a position in the middle of the drive. He had chosen six big lads to stand with him, just to form a decent-looking group. Two white plow horses went some way to block the avenue, enormous animals with twice the muscle and weight even of a warhorse. The way things were, Derry doubted any of the visitors would stop for just one man. The foul weather didn't help, nor the fact that the castle was in sight, with all its promise of warmth and safety. He raised his hand, palm out, standing tall and with as much confidence as he could muster while the rain stung his skin. At his side, his friend Wilfred Tanner raised the royal banner, a splash of red and gold that could be seen from far away. The bony little smuggler stood with quivering pride at being allowed to hold the king's colors.

It was barely an hour past noon, though the clouds overhead had reduced the great drive to a dark gray. Derry stared ahead at the approaching riders, observing the moment when they spotted him and called back to the duke they protected. Derry could not see beyond the first couple of ranks, but somewhere in the mass of soldiers was the man he needed to reach.

"In the name of the king, hold!" Derry bellowed over the wind. He muttered swear words at the lack of response.

The column trotted closer, jingling toward him with no sign of slowing. If the man who led them gave no order, Derry knew they would ride straight through his miserable group, scattering them. God knew, there was suspicion enough in England that year. Every minor baron, every knight and his neighbors seemed to be gathering men and buying weapons. The cauldron was likely to spill, with so much heat under it.

When the front rank was just paces from him, Derry heard another voice snap an order. It rippled down the line, though they had at least expected it and halted before he was knocked off his feet. When they stopped at last, Derry could have reached out and touched the damp muzzle of the closest mounts, though he decided not to do so. No rider liked to see another man reaching for his reins.

The downpour increased without thunder, just the heavens ripping open and pouring out a month's worth of rain in a single day. The ground ran with a thousand streams and great sheets of shining water stretched all around them. Rain drummed on the armored column, a tinny roar that rose and fell in volume with each gust.

"Who are you, to stand in the road?" a knight in the second rank called out. "You are in the path of the Duke of Somerset. Step aside."

Derry could sense the readiness for violence in the knights watching him. They had come armed for war and they were twitchy and nervous. As no one had raised a visor, it was hard to see who had spoken. They might as well have been silver statues, half hidden in sodden blue cloaks, drenched almost to black.

"I would speak with Henry Beaufort, Duke of Somerset," Derry said loudly and clearly, "whose father I knew well and whom I once called a friend. I speak for King Henry and Queen Margaret. You see I have no men to threaten you, but on orders of the king, I must speak to Somerset before you enter the castle."

The men in the front rank stared down at him through the slots in their visors. Those behind turned their heads, and Derry craned to see one among them who wore the colors of Somerset beneath his cloak, a sodden tabard banded in blue and white, with gold fleur-de-lis quartered with the lions of England. Derry fixed his gaze on that slim figure, feeling a pang in his heart at the memory of the man's father. One of the knights leaned in to their master and murmured something Derry could not hear. To his relief, he saw the young duke shake his head and dig in his heels, forcing his armored warhorse through to the front. Like its owner, the enormous animal was girded in iron plates across the chest and head, segments that moved with the horse's gait and could withstand almost any blow. Against an unarmed man, the armor itself was a weapon and Derry swallowed, knowing a wrong step would see him gashed.

As Derry stared, the new Duke of Somerset raised his visor, revealing his eyes and squinting as the rain reached them.

"Your Grace, my name is Derry Brewer. I knew your father."

"He spoke of you," Henry Beaufort replied grudgingly. "He said you were a man to trust, though I will make my own judgment. What would you have of me?"

"A word in private, my lord, on my name, my oath of fealty, and my position as servant of the king."

Derry waited under the young man's cool gaze, but another of the knights spoke before Somerset could reply.

"My lord, this smells wrong. To be stopped on the road in the pissing rain? Let us move on to the queen's castle. We will hear the right of it there."

"It *is* urgent, my lord," Derry added in reply, waiting. "I am unarmed."

The suggestion that Somerset held back from anything like fear or caution was enough to prick him to immediate anger. He dismounted, striding up to Derry and deliberately standing over him, threateningly close. In response, Derry turned away and led the young man a dozen paces clear of his men. They bristled at every step that took their master away from them, ready to kick their horses into murderous action at the first wrong move.

"What do you want?" Somerset hissed at Derry, leaning in close. "I am summoned here with nothing more than a Royal Seal demanding my presence. What must you say to me that keeps me out in the rain?"

Derry breathed in relief.

"There is a man in your company, my lord, a man who passed papers to Earl Salisbury not a month ago. My people watched him do it and then followed the one he met."

"A traitor?" Somerset said in surprise. "Why then did you not bring me the news before?"

Derry found his cheeks growing hot, despite the freezing rain.

"It has sometimes been of use to know which men are false, my lord, without rounding them all up. In such a way, they can be made to feed the wrong path to their masters, if you follow me."

"Yet you stop me now," Somerset prompted, glaring at the bedraggled spymaster before him.

"You will hear plans in Kenilworth that are not for his ears, my lord. I thought it would be easier and quieter to make the problem vanish on the road, instead of in the queen's presence."

"I see. What is this man's name, to be damned on your word alone?"

Derry winced at the young lord's tone of suspicion.

"Sir Hugh Sarrow, my lord. And there is no doubt in this, none at all. Send him back, if you wish, though he will know and disappear to your enemies if you do."

Somerset cast a glance back at his glowering men.

"Sir Hugh? He was one of my father's men! I have known him since I was a child!"

"Even so, my lord. He cannot enter the castle and be allowed to hear what is for your ears alone. Your father trusted me, my lord. King Henry and Queen Margaret trust me still. This is my work—to find traitors and use them, or to break them."

"My father may have known you, Master Brewer. I do not. If I refuse?"

"I regret to say you will be turned back from the castle gate." Derry had to struggle to breathe easily, aware that men like Henry Beaufort were used to absolute obedience to their slightest whim. "You may not enter with that man free, my lord. On your order, he could be trussed and bound, taken to a cell while you speak to the queen. I would welcome the chance to question him, but he is your man. And it is your choice."

Derry started as Somerset turned and roared at his men.

"Sir Hugh Sarrow! To me, here."

The ranks shifted and clattered, as one man came to the front and dismounted, walking stiffly toward his master and Derry Brewer.

"Remove your helmet, Sir Hugh," Somerset said.

The knight revealed a narrow, worried face, part-obscured by mustaches as his brown eyes flickered back and forth between the two men.

Somerset leaned close enough for Derry to feel the warmth of his breath.

"I am loyal to the king, Master Brewer. My father's death cries out for vengeance still and I will not be denied it. If this is a test of my loyalty, you have my answer." With no warning, he drew his sword and swung, turning from the hip and putting all his strength into a strike against the knight's bared neck.

The blade caught the edge of the man's gorget before cutting into flesh, striking a spark that was washed away in blood and rain. Sir Hugh staggered at the force of the blow. His face drained death-white and he raised a hand to his throat in wide-eyed shock, then fell with a crash into the mud.

Derry stared at the young man before him, seeing a rage that had been completely hidden before.

"There is an end to it," Somerset said. "If you have nothing else for me, Master Brewer? I am wet and cold and I would yet hear what awaits me at Kenilworth."

"Thank you for your trust, my lord," Derry said, shaken. He made a gesture to his companions and they removed themselves from the path of the column, pitiful obstacle as they had been. Somerset stalked back and mounted his horse once again. The column rode past Derry with dozens of armored helmets turning to fix him with suspicion and dislike. He stood carefully back from their path, his work done.

When they had passed, Derry signaled to his men. They tied the armored corpse to the plow horses and dragged it behind them through the mud, heading back into the castle.

MARGARET'S EXPRESSION WAS INTENT as she watched Derry Brewer and another man enter and bow. The spymaster's hair was rain-slick, though he had changed into dry clothes before coming into her presence. Whatever warning Derry may have given, his companion was clearly terrified at finding himself under the scrutiny of a queen of England. The man at Derry's side was stick thin, with a brush of unkempt brown hair that looked as if he'd tried to smooth it with spit and a palm. He trembled as he tried to copy Derry's action, pressing one leg out before him and dropping low over it. To Margaret's hidden amusement, Derry had to reach out and steady the man before he toppled over.

Despite the storm that battered the castle walls that day, the long summer of '59 had baked Kenilworth, cracking the plaster and turning green pastures to dry, brown fields as far as the eye could see. Margaret loved the place.

Three years before, twenty-six great serpentine guns had been winched up to the stone walls and towers, enough to fill a quarter mile with iron roundshot—and broken flesh and metal, if an enemy dared approach. Margaret had given no warning to York or Salisbury of her intentions, no sign that she was not utterly content with her lot. She had taken only Derry Brewer into her confidence, the one man she trusted. Together, they had arranged for Henry to come out of his rooms in the Palace of Westminster, suborning his doctors with the need for fresh, country air. As soon as they were clear of London, Margaret had rushed him north before anyone else knew what they were planning. She had received a hundred indignant letters and heralds over the three years that followed, but what could York do? There could be no new parliaments called without the king. Law and order in the country began to fail and crumble, yet Kenilworth was a fortress. Even York would not dare summon an army to take King Henry from his own wife.

"Approach, Master Brewer," Margaret said. "And bring your . . . companion with you, that I may judge the quality of men you employ in my husband's name."

Derry straightened up, seeing the hint of mischief in his queen's eyes. A smile came easily to him.

"This wondrous fine specimen is Wilfred Tanner, Your Highness. He has been useful to me this last year. He was a smuggler, once, though not a good one—"

"Derry!" Tanner hissed at him, horrified to have his previous profession spoken aloud.

"—but he is now in royal service," Derry went on smoothly, "traveling with me around the country to collect your indentures." He held up a leather satchel, stuffed full of parchment. "Another fifty-odd in here, Your Highness. Signed statements of men who will join the Gallants, on their oaths and honor."

"I am well served in you, Master Brewer. My husband has spoken often of your loyalty. If he were present, I know he would express his gratitude for all you have done these past years."

Mentioning King Henry brought a crease between her eyes, Derry noticed. Margaret was not yet thirty years of age and had grown extraordinarily beautiful in the years since her marriage. Her hair was dark, a shining braid that hung almost to her waist. As he stared at her, Derry wondered idly if Margaret knew the effect she had on men. He suspected she did, to the last pennyworth. She sat on a carved wooden chair, wearing a dress of dark blue silk that subtly emphasized her figure. No second child had come to strain those seams, not in the six years since the birth of Prince Edward. Derry tilted his head a fraction to observe the queen, experiencing no flutter of passion, but simply the pleasure, almost awe, that comes from a man gazing upon a fine woman. Light from one of the large windows ran across the queen, making her eyes shine and filling the air around her with golden motes.

"These new men to our cause," Margaret asked, "are they Queen's Gallants? Or my husband's?"

"These forty-six are sworn to you, my lady. Wilfred passed out your swan's badges and I can report they are worn with great pride. I think I will need another gross when I go out again. In some places, they have become the height of fashion, with many men making a gift of them to their wives."

"When we call though, Master Brewer, they must wear my token, or my husband's Antelope. Yes? Whatever the fashion, our Gallants must know each other by their badges."

Derry waved a hand airily.

"Queen or King's Gallants, they serve the Crown, Your Highness. It has been a joy to me to see the fervor in the towns and villages. I am treated like a visiting nobleman myself, whenever I'm sighted on Retribution."

"Sighted on . . . ? Ah. Is that not a rather fanciful name for a horse, Master Brewer?"

"In truth, he is a vengeful beast, my lady. It suits him rather well, as the work suits me. Wilfred here has won more than a few sweethearts, just by carrying my bag of paper and badges."

Margaret laughed and Wilfred Tanner blushed furiously, an elbow poking at Derry, though he was out of range.

One of the queen's stewards entered the audience chamber behind the two men, sweeping silently through the great doors on felt shoes. When he addressed his mistress, Derry and Wilfred Tanner both started in surprise. Margaret knew weapons were forbidden in her presence, so it was with some interest that she saw their hands dart to different parts of their tunics and sleeves. Both men recovered quickly, exchanging a sheepish glance.

"Your Highness. Henry Beaufort, Duke of Somerset, and Sir John Fortescue, Chief Justice of the King's Bench," her steward announced, stepping back to allow the two men into her presence.

In response, Derry bowed once again.

"May I remain, my lady? I would hear these men, in my role as your counselor."

Margaret inclined her head, allowing Derry to guide Wilfred Tanner to one side. They stood meekly, though Derry Brewer watched from under lowered brows. At the end of the chamber, two very different men entered.

Henry Beaufort, Duke of Somerset, was just twenty-three years of age. As one who had known his father well, Derry could discern few traces of the old duke in the son's face, though he knew by then that the bland expression concealed a terrible anger, still burning bright after four years. Beaufort was perhaps a fraction taller than his father, Edmund, had been, coming forward with a lithe step into the queen's presence. Beards had come back into favor in the four years since the battle of St. Albans and young Somerset appeared to be growing one with indifferent success, a confection of dark brown and ginger, with the ends of his mustaches curving slightly upward over his mouth.

"Your Highness," Somerset said, sweeping into a bow that was more elegant than Derry's had been. The duke's gaze settled on Derry for a heartbeat as he rose straight, acknowledging the spymaster.

"My lord Somerset, I welcome your presence," Margaret said. "Abide just a moment while I greet your companion."

Derry saw a flush come to the young man's cheeks and raised his eyebrows in interest as Somerset stood aside. The duke had not taken a wife and Derry wondered if he should counsel the young man to be cautious in making cow-eyes at the queen where another might see. He recalled the sudden violence he had witnessed on the castle avenue and decided against it. Derry supposed the man was handsome enough, in an uninspiring sort of way. Derry caught himself smoothing down his own locks of hair, then shook his head in amusement at the foolishness of men generally.

Entering behind the young nobleman, Sir John Fortescue was dressed entirely in black, from the voluminous robes he gathered at his chest down to a few inches of woolen stockings and black leather boots beneath. At sixty-two, his face was almost unlined, the flesh full. It reminded Derry of the members of some monastic orders, who spend so much of their lives in slack-faced prayer that they do not age as other men. Though Fortescue wore no beard, a slim mustache sat above his lip, dark in the center and white toward the ends of his wide mouth. It went some way to disguise the missing upper and lower teeth on one side of the jaw, giving him a wry expression even when he was at rest. The teeth he retained were strong and yellow, but fully half his mouth was just gum. Derry caught Fortescue's flickering glance in his direction. The king's Chief Justice was famously observant and, in that single instant, Derry felt he had been assessed and dismissed, with the still-cringing Tanner at his side. No doubt Fortescue would observe the signs of Somerset's infatuation with the same cold eyes and twisted smile.

"May I approach, Your Highness?" Fortescue said. His voice was strong and firm, as might befit a man used to addressing a court as Chief Justice. Derry noted the slight hiss on his sibilant sounds as the man's tongue found space where teeth would once have been.

"You may of course, Sir John," Margaret replied. She saw Fortescue glance at the others in the room and spoke before him. "You may also trust those you meet in this place, or none at all. Is that understood? However unfamiliar you are to one another, I know you all for loyal men."

The four visitors spent a moment in silence, each considering the others. Both the duke and Judge Fortescue frowned at Wilfred Tanner, who scratched his jaw and appeared to want to be anywhere else but in that room. Tanner had met a judge or two in his life.

Margaret lost patience with the tension between them.

"My lord Somerset, gentlemen, *friends*. In the king's name you each play a part in a greater enterprise. Master Brewer here has spent two years on the road for me, gathering loyal men aggrieved at the ill treatment of the king by his most powerful lords. York, Salisbury, and Warwick have mocked the throne, mocked England and the Crown. There, I have declared myself. They took arms to make bloody murder on the king's own noble counselors and yet the heavens did not strike them down. They thrive still, strutting like bantams while better men lie under the sod."

Margaret realized she had clenched one hand into a fist and released it, seeing her white fingers open like a flower.

"I have not slept a night since then without thinking of some punishment for those men. Sir John came to me to explain the law, but what is the law, even the law of England, if it cannot be enforced? How many do you have sworn to my Queen's Gallants, Master Brewer? How many is it now?"

Derry blinked. The woman who sat so still to lecture them had lost all trace of lightness. He saw again the young queen who had received the news of her husband's wound and the rise of York over all. Not grief, but a frozen rage. Though she had certainly been broken, it was into pieces sharp enough to cut.

"Nine thousand men will wear the swan, Your Highness. I . . .

cannot answer to their quality, for the most part. Though some eight hundred knights have pledged to you, the rest are farmers and smiths and squires. They need good men to lead them, but they have given their oaths to stand for your cause."

"And the second of our great enterprises, Master Brewer? Tell Sir John how many men will wear my husband's antelope when the king is threatened by his enemies."

"Eight thousand, Your Highness. From Dorset to Northumberland, they have been training to march and fight. They merely await the king's command."

"Thank you, Master Brewer," Margaret said. "Well, Sir John? Is it to your satisfaction? Do such numbers please you?"

Sir John Fortescue had listened in fascination. He bowed once more, a smile playing around his lips.

"Your Highness, I am overwhelmed. I believe it is enough. No, I am certain."

The judge might have gone on, but Henry Beaufort cleared his throat. He may have been only four years a duke, but as far as Derry could see, Somerset already had some of the arrogance of the breed. The young man raised a single finger and, in response, the king's most senior judge closed his mouth with a snap.

"Your Highness, that is welcome news," Somerset said. "I am honored to be included in this circle." He glanced at Wilfred Tanner then, allowing an expression of doubt to cross his face. "I would accept any position of authority in such a . . . what did you call it, my lady? Such a 'great enterprise.' You may depend on my loyalty, to the last horns blown."

"Oh, I do, my lord Somerset," Margaret replied coldly. "There is no middle ground in this. It has been too long in the planning. This very morning, I have met Lords Buckingham, Clifford, Gray, and

Audley. My husband's nobles will stand either with him, or in his path. I tell you now, he will not allow mercy to be shown to those who make the wrong choice."

To Derry's private pleasure, Henry Beaufort held up his finger once again, asking permission to speak. Margaret's mouth tightened, but she nodded to him.

"Your Highness, if these armies will only march when the king is threatened, I have to ask, where is the threat? Even without a parliament, York seems content with all he has won. Warwick is in Calais. Salisbury holds his feasts and hunts, but not one of them could be said to threaten His Majesty directly."

Margaret's expression grew bleak as Somerset spoke, her previous warmth vanishing.

"Yes. They consider all the battles won. It is a pretty point and one that vexed me. I thought I should never overcome it until Sir John explained Attainder to me. That is the spark that will bring them out, my lord. That is the stone to break their heads."

Somerset nodded, touching his finger to his lips. It was clear enough to Derry that the young duke had no knowledge of the term. All the men there turned to Fortescue as the man worked his half-empty mouth, showing pleasure at their attention.

"It is a law for traitors," Fortescue said. "Long in the annals but rarely used, perhaps because of the power it allows. With the king's Seal on a Bill of Attainder, a nobleman is made common. His titles are void, his succession is denied. All property passes back to the king. It is, in short, the death in ashes of a noble house."

"York will never allow it to be issued," Derry said immediately, just as he had agreed with the queen in a private meeting. To his exasperation, Sir John wagged a finger at him, smiling.

"Attainder was created for the most extreme threats to the royal house, Master Brewer. Those who wrote it into English law under-stood that there would be occasions where time was short and traitors perilously close to success. There is very little burden of proof required. Though it must come before a parliament at some point, it can be sealed into law and the action begun with no more than a quorum of lords and the king's agreement."

For the benefit of Somerset, Derry rubbed his forehead as if in thought, making a pretense of hearing it all for the first time.

"Sir John has prepared the writ," Margaret said. "My husband has agreed to add his Seal. Lords Percy and Egremont have lost as much as any other with the death of their father. With you, my lord Somerset, they will command my husband's Gallants." Her tone offered no opportunity for him to refuse and Somerset bowed his head. "Once begun, gentlemen, Attainder cannot be undone. It is a call to arms. The house of York will fall, or fight—and *still* fall."

Her voice trembled as she spoke, as well it might, Derry thought. York would come out like a mad dog when he heard of it, that much was certain. The queen would bring about a war with just a piece of parchment.

Margaret went on, her eyes glittering to have reached this point after months and years of preparation.

"My husband will summon a council of loyal lords to Coventry, to hear the bill read. No more of London, gentlemen. Coventry is but five miles from this place. It will do as our heartland. Master Brewer, you will call the men who have sworn their service and lives to the Crown. Use whatever words you wish, but bring the last of them to the field and have them train. I have a commander for my own Gallants in James Tuchet, Baron Audley. My husband will take the field himself with his army."

"I know Lord Audley," Derry replied. "He is a veteran, a white-beard in service, Your Highness. I have no quarrel with your decision. I must ask though, if King Henry is well enough for what lies ahead?"

As he spoke, Derry looked down in embarrassment. He and Margaret had agreed that he would ask the question, though he did not enjoy that part of his role, nor the lies the queen would surely tell. The king was most notable for his absence, with such great affairs being decided around him. Derry could almost feel Margaret's gaze sharpen.

"My husband is eager, Master Brewer. His health has been inconstant, but he grows stronger every day. Have no fears on his account." She waved a hand as if to dismiss the idea. "I have bought another batch of pikes and lead clubs for my Gallants, stacked high in the storerooms of Kenilworth. I would have you inspect them and arrange for them to be taken where they are needed. In a month, send out news of this Attainder of York. You will let your whisperers do their work, so that York and Salisbury learn of it as well. They will come, then. And they will be met."

"Your Highness," Derry said, accepting his orders. As he stood there, he could not help but recall the last great plan of the royal house—to secure a truce and a wife from France in exchange for the territories of Maine and Anjou. Derry had been one of the architects of that, and the queen before him was part of the result. Yet Lord Suffolk had been killed, London had been invaded, and almost all English land in France had been lost. He could not help the shiver of fear that ran through him at the thought of another scheme to move nations and noble houses like pieces on a board. The ripples from that earlier catastrophe had led to where they stood on that day—and were still spreading.

Putting aside his misgivings for the moment, Derry dropped to one knee, copied instantly by Wilfred Tanner, while Somerset and Sir John Fortescue looked on.

Margaret brightened once more, casting off the cold expression of authority.

"There is a meal laid out for you all. I would be pleased to have you join me. I do not doubt you have questions still to be answered. Please, follow my steward and I will join you at table."

That evening, after the compline bells had rung out in the castle chapel, Margaret dismissed the last of the men who had come to visit her that day. She had seen two dozen soldiers and lords, as well as merchants given the task of providing weapons and supplies for two armies. Their faces swam before her as she carried a small lamp along the corridors to her husband's rooms, high up in the east tower of the castle.

She murmured a greeting to the guards at Henry's door, slipping inside and passing through the outer chambers. The only noise was the swish of her dress and the soft tapping of her leather shoes on the stones.

"Who is there?" Henry called out from within.

Margaret smiled wearily at hearing his voice. It was a good day if he was awake and alert. King Henry slept for extraordinary lengths of time and could easily be senseless for an entire day. His few waking hours were often spent in the chapel, with his hands clasped tight before him. Weeks or months could pass with barely a spark of life beyond those movements, with food and drink chewed without recognition and his eyes blank. The better times came slowly, like a man waking from deep slumber. She had lost count of the occasions when his energy had returned and given her hope, only to fade once more. On any given day, she might find him dressed and vital, talking animatedly about their plans. Such episodes of recovery lasted a day, or a week, or even a month before the stupor would drag him back and he would once again drown and be lost. She never knew what she would find each night.

She still mourned the loss of her love for him. It had not vanished in a single night and there were times when she felt embers of affection amidst the colder sadness. She had been a mother to him more than a wife, for as long as she could remember. Perhaps that was the heart of it. Like so much else, her love for Henry had been allowed to drain away over the years, dragged out thread by clawed thread, until she was empty. The strange thing was that it did not matter. Whether she was a mother or a wife to him, she knew she would not rest until his enemies were cold and in the ground. York had left her with nothing else and she blamed that man for plunging Henry's head under the waters once again. When she recalled the way Henry had been before St. Albans, the brightness and promise in his eyes then, her heart would break anew. He had been given a chance to live, to be alive—and York had stolen it from him, holding him under in his grief until he was gone.

"It is I, Henry," she said. "Margaret."

To her surprise, he was sitting up in bed with books and papers spilled carelessly around him.

"I heard men's voices, earlier. I wanted to rise and go out to them, but . . ." He shook his head, unable to explain the lethargy that stole away his will and made the simplest task take an age.

Margaret swept her skirts under her and sat at his side, looking over the papers around him on the coverlet. He saw her interest and waved a hand over them.

"Bills of Attainder, my dear. And the Great Charter, by my foot. I had them brought to me, though I do not recall asking for them."

Margaret covered her irritation by gathering them up. She vowed to chastise whichever servant had brought the documents to her husband. In conditions of strict secrecy, she had ordered a huge number of papers sent from the archives in London, hiding the ones she really wanted in hundreds of others. Then at the last, the final, vital packets had been given into Henry's hands instead of her own.

"I asked for them, Henry. I did not want you to be troubled with mere papers, when you are still unwell."

"No, they caught my interest!" he said brightly. "I have spent the day reading them. These Writs of Attainder make stories of horror, my dear. I shiver still at what they brought about. Have you read the execution records of the Despensers? The father was cut into pieces and eaten by dogs, the son—"

"I do not wish to hear it, Henry," Margaret replied. "I'm sure they deserved whatever fates befell them, if they stood against their rightful king."

"I think they stood with him, Margaret. The Despensers supported the second King Edward, but after the Attainder was issued against them, the son was dragged, then his flesh was knife-carved with verses against sin, then—"

"Henry, please! No more. You make me shiver to hear such things. You should rest, not inflame your thoughts with terrible imaginings. How will you sleep now, with such pictures in your mind's eye?"

The king looked crestfallen.

"As you say, Margaret. I'm sorry. I did not mean to distress you. I will put them aside."

Margaret continued to gather up the papers in a great sheaf, tucking them under one arm. One of the bundles was held by an old iron clasp and it snagged her finger, making her hiss in pain. Red drops of blood spilled from the tip and she heard her husband take a sharp breath, distressed as he looked away. She sucked the finger, angry with herself as she saw a single red spot remain on the white coverlet.

After St. Albans, her husband had developed a terror of seeing blood. He had not yet noticed the mark, but when he did, he would not sleep again.

Taking the papers with her, Margaret rummaged in the chest at the foot of his bed and pulled out blankets and another cover, quilted and thick against the cold.

"Lie still, love," she said, moving with quick efficiency. She threw off his layers and replaced them, glimpsing his bare legs beneath his shift. Henry settled down, the lines of tension leaving his face. He yawned as Margaret sat once more to stroke his brow.

"You see? You have made yourself weary," she said.

"You will not take the light though, Margaret? I do not like waking in the dark."

"I will leave it here, by your bed. Your servants are always within call."

She continued to smooth his forehead, and his eyes closed.

"I love you, Margaret," he murmured.

"I know," she said. For no reason at all, her eyes filled with tears.

When his breathing was steady and she was sure he was asleep, the queen took the papers to another room, where she brought a lamp close to a table and sat to peruse the fate of the Despenser family and the result of the Bill of Attainder issued against them. When she read the vital document had been ordered by a French queen come to England to marry Edward the second, Margaret sat up straight. History had lessons to teach and she could almost hear the voice of her countrywoman a century before. Margaret didn't move from that spot, rapt and fascinated, until the sun rose.

CHAPTER 19

Salisbury rubbed his freshly shaven face with a cold, wet cloth, closing the pores and easing the sting of Rankin's razor. He had made no bets with his retainer that morning, instead enduring the scraping in perfect silence until he could rise and dismiss his servant. At sixty, Richard Neville was feeling his years. He spent an hour of each morning in sweat-soaked exercise, keeping his sword arm strong and his joints supple. He had never been a heavy man and though the skin of his jowls sagged in sharp creases, there was as yet no fat to make them plump. Even so, age was the great weakener, no matter how he worked to stall its progress. There had been a time when every decision was clear and he could see far, knowing exactly what he wanted and how best to bring it about. He could only shake his head in memory of that youthful clarity. Life had been simpler, once, when his task had been to keep his family strong and spread the Neville bloodline throughout the noble houses of England.

His wife, Alice, came bustling into the room as Rankin scurried out, taking in her husband's mood as she placed a bowl of fresh apples on a dresser. Middleham Castle was blessed with fine orchards and the cider made there was good enough to be sold. It was typical of her husband that he did not do so, allowing his servants to age barrels of it in the castle basements for their own pleasure.

Alice watched as Salisbury finished wiping his face and neck. She could see he was distracted, looking around vaguely for a place to put the cloth, until she approached and took it from him.

"You look troubled," she said, reaching out and touching him on the arm. They had been married for almost forty years and grown old together in what he called the "gentle harness." It was a phrase he had used many times to amuse her, one of many he would utter just to see her smile. The humor may have been lost over the years, but the memory of it and the affection remained.

"Is it any wonder, with such things to trouble me?" Salisbury muttered. Standing by the window, he could see the golden farmland around Middleham, stretching to the horizon and populated by small figures of men and women and horses, cutting and gathering sheaves of golden wheat on the earl's fields. On another day, the sight might have brought him pleasure, an image of the world working as it should, with men drawing goodness from the earth and looking forward to a flagon of ale as the sun set. As the first touches of autumn bronzed the trees, he stared through it all and much further.

There was no need for Alice to wonder at the source of her husband's strain. Ever since the messenger had arrived two days before, the castle had been in an uproar, with a dozen other men going out on fast horses to call in knights and men-at-arms, wherever they laid their heads.

"Richard of York is my oathsworn lord," Salisbury said. He spoke almost to himself, though he turned his head and touched his wife's cheek. "I raised him up, close enough to take the throne. And at the end, he did not reach for it. If he had, there would be no threat to us now, no whispers of this Attainder that could destroy us all. Damn his indecision, Alice! How many times must a man be given a crown before he closes his hand on it? York could have made himself king at St. Albans and that would have been the end. He was too meek, or too cowed with the walls of an abbey all around him. Now? Four years have passed in peace and all we have gained is to let the king grow strong once again—or rather, to allow his queen to tighten her grip. And now this! The house of York shaken to its foundations by the king's own Seal and I have *no* choice, Alice! No choice at all. I must take the field once again. I must take arms and risk everything I have made, when it should have been settled long ago."

"You will not fail, Richard," Alice said firmly. "You never have. In all your dealings, the Nevilles have prospered, by your hand and your wits. You have been a fine shepherd to them all—aye, and to others who do not have our name. You said yourself you have raised more soldiers than any other house could bear. You have not been idle in the years of peace! Take heart from that, from the foresight that made you bring so many to your banners while other men drowsed!"

Salisbury grunted, pleased that his wife would say such things to him. He had never been a boastful man, but he enjoyed her appreciation of his skills, even if such things were said only in private.

"My father told me never to fight the same battle twice, Alice. He warned me that if I won, I should be sure to crush my enemies so completely they could never rise again."

"And if you lost?" she asked.

Salisbury smiled in memory.

"I asked the same question. He said if I lost, I placed my fate in the hands of other men. The answer was always *not* to lose." He sighed then, shaking his head. "Yet here I am, bound to support York in war, where a single blow or arrow can end it all. I am too old for this, Alice. I feel it in my stiff joints, in my slow thoughts. It is a path for younger men to walk. I would rather stay here in peace and watch the crops gathered in."

Alice knew her husband well enough to choose her words carefully, prodding his vanity to bring him out of his somber mood.

"Perhaps, then, you should let our son command the men. Have you news of Richard coming back from Calais? If he were here, you know he would not refuse, love. He would carry the Neville banners, with those of Warwick."

Alice watched her husband's jaw clench, his gaze sharpening.

"He is a fine commander," he said. "My heart swells when I think of how he led his men at St. Albans."

"And yours, love. They followed him when he blew the horns. You have told me how well he looked in his red."

Salisbury chewed his lower lip at that memory, his chin jutting out a fraction as he raised his head.

"Yet he is young, still—and perhaps not yet cunning enough in his youth," he said.

Alice hid her smile as she nodded.

"And he has spent three years in France, while I have kept my eye on all the whisperings of this Lancaster court. No, I should command, Alice. Warwick will have his time, not long from now. He did not come to me with news of these Queen's Gallants marching and training. These King's Gallants riding through the north and gathering bows and pikes and clubs of iron. Where would we be without the men I pay to pass on such things to me? Lost, Alice. God knows whether the king will ever leave his bed now. I have no one in Kenilworth to tell me how he fares, not for a year. Two strong young men both killed in accidents? Young John Donnell found hanged by his own hand, when I knew him for a cheery soul with no dark moods at all? Sir Hugh Sarrow found dead in a house of ill-repute? It was passing strange for a man to take such a cut in his bed, Alice. I knew two years back that I had to gather knights and men-at-arms, no matter the ruinous cost. They tried to pluck out my eyes. Yet I knew. If they would have me blind, there had to be something they did not want me to see. No, it is the queen, that she-wolf, behind this threat, not Henry. That poor, broken man is at her mercy—and the mercy of her courtiers and council. I do not doubt the Percy sons still smart at the loss of their father. They have planned for this—and *I* must answer them, or see my life's work thrown onto the fire."

"Very well, Richard," Alice said. "I am pleased to hear you say it. You will keep our son safe, I hope?"

"As best I can," he replied. "God willing, we will make an end." He dipped his head a fraction, so that shadows played across his eyes. "I tell you, Alice, if Henry must fall, I will not shrink from it, as York did. Not with my house and titles in peril. I will strike the blow to finish this war of whispers and secrets. For if York is broken, Salisbury will be next—and then Warwick. One Attainder will lead to others and we will be scorched out of England. I would die first, before I allow that."

"Old fox," she said, stepping into his embrace so that he folded his arms around her and rested his chin on the top of her head. "Come back safe to me, when it is done. That is all I ask."

"I will," he said, breathing deeply with his lips pressed against her hair. He could feel her tremble beneath his touch. "Whisht! Have no fear for me, love! I have three thousand men—and York, two thousand more. Our son will bring twenty hundred in their red coats, almost half that number from his Calais garrison. Seven thousand, Alice! And not country men more used to scythes and mattocks, but good soldiers in mail. An iron knife, my love, to strike or block the queen's forces. Have we not been called to a Great Council in Coventry? By the king's own order, I have his permission to march my army across the land, more fool them for allowing it. We will not move by night, but in the day, a gathering at the king's command. I tell you, before the first frosts, I shall break these enemies. I will rout them and scatter them like the weak seed of a weak line that they are. On my honor, Alice, I will."

THE SEA WAS TWENTY MILES BEHIND, though Warwick could still smell it in his clothes, that mixture of ancient damp and clean salt that somehow never failed to raise his spirits. His skin had been lashed with spray on the crossing from France and he could taste the bitterness on his bare forearm. In the ring of torches, he raised a pewter flagon and cheered with the men as Edward of March sent another growling knight crashing onto his back. Their first evening on English soil for almost four years had been much longer for the six hundred Calais men. Some of them had wept or danced as they reached the land of their fathers, reaching down to touch and pat it or gather up a scrap of dust to put in a pouch. They had suffered through the fall of France ten years before, as well as entire seasons without pay, when all England seemed to be about to go up in flames. They were not young, any of them, but grizzled veterans to a man, too long denied the comforts of home to remember any softness. Their captain, Andrew Trollope, had been forced to knuckle tears out of his eyes when Warwick told him he would travel home at last.

Warwick watched with pleasure as York's son ducked a wildly swinging staff and hooked a man's leg with his free hand, heaving him up to send him staggering into two more. There was always danger in a mêlée, even one with wooden staffs rather than spiked maces or blades. Yet at a few months shy of eighteen, the Earl of March made more experienced knights look like children—and the watching men loved him for it, cheering each blow. Warwick could hear Edward laughing in his helmet, the sound of it surprisingly loud and deep for such a young man. Not for the first time, Warwick looked forward to seeing York's face when he first caught sight of the giant his son had become. Standing four inches over six feet and with a huge frame, Edward overtopped even the legendary height of his namesake, the king known as "Longshanks." Warwick had been forced to employ the best armorers in France, just to encase the earl in iron as he grew. Yet where other boys might have been weakened by such a surge of growth, March had come to his manhood among the Calais veterans, training with them every day and learning every vicious trick they could teach for the field of war.

Warwick could see the young earl's two most loyal companions cheering with the rest, watching each move with expert eyes. The smith, Jameson, was one of the biggest men Warwick had ever seen, though even he had to look up at March when they met. Sir Robert Dalton had taken over the sword exercises of the entire Calais garrison, claiming he had never seen such rust and sloth in all his life. Their loyalty to the son of York was visible and obvious, mingled with pride as they watched him fight. The earl would be a terror in war, Warwick was certain of that. He stood head and shoulders above most full-grown men and could strike with such force that one blow was usually enough.

At Warwick's side, Captain Trollope was grinning merrily, already drunk on the ale and mead they had found in the first tavern on the coast that morning. The Calais men had come forward quickly enough then to roll the barrels along the street as they left the sea at their backs.

"No one bets against him, any longer," Trollope said, raising his mug and clinking it against Warwick's. "Your health, my lord. I won a fair bit at first, but now? Not even when he takes on three or four."

The last of the struggling knights saw an opportunity to grip the leg of the young earl. He dived at it, only to find himself lifted entirely into the air and dumped with a crash of metal that left him stunned. His hands waved feebly, like a beetle turned onto its back. The crowd of soldiers shouted their appreciation and Warwick had to smile as March came staggering over to slump with a crash onto the grass beside him. He was panting, heat coming off him in waves as if they sat too close to an oven. Warwick saw Sir Robert and Jameson rise from their place in the circle of torches to join their young charge. He signaled for fresh flagons of ale for all three.

York's son wrestled with his helmet and complained with a muffled voice that the thing had buckled. He brought more and more strength to bear on it until the metal squeaked and something snapped, revealing his flushed face and a mane of wild black hair.

"By God, I thought that would never come off! I'll need to have the armorer look it over before I wear it again. Did you see, Richard? Captain Trollope? Ah, Sir Robert! Sit by me, if you would. Did you see that last one? I could have thrown him over a barn. He almost had my leg though, if he'd been strong enough to lift it."

Warwick could smell ale on the earl's breath, sweet and strong, as he panted. He passed a full flagon into the armored hands, watching with amusement as Edward sank it to the dregs and then folded his lips in to catch the froth. It was odd to look up at a man when they were both sitting. Since his last burst of growth, Edward had begun to carry a weight of muscle that made experienced warriors want to look at their feet in his presence. Combined with his youth, it might have made him terrifying, if not for his good nature. Trollope had compared him more than once to one of the Calais mastiffs—huge dogs brought over from England as a breeding line a century or so before. The massive beasts had no malice in them, perhaps because no other dog could make them afraid.

While Warwick fretted over the letters from his father that had called him home, York's eldest son seemed to think it all a grand adventure, rooted in his desire to see his father and mother once again. Warwick blinked as March gave out a great belch, wondering if he should perhaps remind him that the manners of a garrison might not do in courtly circles. Warwick shook his head with a wry smile. At thirty, he was not Edward's father, nor the father of any young man, though he might have wished it so. He had two daughters in the care of his wife and when he looked at York's great plow horse of a son, it was hard not to feel a twinge of regret. He put the sadness aside. There was time yet to breed a clutch of boys and, in truth, Edward was more like a younger brother, looking to Warwick for approval in everything he did.

Warwick and Captain Trollope exchanged an amused glance as the earl downed another two flagons as large as the first, slopping beer down his chin and chest.

"We'll be up and marching early, Edward," Warwick said, despite his better judgment. "You'll be hard-pressed to keep your seat with so much ale in you."

"I have a rare thirst, is all," he replied, signaling for a fourth to be brought to him. "It dries the throat to be heaving men into the air."

Warwick chuckled, giving up. From experience, he knew the next day would find the earl groaning and demanding to know why they hadn't stopped him, though the truth was that he was never easy to stop, in anything he chose to do. For all Edward's good cheer, he had a temper well bridled and checked in him. Men sensed it as they edged away from his presence. Like a Calais mastiff, no one with any sense ever wanted to see that temper unleashed.

To Warwick's surprise, Edward turned his fourth flagon over on the grass and waved away the servant who would have refilled it yet again.

"Very well, enough. My senses swim and I will not be the laggard who holds us back tomorrow. How many days to Ludlow, before I see my father?"

"Eight or ten, depending on the ground," Warwick replied. "The roads are good and we can make twenty miles a day, more if we cut west past London."

"It will be eight, then," the young man said, closing his eyes for a moment as the ale made him dizzy. "My father needs these men and I will stand with him. I'll set the pace, Warwick. You'll just have to match me."

Warwick accepted the boast without comment, knowing March was more than capable of making good on it. The archivists at Calais had explained what Attainder meant. The threat to the house of York could be made to encompass the Earl of March as much as his father. The estates and incomes Edward already owned could be taken, as well as the more grievous wound of being denied the name of York and the dukedom he hoped to inherit.

Captain Trollope shifted, easing legs grown stiff as he sat. At fifty years of age, he felt old and about as moss-covered as a mountain compared to Warwick and the son of York. Yet the two young men had brought him home to England and he was intensely grateful for it.

"I pray, my lords, that this Attainder can be struck down without recourse to arms. We heard of St. Albans, even in France, how York saved the king from his dark counselors, wrenching him from their grip and bringing him to the abbey for sanctuary. It was a noble deed. The king's father would have loved the man who saved his son, I do not doubt it."

"You knew King Harry?" Warwick said, raising his eyebrows.

The captain shook his head.

"I was but a boy when he died, my lord, though I wish I had. There was never so fine a man as old King Hal, who won France for us."

"Though men like Somerset and Suffolk lost it, just as surely," Warwick replied. "The truth is as I have told you. This King Henry is just a boy, for all he wears a man's frame. He is surrounded by courtiers and lords who act in his name, each one a king as it pleases him. My father Salisbury saw the truth of it when he broke Percy and Somerset. Now they have grown bold once again, coxcombs teased and plucked upright by a French queen."

Captain Trollope flushed and looked away rather than reply. In normal times, Queen Margaret was held beyond all blame or censure, considered to be far above the sordid maneuvers of the lords and courtiers of England. Even the suggestion of a criticism made the captain uncomfortable. Before Warwick could smooth his ruffled sensibilities, Edward spoke. After so much ale, his voice was too loud, though he did not open his eyes.

"If Attainders are to be issued, it should be against Percy, Egremont, and Somerset. Our fathers took the heads of serpents, but their sons have replaced them. Better to have burned those names from the rolls, so they could not rise again. I will not make that mistake, when this is done." He opened his eyes then, red-rimmed and glaring at the men around him. "My father saved the king and will again, but he showed mercy to houses that should have been attainted and broken. *I* will not."

A moment of silence followed and Warwick pressed his lips tight, though the young man's arrogant speech irritated him sorely. To his surprise, it was Captain Trollope who answered.

"The Englishmen of Calais will stand with you, my lords. We have given that oath. Not against the king of course, which would be its own treason, but certainly against those who use his name."

Warwick saw the concern in the older man, overwhelmed by all the talk of politics and noble houses. Nothing was as simple as a clear enemy to be faced and crushed.

"King Henry will not take the field," Warwick said firmly. "He is like a child, or a monk, given to prayer and sleep from sunrise to darkness. You need have no fear for your loyalties or your oaths, while King Henry sleeps safe in Kenilworth. All that lies ahead is to meet and vanquish those who would rule in his name, as you say. We will go to Ludlow and they will come to us. It will be a hard and bloody business, but we'll be standing when it's done."

"We'll destroy them," Edward added, lying back on the ground and yawning. "And York will go on. I will remember my friends then—and my enemies."

THE MESSENGER REACHED KENILWORTH in the middle of the night, rousing the castle and bringing Queen Margaret from her bed. Still in a sleeping robe, she met the young man in the audience hall, standing with her hair bound and her face creased and pink from sleep.

"Your Highness, I have word from Baron Audley. I was told to say the word 'Retribution' to you."

Despite the tension, Margaret chuckled. She knew only Derry Brewer could have suggested the name of his beloved nag as the password for such a serious business. The messenger looked blankly at her.

"Speak then," she said. "It will do."

The rider was an experienced man. He closed his eyes and recited the words he had been told to memorize rather than risk their interception if they were written down. Unbeknownst to him, another messenger would appear within the hour carrying the same message— Derry's surety against one of them being lost.

"Your Highness, Salisbury is moving. He has begun to march south to Ludlow. The Queen's Gallants will stand in his path, preventing him from joining his men to those of York. The whereabouts of Warwick and March are not yet known. Lord Audley asks respectfully that Buckingham, Percy, Egremont, and Somerset are informed and the King's Gallants are made ready to take the field. Beyond that, God's blessing and good luck."

The messenger opened his eyes, sweat streaming from him in relief at having fulfilled his commission.

"Will you return to Lord Audley's side?" Margaret asked. The man nodded, standing up straight despite his weariness. "Tell him that the Percys and Somerset are with the King's Gallants by Coventry, armed and ready to march. Buckingham and my husband will take the field with them. Give Audley God's blessing and wish him all good fortune. That is all. Now, I would see you fed and rested, but time is short. My steward will find something for you to eat as you ride back."

"You are most gracious, Your Highness," the messenger replied wearily, closing his eyes once more as he murmured the message to himself, committing it to memory. He left the room at a run, leaving Margaret to bite her lip and consider what she would have to say and do to rouse her husband. Henry was the key to it all and he had not worn armor since St. Albans.

CHAPTER 20

The Queen's Gallants were a motley group, Baron Audley thought privately. Many of them had been raised from his own county of Cheshire, as well as Shropshire and the surrounding counties, brought out from villages in twos and threes and dozens. Some were mere hedge knights, with no badge or livery beyond the queen's silver swan pinned to their breasts. Those men at least were trained for battle, poor and ill equipped as they were. The rest were farmhands and smiths, builders and butchers and squires. They had come from all walks of life, with only loyalty to the king and outrage at York in common.

Derry Brewer was the link between them all, Audley mused, watching the spymaster trotting his bony horse through the camp toward him. Brewer had been the man who'd ridden into villages and set up his recruiting post, calling for loyal men to defend the king and queen. With Wilfred Tanner, it had been Derry who rode out to isolated farms, accepting the indentures of sons and brothers and fathers, anyone who would make their mark and accept a silver badge in return. Audley's task had been to turn boys and gentlemen squires into soldiers over the previous months. Some of them had been in his care for half a year or more, while the most recent recruits were still unsure which end of a pike they should hold. It made for chaos and as they'd come together over the previous few weeks, Audley had found Brewer to be a useful enough aide. It was just unfortunate that the man's memories of large-scale battles were all personal, with little sense of the sweep of tactics in the field. Brewer had been a foot soldier as a young man, with no better view of a battle than the ranks afore and behind as he marched. Perhaps for that reason, Derry had refused a formal position in the Gallants, telling Audley that he had too many roles already and could not bear another. The baron smiled to recall the man's cheek as Brewer reined in at his side.

"They are shaping up well, my lord," Derry said, dismounting. "I have not seen so many since France. I was told the queen's arms and mail have reached you. Are you satisfied?"

"No. I will not be satisfied until I see Salisbury's head on the ground," Audley replied. He was aware that many of the men were within earshot and raised his voice to reach them. "But they will stand, these Gallants. We have three times the number marching with Salisbury and he does not know what awaits him. I would stake my life on these men."

Those who heard him grinned at the veteran commander with his white mustaches and beard, repeating his comments to those around them.

"In truth, I would rather take these men against Ludlow—and York himself," Audley went on in a much lower voice. He raised a hand to forestall Derry's objection before it could begin. "Yes, I understand it serves the cause to break Salisbury before he can join hands with York and Warwick. It is the merest common sense. Even so, I chafe. York is the true threat against my king. He is the man they would all see sitting on the throne instead of its rightful occupant.

York is the heart of this rebel faction and I would see him punished and attainted. Indeed, I have waited four years to see it."

With another commander, Derry might have clapped him on the shoulder, but Audley was a stiff old man, not given to display or intimacy of any kind. Instead, Derry bowed his head.

"You will, my lord, I don't doubt it. As soon as we have broken Salisbury, we can swing south and join the King's Gallants. Before the year is out, we'll pluck the thorn."

"That is rash, Master Brewer," Audley said, shaking his head in reproof. "This is no jaunt, no merry march through woodland. Salisbury's men are long-trained and armed with good iron. If we did not outnumber them by so many, I would not be confident."

"But we do. And you are," Derry said, his eyes twinkling.

The older man grunted.

"Yes, well. We'll see. Salisbury can't reach Ludlow without passing us. Yet the man is cunning, Brewer. I saw his work in the far north and he is no one's fool. I make it a rule never to count the banners taken until the battle is over. That is all I have to say to you."

While the two men talked, the vast army of Queen's Gallants had formed up in its three main groups, captains and sergeants bullying them into place. To Audley's eye, it was still ragged work, with too many individuals wandering out of position. Yet the vast force that formed on Blore Heath was at least confident and well fed, nine thousand strong young lads pledged to the queen herself. Their fervor had surprised Derry at first. The badge of her silver swan had begun merely as a device to separate the two armies, as a way of telling them apart. It was too hard to split large forces in the midst of a campaign, and war could call for fast movement and response. Yet the swan badges had been taken up with enthusiasm and pride. The young men of English villages and towns had enjoyed the idea of fighting for a beleaguered queen, taking up her cause as their own. Derry had been forced to deny hundreds asking to wear it, giving them the king's antelope badge instead.

Twelve hundred of the Gallants carried good yew bows, each weapon matched to the owner's height and worth half a year's wage or more in silver. Derry might have wished for archers like Thomas Woodchurch, but he did not have them. Yet bowmen of lesser quality were to be found in every English hamlet, with archery butts hammered to pieces each Sunday. The Gallant archers could fill the sky with shafts when the time came, then again and again, as fast as a breath. Some seven thousand more wore mail and carried axes or iron maces: clubs to smash helmets and heavy blades to kill men once they were down. At the rear, eight hundred knights rode at stately pace. Derry had wanted three or four times that number, but warhorses were a fortune on the hoof and only wealthy men rode to battle. It had cost the king and queen huge sums to provide horses for the hedge knights—men with the skills who could not afford the accoutrements of war. Derry had last looked over the receipts a year before and he refused to do so again, while a torrent of silver still poured out of the royal treasury. Mail shirts and helmets on their own were ruinously expensive. It made sweat break out on his skin even to think of the costs, but there could be no half measures. York's wealth was legendary and he would certainly not stint when it came to supplying his men.

Audley signaled to his servants and they brought his mounting step and his horse, a dark brown gelding that snorted and stamped. Derry was grateful the animal was considerably younger than its owner as he mounted his own, delighted once again to sit in the saddle of Retribution.

"I have chosen this spot with care, Master Brewer," Audley called. "Blore Heath lies in Salisbury's path to Ludlow. You see ahead there? Half a mile or so, that hill with its strip of oak trees and gorse? We will wait in the shadow of that great hedge and, when we come out, we will surround Salisbury's three thousand and cut them to pieces."

"That sounds a little rash, my lord," Derry replied.

Audley raised his eyes to the pale autumn sky.

"Even so. I have waited for this for a long time. The king's honor has been tainted by traitors, forced to retreat to Kenilworth when all England is his. I am content to be his mace, Master Brewer, his instrument. God willing, we will stop them here." The baron dug in his heels, choosing to ride alongside the marching Gallants and be seen.

AT LUDLOW CASTLE, York stared over the battlements, looking north to where he hoped to glimpse Salisbury's army marching in his support. To the west, he could hear the rushing River Teme, winding round the castle, with the village and bridge of Ludford crossing it to the south. He turned a full circle, breathing deeply of the damp air and trying to find peace. The castle had been in an uproar ever since the letters from Salisbury had come in. York grasped the stones hard enough to hurt as he considered the betrayal of his house and name. King Henry would have had no hand in it, he was certain of that. It could only be the French queen who sat rubbing silk threads and making them all dance. He had known she was his enemy ever since she had stolen the king and hidden him away in Kenilworth. That was an old, remembered rage, a move so rash that he could never have predicted it. It could only be her influence that gave weaker men the nerve to act against him. Attainder! The very word was a poison, a threat he must answer without mercy, no matter who had first begun the path. The cool breezes of evening helped his temper, but he would not hold back as he had done at St. Albans. If the king fell into his hands once again, he told himself, his sword would speak for him, answering with a single blow all those who dared to threaten his name and his house. York could still feel the horror that had stolen upon him as his scribes had dug out their records and described the terrible reach of that single document, sealed by the king. The end of a royal line, the end of a king's great-grandson, never mind the titles York would not be able to pass on.

That thought turned his mind to his extraordinary son, returned with Warwick two nights before. York had thought he might burst with pride when he saw the sheer size of the man Edward had become. None of his other sons had achieved such a height or breadth. The youngest of them was still cruelly twisted, though at seven, young Richard had at last learned to clench his lips tight over his shrieks. The contrast between the sons of York had never been more obvious and York had praised Edward at a feast, catching sight for an instant of Richard watching them both. He'd waved the scowling little boy away then, with such great matters to discuss. The house of York had never been stronger, to have such a warrior as the heir—at the moment when the peril was greatest.

York reached for a jug of Malmsey wine he had placed carefully on the stone battlements. He was drunk, he knew, yet for just one night it felt right to blur the edges of his worries, to let them drift away while he stood in the cold and sank cup after cup. It seemed the garrison of Calais had brought many good things home. Warwick too seemed to have hardened in his time away. Salisbury's son had spent his time well, raiding foreign shipping in the Channel, ships from Spain and Lübeck, or any other nation whose captains dared to risk their vessels along that coast. In York's estimation, Warwick had returned a leader, rather than simply one who had inherited a title through his marriage. No one who saw him now would ever question his right to command again.

"And against us, mere swans and antelopes," York muttered. Warwick's two thousand had glimpsed marching columns as they'd approached the lands around Ludlow. They had not been challenged, not with so many men, but the truth was that the country was in arms and York had no idea of the numbers that would stand against him. He thanked God he and Salisbury had gathered and trained so many in the years of peace. Once Salisbury arrived, they would have seven thousand soldiers, enough to stand against a host of the "Gallants," made fools on romantic ideals and the queen's favor.

As his drunkenness became sour, York wondered if Margaret would tie her husband to a horse and parade him while the men cheered. It grated that Kenilworth was a fortress, closed to spies and messengers alike. For all York knew, the king had recovered from his illness to the point where Henry could ride with banners. The thought was like a cold knife sliding between his ribs and he drank again, finishing the jug and feeling his senses swim. He could trust Salisbury and Warwick. He could trust his son and the Calais men he had brought to Ludlow. The rest of the country would see only that the king was threatened once again. The name of traitor would be hissed in York's ears wherever he went, unless he fulfilled their darkest mutterings and took the throne himself.

He nodded, turning back to the north and peering out, lit only by the spinning stars above.

"Come, old friend," he muttered, raising his cup to Salisbury and slurring. "Come to me and let me do what I should have done before. I will not turn aside this time."

THE KING WAS WEEPING, tears making him blind as Margaret and two servants wrestled him into his armor. Margaret was already flushed and embarrassed by her husband's reaction, though the men with her had tended Henry for years, at Windsor and Kenilworth.

She was rougher than they were, tugging Henry's limbs back and forth and pressing hinges closed one by one.

"Leave us now," she said, brushing irritably at an errant lock of hair that curled across her face.

The two servants scurried out without a backward glance, leaving the king and queen alone. Henry's armor creaked as he sat back on his bed. Margaret knelt before him, raising her hand to touch his face as he blinked and stifled sobs like a child.

"There will be no blood, Henry, I have *told* you," she said. In her frustration, she had to fight the urge to slap him. "You must ride out with your Gallants. You must be seen in your armor and with your banners flying. Somerset and Buckingham will command, with Earl Percy and Baron Egremont. I will be there at your side the entire time."

"I cannot," Henry mumbled, shaking his head. "You do not know what you ask."

"I ask only that you act like a King of England!" Margaret snapped.

The words stung her husband, but the drowning was strongly upon him and his face fell slack, the spark of awareness sinking to blankness in his eyes. Margaret lost patience entirely then, shaking her husband hard so that his head lolled.

"Be sharp, Henry! I have moved the entire country to bring you to this place. I have spun England around Kenilworth, like a stone on a string. I have bribed and promised and threatened dangerous men, but you must have the *will* in the end, or you will lose it all. And what will your son's life be worth then? Not a candle in a gale, Henry. Not even that. Stand for me, now. Rise up and stand straight in your armor. Take up your sword."

Henry did not move from the spot where he sat slumped, staring into nothingness. Margaret rose to her feet, looking down on him in anger and despair. Eight thousand men had pledged themselves to fight for the king. Six thousand of them were soldiers brought in by his lords. They had all come, from Somerset and Northumberland to a dozen minor lords like John Clifford, made baron after his father's death at St. Albans. Yet a quarter of the king's army were raw recruits from the towns and villages, no more experienced than her own Gallants. Simply by being present, Margaret knew Henry would give iron to their backbones, would make them stand when the cannons fired and arrows flew and their bowels dissolved in terror. She had clung to the hope that putting Henry in his armor would enliven him, no matter what stage of his illness had him in its grip. The king's doctors had talked of rousing potions hidden in brandy that would excite the blood and drag him back from wherever he hid. She had hoped not to use them, but perhaps there was no other choice.

"Oh, *lie* there, then. Let your tears rust your armor," she said, her fury lending spite to her voice. "I will be away for three days, four at the most. When I return, your doctors will dose you with fire in your veins. They'll *make* you stand! Can you hear me, Henry? If you spend the rest of your life in this weak drowse, you *will* ride against York this month. For me and for your son, if not for yourself."

Her husband looked up at her, his eyes wide and innocent.

"I will, if you ask it of me, Margaret. As you say, if I must, I will."

She felt her fury mount until she was certain she would slap his face. Without another word, she swept out of the rooms. The stewards of the king's bedchamber waited in a huddle further down the hallway and Margaret strode up to them.

"I will be absent for a few days now. Excepting your own selves, no one will speak to the king while I am away. Not a single soul, until I return. Have Master Hatclyf ready to purge and dose him next Tuesday morning. He will rise then, to join his lords and the King's Gallants. Is that understood?"

The men bowed and mumbled their assent, sensing her anger and cowed by it. Margaret went past them, heading down to the stables where three horses were saddled and waiting. Her own Gallants would fight soon, the first army sworn to her that she had ever known. All else would wait while she witnessed that battle and saw the first triumph of Lancaster, so long kindled from the embers. It was Friday evening and she would race to see them destroy Salisbury at Blore Heath. Not even Derry Brewer knew she would be there, riding with just two swordsmen to keep her safe from brigands on the road.

CHAPTER 21

Blore Heath was vast, open land, mile upon mile of scrub gorse and brown grasses. Salisbury's three thousand had made good time over the previous six days, cutting across country and using the main roads only when they matched the direct line southwest to Ludlow Castle. With foot soldiers and cavalry alone, he could have covered the distance in four hard marches, but his carts had slowed his progress to a crawl on boggy ground. He'd suspected from the beginning that this would be no raid or single clash of arms. For all Salisbury knew, he would not see peace and home again for a year or more—so he moved at the pace of his slowest cart teams, carrying food and equipment, tools, spare mounts and small forges, everything he might need for a campaign. The alternative was to rush into battle unprepared, or to depend on York for aid and materiel. Each morning, Salisbury fretted at the lost time, then made the decision once again and pushed on with the carts bringing up the rear. Half the previous day had been lost wrestling the heavy wagons down and across a streambed, though hundreds of men had made the work light.

At least the heath was dry land, with brown rolling hills stretching away south. Salisbury had good maps with him. He had chosen the shortest path to Ludlow and pressed on at the best speed they could make. When one of his forward scouts came galloping back in, his marching ranks were already halfway across the heathland, scattering sheep and heading toward a brook with no bridges marked. Salisbury's thoughts lay ahead to crossing that obstacle and he looked up with a frown as the rider reined in. Two more were racing closer and he felt his pulse quicken.

"Armed men lie ahead, my lord. I saw pikes and flags across a dip in the land."

"How many?" Salisbury replied, staring out as if he could see through the folds and hills of the heath ahead.

"I could not see, my lord, though it was a great number. I caught sight of them and returned with the news."

Both turned to the next man riding in. He was panting as he touched his forelock.

"How many?" Salisbury snapped again. The third rider was coming at full gallop and the news was already spreading through the marching ranks.

"Twice or three times the men here, my lord."

The second scout pointed as he spoke.

"They are hidden by that hill and the line of gorse and trees you can see there."

Salisbury called a halt then, his order passed from captain to captain until the entire mass of men stood still on the heath grasses, all too conscious of the lack of cover all around. The third scout confirmed the numbers and Salisbury swore to himself. He had hoped they were wrong, that such a host could not have been brought together by those standing against him.

"Very well. Go out again and examine the land between us. Find me a crossing place over that brook." Salisbury turned to the other scouts. "You two—get as close as you can, but if they give chase, stay out of range. I need your eyes to watch them. Go!"

The three riders raced off once again and Salisbury was alone to fret and worry. Without the scouts, he would have walked right into an ambush large enough to see him killed. He wanted to withdraw against such numbers, but he clenched his jaw at the thought, knowing he could not. Unless he reached York and supported him, the king's armies would besiege and destroy his closest ally. It would not be long then before they came to Middleham with their Writs of Attainder. Salisbury gripped the high point of his nose, between his eyes, screwing his face up around the fingers. His son Warwick would have reached Ludlow by then and all Salisbury's choices vanished on the breeze. No matter the odds, he *had* to fight. He muttered a prayer under his breath, one that was little more than a blasphemy, then called his captains to attend him.

Sixty men rode to the earl's position in the vanguard, their faces drawn and serious. The news had already spread and Salisbury saw some of the common soldiers reaching down to touch the ground. He frowned at the superstitions of those who would tell soil to be ready for their blood.

"Have the carts brought up to our right flank," he ordered, speaking with deliberate confidence. "We have seen the trap in time." As he spoke, he recalled his son's wedding party and the Percy army that had sought to destroy him then. On that day, he had won by withdrawal, by making them fail against him. Some of the tension left him. He did not need to crush the army he faced. He had only to survive the clash and go around them. His carts could be abandoned and he knew he could maintain a fighting retreat to Ludlow, no more than two days to the south. If he sent his scouts ahead, York might even march reinforcements out to meet him. There would be a way through, if he could just find the right moment to disengage and push on.

The carts came rumbling up from the rear, forty-two heavy wagons loaded down with arms and armor, food and horseshoes, everything he had thought he might need. Their best use then was as a blockade to protect his flank, but Salisbury knew that he could not dig in. He had to reach Ludlow. He had to go on. Yet he saw his men brighten as the solid barrier of carts took shape and he nodded briskly to himself. He had run the Scots ragged on the northern marches for years. Salisbury had fought in dozens of actions in his life, enough to know numbers were not the only key to victory. Discipline and tactics mattered just as much. Perhaps it was time to see what sort of men stood for the king.

"Archers to the fore!" he bellowed across his men. "Slow advance into range. We will show these farmers how a real army fights."

The men cheered dutifully, though as they lurched into step once again, he still saw some of them dipping down across the ranks, touching the dry grasses and crossing themselves with muttered prayers. The teams of carthorses were whipped on with them, guarding their right flank with wood, wheels, and iron. His archers strung their bows and readied quivers on their hips, running their hands through the white goose feathers and swinging their free arms to loosen the muscles. Salisbury untied his shield from where it lay across the haunches of his mount, tugging it onto his armored forearm and taking some satisfaction from the weight. He did not have to win, he reminded himself. He had to get past. After that, the bastards could have his carts and chase him all the way to Ludlow, for all he cared. The brook grew as he approached it, until he was forced to call a halt once more, swearing softly. The river had eaten away at the ground for God knew how long, so that there was a four-foot drop from the banks to the rushing waters, then another steep bank to climb. It would have been a difficult obstacle if they'd been alone on the heath. Salisbury looked up then, seeing a cloud of arrows launch like sparrows from behind the trees and hill ahead.

AUDLEY WAS SATISFIED. The force he faced was barely a third the size of his own. Better still, he had chosen the best spot for miles to defend. Even to reach his position, Salisbury would have to cross the brook, climb a steep hill, and do it all while shafts rained down on his forces. Audley watched as arrows rose on both sides, seeming to float at first and then accelerate as they dove and struck. Most fell short and the few that reached his position on the crest of the hill vanished into gorse bushes without a single cry of pain sounding from his men. The corners of Audley's mouth raised in grim appreciation. There was one last card to play and he had found the right place to lay it down.

"Cannon teams. Fire on the enemy!" Audley shouted over his shoulder. He turned back immediately to watch, flinching despite himself as cracking roars sounded on his left and right. He could see twin black blurs flicker toward Salisbury's forces, vanishing into the ranks of armored men beyond the brook. One appeared to have no effect at all while the other must have skipped and bounced, throwing men down so that its flight could be seen in the sudden collapse of bodies. Audley whistled to himself, wishing only that he had a dozen of the heavy weapons instead of two.

"Again! Fire again!" he roared. "Aim for the center!" The teams rushed around like ants on a carcass and he was glaring at them as minutes passed and they were still not ready.

Salisbury had not been idle when he saw how exposed he was to their range. The entire middle section of Salisbury's forces was pulling back, leaving dead men behind in ones and twos to show where roundshot or arrows had struck.

Audley showed his teeth as the cannons fired once again, crashing across the still air. That second shot was less lucky, with one ball disappearing into the ground and the other killing a single man as he turned to run. Salisbury's forces jerked into greater speed even so, beginning to panic. Audley turned sharply as the Queen's Gallants roared wildly, driven to instant frenzy by the sight of their enemies running before them.

"Hold steady there!" Audley bawled at them. "Captains! Hold them back!" To his fury, the captains could do nothing. Some of his men were already running over the edge of the crest, racing down the other side toward the brook. Audley cursed, his voice growing hoarse as he bellowed for the rest to stay in their position.

Thousands of men poured past him, their faces wild with battle-lust and excitement.

"God damn it!" Audley said. "Bring my horse, quickly!" He was buffeted by the mob his men had become, throwing away all the advantages of the land in their desire to kill a fleeing enemy. Audley was just about alight with rage at the stupidity and fecklessness of the Gallants, but there was no help for it. He had nine thousand to the enemy's three and he could not let them shriek themselves into a rabble against well-trained soldiers. As he mounted, he saw the first of them plunging into the river, leaping down from the banks and crashing through the running water in great surges of spray.

Ahead of them, on the rising ground above the brook, Salisbury's forces came to a halt and re-formed in good order. Audley felt his heart pound with fear as they began a steady march down toward his men, still struggling through the water and over the banks.

In a single, mad rush, his Gallants had given away all their advantages but one. They still outnumbered the enemy, but Salisbury's soldiers were marching downhill against tiring men.

Audley kicked his mount down the slope, reaching the brook and crashing into it at a dangerous speed. He shouted for the Gallants to stand and hold as he went, but the river was wider and deeper than they had known and men struggled in it, exhausting themselves as the numbers piled up. Hundreds stood shivering, calling to those ahead to move on while they waited to clamber up in turn.

Ahead, Salisbury's first rank struck, a wall of sword and axemen holding shields before them. On the wings, Audley could see their horsemen in formation, waiting to counter his own mounted knights and sergeants. They had come down to the brook in slow procession, the more experienced men immune to the urge to chase. Audley could not let his cavalry remain on the far side, though he cursed his luck and the poor discipline of the young fools he led. He dragged a horn from where it bounced by his knee and blew a double note to charge. It served to bring some calm to the foot soldiers as well, who turned and saw Baron Audley was present to command them.

Salisbury's forces pushed forward step by step, commanding the hill above that side of the brook and killing anyone who made it across to stand against them. For a time, the slaughter was appalling and a shiver of fear rippled through Gallants who could see only death ahead. Thousands were still dry, unable even to reach the river in the press of shouting, angry men. Audley had forced his mount through them and gathered a dozen captains, with four or five hundred men finding the wits to stand and hold while the rest came out of the river. Salisbury saw the danger, and his horns could be heard blowing across the heath as his men pressed the Gallants cruelly and his archers shot from the wings until the river began to run red with tumbling bodies.

The men around Audley were cut down by a solid line of mailed soldiers, killing with terrible efficiency. He heard the thunder of hooves as Salisbury's cavalry engaged his own, hammering together hard enough to shake the ground as the two armies struggled on. One group of riders cut straight through his hedge knights and swung in against the flank of the Gallants, sweeping them away until they reached Audley himself. He barely had time to raise his shield and sword before an ax crashed against his chest, hammering a great dent in the plate and making him blow blood. He felt his strength falter as he swung his sword down from behind in a great strike that cut his opponent at the joint of his neck and shoulder, sending the knight reeling. Two more came crashing in and Audley saw a mace raised. He could not bring his sword back in time and the heavy iron club stove in his helmet, breaking his skull and toppling him to the ground.

The Queen's Gallants were pressed on all sides, with arrows still punching into them. Those yet to cross the river lost their desire to take another step against such a terrifying enemy and instead began to move back. Two thousand of the Gallants still fought on around Audley's body, some of them calling to those behind in desperation as they watched them stream away. They knew by then that they would be slaughtered if they ran back to the river so they fought on, falling by arrow or better-armed men cutting them down. In their fury, they cut holes in Salisbury's lines, but it was never enough and the holes closed with shields again and again until the last of them were butchered and sent tumbling.

The cold brook waters drained the blood from all the bodies in it, piled so high in places that a man might almost have walked across on broken corpses. Salisbury's men never crossed the brook, contenting themselves with the slaughter of all those who stood on their side and ignoring the rest.

When the fighting ceased, Salisbury came right down to the water's edge. The sun was beginning to set and he looked across the river to the rising hill and wondered idly if the cannons were still on the ridge. There was no sign of any of the Gallants there. They had all fled.

He cracked stiffness from his neck, though he had not struck a single blow during the fighting. Perhaps a thousand of his men had been killed, a loss he could not afford, no matter what victory they had won for him. Three times as many, or more, lay dead around the brook and in it. His men were already gathering great armfuls of the silver swan badges, laughing at the loot and yelling to their mates to come and collect more.

He called his captains away from their search, fixing them with a stern expression as he decided to ignore the men's bulging pouches.

"Get my carts across this damned river before dark. We'll scout the Gallants' camp, but we must press on." He knew they expected some word of congratulation, but he had lost a third of his army, men he and York needed desperately. He felt no joy of it.

"My lord, will you give us time to see to the wounded?" one of his captains asked. Salisbury glared at him, angry at the decisions he was being forced to make.

"I see no Percys here, no Somersets. There is another army in the field and I must reach Ludlow. If they can walk, they must follow us at a slower pace. Leave a good knife with those who will not last the night. We have lost half a day here, gentlemen. We cannot lose more. Be ready to march."

His captains nodded, losing their grins and taking up the responsibilities of their rank once more. One by one they turned away, looking over the slaughterhouse they had made of the heath and the river that would run red for days afterward.

MARGARET ROSE to her feet from where she had crouched perfectly still for so long. It was hours since she had settled into that spot, a hill to the east of the heath that gave her a good view of Audley's forces and then the army of Salisbury as it crossed the land. She was white with horror at what she had witnessed, a vision of cruelty and violence that continued to flash pictures into her mind in the twilight, making her want to brush them away like flies landing on her skin. In her imagination that morning, she had expected neat formations facing each other, not the chaos and screaming madness of men crushed and drowning in a river, hacked down and shot from close range by laughing, jeering enemies. She shook her head, trying in vain to clear it of the memories. Those men had sworn an oath to her and worn her swan. They had come to that place in trust and martial spirit, ready to fight for the king and queen against foul traitors. As she dragged her eyes away, she could still see the dark stain in the waters as the brook leached their life's blood. Margaret shuddered, feeling small and cold herself with the twilight closing in. She did not know what happened after a battle, whether Salisbury would stop to bury the bodies, or whether he would press on to Ludlow. There were still dozens of his horsemen milling around on the hillsides and she was struck by a sudden fear that one of them might see her and give chase.

Her throat dried and she fluttered her hands at the thought. Two men waited for her at the bottom of the hill. She had not let them climb the slope to watch with her, knowing that to be spotted by anyone was to invite disaster. They had seemed strong and fearsome warriors that morning, but as she climbed down, they looked as frail as any of the other men who had died that day.

Margaret mounted without a word, not trusting herself to speak. Behind, she heard some horn blowing once again and she shrank in the saddle, the growing shadows making it feel as if she was already being run down by huntsmen. Leaving the heath behind, they rode a mile and she looked back more than once.

In the first village they passed, Margaret saw the forge light of a smith, still working at his trade, though the hour was late. Her mind was on the threat of pursuit and the delight Salisbury would take in her capture. She almost rode on and then reined in sharply at the sound of hoof nails being hammered into place.

"Fetch out the smith," she said, relieved to hear her croaking voice was firmer than she had expected.

The man who came out at her order was wiping his hands on an oily cloth. He took in the fine cloak of the beauty staring down at him and chose to bow deeply.

"Do you need a shoe, mistress?" he called. He reached out to pat the neck of her horse and froze as one of her guards drew a sword, a sound the man knew very well.

"I need them all taken off—and reversed on the hooves," Margaret said.

Her mother had complained of poachers doing the same thing when she was a little girl in Saumur. Anyone riding after them would find a set of tracks heading the wrong way and take another path. It was a simple enough trick, though the smith stared in surprise, glancing off at the road behind them. Margaret could see him guessing they had come from the battle fought that day, confusion and a little fear written clearly on his soot-dark face.

"Pay the man for the work, a half noble," Margaret said.

The smith's eyes widened and he snatched the gold coin out of the air as it was flicked to him, patting it away carefully. Margaret dismounted and the smith kept his silence, lifting each hoof and yanking out the nails with quick neatness, dropping the bent ones into a pouch to be straightened and replacing them with a dozen more, hammered in hard. He did not dawdle, made nervous by the glances thrown down the road behind the small group. In just a short time, all three of the horses had been shod in reverse and they mounted again. Margaret hesitated, unable to resist a word before she left the man behind forever.

"You have served the royal house well, Master Smith," she said. "In the king's name, I ask that no one else hears what you did tonight."

The smith was very aware of the armed men watching him. He backed away, nodding and holding his hands up until he was safely in the smithy, warmed by the forge.

Margaret dug in her heels. Night had come while she waited, but the moon was up and it was a good road and a clear sky. She kicked hard for Kenilworth, safety, and home.

CHAPTER 22

S alisbury's men limped into Ludlow, footsore and weary beyond belief. The earl they followed had forced them on for fifty miles, driven by the terrible fear that he would find York's castle under attack. They'd arrived barely able to stand, never mind fight, but there was no sign of a besieging army. Salisbury passed on his thanks to his captains, allowing them to make camp alongside the four thousand already there.

York's soldiers watched as Salisbury's starving men clustered around cooking pots, or simply lay down on the open grass to sleep. The newcomers had no carts with them after the forced march. As the moon appeared low in the sky, hundreds of York's sergeants walked over to the huddled groups of weary men, passing out spare blankets and sharing water, ale, and meat, whatever they had, in exchange for news of the battle.

The arrival of Salisbury's army brought a heightening of tension across the great camp around Ludlow. New lines of wooden spikes were hammered into place and many of the men blessed the river that ran round the west and south of the castle, forcing any enemy to come from the east.

Salisbury's carts arrived the following day, allowing his men to set up tents and give back some of what they had been lent. The walking wounded from the heath came in a day after that, staggering along and collapsing with relief at the sight of acres of tents around the York stronghold. Fully eight hundred men were missing from the rolls called, while many others were little more than a drain on the healers and their supplies.

On the evening of the third day, York's scouts rode in with the news they'd all known would come. The King's Gallants had been sighted twelve miles off. Every man of the six thousand at Ludlow ate a good meal, repaired any broken kit, and sharpened his weapons. Those who had horses tended to them, while the host of archers took up position on the flanks of the castle. Salisbury's carts were made into a barricade once more, blocking the southern approach from Ludford, across the bridge.

As night fell, York's army settled down into disturbed sleep, jarred from it by single cries and bad dreams before they pressed their eyes shut once again and tried to lose the dark hours. Ludlow was the stronghold, but the river protected their backs as much as the stone walls behind them. Every soldier knew that, at the last, they would be allowed to run inside the walls for protection—but if it came to that, the battle would be lost and the castle would surely fall. They were the shield and the sword, not Ludlow's battlements. The guard shift changed at midnight and, by then, a light frost made the camp sparkle. The guards stamped and blew on their hands, watching for the dawn.

The moon vanished to the south, its brightness fading quickly. As the sky eased from starlight and blackness to the first shades of gray, Salisbury and Warwick climbed the stairs to the highest point to stare east. York and Edward of March were already there, talking in low voices as Neville father and son reached the top step.

"Come here and you will see them," York said, beckoning.

Salisbury squinted into the gloom, spotting tiny points of light in the distance, shifting and darting back and forth.

"How many?" Salisbury asked, as much a question to the younger men with sharp eyes as York himself.

"However many you left alive at the heath—and the king's forces," York replied.

He had railed and shouted on the first evening, when he heard how many Salisbury had allowed to escape. His friend had endured the tirade, knowing it sprang from fear. It was true Salisbury might have tracked and butchered the Queen's Gallants streaming away from him. He might equally have been overwhelmed by them as they regrouped and fought back. He had chosen instead to follow through with the original plan and reinforce Ludlow. There was no point in wishing for different choices to have been made.

Far away, the line of torches grew and grew, spreading across the horizon until the four men could only stare in grim silence. York knew the land to the east better than anyone and he was most affected, rubbing the back of his scalp and shaking his head.

"It might be a trick, still," he said. "Men far spaced perhaps to carry the torches, making them seem a greater host than they truly are."

He did not believe it and none of the others replied. The sun would reveal the extent of the king's army facing Ludlow.

"Ludlow has never been breached," York said after a time. "These walls will stand long after us all, no matter how many tanners and squires they have found to march against it this year."

The sky behind the approaching army was brightening slowly, clear and pale. York stiffened as he began to make out the dark shapes of cannon being trundled along with the host. Once he knew to look for them, he peered further, leaning out over the stones until Salisbury wanted to take his arm before he fell. A dozen heavy serpentines had been dragged toward Ludlow, each one capable of smashing an iron ball through a full mile of clear air. Against castle walls, even those of Ludlow, they would wreak terrible destruction.

"They've come to break us," Salisbury murmured.

He sensed York's anger at his words, but the light before sunrise was strong enough for them all to see the extent of the king's forces. They could barely make out the noble banners in the soft gray, but the numbers were appalling, at least twice the men they had gathered in the name of York.

"I see the Percy colors," Edward said, pointing. "Lord Gray is there. Exeter. Buckingham. Somerset on the left, do you see? Is that the banner of the Cliffords?"

"It is," York replied. "A great pack of curs and fatherless boys, it seems. I should have killed Buckingham at St. Albans, when he was laid out with his face split in two. Look for the king's lion pennants. Or the queen's swan. That wolf bitch will be among them, I am certain."

At the distance of half a mile, the royal army halted, blowing horns to wake the dead, or at least any Yorkist soldiers who might somehow have slept through the clash and rumble of their approach. The ranks of torches were extinguished as full dawn came and York and Salisbury could only stare in dismay as dozens of armored knights rode up and down the first rank, carrying the streaming banners of all the houses they represented, led by three gold lions on red. It was a display meant to intimidate and shock—and it did its work well.

In the front rank, the cannon teams raised the immense black iron barrels and placed wooden blocks under them. York clenched his right hand as he saw braziers lit and men scurrying with bags of corned black powder. Right across the king's army, thin streams of smoke rose into the clear air. The men on the battlements heard the order, a single voice that was answered with a crashing thunder and such an explosion of smoke that half the royal force vanished behind it.

No iron balls soared across the distance between them. The flame and smoke had been a warning and a demonstration of power. No one who saw it was left in any doubt that the next volley would tear men apart and hammer castle walls. Yet it did not come. Instead, a single herald rode forward beyond the rest, accompanied by six men. Two of them blew horns while the rest carried royal banners, the lions fluttering. They reached the edge of York's forces and the herald declaimed at the top of his voice. Few of his words reached the battlements, though the four men above craned to hear. York watched sourly as the herald finished his speech and continued out of sight, heading into the castle. He would be allowed to enter, to deliver his message to the master of Ludlow.

York turned to the earls standing with him, his eyes resting at last on the son who towered above them all in his armor. Like the rest of them, York was pale, his confidence shattered. He knew the king's herald would be brought up to him and he spoke quickly before they were no longer alone.

"I had not thought to see Henry himself come against me," he said. "However they have done it, I do not know if the men will stand, not now." The anguish felt by that small group on the battlements would be flooding through every soldier below. It was one thing to raise arms against another lord, especially those York accused of being traitors and manipulators of the king and queen. It was quite another to stand against the King of England himself in the field. They could all see the pavilion of flags and banners being raised in the center of the line.

"Half of them are farmers' sons," Edward said into the silence. "They can be routed, just as they ran at Blore Heath. Let Warwick and me take our two thousand against the flank. We'll roll them up, while the rest assault the center. Our men are veterans, sir. They are worth two of those men or more, each one." Even as he spoke, the Earl of March could sense the despair in Salisbury and his father. He looked to Warwick for support, but even he shook his head.

Salisbury glanced to the top of the steps, gauging whether he could yet be overheard.

"My father suffered many raids into his lands," he said suddenly, "all led by the same Scots laird. Ralph Neville was a cautious man, but on one occasion he found himself outnumbered, caught in the open. He knew if he stood and fought, he would have lost it all."

The three men with him were listening as Salisbury peered again at the steps.

"He sent his serving men forward, three big lads with two chests of silver, leaving them alone in a meadow while the clansmen crept up like the wolves they are. Perhaps it was their unexpected good fortune that made them wary, or simply because they had already learned the earl was a cunning enemy. The laird's men expected a trap and by the time they realized there was none, my father had retreated to a stronghold and was out of their reach."

"What of the silver and his men?" Edward asked.

Salisbury shrugged.

"They were all taken. The men were killed and the silver spirited away to the laird's longhouse. They drank themselves to a stupor at the wealth they had won and they were still asleep when my father's men fell on them from the darkness. He had brought more than enough for the work and they'd followed the tracks of clansmen carrying the heavy chests, right through field and forest. My father's men killed the laird in his home and slaughtered his bondsmen before they could rise and defend themselves. In the morning, they took back their chests and returned across the border. It was a memory my father cherished in his final years. It kept him warm in the cold, he said, to remember their surprise."

A clatter of footsteps made Salisbury raise a hand in warning to them all, snapping his mouth shut on whatever else he might have added. The king's herald was dressed in pink and blue, a jay among crows on that roof. He was panting and he bowed elaborately, acknowledging the three earls and York last of all.

"My lords, I speak for his Royal Majesty, King Henry of England, Ireland, and France, Protector and Defender of the Realm, Duke of Lancaster and Cornwall, God's blessing on his name." The herald paused, swallowing uncomfortably under the cold gazes of the men he addressed. "My lords, I am to say that the king will pardon all those who have taken up arms against him. He will show mercy to any man who accepts his pardon without delay." He had to summon his nerve to go on, a sheen of sweat appearing along his brow. "Excepting only the Duke of York, the Earl of Salisbury, and the Earl of Warwick. Those men are declared traitors and must be handed over to the royal forces and the king's own authorities."

"What of the Earl of March?" Edward demanded, honestly affronted that he had not been mentioned.

The herald looked nervously at the enormous man, shaking his head.

"I was not told to say that name, my lord. I . . . cannot . . ."

"Go, sir," York said suddenly. "I will send my answer at noon, with my own man. Will you return to the king's side?"

"Yes, my lord. His Highness awaits what answer you would have him hear."

"King Henry stands then, in the host? He is present on the field?"

"I saw him with these eyes, my lord. I swear it. I will await your answer, if you wish."

"No," York replied, dismissing him with a sharp gesture. "Return to your master."

The herald bowed again and vanished, escorted down through the castle by York's staff.

Salisbury could see York readying himself to snap furious orders. As the herald left, he spoke quickly.

"My father's tale is the key to this lock. We cannot stand today. We do not have the men or the walls to resist such an army."

"You'd have me *run*?" York demanded, rounding on his oldest friend.

"Has the king not offered a pardon?" Salisbury replied instantly. The herald had aided him, unknowing. Yet Salisbury still had to find words that would placate York's prickly honor. "Tell your captains to wait for your return. Tell them the king is just a puppet of the Percys, or a pawn of his French queen." He held up his hand and spoke more loudly as York began to argue. "Tell them you will come back in the spring and that a leader chooses the place he will stand—and does not let his enemies choose it for him! God knows, the king is not popular. He has hardly left Kenilworth in—how long now? No parliaments called for three years, no order in the land. There is little love for him—more for you. Let your men and mine have their pardons, Richard! Let them return to their homes, knowing that this is just a breath between blows, before we break this royal rabble into pieces, lord by lord, man by man!"

York stared, his mouth slightly open. He looked as if he wrestled with betrayal, and Salisbury's son added his voice to the argument.

"We cannot win here," Warwick said softly. "You know that is the truth. We could *die* here, in all certainty, but I would rather we give them their small triumph—and then come back and fall on them when they are drowsing and drunk on their success. The final victory is what matters, my lord York, not how it comes about."

The anger seeped out of York and he let his head droop, leaning back on the stone battlements. Ignoring Warwick, his eyes beseeched Salisbury.

"You think we can return, after such a loss?" he said, his voice hoarse with pain.

"They have surprised us here. We will surprise them in turn. There is no dishonor in such a course, Richard. If there were, I would blow the horns with you and settle it today, one way or the other. Would you have me throw my life away in this place?" Salisbury raised his chin. "If you give the order, we will fight to the last man. We will strike hard at the king's—"

The tramp and jingle of men in mail interrupted him and all four looked over the battlements to the gathered armies far below. Warwick exclaimed as he saw the colors of the marching soldiers.

"What are they doing?" he said in shock. "That is Captain Trollope leading my men away! What is he . . . ?"

He fell silent as the ranks of six hundred Calais veterans raised a white banner and approached the king's forces. They were met with a hostile bristling of pikes as well as knights and lords riding out to meet them. As Warwick watched in disgust, the ranks parted to allow the marching column to pass through.

"God's wounds, that's the end of it," Salisbury said. "We needed those men." He turned to York. "It is no small thing to stand against the king, my friend. If you'll depart this place, we can prepare our captains for our return. I will not be idle, I swear it. I'll send each one a letter swearing my loyalty to the king and asking only that he defends Henry from evil men."

"I cannot walk away!" York shouted, silencing him. "Do you not understand? If we leave tonight, we will be attainted, every one of us! York and Salisbury, gone! Warwick, gone! March, gone! My life's work, my house, my name, blackened by their writs, destroyed and broken! Damn you. Damn King Henry and his French bitch. I would rather die here, with these walls at my back."

"I would rather live," Warwick said, speaking firmly across York's grief. "I would live so that I can overturn any law they make. I would live so that I can hold Parliament in my hand and make them tear up these Writs of Attainder. And I would live so that I can take my vengeance against my enemies, with men who understand that York too is a royal line. That is what I would do, my lord. Yet my father spoke the truth. If you wish, I will stand with you as the soldiers despoil your home and those you love. I will remain at your side as they are let loose to rape and torture, to burn and shatter everything you hold dear. That is my oath and the strength of my word. My fate lies with you."

York looked around at the three men waiting on his decision. He was trapped, caught between two paths, each so appalling that he could only stare and shake. After a long time, he nodded.

"I have friends in Ireland, still. Men who care nothing for Attainder and who would protect me in my estates. Will you come with me?"

"Not I," Salisbury said. "Calais will keep me out of the clutches of the king's officers, but it is close to Kent. Close enough to leap over on a dark night next year."

"Warwick?" York asked.

"Calais," Warwick said firmly.

"Edward?" York said, turning and looking up at his son, standing there like a tree above them all. The young man squirmed, caught between conflicting loyalties.

"If you will allow it, father, I would rather return to France. There's nowhere better placed to gather an army and cross back."

If his son's choice was another blow, York did not show any sign of it. He nodded, clapping Edward on the shoulder.

"There is a path and a bridge across to meadows, to the west of Ludlow. It's a quiet route and it will take us far away. I must speak to my wife before I leave, as well as my captains. They must be told what to expect. What say you to April, six months from now, for our return?"

"Give me nine months, my lord," Warwick replied. "Nine months and I will gather enough men to win back everything we have lost."

York nodded, feigning confidence against a chilling desolation that numbed his limbs.

"Very well. I will expect to hear you have landed on the first day of July, on your souls, all of you. Give me your oaths that you will set foot on English soil in July next year, or be ever known as faithless men, oathbreakers. With God's blessing, we will pay them in full for this disgrace."

All three earls gave a private vow, gripping Richard of York by the arm and kneeling on the battlements. In somber mood, they left the heights then, to arrange for their escape.

As evening came, torches were lit across Ludlow Castle and all through the village of Ludford to the south. The great gates of the fortress were thrown open and the first ranks of armored knights rode in, carrying the banners of the noble houses they represented. Duchess Cecily of York stood to meet them in the open courtyard beyond the gates, stiff and still as armed horsemen swept by her, seeking out some sign of her husband, or the first breath of a trap. They tramped and rushed all over the castle, kicking in doors and reducing the servants to terror as they quivered with their heads down, expecting a blade to land at any moment.

Two hours passed before Queen Margaret entered Ludlow, riding ahead of a hundred of her Gallants. She sat side-saddle on her horse and it was Thomas, Lord Egremont, who helped her to dismount. Her face was icy with disdain as she reached York's wife and regarded the older woman with cold fascination.

"Your brave husband has run, then," Margaret said. "A coward at the last."

"And yours is nowhere to be seen. Is he sleeping, or at prayer?" Cecily replied sweetly. Margaret's eyes narrowed as Cecily went on. "You have won tonight, my dear, but my husband *will* claim what he is owed. You must never doubt that."

"He will not have this place," Margaret said, gesturing to the stone walls all around and smiling at the older woman who had once intimidated her. "Ludlow will be sold now York is made common, with every other stone and scrap of land he once owned. Where will you rest your head then, Cecily? With no servants to tend you, or any name beyond wife to a traitor? I have seen the writs, with my husband's Seal proudly on them. You will not find shelter with Salisbury, or with Warwick after this month. They are all subject to Attainder and that foul trinity is cracked apart."

Cecily of York shuddered as if the words were blows. Not far off, they could both hear yells and screams as the king's soldiers tore through the village of Ludford, unrestrained as they followed orders to search for York.

"I married a man, dear," Cecily said, "rather than a child. Perhaps if you had done the same, you might understand why I am not afraid."

"I married a *king*," Margaret snapped, driven to fury by the woman's calm superiority.

"Yes, you did. And he lost France in return. I do not think it was the best bargain, dear, do you?"

Margaret was tempted to strike Cecily of York in her anger. She might have done so if the woman's young children had not been herded out around her. The eldest, Edmund, had one arm around two younger sisters. At sixteen, he had most of a man's growth, though he wore only a belted tunic and hose and bore no weapon. Edmund carried the smallest lad on his hip. Richard was awkward there, clinging to his brother like a frightened cat and staring around with wide eyes.

Cecily turned to them and held out her arms for the lad.

"Come here to me, Richard," she said, smiling as he almost leaped from his brother to her arms so that she staggered under his weight.

The little boy winced as he clambered to a safe position, making a low, animal groan until Cecily kissed him on the forehead. She turned back to Margaret then, raising her eyebrows in silent question.

"I must take my children away now, unless you have more to say to me?"

One of the little girls began to sob and wail at the sight of so many strange soldiers in their home. Cecily shushed her, waiting for the queen to allow her to go. Margaret bit her lip, but she took no joy in dismissing York's wife. She was left staring after them as they walked out through the gates, confused by her own envy and sadness.

CHAPTER 23

Margaret breathed deeply, enjoying the smells filling the Palace of Westminster. Christmas was just three days gone and though December the twenty-eighth was Herod's day, where the old tyrant had ordered the death of children, it was also the day the royal kitchens would bake all the remnants of venison into pies and send them out. They took the "umbles": the liver and the heart, the brains and feet and ears, simmering them all into a rich gravy before sealing them in pastry. The royal kitchen staff then carried them out to a shout of triumph from those gathered outside the palace. The umble pies would be cut into thick slices and born off still steaming for families to enjoy. Margaret had tasted a slice of one and found the thick juice took a while to work from her mouth and teeth.

She looked down on the crowd from a high window, content to observe them as the line of cooks came out, each bearing a tray and a heavy pie, with knives on their hips to cut the shares. There were no children in the crowd, she noticed. On Herod's day, they were often beaten in memory of that king's cruelty and the boys and girls of

London made themselves scarce as best they could, keeping their heads down and getting on with work in silence, rather than remind their masters of the tradition. Men and women were there, smiling and lighthearted as they clustered around the line of cooks. Many had brought their own cloths and baskets to carry a piece away.

Margaret ran a hand over her stomach, feeling the heaviness there from all she had eaten over the previous few days. She had sat through a Christmas service in Westminster Abbey with her husband nodding beside her. Carollers had gathered outside to dance and sing for the birth of Christ, banned from entering the churches for how they disrupted the congregation. They had begun a scuffle, she recalled, fighting in the street until her guards had gone out with cudgels and sent them roughly on their way with kicks and blows.

Derry Brewer cleared his throat behind her and Margaret turned, smiling at the sight of him in his best, brushed garments. It was hard to reconcile the image of the man who had just entered with the thin and shivering monk who had come to her in Windsor, five years before. Derry had put on weight in the intervening time, his waist and shoulders growing heavy. Yet he looked strong still, like a boar who had not lost its cunning with age. She touched her own stomach lightly at the thought. Grief and worry had helped her to avoid the same fate, perhaps because her womb had remained unfilled, after Edward. That thought was a pang of sorrow, and she forced a smile to greet her spymaster.

"What news, Derry? My steward told me there would be children beaten through London this afternoon. I think he was playing with me, knowing I spent my childhood in France. Is it true?"

"It has happened, my lady, if the apprentices have grown rowdy and their masters have lost patience. There have been riots before, on this day. Not every year, though. If your wish is to see such a thing, I can certainly arrange it for you."

Margaret laughed and shook her head.

"Would that all my desires could be met in such a way, Derry. That is how I imagined being a queen, when I was a girl, crossing the Channel for the first time." Her words brought back a memory of the man who had brought her to England, William de la Pole, Duke of Suffolk. Sadness came to her eyes then, in his memory.

"How goes your work, Derry? Is the fleet ready?"

"I have every shipwright on the south coast working night and day. New vessels or the old repaired, the fleet will be finished, my lady, by the spring. We'll have ships to take an army such as France has not seen since '46. It will be enough to scorch Salisbury and Warwick and March out of Calais, I am certain. If they have gone further into France, it will be alone. The French king would never allow English soldiers to march or camp on his land. We'll secure Calais for the Crown, my lady, never doubt it. We'll deny that stepping-stone to the king's enemies, whatever they intend."

"And after that, York, in Ireland," Margaret said.

It was spoken as a half question, and Derry answered it as he had a dozen times before.

"My lady, you know I have said Ireland is a wild place—and York is well loved there, from his time as King's Lieutenant." He cleared his throat uncomfortably. "He has friends in Ireland who believe the house of York . . . well, that it should be the royal line. They will resist, their men with them. My lady, taking a fleet across twenty miles of sea to Calais is no great step. We can blockade that port and land an army, cannon, anything we need, though I hope they will surrender before we are forced to breach the walls. I do not want the French king to feel he has another opportunity born from our strife! Ireland . . . is somewhat different, my lady. To land an army on that wild east coast would be a proper campaign, a year or more away from England when those men might find some better use at home. The

Irish are sullen folk. Their lords will resent the challenge to their authority and just one spark could set off a rebellion. I have said I cannot recommend such a course, at least this year. Please, let me consider York once again when we have Calais in our grasp. God loves those who plan too far, my lady. He loves to show them the cost of their ambitions."

Margaret pursed her lips, making a moue in her frustration.

"I cannot let that bird rest," she said. "He escaped when we had him at bay, scorning all my Gallants. Can you understand, Derry? I saw Salisbury slaughter good men who had come to the field with my badge, for love of me. Where is the punishment for that foul day? Where is the justice, with Salisbury and his son safe in France, York in Ireland? I want them brought home in chains, Derry! For all they have cost me, for all they have threatened."

"Your Highness, I know. It would be Christmas once again, if I could see York and Salisbury brought back for trial. I was at St. Albans, my lady. I know the debts they have run up—which remain. They will be paid, I swear it. With sixty ships, packed full of men and cannons, we'll dig them out like foxes. I ask only for your patience."

Margaret nodded stiffly, waving a hand to dismiss him. Derry bowed, feeling his back twinge. God, he was getting old! He considered all the things he had to do that day and whether he could fit in an hour of sword practice with one of the king's guards. He had learned to ride like a knight, after all. He had decided to learn to fight like one, though it hurt his pride to be knocked about like an unruly child. He made a decision, determined to work up a sweat, no matter what it cost him.

Margaret had turned away to the window as he left, smiling once again at the sight of London crowds. The new year was just days away and she had high hopes for it, more than any of those gone before. First Calais, then York, wherever he had hidden himself. Her husband's enemies would be hunted down and Henry could live out his years in peace. England would be stronger for all the suffering, Margaret was certain, just as she had grown strong in the forge-heat. She could still recall the innocent she had been, a slip of a girl who spoke in broken English, a mere whisper of the woman she had become.

For a dark January night, the sea was calm. It had to be, for what Warwick had in mind. He and his chosen men had fretted through three days of a terrible blow raging across the Channel, taking comfort only in the fact that the royal fleet would never be able to come out of port in such rough seas.

The year 1460 was still young, with just three months having passed since their flight from Ludlow. While York sailed for Ireland, Salisbury, Warwick, and Edward of March had slipped over to France in a herring boat. That had been the lowest point for all of them, though the three earls had thrown themselves into plans for their return almost as they set foot in the Calais fortress. Salisbury's brother William, Lord Fauconberg, had visited them later, bringing a hundred men with him and two sturdy caravelles to be tied up in the sheltered docks. As one who had been favored among Henry's supporters, Fauconberg had also brought news of a Lancastrian fleet being assembled in Kent, ships to land ten thousand or more in the spring. If there had been any doubt in their minds about the future path, his words had dispelled them. The Writs of Attainder had been issued, and they would not be left alone in their exile.

The port of Sandwich was quiet and still in the small hours of a frozen winter morning. Warwick and Salisbury walked together along the deserted quayside, with Edward of March just a step behind. Some forty men followed in staggered groups of six or a dozen at a time. In all, two hundred veteran soldiers had crossed to England that night, wearing simple, rough clothes of wool and leather. Armor or mail would only have been a hindrance for the sort of quiet work they planned. In the darkness, they had a chance to pass for king's crews or Kent fishermen. Yet Sandwich had been raided by the French many times over the centuries. Enemy ships had slipped across that channel before, and Warwick was only surprised the church bells had not already begun to toll a warning across the town.

Their luck held for an age. They had tied up four small ships among the shadowy royal fleet, some forty at anchor, with no more than a few lamps swinging between them all. The town itself was black against the night sky, with so many of its inhabitants used to rising before dawn. Warwick and his father had timed their crossing to arrive when the fishing crews were asleep, and the king's sailors would still be sleeping off their ale.

Warwick turned sharply at a strangled yell from one of the merchant cogs, all creaking in their berths. He could not tell the source. The ships tied up along the dockside were so close together, his men had been able to clamber onto one and then step across to the next. For those anchored further out, small boats carried Warwick's men to ladders set in the wooden walls, creeping aboard as silently as they could manage. At that moment, they were sprinting across dark decks in bare feet, clubbing or knifing the poor souls left to guard them as quietly as they could. The king's crews were all ashore and each ship held just a few young men given the task of tending a lamp and keeping watch against the French.

Warwick was looking out to sea and he jumped as his father gripped his arm. Lamplight was approaching along a side road leading toward the waterfront. Perhaps because of the presence of so many of the king's soldiers in town, the local watchmen were less alert than they might have been. As Warwick and March darted forward, they could hear snatches of laughter and conversation, some story of the Christmas just past. Warwick could sense the huge shadow that was Edward of March at his right shoulder. Dressing the young giant in fisherman's wool had been a lost cause. No one could look at him and not know he was a soldier.

There were six men in the small group that rounded the corner and came to a shocked halt. Warwick could see one of them carried a large handbell to rouse the town. He swallowed. The two groups stood frozen, staring at each other.

"The French!" one of the watchmen hissed, raising the bell.

"Shut up, you fool," Warwick said sharply. "Do we *look* French?"

The man hesitated, up on his toes as if he'd sprint away at any moment. The one leading them pulled back the shutters on his lamp, the gleam revealing some of the shadowy men trotting up behind Warwick. The watchman cleared his throat carefully, knowing that the wrong word would surely get him killed.

"We don't want any trouble, whoever you are," he said, trying to put some authority into a voice that was strained and shaking. The man's eyes flickered to Edward, sensing his readiness for violence.

"Earls Warwick, Salisbury, and March," Warwick answered. He didn't care who heard they'd been there. All he wanted was to get the ships away and be gone by the time the sun came up. It wasn't as if the royal crews could chase them in fishing boats.

The watchman leaned closer, staring. To Warwick's surprise, he smiled. Without turning around he muttered a command to those with him not to run.

"You'll need to tie us up, then," he said. "Or the king's men will see us hanged in the morning."

"Sod that, Jim!" the bell-carrier hissed at him. "They'll flog us anyway."

"You'll survive," the watchman snapped. "If you sound that bell, Pete, I'll batter you meself."

Warwick had been frowning as he followed the exchange. He'd expected a quick, brutal scuffle with the watchmen, then perhaps a race to the last ships in the dock as the town came alive to repel invaders. As the furious whispered argument went on, Warwick glanced around at Salisbury and March. York's son shrugged at him.

In frustration, the one with the lamp suddenly rounded on his companion, reaching for the clapper of his bell and snatching it out of his hand with a dull clunk.

"There you are, my lord. We won't give you any trouble."

"Do I know you?" Warwick asked.

"Jim Wainwright, my lord. We've not met, though I do remember you chasing me along an alleyway a few years back." Wainwright grinned oddly, showing missing teeth. "I was walking with Jack Cade then."

"Ah," Warwick replied warily, understanding at last. Thousands of Kentish men had come home with their spoils after that terrible night. He wondered how many of them still remembered the rebellion with fondness.

"It ain't right what they did to Cade and his mates," Wainwright said, raising his chin. "These boys don't know what it was like, but I do. We were pardoned by the queen, my lord, all sealed and fine—and then they still sent Sheriff Iden to hunt us down. I lost good friends to that bastard. Men who'd been pardoned, just like me." He took a moment to glare back at his companions, making sure they were not trying to sidle away. "We've all heard the king's crews talking about the rebels in Calais. I reckon you were on the wrong side once, but perhaps you've learned better by now, eh?"

"Perhaps I have," Warwick said faintly, making the man chuckle.

"That's what I thought, my lord." Wainwright looked to his left as a black ship eased away from the dock, the sail heaved up onto the yard by silent figures.

"It's the ships, is it? You're after the king's ships?"

Warwick nodded, surprised to hear Wainwright chuckle aloud.

"They'll be furious in the morning, I know that much. It seems to me, though, that I'm not going to side with king's crews. Not when I've a chance to pay them back for Cade." Wainwright scratched his chin as he thought. "And if you need men, my lord, you could do a lot worse than look for them in Kent, that's all I'm saying. There's more than me who still bear a grudge or two about that night. There's some who don't like what happened at Ludlow, neither."

"What of Ludlow?" Warwick said softly. "We left when there was no hope, not before." He saw the watchman looked embarrassed.

"Word is the king's fine, brave lads were let loose on the village there," Wainwright said. "Worse than French raiders. It was the talk of the country at Christmas. Ravishment and killing of innocents. Terrible thing. King Henry didn't stop it, or even try to, so they say. I tell you, my lord. You just call 'Kent' when you're ready and see what happens, that's all. We don't like to hear of king's men killing women and children and that's the truth. You'll get more than a few volunteers for a spot of vengeance—and we're the ones who broached the Tower, don't forget. We might not have mail shirts and that, but then a Kentish man don't need one. He's in and out quick."

Salisbury had listened to the exchange without a word. He looked up to the turning stars above and tapped his son on the shoulder.

"We should go on," he murmured. "Tie these men and take the last of the ships."

Even as they'd been talking, the dark rows of cogs and caravelles had thinned like teeth being drawn, more and more of them with ropes hanging loose, easing out onto the deeper waters beyond. No more than half a dozen remained, their lamps snuffed and their decks cleared.

Warwick nodded. He'd been expecting a fight on the docks and was still ready for the sound of church bells across the town. It was time to leave.

"Thank you, Master Wainwright," he said. "And I'll remember what you told me."

"You do that, my lord. Kent *will* rise for a good cause. For a bad one too, mebbe, but a good one's better."

It took only a short time to truss the six watchmen. With apologies, Warwick had two of his soldiers add a set of bruises to the faces of a couple of them, though he spared Wainwright that. It was only an hour or so to dawn and he knew the watchmen would be found at first light, with a bloody nose or two for show.

Warwick sent his father and March to different ships, each taking command of a small crew. He waited to the very last before leaping onto the final vessel and taking position at the tiller to steer her out. The tide was turning and it took only half a dozen men to raise the single sail and catch the morning breeze. They left a long and empty length of dock behind them, and Warwick looked back and laughed as he went.

The waves were less calm beyond the shelter of the port. The men from Calais were spread too thinly among the ships they'd captured, so they used the smaller boats to take ropes between them. One well-manned ship could tow another easily enough, with the sun rising and France clearly visible across the Channel.

With the sails up and billowing in the wind, Warwick felt the desire to sing a sea shanty he recalled from his youth. His voice rang out across the waves and those who heard and knew it sang with him, grinning as they worked the sails and tillers, guiding their prizes back to Calais.

CHAPTER 24

Spring came to the French coast, bringing gentle breezes and blue skies filled with wheeling cormorants and gulls. The stolen fleet had proved vital for sailing up the coast of England to collect soldiers and lords loyal to the Yorkist cause. By June, the Calais fortress was heaving with English soldiers, packed into every spare space and stable. Two thousand of them would cross and invade, leaving eight hundred behind. As the last piece of English land in France, neither Salisbury nor Warwick wanted to be the ones who lost the fortress in their absence. The Calais walls had to be well manned, no matter what else was at stake.

Warwick had not been idle in the months since his jaunt across to Kent. The watchman's words had interested him and there was rarely a night that went by without some small cog slipping over on the dark waters, filled with the best speakers he could find. As the spring passed, Warwick's men were to be found in every Kent town and village, calling out for those who wished to avenge Jack Cade and repay the savagery of Ludford. Ten years before, Cade had entered London with some fifteen thousand men. Though some of them had been from Essex and other parts, the king and his officers were no more popular in Kent than they had been a decade earlier. A new generation of boys had grown up under the yoke of cruel punishments and brutal taxation. After the dark news of Attainder carried out on York, Salisbury, and Warwick, every report Warwick received went some way to revive his spirits.

By the end of June, they were ready. Only bad weather kept them in port then, the sea too rough to risk a crossing. Mindful of his oath to York, Warwick fretted for every lost day, but the gales had to blow themselves out. His fleet of forty-eight small ships could carry all two thousand across in one great surge, with half the Calais garrison suborned to bring the ships back to France. After the desertion of Captain Trollope to the king's side, those men could not do enough to aid the earls.

As they trooped into boats and rowed out to the ships, it intrigued Warwick to think of men like Caesar, who had been forced to build a fleet to take his legions across to Kent, fifteen hundred years before. The target was the same: London. As well as a royal garrison they dared not leave at their backs, London meant Parliament and the only group with the power to reverse the writs of Attainder. London was the key to England's lock, as it had always been.

The wind was blowing hard toward the English coast as the fleet launched. Gray clouds were low overhead and a constant drizzle chilled the men packed into the ships. Yet it was only a single leap and they could see the landing spot after just an hour or so at sea. One by one, the ships came in under as much sail as they dared raise. The captains could not beach the vessels for fear of staving them in. It took time to land men by boats and, all the while, the local militia could be seen rushing along the quays and docks, gathering men to repel the invasion. There were too few to hold back so many boatloads of men landing at once. A brief struggle developed before the militia gave up, leaving bodies on the quayside and more men haring away.

Warwick landed a little further along the coast, establishing a defensible position on a long shingle beach and putting archers out. Unchallenged, he and his men marched back to the port of Sandwich and filled it, watching as ships turned and raised sail, tacking into a rough sea and rising wind. Even then, there were hundreds of small boats still being rowed to shore, in such numbers that they bobbed together like driftwood. Some were unlucky, the fragile craft turning over as they caught a wave. Men who went into the surf in mail shirts were not seen again.

Close by the spot where Warwick had touched the land of his birth, two of the merchant cogs were driven right up on the shingle. As the ships leaned and settled, their captains ran plank bridges out from the lowest point of the deck so that they could walk a dozen blindfolded warhorses to the ground. Those ships would rot where they lay, but men like Salisbury were too old to march the sixty miles to London.

The sun was setting by the time the last of the fleet vanished into the mist and clouds on the Channel, leaving them alone. In a thin drizzle, the men settled down to fires on the beach and docks. They ate and drank and covered themselves as best they could, trying to snatch a few hours of sleep.

With the sun's return, a column of men came marching through the town. Soldiers were leaping up all around Warwick, ready for an attack. Yet it was not the local militia returning to repel his men, or even some part of the king's forces. Word had already spread of the landing and hundreds of Kentish men had come with their axes and pikes and cleavers. They halted by the docks and Warwick could only smile, accepting watchman Jim Wainwright into his service at fourpence a day. The earls' army began to move west and those first few hundred became thousands, with every town they passed adding to their number.

On horseback, Warwick and his father acknowledged the cheering crowds in towns and villages, Kentish families greeting them as saviors rather than enemies of the Crown. It was dizzying, and Warwick could hardly believe the success of his recruiters. The men of Kent had risen once more and this time *he* was the spark. He could not help wonder how many of them knew he had fought against them on the last dark night they had entered the capital city.

The irony of it all was not lost on him. In the very steps of Jack Cade, he would have to gather them in Southwark and cross London Bridge, heading for the Tower and the only force able to stop his progress.

THEY REACHED the southern banks of the London river on the afternoon of the third day, after three hard marches. Warwick had ordered a count and found more than ten thousand men of Kent had joined him. They might have been unarmored and untrained, but Cade had used such men well enough. Warwick remembered that night of blood and chaos all too well.

With his father and Edward of March, Warwick walked right to the southern end of London Bridge, ignoring the city crowds watching like it was a day at the fair.

"I see no king's men," Salisbury said. "Ours are weary, though the weakest fell behind a day ago. I would take them in." His pride was clear as he looked to his son, accepting that the decision would be Warwick's.

The vast host of Kentish men had come because of Warwick's recruiters. They looked to the young earl for command, not his father. York's son did the same, and Salisbury had experienced a revelation when he had seen the landing parties. He could trust his son to lead. It was something of an effort, but he had never been the sort of fool to grasp authority beyond its natural time. For all Salisbury's experience in war, he had discovered he would step back for his heir, if for no other man.

Warwick sensed his father's satisfaction and gave private thanks for the years he had spent in Calais. Every father remembers when his son stole or lied, or made a fool of himself with young love. To have been given even a few years apart had allowed Warwick to be tempered away from that stern eye.

"The best reports we have give the Tower garrison as a thousand strong," Warwick said. "They might surrender, though I have little hope of it. I know only that we cannot leave them to sally out of London behind us. We'll either force a way in, or bottle them up behind their own walls. You both know the plan. Speed is all, if we are to have any chance of success. Every day we lose here is one more for the king's forces to grow and make ready."

He did not mention the Bills of Attainder that had been committed to law. At that moment, on July the fifth, 1460, all their titles and estates had been torn from them. Though none of them spoke of it, they felt the loss like an open wound, bleeding them white. Yet after Ludlow, the king's army would have dispersed back to farms and manors. Warwick and his father were gambling on a single strike up the country, on reaching King Henry before his lords could gather once again. Anything in law could be overturned after that, once they had the king and his Royal Seal.

Edward of March had listened, observing the pride between father and son. He stood like a statue in his armor, wearing no helmet. He too had ridden from the coast, his horse more suited to pulling a plow than bearing a man. The animal cropped grass some way back, while the restless sea of Kentish men stamped and waited among the armored ranks. There was a sense of anticipation in the air; they could all feel it. Once across that bridge, their pleasant march through the countryside would be at an end.

"I'm not spending another night on cold ground when I could rest in a fine bed and enjoy meat and ale," Edward said. "The men have come this far today. Tired or not, they'll march one more mile."

In comparison to Salisbury, Edward was still fresh, his strength and stamina almost without limit. Each dawn, he'd been the first to rise, bounding to his feet and pissing happily before he was pulling bits of armor into place and yelling for servants to bring him food. Warwick could not fault him for his enthusiasm, though in truth the energy of the young earl could be wearing after too long in his presence.

"Very well," Warwick said. "I see the two of you won't be satisfied until we are in the city. Bring the knights and men in armor to the front, Edward. Cade faced archers and I want shields ready."

"It looks safe enough," Edward said, peering between the houses and shops on their side of the bridge. "I could walk across right now."

He took a pace, and Warwick's expression darkened.

"When you are in command, you can do as you wish, Edward. Until then, you'll do as I damn well say."

The young earl met his eyes without embarrassment, letting the moment of silence stretch.

"Have someone else fetch the knights, then. I will be first into the city, I think. For my father's honor."

Warwick had tensed under the giant's stare. He colored slightly, setting his jaw and whistling for a runner to take the order. His authority had been challenged in front of his father, but the truth was that it would take a lot of men to stop the Earl of March if he decided to make a point of it. It was not a time to quarrel and Warwick chose discretion, though his voice was strained as he passed orders to assemble.

Men-at-arms came running up with shields and weapons ready. Behind them, the host of Kentish followers gathered and swirled, the veterans of Cade's army exchanging stories of the last time with anyone who would listen. The mood was light and only Warwick walked stiffly as the horns blew and the first ranks stepped onto the wide street that ran down the center of London Bridge.

They had entered the city and the crowds still cheered and waved as they crossed the river and reached the streets beyond. Warwick roared an order and the vanguard of armored men swung right, heading toward the Tower and the royal garrison.

CHAPTER 25

L ord Scales was bright red with strangled emotions as he strode
along the walls of the Tower of London, looking down at the
streets below. From that great height, he could see the army
gathering a mile away across the river. He felt a shudder run through
him at the sound of horns, signaling they had entered London. At
that moment, he would have given anything for another thousand
men.

The memories of Jack Cade's rebellion were still raw, for all it had
been a decade before. He had dwelled on that failure to defend the city
for a long time, not least for his part in it. With no effort at all, Scales
could recall being witness to hundreds of murders, as rioting men
turned the city into a charnel house. Order had broken down completely on that appalling night. The thought of seeing anything like
that ever again made his old heart thump painfully and his fists clench
to cramping. He knew he was working himself up to apoplexy and the
danger of collapse. His doctor had warned him about his color, his
humors out of balance as old age squeezed out his strength. Yet only
anger controlled the terrible fear that made sweat pour from him.

His reward for that night ten years earlier had been a pension of a hundred pounds a year and the use of a royal merchant ship. Scales had made himself wealthy on that trade, buying and selling small cargoes of cloth and wool. Command of the Tower garrison was his last post going into retirement, a sinecure, with a generous pension and a household of servants to tend him. At sixty-three years of age, Scales knew he was no longer a man to go out and face a screaming riot with sword and shield. He felt his weakness in his aching joints and every softly wheezing breath.

Along the walls, cannon teams waited for his command. His one comfort was that the defenses had been made much stronger since Cade's rebellion. If an enemy force tried to break the gatehouse, he had heavy guns to sweep the street clear in bloody rags. Torsion catapults of a design any Roman legionary would have recognized were also there along the battlements, ready to spring the most terrifying weapon he controlled over the walls, much worse than the guns of bronze and iron. Scales crossed himself, kissing the ring on his finger that held the crest of his family. He would not allow the Tower to be breached. He almost smiled at the thought of what he could unleash against the men of Kent this time.

"Let them come," he murmured, staring into the dim haze across the river where so many still waited to cross. At the distance of a mile, he could see the Kentish mob as a stain on the land, shrinking in as they entered his city. The people of London were making no effort to stop them, he thought, seething. A man might expect them to remember the terror and damage from the last time, but no, he could hear cheering on the breeze, fools waving their caps at men who would light the capital on fire. Well, they would not have the Tower, if London burned down around it. Scales swore it to himself.

It was cold comfort. His job was to defend the good people from the mob and he could not help them. Beyond a few scattered aldermen and their personal guards, he knew he commanded the only soldiers in London. He clenched his jaw, his eyes cold and calm. The king's nobles were all in the north, either on their own great estates or around Coventry. Scales had too few men to sally out, no matter what horrors he would see from the walls. All he could do was honor the exact wording of his commission and hold the Tower until such time as reinforcements reached the city. Once again he looked down the line of cannons facing west over the streets. The river ran along the southern walls, with no bridge there to make him fear them coming at his flank. The Tower was a fortress and it would speak in tongues of fire to anyone who approached.

"Stand ready for my order," he bellowed, hearing his voice echo across the ancient stones. Eight hundred of his men tensed to wait. The gun teams checked their braziers and slow-matches one last time, the iron shot and bags of corned powder already in place. The White Tower loomed over them all and Scales remembered the carnage and blood-spattered ground he had seen all around it before. He shook his head. It would not happen again.

Warwick, Salisbury, and March rode abreast along Thames Street, heading east to the Tower. Their slow progress went some way to block the crowds behind them, though more and more people ducked under and around the horses, rushing on. All three had their swords bared and ready, carried along on a tide of shouting Londoners who seemed to have been waiting for an opportunity to unleash their own anger, regardless of whatever the earls or the men of Kent intended. Warwick saw hundreds bearing cudgels or long knives, rushing from street to street. His horse was buffeted by those trying to shove past and he struggled to understand what was happening.

He had wanted to be the spark for rebellion, it was true. He had not known he was sitting on a keg of black powder as he lit the match.

There was no question of leading the crowds anywhere. They all knew where the king's garrison was and they streamed toward the Tower with Warwick's army, beckoning them on. Women and children ran with the mob and the pace increased moment by moment until Warwick and his father found themselves trotting to keep Edward of March in sight. Sir Robert Dalton and the big figure of Jameson loped along on either side of the young earl, watching for any danger. Edward rode obliviously, clearly delighted by the chaos as he moved with the tide.

There had been no parliament called for more than three years. Far behind them, the Palace of Westminster was shuttered and damp, unwarmed by fires or the words of men. Warwick knew King Henry had been hidden away in Kenilworth, but not how the rest of the country had fared without the beating heart of his government. It seemed the king's officers had been cruel when left to enforce the laws on their own. There was mindless rage all around him, and Warwick began to wonder if he could even control what he had begun. When Cade had entered London, the good citizens had barricaded themselves in their homes. This time, they led the way.

The mob grew and grew, filling every side road, courtyard, and alley with struggling figures, all converging on the Tower and its garrison of hated king's soldiers. The land was clear around the walls there, a vast space of stone flags that Warwick recognized as a killing ground even as he was forced out into it. The crowd screeched and bellowed their anger up at the Tower battlements, looking to the Kentish men as if they expected them to march right up to the gatehouse and kick it down.

Warwick reined in with his father, making a still place in the swirl of rushing people before they could be pushed against the Tower it-self. Even then, the warhorses stamped and skittered left and right, made nervous by the noise and press of men all around.

Salisbury was staring up to the highest point of the outer walls, narrowing his eyes at the sight of dark figures and rising streams of smoke. The black mouths of cannon loomed out over the crowd, pointing down at them. Still, the people poured in, more and more of them in wild disarray, filling the open space until there was hardly room to move.

"Do you see the guns?" Salisbury shouted to his son, pointing. Warwick nodded, the noise too great to reply. It was chaos and he could see some of his captains beating men back with clubs just to make space for themselves. Those men were growing afraid in the heaving and shoving of too many packed around them. Already, they were red-faced and hoarse with shouting, pushing men away.

"Let them have axes, these men of London!" Salisbury shouted at the top of his lungs. Some of the mob heard him and cheered. "Let them cut their way in through the gatehouse!"

Warwick could hear only one word in three, but he gestured for his men to move forward to the weakest point of the Tower fortress. Cade had forced his way in once. They would again.

High above, Warwick heard a single voice call an order, with doz-ens more replying. He looked up, suddenly afraid.

SCALES GLARED POISONOUSLY as the crowd swelled out into the open ground around the Tower. He was seeing a true mob, common men driven wild at the chance to break and destroy. All his life he had stood for order and stability and now there they were, a horde of wide-eyed fools come to tear it all down. Armed soldiers in mail struggled among them like pebbles thrown into a river. Hundreds of

Kentish men bawled Cade's name, as if they could bring him back from the dead with sheer rage.

More and more of them came, and Scales could feel sweat run from his armpits beneath his tunic. He could *feel* the hatred of the dispossessed as they howled up at him. Men who saw no value in the king's law, who would throw it all aside in an orgy of violence. He had feared the damage they might do away from his reach. Instead, they had come to him.

He leaned forward, gripping the stone wall and staring down. Dozens of men carrying axes were gathering in wedge formation, their intention obvious as they tramped through the crowds, heading for the Tower gatehouse. Scales swore as he saw two men on horseback at the rear, a small island in the swirling madness. He thought he could feel the gaze of those horsemen on him. Scales shook his head in disbelief as he recognized the tabard colors of Salisbury and Warwick. A spike of fury shuddered through him at such a betrayal by king's earls. No, he remembered suddenly. They had been made common.

Three of the cannon along the walls had been loaded without round shot. As the mob filled the open ground below, Scales filled his lungs.

"Warning cannon! No ball!" he shouted, his voice echoing back from the White Tower behind him.

A triple crack sounded, belching long spits of flame from the barrels and wreathing the teams in gritty smoke. Scales lost sight of the mob below as the cloud passed. He heard screams, but when it cleared, they were pressing forward in a spasm. Axes were rising and falling against the outer gate and he swore aloud, not caring who heard him.

No. He would not lose the Tower. Scales was pale as he looked up, seeing the faces of the gunnery teams waiting for the order. They were afraid, with every right to be. Not one of them would survive the madness if he allowed it inside.

"Bring up the wildfire," Scales ordered. Men ran down the wide steps along the wall, crossing to the storerooms and returning at a much slower pace. Each one held a large clay pot, with both arms around its girth. They cradled them like children and they were sweating, terrified of dropping them onto the stones.

Scales could feel his heart skipping in his chest, so fast that it blurred his vision and made him dizzy. He leaned over the battlements and shouted for the mob to get back. They snarled and cursed up at him. The thumps of axes and hammers went on and he stood away from the edge, unable to watch.

"Cannon. Load ball and fire!" he said, too quietly. The gun teams could not hear him and he walked along the battlements, repeating the order so that they set to in a flurry of activity. He did not look down again as the first guns thundered, followed instantly by screams. More and more of the cannons on the walls poured shot into the massed crowd, tearing them apart.

Scales stopped by one of the small catapults, resting his hand on the great twist of horsehair that was the spring, thicker than a man's thigh. The clay balls were in place, with rags dangling from the top of each one. Three of them were spaced along the walls and Scales crossed himself, muttering a prayer as he nodded to the men watching.

Each dangling twist was lit and the catapults released almost instantly. No one on the walls wanted to be close to that foul substance once it was aflame. Even the cannon teams stood back from their weapons, ready to run if one was broken and spilled.

The smoke was still thick in the air and Scales watched as the heavy clay balls went soaring out, dropping quickly as streaks of brightness in the fog. He closed his eyes.

The sound of the crowd seemed to drop away to stunned silence for a single beat. Then the screaming began again and this time it built and built, the noise of insanity. Flames lit the gunsmoke and soared up at furnace heat, burning any living thing they touched. Scales shuddered. He had overseen the production of the wildfire himself, a foul blend of naphtha and niter, sulfur and burned lime. It stuck to whatever it touched and it consumed all flesh. Water merely fed the flames and could not put it out. He thought he could hear splashes as burning men threw themselves into the Thames, then screamed as they drowned, finding the fires of hell still eating at their skin.

Scales raised his chin. The gun crews were staring at him, waiting for fresh orders. He did not meet their eyes and went back to his spot on the walls. He clenched his right fist at the sight of the crowd streaming away like rats. Some of them still burned, staggering and wailing, setting others alight with their touch until their voices were choked by flame. The smell was sickening and Scales could hear some of the gunners vomit as they realized what it was. He breathed hard in satisfaction. As ugly as it had been, the mob knew by then what awaited them in their madness. The Tower would be defended with fire and iron. It would not fall.

Warwick saw the first empty flames spitting across the heads of the crowd. He looked again at the number of cannons facing them and turned, white-faced, to his father.

"Pull the men back! We don't need to break the gate, just to hold the garrison in London. If they'll fire on their own, we have no choice."

Salisbury sat stunned as he saw how many women and children were in that heaving crowd. He looked up in disgust at the battlements, unable to believe the commander would slaughter the people he was sworn to protect.

In ignorance or terror, the vast mob pressed even closer to the Tower walls. Salisbury could see axemen attacking the gatehouse and knew they had to be called back. He pressed a horn to his lips and found himself panting too hard to use it. Instead, he tossed it to his son and watched as Warwick blew a falling note, repeating the call for retreat.

Above them, white smoke billowed again and a rolling thunder began. Iron balls that could cross a mile of air were sent crashing through the crowd, killing dozens at a time in great bloody smears. The sound of the people changed to a moan then, an animal sound of distress as they began to push away from the Tower, searching for any path out of that open space. The rippling cracks kept sounding and nowhere was safe.

Warwick jerked his head up as something snagged him, leaving a line of blood on his cheek as if he had been caught by a blade. An iron ball had ripped through the crowd near him, too fast to see. He was thanking God for his luck when his horse coughed, spraying blood from its muzzle. Warwick threw his leg over and stood clear as the animal sank to its knees. Wherever the iron balls struck stone, splinters filled the air, ripping through the packed crowd. In desperation, Warwick blew retreat again and was almost knocked down as a man and woman rushed blindly past him, heading away.

Over the sounds of pain and rage, no one heard the catapults. Warwick saw three black balls leap out from the battlements, moving much more slowly than the cannon shot, so that his eyes fixed on them in confusion. He saw them vanish into the crowd and a breath of warmth bloomed, rolling across the open space. Three pools of fire erupted, liquid flames leaping and splashing over the struggling crowd.

They surged away from the heat in complete panic and the screaming of those caught was raw and pitiful to hear. Warwick stayed close to his father's horse, but they were both shoved back. He caught sight of Edward of March, unhorsed in the flood of rushing men. Though Jameson and Sir Robert still guarded him, even those three could not resist the flood of people pressing to get away. March struck out around him, clearing a space. No one who fell in that mad rush would ever get up again, their bodies trampled and crushed as the mob streamed back from the walls.

Hard voices called in outrage at the edges of the square, shouting for others to follow. As far as Warwick or his father could see, it was the Londoners themselves, gesturing back to the bridge. Thousands broke into a run as they left the Tower behind and it was all Warwick could do to press against a wall with his father's horse and let them go past. The killing ground emptied as quickly as it had filled, leaving smears of broken flesh, rings of burning bodies and black smoke. Above their heads, men leaned over the walls, pointing and shouting.

Warwick saw Edward of March staggering past him. The smith, Jameson, was at his back, though Sir Robert Dalton had vanished somewhere in the crush. Warwick reached out to snag Edward's chestplate, dragging him out of the clutches of the crowd. Jameson came with him, resting one arm against a wall and blowing hard.

March nodded to Warwick in wide-eyed thanks. His great strength had counted for nothing in that crowd and he had been frightened for the first time in his life. The multitude still rushed past them all, and the three earls could only pant and look on. More of their men struggled to that spot, until around forty had gathered against the walls. Dozens had been right at the base of the Tower when the wildfire crashed among them. Those flames still burned, flickering on bodies and stone like living things.

"We should get further back," Salisbury said. He was pale and exhausted-looking, worn down by fear and the battering of the crowd.

A side road lay just a dozen yards away from the open space around the Tower and the three earls made their way to it, seeing the gray Thames at the far end. Their men came with them, casting nervous glances behind as they went.

"Go on," Salisbury said, guiding his horse along it.

They were safe from the Tower cannon, at least. Six or seven houses long, the tiny street ended at the river and they could all see blackened corpses floating on the surface as they stopped. Some of the soldiers began to point and Warwick looked up to see a moving mass of men on the far side of the river. The Londoners had already crossed the bridge and made their way back along the opposite bank. He thought at first that they were still running in terror. It made no sense, and Warwick stared.

There were many buildings on the other side of the river, businesses and homes that had spilled across from the city, taking valuable land around the only bridge. Storehouses and meat markets thrived there. Warwick caught glimpses of the torrent of men as they passed between houses of wood and brick.

"What are they doing, over there?" he heard March asking.

Warwick could only shrug. Londoners knew their city better than he ever would. He could see the running men gathering in one place, using their weapons to break into one brick building, squat and low, as it stood on the banks of the Thames.

"It must be for weapons," Salisbury said. "Is there an armory there?"

One of the nearby soldiers swore suddenly. Warwick recalled he was a London man and he called him forward.

"I know it, my lord," the man said, his face awed. "It's a royal depot, where they make cannon."

Every man there turned in dawning amazement, in time to see a black gun carriage wheeled out along the bank path, pushed by a great knot of Londoners. The length of iron it carried could have been one of those that had torn through the crowd. Despite its ponderous weight, the roaring mob pushed it on and on, until it faced the Tower's southern wall, where no guns were.

They had found bags of powder and other men staggered along with round shot held in their arms. Warwick craned out as far as he could, catching a glimpse of scurrying figures on the high walls of the Tower. The river was a quarter of a mile wide, but the rushing water would be no protection.

The first ball cracked out, smashing into the Tower walls and falling back with lumps of stone and masonry dropping onto the paths below. The water of the river rippled as a thousand smaller pieces struck and sank. A savage cheer went up from that side of the river, but it was not a joyous sound, rather the cry of wolves, meant to terrify. It took an age between shots, but a second cannon had been brought out from the royal works and pointed across the river. The iron balls smashed hard against old stones again and again, until a huge crack could be seen and part of the curtain wall crumbled outwards.

Warwick watched, stunned, as the men of London adjusted their aim and blew out another piece the size of a horse with a single shot. Smoke and dust hid the extent of the damage for a time, but when it cleared, the sight pleased those who had worked so hard for it.

They abandoned the guns where they stood and began to stream back along the bank to London Bridge. Warwick had no doubt they would be returning to that spot and shook his head, imagining the slaughter that would surely follow.

"That's it now," he said to his father. "They've made their breach. Will you stay to keep order? I've lost enough time here already and my aim is more than one Tower, or London herself."

"Go, by God," Salisbury said, looking from his son to Edward of March. If anything, Salisbury was relieved at the chance to remain, rather than trying to force his old bones another eighty or ninety miles to Coventry. "Leave me a few hundred soldiers and I'll keep an eye on the mob, though I think their anger will burn as long as the wildfire. God's bones, I never thought to see that filthy muck used against my own people. Someone will suffer for it."

The older earl sat back as his son and March raced off with two dozen of the men, already raising the horn to call in the rest. Salisbury knew it would take forever to bring the Kentish lads to order and then turn them onto the road north. He was proud of his son then. In all the chaos, Warwick had not lost sight of the path. Whatever horrors they had witnessed, London was just a step and the beginning of it.

DARKNESS WAS EDGING closer by the time Warwick and March had their army gathered once again on the north side of the city walls. Over the hours of twilight, something like calm had been restored among them, though a number of the Kent men had looted ale and others stank of smoke and stood stupefied at what they had witnessed.

The captains had been busy gathering the men and had to batter a few before they would agree to leave the city. They had witnessed the sort of violence against innocents that made them cry out for vengeance. Women and children had been burned in that crowd by the Tower and they wanted to see blood in return. Warwick had harangued a dozen surly groups, reminding them that they had come to strike a blow against the king himself. That was enough for most and Warwick could see how they took a grip on their axes and imagined using them, paying back something of what they had seen. He did not doubt the fervor of the Kentish men, frightening in its intensity.

The church bells were ringing across London by then, led by Old Edward's muffled note at the Palace of Westminster a mile away. The air was warm and thick with darkness around ten thousand men. The road lay at their feet, good Roman stones. Warwick could only wish he had the time to take some of those London cannon with him, but such lumbering things would be left far behind. Speed was the key to it all, he knew it. His men had found two carthorses in a stable by the city wall. The animals snorted and whickered, less than happy at the weight of armored men on their backs.

"Sixty miles!" Warwick bellowed suddenly to the men all around. "Just eighty miles on fine roads—and you will see the king's own army, quaking in fear. Men who have taken everything from me— and men who would take everything from you. Cry 'Warwick,' cry 'March!' Cry 'York' and 'Jack Cade!' Will you walk with me?"

They growled and stamped in response, and he led them north.

CHAPTER 26

Thomas, Lord Egremont, preferred to look down at his boots rather than face the anger of the queen. He stood under a huge swathe of canvas, aware of the six-year-old prince tugging at his mother's skirts and demanding her attention, asking question after question while Margaret glared at Egremont and ignored her son.

"Your Highness," Thomas tried again. "I have sent my fastest scouts to my brother. I cannot give them wings, but he will already be marching his army here to support your husband. Beyond that, I have the men with me and my own personal guard."

"Not enough!" Margaret said. She turned suddenly to Edward, grabbing him by the arm. She could see she had startled her son and gentled her tone with a visible effort. "Edward *dear*, would you please find something else to do besides asking all these questions? Go and find Lord Buckingham. He wanted to show you his new armor."

The little boy dashed away in excitement, leaving Margaret to face the younger son of the Percy household. Thomas already missed the boy, for the useful distraction he had been.

"My lord Egremont, if you cannot promise me the numbers we gathered at Ludlow, I have no choice. I must take my husband back to Kenilworth and wait to be attacked! The King of England, Thomas! Forced to run from a rabble of traitors!"

Egremont shook his head. He suspected Margaret said such things to shock or shame him, though he could not disagree with her assessment. Royal scouts had raced north from London with the news of a Neville army as soon as they had been sighted on the south bank of the Thames. The exhausted riders had reached the royal camp by Northampton two days later. God alone knew how much time they had gained, even exchanging horses at taverns and almost killing the animals they rode. If the Yorkist earls lost only a little time in the capital, they would still have to come at the pace of marching men. The royal camp had been in a panic ever since the news came in, with every spare rider haring off to summon soldiers and nobles back from their estates.

"My lady, I understand your anger, but if you do retreat to Kenilworth, it would allow enough time to bring more Gallants back from their farms and homes. My brother and Lord Somerset are already riding. In two, perhaps three days, we will double the number standing with us now. It will not matter then if these forces of York have besieged your castle. Sieges can be broken from the outside."

"That is your advice then, Lord Egremont?" Margaret said in disbelief. "After the Attainder of York, Salisbury, and Warwick? After the death of those noble houses and the scattering of their titles and lands? After a great royal victory at Ludlow and seeing the king's enemies flee into the night, you'd tell me to retreat?"

Thomas looked away.

"My lady," he said at last. "No, I would not. We have time—and we have five thousand men. Lord Buckingham, Baron Gray, and I are sufficient protection for the king in the field. Yet if you did decide to take your son and King Henry to safety, I would be happier. I cannot predict the outcome as things stand. Salisbury and Warwick will be marching north by now. We do not know how long they stayed in London, or whether they went out to their old estates to swell their ranks. We do not know their numbers, or the quality of their men, though I expect it to be poor. It shames me to suggest it, but Kenilworth is only thirty miles away. I would not be so concerned if I knew the royal family was safe."

Before Margaret could reply, Lord Gray entered the tented pavilion behind Egremont, bowing deeply to the queen. Older than the Percy son, he dipped his head the merest fraction in greeting. Margaret did not know if Lord Egremont knew of Gray's unpleasant appetites. Whatever the reason, neither of the two men had found much to like in the other.

"Your Highness, Lord Egremont, my riders report the forces of Warwick and March." Gray paused for a beat, working out how far they might have come in the time it took his scouts to race back with the news. "They are around . . . ten miles to the south, moving quickly. Will King Henry give me my orders?"

Despite her shock at the news, Margaret glanced over her shoulder, to where Henry sat, leaning back on a couch at the rear of the tent. His eyes were open and he wore plate for the battlefield, but he did not move or acknowledge their interest. A brief spasm of distaste passed across Gray's face when the queen's eyes were not on him. He had come to serve a king recovered from his weaknesses. Instead, Gray had found a dazed child, utterly unaware of what went on around him.

Margaret sensed the baron's irritation and spoke more sharply than she intended.

"Ten miles?" She looked at Egremont and saw he was as dismayed as she was. "How many men are coming, Lord Gray? Do you know that much?"

"Eight to twelve thousand, Your Highness. Some of them in mail and armor, most without. My lads reported a mob, led by half-decent soldiers."

"Then your orders have not changed, my lord. Defend the king. Hold the ground. Is that clear enough for you?"

Gray clenched the muscles in his jaw, nodding stiffly. Once more he glanced at the seated figure behind them, the king's armor gleaming in the shadows.

"Yes, my lady. Quite clear. Thank you," he said, turning on his heel and vanishing into the sunlight.

"Nasty old sod," Egremont muttered under his breath. He was still thinking how such numbers could be withstood, his eyes vague as he chewed the inside of his lower lip.

"Well, Thomas?" Margaret demanded. "What must be done? Shall I have my servants fetch Buckingham?"

"They are much closer than I thought they would be, my lady," he said. "They must have force-marched up the Great North Road with hardly any time lost in the city. They will surely be weary and that is to the good. Yet the numbers . . ." His voice trailed away and he shook his head once more. "This army is almost upon us. There will not be time now for my brother to bring his men, or Exeter, or Somerset, or any of the others. Unless they arrive in the next hour, we have only those with us at this moment—and my lady, they are not enough." He wanted to call Gray back to hear how many of the approaching army were on horseback, his hand clutching at empty air as he thought quickly. "You should leave now, Your Highness. Take your son and your husband and ride for Kenilworth."

"When my husband is unwell, Thomas, he cannot ride."

The strain showed in Egremont's reply, his rush of anger startling her.

"Then save yourself and your son, my lady. Save something! Take one of the supply carts and lay King Henry in it! Do you understand? They outnumber us on open ground. We can plant stakes and yes, we might hold them for a time, but it will be hard and bloody, with no man knowing the outcome until it is over. Would you have Prince Edward witness such a thing? I am your man, Your Highness—and I have my own scores to settle with the Nevilles. Leave me to fight for you and for the king."

Margaret had paled as he spoke, unused to such a tone. Her eyes were wide at the fear and tension she saw in him.

"Very well, Thomas. Find my son and have him brought back to me. We'll need three horses saddled. I will see to my husband."

Released as if from a trap, Lord Egremont raced away. Margaret crossed quickly to where Henry seemed to watch her. Slowly, she lowered herself at his side, looking deeply into his eyes. On impulse, she took his arm, feeling the cold metal slip under her fingers.

"Did you hear? Can you stand, Henry? It is not safe now. We must go."

"As you say," he whispered, barely more than a breath crossing his lips. He did not move.

"*Henry!*" she snapped, shaking him. "Get up, now, to ride. Come on."

"Leave me here," he murmured, pulling away from her. Some life came back into his eyes and she wondered again how much he truly understood.

"I will not," she said. Her head jerked up in shock as she heard horns blowing in the distance. Panic surged in her, making her tremble. How could they be so close? Lord Gray had said ten miles! She left her husband and went out into the sun, staring at a distant column of men approaching the royal camp. Either Gray had somehow been wrong, or the men of Kent had run the last few miles. Margaret shook her head in confusion and rising terror, looking back into the gloom of the tent. She trembled as she stood there, caught between needs that tore her in two.

The sound of hooves and harness announced a servant arriving with horses outside the tent. Margaret could have wept with relief as her son, Edward, ran inside, his eyes bright.

"Bucky says there's an army coming!" the little boy hooted, bouncing from step to step. "He says they're right bastards!" He mangled the last word deliberately, mimicking the slurred speech of a man who had suffered a cleft palate at St. Albans and could no longer speak clearly.

"Edward!" Margaret snapped immediately. "Lord Buckingham should not have taught you such a term and he is too good a man to be mocked." She spoke almost without conscious thought, distracted by the problem of getting her husband away to safety. Closing her eyes for a moment, Margaret felt herself trembling. Outside, the noise of marching men grew louder and louder, jingling and stamping. Voices called across the field, warning the king's forces to be ready. She ran back to her husband and kissed him hard on the cheek.

"Please, Henry. Get up now. There are soldiers coming and there will be fighting. Please come with me."

His eyes closed, though she thought he could still hear her. There was no time left. She chose between her husband and her son, her heart breaking.

"No, then," she said. "I'm sorry. I must see Edward safe. God keep you, Henry."

WARWICK'S HORSE had suffered under the weight of an armored man. He had flogged and spurred it raw to reach Northampton and he knew he would have to dismount to fight. The animal was more used to pulling a cart of malted barley for the London brewers. The crash of arms and smell of blood would surely see it bolt.

At his side, Edward of March rode an even more unfortunate animal. Rather than see his horse collapse, March had been forced to remove his armor. Each piece had been taken up with pride by the men around him, sharing the weight of iron between them while the young earl rode on in brown wool. His face was so flushed that no one had dared say a word about it.

A shout went up from the front ranks as they sighted the king's army. They had marched hard and far to reach that place, but the reward was there to be seen. King Henry's lion banners fluttered in an open field, on the grounds of an abbey. The royal army looked small in comparison to the great column that had come north, but Warwick could see the king's soldiers wore mail and his heart sank at the sight of hundreds of horsemen and archers. His Kentish men had no pikes to stand against cavalry, and numbers would take them only so far against well-trained soldiers. He felt fresh sweat break out on his skin and, for once, he wished his father were present. He had decisions to make that would mean victory or complete destruction. The sun was not yet at noon and he could not shake the sense of dread that rose in him.

"Will you take Baron Gray at his word?" Edward of March said, easing his horse closer.

As the most senior lord, the command of the army was Warwick's. He had not forgotten Edward's sudden disobedience at London Bridge, but there was no one else.

"That is the damned thorn, Edward," he replied uneasily. "How can I trust him?"

Lord Gray's scouts had been tracking them all morning and part of the previous day. One of them had come in with his hands held high and open to show he intended no treachery. He'd brought an extraordinary offer and Warwick was still uncertain if it wasn't some trick to lure him in against the strongest wing of the king's men.

"What's to lose?" March replied with a shrug. "He wanted a red banner raised, so have it raised. He'll either follow through on his word, or we'll cut him down with the rest."

Warwick held back from allowing his irritation to show. Edward was very young and had not yet seen all the villainy of men.

"If he is true to his word, we'll attack his force on the flank. You see them there? But if his man was lying and it is some sort of trap, Buckingham will have all his best fighters in that place, ready to tear us apart."

To his exasperation, Edward of March chuckled.

"Let them! I'll lead the charge when I have my armor on. One way or another, we'll go through them."

Warwick called a halt and dismounted, guiding his exhausted horse off to the side as the column widened out. He'd set his captains to lend some discipline to the Kentish recruits. They could be heard bawling orders at the top of their voices, aware that the two earls were watching. Piece by piece, the marching line took up a new structure in long ranks and squares, facing the king's army less than half a mile away across the open land. Warwick could hear warning horns sound in that camp, with servants and horsemen running everywhere. Eight hundred yards separated them, enough to make out the broad banners of Buckingham in the center. An abbey stood in the near distance and Warwick could see the dark figures of monks watching them maneuver.

Behind the king's forces, a river ran fast with summer rain. Warwick had no idea if there was a bridge there, but it meant Buckingham's men would not find it easy to retreat. The king's flags were still flying on his pavilion and if his presence was not enough, the river would force them to stand and fight to the last man. Warwick found himself wondering if the queen was close by. His memories of her were more tender than anything he felt for the king who had attainted his family. He shook his head, remembering his father's certainty that the queen was the snake wrapped around Henry, more than any of his lords.

"Slow march to a quarter mile!" Warwick ordered when they were ready. It had taken an agonizingly long time for them to form up, but they were fit and eager to engage the king's men. They stepped forward, brothers and sons of Kent together in the lines. Sixteen hundred mailed soldiers made the first two ranks, an iron hammer with an oak shaft of Kent rebels behind. Warwick could feel the desire to charge rising in them. He headed it off with sharp commands, keeping them in line and walking at a slow pace. He needed to be close, to observe the enemy positions.

The thought snagged in his mind, making him blink. He was marching toward the King of England and the man was somehow his enemy. Just a year before, he would have laughed if anyone had imagined such a scene. Yet the Bills of Attainder had been passed and there was no Warwick any longer. His men were careful to use the title when they spoke to him, but he had lost it all, along with Salisbury and York. Edward of March strode along at his side, gripping his sword and clearly imagining red-handed slaughter.

They halted once more, with the abbey much closer on their right flank. Beyond the river, Warwick could see the city of Northampton itself, its walls and churches dimly visible. He strained his eyes in every direction, seeing a forest of stakes around the royal forces as well as archers on the wings. In the terrible silence, Edward of March sat on the grass, allowing Jameson to pull on the last pieces of his armor. Sir Robert Dalton had not been seen since London. March only recalled him being yanked away into the mob, suddenly gone without even a cry. The young earl felt the man's absence at his side, making him uneasy.

Warwick saw smoke rising from braziers among the king's soldiers and swore softly to himself. The men with him had seen the effects of great guns on a crowd, the memories still fresh and terrible. To face such weapons without flinching took a kind of madness, combined with the belief of all young men that it would always be the one next to them who fell. It made no sense at all, but he could see the Kentish lads scorned the forces ahead. No fear at all! Warwick looked closer at the men of Kent and saw they were ready to rush forward at a single word, many of them staring at him, waiting for him to open his mouth. They wanted to run in and begin the killing. He had a sudden understanding of why the French had failed so many times to break such armies. He could see it in Edward's foul curses and jerky movements, in the way the Kent men gripped ax shafts, twisting their hands around the wood like they were strangling children. They *wanted* to fight. They wanted it to begin. He would indulge them.

"Forward!" Warwick called.

His captains all knew the first maneuver against the king's men. With the armies so close, it would not do to have his orders shouted across the field, alerting Buckingham to his intentions. Instead, Warwick marched straight down the center, closing the distance at a good pace.

Arrows rose in a cloud from both flanks and Warwick felt the sick terror of them. Only his front ranks had shields and the king's archers lofted shafts over their heads, wounding or killing dozens with each whirring volley. Almost worse were the cracks of thunder as cannon spat flame. Blurs hammered through his men, and arrows sank into the earth before his feet. More and more flew, buzzing and thumping into flesh and iron. There were cries of shock and agony falling behind, but he didn't look back. At two hundred yards, every instinct screamed to charge and kill. His front ranks lurched into a slow run, breathing hard.

"Red banner!" Warwick called, waiting until his herald raised the scarlet cloth on a pike-pole, holding it high for ten steps before tossing it down. It would mean nothing to Buckingham, but that was the signal Lord Gray had requested. Warwick would learn whether the man had made a fool of him in just moments.

At a hundred yards, Warwick called fresh orders to swing left. The arrows were chopping men down at short range by then, snapping through mail and hammering shields. Warwick found himself relieved he was not on horseback to be an obvious target for them. His front two ranks showed their experience as they swung over, holding formation. The Kentish lads followed in their wake, angling sharply across the field to aim themselves at Buckingham's flank. They left behind a trail of dead and screaming wounded.

The king's bowmen were protected by a field of stakes that might have stopped cavalry, but not men on foot who simply stepped around them. The archers were not prepared for the best part of ten thousand men to come howling at them in a sudden rush, hacking into their midst as they shot and tried to duck out of the way. The approach under arrow fire had been terrifying, the toll of injured or dead into hundreds or even thousands. Those men were swallowed up in a tide of red rage, torn apart by sword and axemen, too far gone in anger to have any caution at all.

Whoever commanded the cavalry on that outer flank chose to pull back rather than let his men stand to meet the charge. While the archers were cut to pieces, the officer's intention would be to circle and strike against Warwick's own flank, pinning them between the king's main force and armored horses. Without mounted knights of his own, Warwick could not block them. His men had to ignore the moving horses, crashing shields instead against the standing ranks, pressing in toward the center.

Warwick had kept his word. He waited, and his men held steady for new orders. For a time, they were content to shove forward with a shield line. Some were killed, on both sides. In the heat of engagement, the men were close to berserk and could not hold back. Yet the two front ranks kept discipline and the shield line held.

Ahead of him, Warwick saw Lord Gray turn his horse right around in the midst of his men, gesturing away from Warwick's forces and signaling an attack on the center. A great roar went up from every throat on the field. Warwick's men cried out in savage triumph, while Buckingham's forces shouted in horror at the betrayal. The center faltered and Warwick found himself surging forward in a great rush, almost falling into the gap left by those his men had pressed against. Lord Gray too had kept his word.

Edward of March ran through a dozen ranks of allies to crash against the milling center, smashing shields to splinters in huge blows. Warwick almost stopped to watch in awe at the sight of the massive warrior throwing men back in wrenching movements, making himself and Jameson the point of a wedge of soldiers, cutting deep into the ranks around Buckingham.

Warwick looked back for the cavalry he still feared, only to see them standing in a compact group some way off. Gray's men, he saw, breathing in relief. They would not take part.

Faced with the betrayal of Lord Gray, Buckingham's soldiers broke. They tried to retreat in order, hampering each other and dying in droves as they were harried and cut at every step. Warwick saw his Kentish men pour in, engaging anyone they could reach and cutting axes into those who turned away and ran. It was butchery and madness, but the ten thousand could not have been held then. They had come a long way to fight the king's soldiers and they knew they had them beaten.

At the center of the king's army, Warwick saw Buckingham unhorsed. Edward of March raced over, crashing into a cluster of knights with his sword and shield. With his gaze fixed on the fallen duke, March knocked them away in great sweeping blows, two or three falling onto their backs. Those men began to struggle up with murder in their eyes, but Jameson was there at March's side with his sword ready and no one challenged the young giant who treated them so carelessly. Warwick was still a dozen paces away when Buckingham came to his feet and raised his sword once again. The duke's ruined face was hidden beneath his visor, though Warwick noted he was holding his left arm against his side, protecting broken ribs.

Edward of March nodded to him, waiting with both hands on his hilt.

"Are you ready, my lord?" March said, his voice echoing in iron.

Buckingham dipped his head in reply and was dead a moment later. March had smashed his great sword down through the duke's shoulder plates, cracking the iron and cutting deep. Warwick left him levering the sword out with his boot on Buckingham's chest. Some of the king's men were trying to surrender, but Warwick had seen the Percy banners of blue and yellow and he did not touch the horn on his hip. The killing went on all around him and March came jogging back to Warwick's side, his armor covered in blood and his companion smiling in grim pride. Warwick looked up at both of them as the young earl pulled off his helmet and rubbed a hand through his hair.

"Did you see me kill Buckingham?" March asked.

"I did," Warwick said. He had liked Humphrey Stafford and it crossed his mind that the man had deserved a better end for faithful service. Yet that was the way of it. He did not think there was a man in England that year who could have stood against March with a sword.

"Egremont is mine," Warwick said.

March gestured, as if allowing him to go first through a door, then spun suddenly as Jameson crashed his sword against a man running at them, cutting through chain mail. March laughed, clapping the big smith on the shoulder and making Warwick think once again of Calais mastiffs. He might have spoken, but he had crossed a hundred yards of bodies and ahead the Percy colors suddenly wavered and fell. Warwick cursed, shoving through Kentish men.

"Egremont! Mine!" Warwick yelled as he went, suddenly afraid that he would be denied his revenge on his family's enemy.

His men moved back, revealing six armored knights around their lord.

Thomas Percy stood with his hands resting on the hilt of his sword, stealing a moment to breathe and rest. He raised his visor.

"Richard Neville!" he called. "Who was once an earl. Who is that great troll at your side, Richard?"

"Let me kill him," March growled.

"If I fall, yes. Not till then," Warwick replied. He was still fresh, kept from the fighting by all the ranks ahead. He realized he had lost his shield somewhere and accepted one that was handed to him by one of his men, tugging it onto his arm. His armor felt light and he was confident, though Thomas, Lord Egremont, was known for his skill.

The Percy lord stepped forward to meet him. The battered knights at his side seemed in no hurry to continue the fight, surrounded as they were. The stillness of that center point crept out across the field so that fighters backed away from each other and king's men threw down their weapons rather than be killed.

"Will you surrender, Thomas?" Warwick said. "It seems the day is ours."

"Would you allow it, if I did?"

Warwick smiled and shook his head.

"No, Thomas. I would not. I just wanted to see if you would try."

Egremont snapped his visor down in response, coming forward. His first blow smacked against Warwick's shield and was then followed by three more, forcing Warwick back. The Percy lord was fast, though the fourth swing seemed to lack strength and he staggered. Warwick knocked the man's shield away and hacked a great dent into his side.

Egremont went down onto one knee, gasping audibly in his helmet. Warwick waited for him. When Egremont rose, his sword came up fast from low down, smashing the edge of Warwick's shield and almost ripping it from his arm. His return strike was against the same spot on the man's side, breaking the plates.

Once more, Egremont dipped to his knee, wheezing. With a groan, he forced himself up for a second time, protecting his side as Warwick brought his sword across in a chopping blow against his neck. Thomas Percy crumpled limply then, lying facedown, with his helmet pressed into the grass. For the first time, Warwick could see the leather hilt of a dagger that had been shoved up between the man's back-plates. Blood had streamed out of him for every moment of the fight and Egremont had surely felt his strength draining away. He did not rise again and it was March who wrestled Thomas Percy's helmet away and revealed his lifeless face, bruised and white.

Warwick looked around him, at the swords thrown down and the bodies on all sides. He felt his blood pound and he took off his own helmet, sending it spinning into the air as he roared for the victory.

Thousands of Kent men echoed him, a great hoarse cry that could have been heard for miles.

Warwick turned to March, feeling for once that nothing the young earl could say would possibly spoil his mood.

"The king?" March said, chuckling at his expression.

"Yes. The king," Warwick replied.

The two men turned as one to face the royal tent behind them.

THEY FOUND KING HENRY sitting in the gloom of his tent. He had removed his armor and sat wearing only black broadcloth, a long tunic and hose all dyed the same color, with no rings or jewels beyond a royal crest picked out in gold thread on his chest. As March ducked to enter the canopy, he shuddered at the thought of the king sitting the whole time in silence while thousands died nearby.

"Your Majesty?" Warwick said. He sheathed his sword when he saw there were no guards around, or even servants to tend him. They had all fled. Henry looked up, frowning at them.

"Will you kill me?" he said. Warwick could see he was shaking. "Will there be blood?"

"We should," March said, stepping forward. He looked around angrily as Warwick took a good grip on his arm. It was like holding a branch and both men knew March could shrug it off.

Warwick spoke quickly, his voice low.

"If the king dies here, his son, Edward of Lancaster, inherits the throne. A boy who would have no love of us."

March grunted in irritation and Warwick's eyes widened as he saw the young earl held a long dagger in his right hand.

"What do I care for that?" March growled, staring at the slender man watching them both. "His is a weak line. I do not fear it."

Warwick felt anger surge in him.

"Care then for your father! He will not be York until the Attainder is reversed. With King Henry alive, his Seal and Parliament will give our families back everything we have lost."

To his relief, March made a grumbling sound deep in his chest and put away the blade.

"Very well," he said. "Yet I think it will come after that. I have no use for a king who would take my inheritance from me."

Warwick let his hand fall, feeling ill at how close March had come to murdering the man who still stared at them with wide, dark eyes. The possibility of violence remained in March's every brooding glance.

"We have what we hoped, Edward," Warwick said slowly. He spoke as if to a dangerous hound who might turn savage at any moment. "We'll take the king back to London and meet your father there. Be at peace. We've won."

CHAPTER 27

York ran his hand over a smooth white square, blank and ready
for repainting. The panels in that room had once been an
unbroken blaze of colors, the arms of every noble house in
England. It had been one of the pleasures of his youth, to come to the
Palace of Westminster and see the crest of his house sitting proudly
with all the others. No longer. The painted panels stretched right
around the four walls of the room, emblems and histories written in
the symbols of ancient houses. Three white squares spoiled the unbroken run. Three that had been ripped out and replastered in palest
cream. The crests of York, Salisbury, and Warwick had been removed
by the king's heralds. It was some consolation that the Earldom of
March was still there, quartered in blue, yellow, red, and white. It
seemed the agents of the royal courts had been uncertain whether
that title should be included in the Attainder, given that it had already been passed on.

Salisbury watched the duke sweeping his hand across the blank
plaster, lost in thought.

"They'll be replaced now, Richard," he said. "The king's own Seal has undone all the lies of his queen. It gave me great pleasure to see all those little Parliament men running to do our bidding."

York blew air, his lips twisting.

"It was a foul thing and it should not have been attempted. Our families *are* England, deep into the bone. Yet I've seen your crest and mine cut from stone and wood, hacked smooth by files and chisels. Those damned heralds were busy while I was in Ireland. Ludlow Castle was stripped, did you hear that? Sandal Castle had tapestries and statues as old as Rome, but they have all vanished, spirited away while I could not defend them. The damage of this Attainder will take me a lifetime to repair."

"I've seen as much, though it gave me some pleasure to take back my estates from those who bought them. Some of my lands are now in Percy hands, think of that! At least you were able to reclaim all of yours. While Henry Percy lives and spites me for the death of his father and brother, I'll never get some of mine without bloodshed."

York turned away from the wall at that.

"I trusted you at Ludlow. And you kept your word. I will not forget it. You and your son brought me back from despair and disaster, such a feeling as I will not endure again for anyone. I will always be in your debt." He held out his hand and Salisbury took it, hand to elbow, gripping the forearm.

Bells across London began to sound noon then, a long clamor that had both York and Salisbury turning to the door.

"How is the king?" Salisbury asked as they swept out into a corridor.

"Well enough," York replied. "Bishop Kempe says he is the most agreeable guest he has ever known. Henry spends his time in the chapel, or reading, so I've heard. He has to be reminded to eat."

"Have you considered what you will do with him, now the Attainders have been struck from the rolls?"

"I have *considered* it many times," York replied, stiffly. "I have not yet come to a decision."

The two men made their way up a set of stairs, passing over the room where the Commons met and into the chamber at the far end. It was already busy with voices, all of which fell silent as York was sighted.

The White Chamber was little more than a debating hall, much smaller than the one where members of Parliament met below. It had benches running along each side and a lectern to address those present. At one side, placed to overlook the room, the king's seat remained empty, a simple oak throne carved with three lions and gilded along the edge.

York's mind was still on his own losses and he barely acknowledged the assembly of lords. They were small enough in number and rank. No Percy had come, no Somerset, no Clifford, nor any of the others who had fought for the king. York recognized a dozen minor barons, Cromwell among them. He paused on the raised step and inclined his head to Lord Gray. The baron had put on a great deal of weight since the battle close by Northampton, York noticed, developing chins and jowls better suited to a bishop. York had heard every detail of Gray's part in that victory from his son and Warwick. It pleased him to imagine the king's forces being told their enemies were miles away when they were almost upon them. More importantly, Gray had kept his word and turned his men against Buckingham at the right moment. Growing fat on new wealth and being made Treasurer of England was small return for such a vital betrayal.

As York stood by the lectern, Salisbury walked down, joining Warwick and Edward of March and some twenty others. They looked up at the duke and Salisbury's eyes widened as York laid his hand on the royal seat, as if he claimed it. He nodded sharply and York smiled.

The expression lasted just an instant, as the other men there saw where his hand lay and what it might mean. York frowned as someone hissed and another growled angry words. He looked up into a cluster of forbidding faces and saw only March, Gray, Salisbury, and Warwick were raising their hands in his support. Four Lords Spiritual were present and, to his irritation, he saw Bishop Kempe shake his large head slowly from side to side. York considered sitting down in the royal seat and scorning them all for their tutting and sighing. The chancellor, William Oldhall, entered from the side and looked horror-struck at the scene before him.

York removed his hand. The tension in the room vanished instantly and the chancellor came across to speak, his voice barely a murmur as the rest chattered like birds.

"My lord York, the king lives," Oldhall murmured into his ear. "As does his heir. These men dare not accept you as things stand, but be assured my work has borne fruit. The good fellows of Parliament have debated the best course forward. If you would take your place, my lord, I promise you, you will be pleased at the result."

With ill grace, York left the lectern and the royal seat and stepped down to the benches. Salisbury made a great show of welcoming him, as if they had not witnessed anything untoward at all.

Oldhall guided them through the opening prayer and then gave florid thanks for the reversal of Attainder on the houses of York, Salisbury, and Warwick. That formal announcement brought forth a cheer from the gathered lords, going some way to ease York's glowering mood.

"My lords, it is my pleasure to pass on the will of the Commons in this matter. The members have sought some way to show their gratitude to Richard Plantagenet, Duke of York, for his service to the king, for keeping King Henry safe and rescuing His Highness from traitors. An Act of Accord has been proposed, naming York as heir to the throne of England. The vote will be held at sunset tonight. If it is successful, the new law will be drafted tomorrow for the king's Seal."

York's brow smoothed and he sat up straight, hardly hearing the congratulations of all the men who had frowned at him only moments before. The cowards in either chamber would not allow him to claim a throne, but they were willing enough to place Henry's fate in his hands and leave any action to him. He felt only disgust for them all in that moment, though they had delivered his greatest ambition. He looked back to the bench behind him, catching the eye of his son. Edward knew what it meant and he was beaming, gripping the wood with his big hands.

York settled back into his seat, feeling a rush of vitality and fresh strength. He had been forced to run at Ludlow. He had seen his castles and his lands given away or sold to men with no right to take them. His very name and arms had been ripped from tapestries and chairs, hacked from wood and scoured from iron and stone across the country. Yet if he would be king in the end, all that would be no more than a bitter season. He knew the presence of an army infesting London was the heart of why the men of Parliament were suddenly so meek and helpful. Lord Scales had survived the wall of the Tower being broken, barricading it from within and escaping bloody vengeance by the London crowds. Scales had held out long enough to surrender to Warwick when they brought the king back. It had not saved him from the vengeance he had earned. It had taken just two days for someone to reach him in his cell in the Tower. York had seen the body, though he had no sympathy for the man after the orders he had given. There was still blood on the streets. More importantly, there was only one force in London that day, and they were loyal to York. He had the king and the city in his grip and Parliament knew it.

He closed his eyes for an instant, feeling an old pain. He had visited Henry at the Palace of Fulham further along the river, praying for hours with him and trying to understand the young man and his weakness. In all their years of dispute, York had never spent enough time with Henry to truly know the king's character. He felt his eyes tighten at the thought of killing him. It would be the murder of a true innocent, the most terrible of sins, no matter how he brought it about. He would be damned, without a doubt, though being damned would make him king. Dredging for the will to see it through, he remembered again how mercy had nearly cost him his life and his house. York opened his eyes once more, the decision made. For propriety, he would do nothing for a time. Parliament would make him heir and before the year was out, Henry would slip silently into a sleep, never to wake. York would be king, as his great-grandfather Edward had been. His son would be king after him.

A further thought came as he drew in a breath, filling him with joy. His son would not be damned for the murder of an innocent. Edward would rule the house of York and all England—and what father would refuse to make such a gift, no matter what it cost? York told himself he would write to Cecily that very day, busy at Ludlow with repairs and overseeing hundreds of craftsmen. He smiled as he imagined her reaction. One more Act of Parliament and they would have everything they had ever wanted. The world would have been put right, after too many years with a weak house on the throne. He might even take back the lost lands in France. Who could refuse his right, when he was king? York felt his mind fill with glorious imaginings and it took Salisbury's sharp elbow jabbing into his side to bring him back and make him listen to William Oldhall and the discussion still going on.

". . . there is as yet no news of Queen Margaret or her son, no, Lord Gray. I have a report that they were seen passing into Wales, but their whereabouts now are unknown." Oldhall showed his discomfort as he glanced over at York. "There are absences today in these benches, empty spaces that speak loudly enough. If my lord York is made heir, I do not doubt we will hear from those noble lords who have not come to London, to this chamber."

York looked down, not caring to hear. He knew the names of those who would support the queen well enough: Percy, Somerset, Clifford, Exeter. It gave him more pleasure to think of men like Buckingham and Egremont who could no longer trouble him.

The news of a new heir to the throne would make Margaret tear her hair in rage when she heard. The image of it twitched at his lips, after all he had endured with Attainder. It was a pleasure as simple as a childhood summer, to think of his tormentors suffering in turn. Margaret had lost her husband. When the vote was passed, she would lose her son's inheritance as well. He chuckled aloud at that thought, interrupting an elderly baron so that he stopped and stared. Salisbury laughed in turn. He had watched York closely as he mused, almost able to follow the meanderings of his mind and enjoying every moment.

MARGARET BLUSHED, pleased at the attention and the compliments. Jasper and Edmund Tudor may have been made earls by her husband, but they still stood in respectful silence in the presence of their father.

Owen Tudor took her hand to lead her in, smiling with such amused devilment that she could well believe he had charmed a French queen once before. He was thirty years her senior and though he was bald and white-haired, he had kept a rare vitality, his good health showing in tanned skin, clear eyes, and a firm grip. He looked like a gentleman farmer, with little sign of the soldier he'd once been.

Prince Edward ran past them all, exclaiming in delight at the feast laid out before them. He bobbed and jumped around as Margaret was seated at the head of the table, coming to his own chair with enormous reluctance. He was nearly seven years old and saw the ride into Wales as an adventure. As one who had grown up in Kenilworth, he had not been overawed by Pembroke Castle. He'd spent the morning racing around at high speed and bothering the servants, who already seemed to dote on him.

Pembroke had been King Henry's gift to Jasper Tudor, but he took a seat one place away from the head of the table, deferring to his father with cheerful good grace. Margaret could see the three Welshmen liked one another. She felt something unclench within her as she sipped her wine and eyed the steaming haunch of lamb brought in as a centerpiece of the table.

"It does my heart good to see a family who are not at each other's throats," she said. "If I had not been able to come here, I don't know what I would have done."

Owen Tudor looked over at her, his eyes crinkling in pleasure at having such a beauty in his presence. He could not resist smiling at the young queen, despite the disasters that had brought her into his son's lands.

"Your Highness . . ." he began.

"Margaret, please."

"Very well. Margaret. I am glad you remembered you have friends here. My family owes your husband a great debt. It cannot be repaid with wine and lamb—even Welsh lamb, which is the best in all creation."

She smiled, and he signaled for another thick slice to be passed to her plate, dripping with juices.

"When my wife passed, Margaret, news of our marriage and my lads got out. I was captured, did you know that? Oh yes. I was taken to Newgate prison for a time, on the orders of Speaker William Tresham. It was only a few months, but I tell you I have never been happier to feel the sun on my skin as when they let me out."

"Why were you taken up?" Margaret replied, interested despite her own worries.

Owen Tudor shrugged.

"They were angry about my marrying King Harry's bride. That was all it took to send soldiers after me. I could have disappeared into the hills, I suppose, but I could hardly see how they'd imprison me for marrying a queen, not after her first husband was in the ground. Yet I think I would still be there if your husband hadn't signed an order for my release, God's blessings be on him. He did right by me and held no grudge against one who loved his mother as much as he did himself." The old man shook his head in memory. "She was the finest part of my life. My Catherine gave me these scoundrels for my sons, and your husband made them earls. I have been blessed beyond anything I could have dreamed when I was young and foolish, though I miss her still."

To her surprise, Margaret saw a line of tears brighten his eyes, quickly rubbed away. It was hard not to like the man.

"I wish I had known her," she said.

Owen Tudor nodded.

"And I wish your husband had kept his strength. I am more than sorry to hear of his illness. Every year brings worse reports. It is a cruel thing he has endured, hard for any man, but much worse for a king. I know, Margaret, how dogs will gather around a wounded deer. They can be cruel."

It was Margaret's turn to feel tears sting her eyes. She looked away, fiddling with a cup of wine rather than allow her grief to turn to sobbing at the pity she could see in him.

"They have been," she said softly. "Henry was captured and good men were killed trying to save him. York has him now, hidden away.

It breaks my heart . . ." She made herself stop before the grief overwhelmed her.

"And yet you could have stayed in Kenilworth, my lady," Owen went on.

Margaret sensed his sons leaning in, their interest sharpening.

"I am pleased and more honored than you know that you came here to us, but I do not yet know why."

"You do," Margaret said, dabbing at her eyes with a cloth. "If I had stayed where I was safe, it would have meant giving up. It would have been the end. Instead, I came to you for an army, Owen. It is like a hot iron against my skin to have to ask, but if you feel a debt, I must call it in."

"Ah. There is the heart of it," Owen Tudor murmured, his gaze unblinking. "Though it is no choice at all, for me or my sons, my lady. We've talked before and there was never any doubt, not if you asked. Is there, lads?"

"None at all," Jasper Tudor said firmly.

His brother Edmund echoed his agreement, the three men made grim by her grief. Prince Edward had fallen silent, staring around him at the serious adult voices. One of the servants stepped in with cut fruit for him to enjoy and he tugged his mother's sleeve to show her. Margaret smiled down at him through tears that would not stop coming.

"I am grateful to you all," she said. "I hoped for it when I thought to come here, but you must know that York and Salisbury, Warwick and March, all threaten my family. I will need to find and raise every man in England and Wales—and beyond—to stand against them."

"Beyond, my lady?" Owen Tudor asked.

"If you will provide the ship, I have thought to sail to Scotland and speak to King James there. He has supported York's cause in the past, but I think I can make him an offer he'd find hard to refuse."

The Tudor sons waited for their father to consider this development. At last, he spoke, nodding.

"I would not like to see Scots come down from their highlands, my lady. They are a fierce race, right enough, and they will certainly be a terror on the battlefield. You must know their king will drive a hard bargain for his aid though. Whatever you have in mind—and I will not ask such a private thing—he'll want all that and a penny more, if you understand me."

"There is no price too high to pay to see my husband's enemies broken," Margaret replied.

"I wouldn't say that to him, my lady, or King James will ask for London—and a penny more," Owen Tudor replied.

She saw his eyes twinkle and smiled back despite herself. She had no doubt then that Queen Catherine had loved him, the bluff and solid Welshman who had eased her grief over the death of her first husband.

"I'll have a ship made ready for you, my lady," Jasper Tudor said. "The storms can be terrible later in the year, but while the summer ends, you should be safe enough. I'll send twenty of my own guards with you as well, to impress the Scots."

"Good lad," his father said. "We can't have the queen and our prince turning up in the wilds of Scotland alone. King James will expect a fine show. Now don't you worry. I'll bring the men of Wales out, my lady. I might even ride with them myself, to show these young pups what an old dog can do."

Jasper snorted and Margaret was touched at the visible affection between them. It was something she had never known and it seemed to bring her close to tears at every moment until she was exasperated with herself. It had probably not hurt her chance of winning their support to have wept at their table, she understood that much. Some men will move heaven and earth to aid a woman in distress.

"You give me hope, Owen," she said, her breath coming in shudders. "I pray my husband will be able to thank you as you deserve."

"It would be my honor," Owen Tudor replied. "He is a good man. The world doesn't need more cunning devils, Margaret. We have enough of those. Are you listening, lad?" He addressed the last to Prince Edward, who nodded in reply, his eyes wide. "I said we need good men to rule. One day, it will be you as king, did you know that?"

"Of *course*," the boy replied scornfully, making the old man grin.

Margaret reached out and twisted Edward's ear, so that he yelled. "Be respectful, Edward," she said. "You are a guest."

"Your pardon, sir," the boy replied, rubbing his ear and glaring at his mother.

CHAPTER 28

Derry Brewer wondered if the Earl of Northumberland was going to have a fit of apoplexy. The wind soared and sobbed around Alnwick Castle, whistling falling notes like a horn blowing retreat. At the head of the dining table, Henry Percy had grown darker and darker, his face swelling like a child holding his breath until he fainted.

"Lord Percy, we have common cause," Derry reminded him. "The queen must find her army where she can, if we are ever to see peace restored."

"But, the Scots! She might as well deal with the devil himself!" Henry Percy said. His mouth stayed open as he shook his head, giving him a foolish aspect that made Derry want to smile. He merely waited for the young earl to find calm. To his surprise, it was Somerset who spoke then, a man who could hardly understand the ancestral resentment of those who guarded the borders.

"My lords, Master Brewer, I would accept any force of men, aye, even the French, if it gave us a chance to right these wrongs. I accept my part of the blame for Northampton. If I had known York's supporters would come north, I would have been there to break them. We all took a debt that day, a responsibility for King Henry's capture."

"My brother Thomas *died* there," Henry Percy snapped. "Do you not think I feel the pain of that? Because of York, I lost my father. Because of attainted traitors, I lost my brother as well." He paused. "Perhaps I have suffered enough to endure the Scots in England, Master Brewer. Though I am only grateful my father did not live to see it." He shook his head in wry bitterness. "I think it would have killed the old man."

"I do not know they will even come," Derry said. "Though I would truly deal with the devil if I thought—"

To his irritation, Baron Clifford snapped a reply, talking over him before he had finished speaking.

"Don't say that, Brewer. Not even in jest, or foolish boast. The devil listens to such airs and promises—and he acts on them."

Derry clenched his jaw.

"—if I thought it would bring us victory. My lords, I have seen York, Salisbury, and Warwick turn disaster into triumph. I have lived to see King Henry captured and held prisoner." He included Baron Clifford in the look he swept over them. "You three lost fathers at St. Albans—and brothers or friends since. All the while, these traitors have grown strong, with every coin-toss falling well for them. The Attainders have been torn up by Parliament. York has made himself the heir to the throne—and how long will King Henry live now that he is a stone in York's boot? I tell you, my lords, this is the bitter heart of it. We will need every loyal man and, if we fail, the house of York will rule forever. There will *be* no Northumberland, or Somerset or Clifford. They will not forgive the Attainders against them if they ever have you at their mercy. Mercy is not a Neville trait, my lords, when they are strong. You know that is the truth. So I *would* welcome Scots and Welsh, even French . . . by God, even *Irish* to these shores if they could restore the rightful king and queen to the throne! I would risk my soul and the last breath in my body to see York beaten. *Nothing* else will do."

The three lords could only stare at the strong emotion revealed in the man before them. Derry Brewer was filthy from weeks on the road. They knew he had traveled to Wales and all over the country, passing word for men to gather. He had been urbane and amused throughout the discussion, but for one moment, he had allowed them to see his anger and his determination.

"Do you know yet where they have the king?" Somerset asked him.

"Not in the Tower," Derry replied. "It is still being repaired, after that fool Scales let the mob blow down a wall. I am only surprised Salisbury allowed him to surrender, with all of London calling for his blood. There's one man whose death I will not grieve, though I fought at his side, once. Using wildfire and cannon on the people of London! I'm told Scales was found with his throat cut in his cell. I'd buy a pint for the men who did it, if they ever find them." He shook his head in disgust. "No, my lord, they'll have the king somewhere close by. I have lads looking, but there are a thousand different houses and no way to know which it is." A memory came to him of racing through the Palace of Westminster, searching for William de la Pole years before. He did not share it with those present, knowing that they would not understand, or care.

"My lords, I think sometimes I have given my whole life to the lamb, to keeping Henry safe from his enemies. It is like a burr under my skin to know they have him and that his life is as fragile as a glass." He closed his eyes for an instant, his brow furrowing. "Perhaps we cannot save him now. But I will see York dead by the end, if I have to climb his towers and knife him in his sleep!"

Earl Percy chuckled, enjoying the spite in Derry Brewer's expression. It echoed his own feelings on the matter perfectly and he gripped the king's spymaster by the arm to show his support. A cloud of road-dust rose around them both.

"We have twelve thousand, Master Brewer. True soldiers with pike and cavalry and cannon. If the queen can bring a few more great hairy Scots as well, I do not think it will come to you climbing any towers. We'll put York's head on a city wall yet."

"I pray for it, my lord," Derry replied.

MARGARET PULLED HER CLOAK more tightly around her shoulders, feeling a bite to the wind that she had not known before. The sea voyage had been almost pleasant at first in the late summer sun, a week of sailing up the coast with nothing to do but plan and watch Prince Edward scamper about the deck on bare feet. His skin had reddened at first and then grown gold with the exposure, though she had kept her own well covered. As they went north, it seemed to have become colder with every sea mile. Margaret had been astonished to see sleet spatter the waves as they came into dock.

She found a country in mourning, with no gaiety at her arrival. The lairds of three clans met her on the docks, bowing deeply as they explained King James had been killed just a week before. She heard no more details as they escorted her deeper into the lowlands, with Jasper Tudor's troop of soldiers bringing up the rear in polished mail. The Scots had not seemed impressed by those men, though she thought it was no accident that they outnumbered her small force four to one, a party of more than a hundred riding away from the border with England.

It took three days to reach a huge castle still being built on the coast, with black crags on one side and screeching gulls in the air all around it. Margaret felt stronger, though her back ached after so long spent in the saddle. She had eaten with the lairds each evening in roadside inns, making light conversation that never strayed into her reasons for coming. They looked on her with pity in their eyes and she had grown angry with them as a result, feeling almost as if she was heading into battle. Time and again she had asked about King James and been gently rebuffed, with sighs and shrugged shoulders, as the lairds fell silent and called for whisky to toast the dear departed.

Margaret dismounted stiffly as rain began to fall, driven in from the sea. She pulled her cloak's hood over her hair and rushed into shelter, shooing Edward before her. There were guards at the gate and every door within, men wearing black tunics who stared at her in fascination. She kept her head up and followed the lairds in until she was taken to a comfortable-looking room deep within the castle. That part of it had been furnished, though entire wings and walls were still unmade. Prince Edward rushed to a window of tiny panes of glass, all held in lead. He stared out at the sea while his mother smoothed her skirts and fixed a loose pin in her hair.

She had not known what to expect, but it had not been the pretty, black-haired young woman who entered the room and rushed over to her without any formal announcement. Margaret stood up quickly and found her hands taken and held.

Mary of Guelders was Portuguese in her coloring, though when she spoke, her accent was a gentle Scottish lilt.

"I wish we could have met in happier times," she said. "But however it has come about, you are welcome here. Would this fine boy be your son?"

"Edward," Margaret said, utterly disarmed. She had expected fierce Scottish leaders, not a woman younger than she was herself, with eyes still red from weeping.

"What a lad! What a fine, dear lad!" Mary cried, kneeling down and opening her arms.

Edward came very reluctantly, allowing himself to be gripped, though he squirmed.

"Now, Edward, you will find my own boy if you run down to the kitchens. Young James is about your age and you must not fight with him, do you understand? The cook will feed you broth, if you ask her nicely."

Edward beamed at that. He held still while she kissed him on the cheek and then raced out of the room.

"James will look after him," Mary said, smiling at the sound of his fading footsteps. "Sit, Margaret. I must hear it all."

Margaret took a seat on a long couch, gathering her thoughts from where they had scattered.

"I heard the sad news from the lairds, my lady. I—"

"You must call me Mary! Are we not queens together? My husband was too in love with his cannon, Margaret. I warned him many times about the foul things, but he did not listen. Have you seen them? They are made for killing, and cruel-looking. And they will explode without warning, tearing good men too soon from the world."

Her eyes filled with tears and, without thought, Margaret reached out and drew her into an embrace. Mary sobbed into her shoulder, mastering herself with difficulty, but finally pulling away and dabbing at her eyes.

"For my husband's men, I have to be cold, do you understand? I cannot let them see me weep, with all of them wondering if I am strong enough to be regent while my son grows. Whisht, listen to me! A daft fishwife with my sorrows. You have known such pain, Margaret. Your poor man taken away by his enemies! I do not think I could bear such a thing, truly I don't."

Margaret blinked at her in surprise, guilt surging up into her throat. She would not speak of the sense of shame that *bit* at her every moment, like a summer fly. She had saved her son before her husband. No, she had saved herself and left him. She would not allow any comfort from lies. There had been spite as well, for a man who would not rouse himself, no matter how she begged him. The shame of that had left Margaret with a desperate need to bring Henry out of the clutches of his enemies. She knew she would do anything, *give* anything to see him again.

Margaret felt walls crumbling as her hands were held. She had thought to be hard and cold, but she had no defense against the kindness of this strange woman, who could go from tears to laughter in a single breath, speech rattling out of her the whole time. Mary saw her trembling and waved a hand as if to brush away sadness.

"We hear it all, my dear. My husband was in favor of York, but I never agreed with him! I think James would have sung a different tune if one of *his* lords marched against him, wouldn't he just? No, you and I are the same. Brought to new homes to be queens, married and sold for a fine dowry. I remember how proud I was when William Crighton came for me, my own Scots warrior, bringing me to James. Oh, damn me, crying again. It is too raw."

"William de la Pole came to fetch me to England," Margaret said faintly. Tears came to her own eyes in reaction. She and Mary smoothed them away with the backs of their hands. Seeing their own action mirrored in the other suddenly made them both laugh.

"Look at us, in our grieving," Mary said. "My husband's men would pull their beards in disgust if they knew. Well, we will not tell them. We'll say we faced each other and spoke like there was ice in our blood. They will not believe it, but we'll say it anyway. A French queen of England, a Portuguese queen of Scotland. We are two rare flowers, Margaret: two sprigs of heather."

"Then I am not ashamed to say I hope for your aid, Mary," Margaret replied. "I need men to come south with me, if I am ever to free my husband."

Mary sniffed and nodded, brushing her hand over her bound hair.

"I knew it when your man Brewer sent James the news of your coming. I think my husband would have sent you back empty-handed, Margaret, but I will not! I would not turn away a sister, though I must have something to show my lairds in return."

Margaret nodded, wondering privately if the woman's tears and affections were not at least partly feigned. Her doubts must have shown on her face, as Mary leaned in and pressed a hand on her arm.

"I won't bargain with you or count the coins. I *will* help, with whatever I can. You must have thought of terms as you sailed. Tell me what you intended, Margaret, and I will agree to it all. You will have four thousand men, a rare crop of bonny lads to fight for you."

Once more Margaret was assailed by doubt and suspicions. If this was negotiation, it was either too simple, or far more complicated than she had expected. She rather missed the gruff honesty of Owen Tudor at that moment, for all the fellow feeling she had been shown.

"I hoped your husband would agree to a betrothal between my son and one of your daughters. Their children will sit on the throne of England."

"Agreed!" Mary said, sweeping her arm through the air between them. "There! My daughter's name is Margaret, named for you. She is five years old and she will make your lad a fine queen when she is grown."

"Named for me?" Margaret said, her eyes widening.

"The French queen of England who kept her husband safe from wolves for so long? What better name for a daughter of mine? I am only sorry we have not met before. I could have helped you, if my James would have let me. He was a rare man. I will not see his like again." A frown crossed her face then, at the memory of her husband. Her head tilted, almost as if she could hear his voice. "I recall he always talked of one place, one thorn in his big paw that he wanted and could not have. Perhaps in honor of his memory, I should add that to our agreement, but no, I will not! I have said I will support you with four thousand men and the betrothal is enough, more than enough."

"What place do you mean?" Margaret said faintly.

"Berwick, on the River Tweed. It is almost Scotland, he said. Right on the borders. It would mean moving the border a single mile, but it would please his shade and I should honor him. His lairds will think me clever if I could tell them I had won that."

"I'm sure they think it already," Margaret murmured. She was certain by then that the young woman had run the conversation exactly along the lines she wanted, but even so, the price was not too high. Losing Henry was a guilt and shame she could bear no longer, no matter what it cost. Just the thought that men like York might hurt him wrenched at her womb and stomach as if she had been kicked. Margaret dipped her head.

"Berwick is yours, Mary. My husband would not begrudge the loss of a mile, compared to all his kingdom."

Once more, Mary of Guelders took up her hands, holding them tight.

"Then it is agreed. You'll have the best fighters in Scotland to come south with you. My husband was the *Clan* Chief, do you understand? The word is 'Clanna,' children. They were all his children and he was a fine father to them. I will pick them myself for beards and muscle and skill with a sword. You've made me your ally, Margaret, as if I was not before. We'll announce the betrothal immediately. Will you sit at table with me now? I want to hear so much more of London and France."

————

YORK COULD HEAR RAIN SPATTERING against the windows of the bishop's palace. The king's room was lit by a fire burning low along one wall and a single lamp of copper and polished iron, placed by the king's elbow so that he could read. Beyond the noise of the rain, the only sounds were the whisper of Henry's hand running across paper and the gentle murmuring of his voice as he spoke the words aloud, his lips moving constantly.

They were alone. The bishop's servants had all been sent down-river to London for the evening, escorting their master so that no one had seen York arrive and shed his dripping cloak. The main door had come open at his touch and he'd walked through empty corridors carrying his own lamp, hearing only his footsteps.

York sat by the king's chair, facing the fire and close enough for any observer to have believed they were deep in private conversation. Though the logs burned low, the room was warm, the walls paneled in the dark gold of ancient oak. York wondered who had been king when those trees were felled. The oak planks had certainly been cut long before the Norman invasion, old even then. Athelstan? Before even him. They could have been dried and polished when the king-doms of Wessex and Mercia had not yet been joined under a single English throne. York thought he could feel the weight of history in that room. He breathed in the odors of wax and smoke as if they were the finest incense.

A small round table sat between them, bearing a single cup, a flask of wine, and a much smaller wooden bottle with a glass stopper. York's gaze was drawn to that collection, watching the raindrops from his cloak scattered around it, gleaming the reflections of the embers, like spilled drops of gold.

The murmuring stopped and York raised his head slowly, seeing that Henry was looking at him in mild interest.

"I know why you are here," Henry said suddenly. "I have endured this sickness, this madness for such a long time, I think whole years have been stolen from me. But I am not a fool. I was never a fool."

York looked away, leaning further over with his elbows on his knees as he sat there, staring down at the polished wooden floor. He did not raise his head as the king spoke again.

"Have you news of my wife and son, Richard? The servants move around me with empty faces, as if I am a ghost, as if they are all deaf. You see me though, don't you? You hear me?"

"I hear you, Your Majesty. I see you," York said in a breath. "Your wife and son are well, I am certain."

"Margaret named my boy Edward, just as you did with yours, Richard. He is a fine lad, always laughing. How old is your boy now, thirteen? Older?"

"He is eighteen, taller than most men."

"Ah, I'm sorry. I have missed so much. They say a son is his father's greatest pride, a daughter his comfort," Henry said. "I would have liked daughters, Richard, though perhaps they will come to me yet."

York's gaze flickered to the bottles on the table.

"Perhaps, Your Majesty."

"My own father died before I could ever know him," Henry said, looking off across the dim gold light of the room. "He took no pride in me, he could not. I wish sometimes that I had known him. I wish he had known me."

"Your father was a great man, Your Majesty, a great king." York's head drooped further. "If he had lived a dozen years longer, so much would be different."

"Yes. I would have liked to know him. Yet I must be content. I will see him again, with my mother. That brings me comfort, Richard, when the illness presses on me. There will be a day when I stand before him. I will tell him I was king, for a time. I will describe Margaret to him and my son, Edward. Will he be disappointed, Richard? I have won no wars, as he did." His eyes were large in the dim light, the pupils black pools of sorrow as he turned to York. "How will he know me? I was just a child when he died."

"He will know you, Majesty. He will embrace you."

Henry yawned, looking around for the servants that were not present, and frowning.

"It is late, Richard. I rise very early now, before the sun. I have been too long at my reading and my head is aching."

"Shall I pour your wine, Your Majesty?"

"Yes, please. It helps me to sleep without dreams. I must not dream, Richard. I see such terrible things."

York broke the wax seal on the wine and removed a paper plug, filling the cup with dark red liquid that looked black in the dim light. Henry seemed to have forgotten him, his attention drawn to the glowing embers as the fire burned down. York might as well have been alone for all he could feel the presence of the other man. Silence filled the room like warm air, thick and sluggish, as York's hand reached for the second bottle. He flicked open the glass stopper on a tiny hinge, but he did not bring them together. Henry's face was lit in gold and shadows, his eyes hooded as he stared into the coals.

York closed his eyes, pressing the heel of his hand against his forehead, the open bottle still held in his fingers.

He stood suddenly, startling Henry into looking up at him.

"God be with you, Your Majesty," York said, his voice hoarse.

"You will not stay with me?" Henry asked, his gaze falling on the cup of wine.

"I cannot. There are armies gathering in the north. Armies I must meet and break. Your servants will have returned when you wake."

Henry took the cup and put it to his lips, tilting it high. His eyes remained on York as he drank and put it down empty.

"I wish you fine fortune, Richard. You are a better man than they know."

York made a rough sound in his throat, almost a cry of pain. He swept out of the room, the small bottle still clenched in his hand. Henry turned back to the fire, pressing his head against the chair's cloth and feeling sleep steal over him. York's footsteps seemed to echo in that empty place for a long time, until they could be heard no more.

CHAPTER 29

Winter lay hard on the land as York rode back along the river to the Palace of Westminster. Rain beat against his skin until it felt as if he wore a mask. There was no moon or any stars to be seen under a low bank of cloud over the city, so York was forced to walk his horse for five miles, warmed only by simmering anger. Even that could not withstand the bitter cold, so that he arrived drenched and stiff at the royal apartments, his teeth chattering and even his thoughts reduced to drifting lumps of ice in his mind. He reached a crackling fire and stood mute before it, pools forming on the rugs at his feet. Dawn was still some way off and he was weary to the bone, to the point of swaying slightly as he closed his eyes and stretched out his hands to the heat.

Salisbury entered the room as York's cloak began to steam. The earl had clearly been summoned from his bed as his hair stood up in tufts of gray and he looked ten years older. Even so, his eyes were sharp as he caught sight of the tall, dark figure staring into the flames as they crackled and huffed. Salisbury knew very well where he had been that night and he ached with the desire to ask. When York turned to him, the man's eyes were red-rimmed and wild and the questions dried in Salisbury's throat.

"What news?" York asked. His hands had turned bright red and slightly swollen as he held them to the fire. Salisbury found his gaze drawn to the outstretched fingers.

"Nothing more on how many they have gathered. In this weather, too many are snugged away in tents or behind city walls."

York scowled at him.

"We need to know."

"I cannot work miracles, Richard," Salisbury said, coloring. "I have six good men in place in Coventry, three in the city of York, but only two now in the whole of Wales—and no word from them for a month."

It had taken years to place informers in the major households of their enemies. After the battle of St. Albans, Salisbury had set about it with a will, determined to match Derry Brewer in his reach and depth of information. Over time, Salisbury had begun to glimpse the difficulties of establishing such a group—and the quality of his far more experienced opponent. All too often his men had been found murdered, almost always as if they had suffered a terrible accident. Yet some had survived, remaining silent and overlooked, until they'd been able to report a massive force forming in the north.

It made little sense. No one fought in winter. Marching armies could not forage as they went. Rain ruined bows and made men slip in clotted muck, halving the distance they could march each day. Numb hands dropped weapons and entire armies could slip past each other on dark, windy nights and never know how close they'd come.

Despite all that, a dozen powerful lords were all bringing soldiers to the same spot, planting banners in the mud and bitter cold. Worse, one of Salisbury's men had come in to report recruiters in Wales, with hundreds gathering under the drenched banners of the Tudors. No one ever fought in winter. Only the fact that Henry was a prisoner could have brought them out to march on London, desperate to save the king.

"Have you heard from your son, Warwick?" York asked.

Salisbury shook his head, irritated.

"It's too early still. It's one thing to call the men of Kent in high summer. Quite another to bring them out of their villages with Christmas on the way."

"London is too far south," York muttered, turning back to the fire. "Too far for me to keep my eye on what they are doing." He saw Salisbury flush as if he had been rebuked and nodded to himself.

It had been Salisbury's idea to make London their fortress, while the Bills of Attainder were reversed. It had made sense for a time, with so many London men willing to come to their banners, to be trained and equipped. After the savage defense of the Tower by Lord Scales, thousands of London lads had volunteered to join them, from the families in grand houses on Wych Street to lads from the heart of the rookeries. They'd spent all autumn marching through the southern fields beyond the river, learning to use pikes and shields.

York clenched his fists and splayed the fingers wide once again, feeling heat ease the pain as blood returned to them. While he and Salisbury had been building an army, it seemed the queen had been out as well, dripping poison into the ears of men like the Tudor earls. He might even have admired the woman, if she had not been so set against him from the beginning. While Margaret lived, while her son lived, he knew he would never be safe.

York wondered where she was at that moment and whether she had heard of his rise to become heir to the throne. It was a small comfort in the black mood that swamped him. His imagination kept returning to King Henry and the room in the bishop's palace, dreading the moment when Salisbury would ask.

"We'll march," York said suddenly into the silence. "I won't wait for them to come to me. We'll take all but three thousand men north. If they are gathering armies, I want to see them. I want to know how many they have. For all we know, they are waiting for spring and we might catch them unaware. Yes. Better than standing here, for others to decide our fate."

"Three thousand can keep order, well enough," Salisbury replied. He lifted another pair of logs onto the fire, busying himself with an iron poker.

"Perhaps they could, but we can't spare them," York said. "I won't leave good soldiers in London. We need a strong force in the path of the Tudors, to change their minds about leaving Wales. My son can settle three thousand around Ludlow to defend the border. He knows the land there. We'll keep a string of horsemen between us, so that any messages can be carried quickly. Another line to Warwick in Kent, as he brings them north. We do not need London now. The taverns are all dry, anyway." York smiled wryly, pleased to see the older man's expression lighten.

"I would like to go home," York said softly. "I have spent too long in the south and I am weary of it. I will be fifty in a few months and I am tired. Do you feel it? I would see my own lands again, even if there is a queen's army waiting for me there."

"I understand. I feel the same, in truth. They've lost six thousand men this year. Too many crops have rotted where they lay, without lads to take in the harvest. Bread costs twice the price now, did you know? Beer is twopence a pint, with barley so scarce. They've beggared the north. People are starving in some places, all for battles they've lost. I think those Gallants have learned the cost of fine promises and a silver badge. They cannot afford another year like this one."

All the time they had been talking, a single question had shimmered beneath Salisbury's thoughts. He suspected he knew the answer already, from York's grim mood, but he chose to speak the words aloud, even so.

"In King Henry, they have a talisman to gather support, a name to bring men in, who might otherwise spend the winter at their hearths. Did you . . . find him ailing?"

York sucked his front teeth, his tongue probing a hole that hurt him.

"He was well enough, when I left him." He did not look away from the fire as Salisbury blew air in grumbling irritation.

"The sickest man in England is still 'well enough'? No one would be surprised if Henry passed in his sleep, but you are somehow certain he is well? For God's *sake*, Richard! You are the heir to the throne! Will you wait for him to die of old age?"

"You don't understand," York snapped at him. "While he lives, we have some semblance of acting in his name. There are still some, more than some, who will fight with us only because we *defend* the king. You were there at Ludlow. You saw Trollope lead his Calais men to the king's side, just as soon as he saw the lion banners! If Henry died, we would be throwing away some part of our armies. Henry alive puts us in the *right*."

Salisbury looked at the younger man in bemusement, hearing the lie and not understanding it. He wondered if York even did himself.

"If Henry had *somehow* died tonight, as we discussed and feared he might, you would be king. You would be crowned in London tomorrow and you would take up that same lion banner. All the lords and common men who feel such awe for King Henry would kneel to you—and fight for you! Sweet Jesus, I knew it when I saw your scowls."

Despite his anger, Salisbury looked around the room, checking no servant had entered who might overhear them. His voice dropped to a harsh whisper.

"You were the one who insisted it could be no other hand. You said you would not allow some thief to break into his room. You said it could not be done in blood. Do you still have the bottle, or did you leave it by his side for his doctors to sniff and recognize?"

Stung by the anger of his friend, York reached sharply into a pouch under his cloak and threw the small bottle into the fire, where it rested unbroken, slowly turning black. They could both hear sizzling begin inside it and a tongue of green flame flicker around the stopper.

"He is like a child," York said, "an innocent. I think he understood what I was going to do and he forgave me for it. It would have been a monstrous thing, to damn my soul for such a boy."

"You would be king *tonight*," Salisbury said, bitterly angry. "You and I would have secured our futures, our families, and our houses for a century. For that, I would damn a thousand souls, my own among them, then sleep like a child after."

"Oh, keep your scorn," York retorted. "This is no game of thrones, but real endings and real blood. I wonder how it is that you would make me king and yet still seek to control my hand. Is it so terrible that I could not murder a child? Do I not know you at all?"

Under York's searching gaze, Salisbury looked down, breathing out and out, until he was empty.

"You do know me," he said at last. "And it is not so terrible. I would have felt the loss if you'd brought me news of his death, not least for love of his father." He held up both his hands, palms out and empty. "Very well, Richard. I will not ask again. Send Edward to Wales and I will ride north with you, though my old bones complain at the very thought. We'll find another way that does not come from Henry's death."

MARGARET LOOKED OVER HER SHOULDER, her eyes brightening as she caught sight of her son. The little boy rode so proudly, with ambling Scots all around him. The lairds had put him on a horse to keep up with them, though they walked themselves. For the first few miles, Margaret had feared for his safety. Yet the one time he'd slipped, a young man had caught him easily, swooping him back into the saddle, with the boy's laughter ringing out.

They might have frightened her, those clan warriors that Mary had chosen to come to England. They were not large men, with some notable exceptions. They wore thick beards of red or black or dark brown, sometimes braided into lengths, with charms woven into the hair. They spoke their own strange tongue among themselves, though a fair scattering seemed to know French. Very few of them knew English, or at least admitted to it, though they could grin and look aside at each other at the simplest question, breaking into sudden laughter for no reason she could understand.

They were fierce enough, she could see that much. Mary of Guelders had not lied when she said she'd choose them for their strength and skill. Each man wore a leine, a long yellow tunic that left his arms bare, stretching to his knees. She'd learned early on from the smell which ones had been able to afford saffron dye and which had used horse urine. Over that warcoat, they pinned a shapeless cloth— a "brat," as they called it—held by a clasp at the neck to make a cloak, or even a blanket to sleep in. Some of those were dark blue, or red, while others were woven in a strange pattern of browns and greens.

She had been surprised how many went barelegged underneath the leine and brat. A small number wore trews like her countrymen in France, molded to their legs with years of wear and all the grease they could rub in to seal out the cold. The rest strode out with hairy legs showing almost to the thigh as they belted the brats tight around their waist, gathering the cloth in folds to march.

The days were short and dark by the time they crossed the border. They walked for all the hours of daylight, then rested and ate, with four thousand men wrapped in the brats like cocoons on the damp ground. Food was very short, though they emptied the stores of any village or town they passed and placed a few good archers at the front to watch for rabbits or winter deer. Margaret felt thinner after a week with them, though her energy seemed to increase, against all understanding, on that poor diet of oats and a few strips of dried meat.

December was well advanced by the time they reached the city of York and the huge army assembling outside it. The Scots seemed to perk up at the sight of tents and armored knights waiting for them, making Margaret worry. She had brought an old enemy into England, for all she had been promised their loyal service. It was too easy to imagine some rash action or shouted jibe and then the young men of Scotland would be fighting the very army they had come to aid.

Scouts were racing ahead of her four thousand, carrying the news. Margaret told herself not to worry, but she saw the laird they followed ease his horse across the line of marching men, heading toward her.

Andrew Douglas could speak both French and English, though he would mutter in Gaelic at the same time, almost as if he carried on a conversation with himself. She did not know his formal position at the court of the Scottish king, though Mary had said she trusted him. The laird was large and solid, one of the few who had chosen to ride, though he controlled his horse with main force rather than any grace or delicacy. He seemed to glare at her as his habitual expression, though Margaret knew in part it was the great hairiness of him, a beard that could have hidden a bird's nest, combined with thick black hair to his shoulders and bristling eyebrows. Beyond his nose and a patch of exposed skin high on his cheeks, the Douglas gazed out from thickets, his blue eyes always shadowed. He was respectful enough in her presence, though his Gaelic murmuring may not have been, for all she knew.

"My lady, it's best I halt the men, before they frighten the hounds, if you follow," he said, adding a low undertone of words she did not know. "I'll need to find a good place for them to rest, near a river—upstream of those lads below, so there'll be no drinking their pesh."

Margaret blinked at him, feeling she might not have understood his exact meaning, but not willing to ask him to repeat himself. For someone with French as her first language, she found the Scottish accent almost impossible at times. She inclined her head to the general idea and he shouted to the men around him in his own language, so that they stopped and unbuckled their swords and axes. Margaret began to worry once again.

"Why are they arming themselves, Andrew? There are no enemies here."

"It's just their way, my lady. They like to hold iron when the English are close. It's just their habit, pay it no mind."

Margaret called her son, watching fondly as he kicked his mount on, red-faced at the gaze of so many on him until he reached her side, panting and beaming. In the distance, perhaps three dozen men had gathered outside the ranks of the army awaiting them, raising banners as they approached at a light trot.

"That is the Duke of Somerset, there," Margaret said, turning to the laird.

"Aye, and Earl Percy," he replied. "We know his flags well enough."

"And I am grateful that the honor of your queen and her son will mean there is to be no fighting between you," Margaret said firmly.

To her surprise, he laughed.

"Oh, we understand a truce—and who our allies are. If you knew a little more of the clans, you'd know to trust these lads."

Despite his reassurance, Margaret found herself growing nervous as the riders approached. She felt a wave of relief to see Derry Brewer riding alongside them, his delight visible.

As the most senior lord, Somerset was the first to dismount and drop to one knee before Margaret, followed quickly by Earl Percy and Baron Clifford. The rest of the men stood in silence while their masters greeted the queen and her son, watching the ranks of Scots warriors with cold expressions and one hand on their sword hilts.

"Your Highness, you are a joy to see," Somerset said as he rose. "Prince Edward, I give you welcome."

"I can only wonder at the price you must have paid for such a number of men, my lady," Henry Percy added, frowning. "I pray it will not be too great a burden." The young earl had the Percy beak, Margaret noted, that great wedge of a nose that dominated his face and made him look like a younger version of his father.

"I believe that is the business of the Crown, my lord Percy," she replied tartly, making him flush. "Now, I must introduce Lord Douglas, commander to these fine warriors."

Earl Percy sensed hostility as Andrew Douglas approached. The Scot made a point of showing his empty palm and then took Percy's hand as if he was granting a great concession. When he had his hand back, the earl turned away from him, staring in disapproval over the rabble of Scots, his mouth twisting as he gnawed an ulcer inside his lip. Margaret could see Derry Brewer was watching the exchange in amusement.

"I have marked a camp, just a little way off the main force," Somerset said, frowning at the tension in the air. "Lord Douglas, you and your men will take the left flank, if we are attacked, close by Clifford and my own men."

"And where will you stand, Lord Percy?" Andrew Douglas asked innocently.

"On the *right* flank," Percy replied immediately, color deepening on his cheeks. "My men and yours have a long history and scores that will not be settled here." His voice and expression hardened subtly. "I do not expect any trouble at all—I have said the same to my captains. I must, of course, forbid any entry to the city by your men. I have already given that assurance to the city council."

"We accept your terms, my lord," Douglas replied. "God forbid we should ever frighten the people of York." The Scot muttered something else under his breath that made Percy darken almost to purple.

Margaret wondered if the earl understood the strange, liquid tongue, after guarding the borders for so long against men just like her four thousand. She took a moment to offer up a silent prayer that she had not brought wolves among the lambs.

"Your Highness," Somerset said, breaking her concentration. "With your permission, I have allocated rooms for you to rest in the city, in a good street. Baron Clifford has agreed to show these men their place."

Andrew Douglas chuckled at that, enjoying some meaning that may or may not have been intended. Before she could be guided away, Margaret dismounted and embraced the Scot, surprising them all so that every man froze and stared into the middle distance.

"Thank you for bringing me home, Andrew. Whatever your reasons, I am grateful to you and to your men. They are fine lads."

She left the Scotsman almost as deeply red as Earl Percy, staring after her. Derry Brewer helped the queen to mount once again. He was grinning as he swung up to the saddle of Retribution and they trotted away, taking half the assembled nobles and bannermen with them. Above them all, rain started to fall once again, hard enough to sting the faces of those who looked up and groaned.

CHAPTER 30

Christmas had come and gone on the road, one of the strangest York and Salisbury had ever spent, away from their families. Though they were marching north to war, neither man could ignore the day of Christ's birth, even if their men would have let them and not considered such an act the worst omen possible.

The presence of eight thousand soldiers descending on his diocese had astonished the Bishop of Lincoln and been far too many even for that vast cathedral on its hill. Huge numbers of men had packed in good-naturedly around the local congregation, while the rest huddled outside, looking up in awe at the tallest spire in England. For once, the rain gave the men a respite. There was no wind at all and the cold deepened, so that the city sparkled in frost and those outside were quickly shivering and blowing on their hands. For a few hours of silence and muffled hymns being sung, it seemed as if the whole world held its breath.

They had lost almost two days cutting across country to the cathedral, but York could see the experience had refreshed the men, so that they walked with less of a load on their shoulders. No doubt

many of them had confessed their sins into that vast and frozen stillness, asking to be forgiven so that, if they died, they had at least a
chance of reaching heaven. He had done the same himself and in that
moment, as he knelt, he had been thankful the king's death did not
lie on his soul. It would have been too much to bear, too much to
forgive.

It had surprised York to find he was enjoying the slow journey
north. The Roman roads were solid flags of stone leading through
moors and dense forests of oak and birch and ash. The marching
soldiers strode to the top of hills and could see for miles across a dark
green landscape before descending into forested valleys and pounding on.

The rain and blustering wind had been almost incessant, dripping
through the trees on either side of the road, dampening the spirits of
the men and making their clothes and cloaks as heavy as armor. Yet
when York breathed in, it was air he had known before, sometimes
driven hard into his lungs. All the politics and problems of London
fell behind and he was enjoying the company of Salisbury, with no
more concern than putting a good number of miles behind them each
day. Food was scarce and after eight days of eating little, York could
pat his stomach and take pleasure from the trim muscle, losing some
of the thickness that had bedeviled the previous few years. He felt
strong and alert, so much so that it was almost a shame to be taking
his men against a hostile army. For all the goodwill he felt, that fact
lay over his best moods like a shroud.

He and Salisbury had picked up another four hundred men from
their own estates as they passed close to them, often single manors
long owned by their families and restored after the Attainders had
been revoked. York's second son, Edmund, Earl of Rutland, had been
among them, seventeen and as proud as the devil to have the chance
to march and fight at his father's side. Edmund did not have the

height or massive frame of his elder brother, but he resembled his father with black hair and dark eyes and stood an inch taller than York. His father greeted his arrival with a shout of joy, though in private, he told Salisbury it felt like Cecily had her eyes on him, through the boy.

York and Salisbury used any spare mounts as scout horses, placing men back along the roads to London and west toward the borders of Wales. Others rode ten miles ahead of them in groups of three riders at a time, so that at least one would survive an ambush and be able to race back. In hostile country, it was the merest sense to have far-ranging riders out before them, like dragonflies swinging back and forth at all hours, taking orders and passing on news of the land ahead. Each day extended the lines, so that when Warwick returned to London in the south, that news was six days old by the time it reached Salisbury. Warwick was coming north behind them with the men of Kent, drawn from their families and grumbling the whole way, judging by the few terse lines he sent to his father.

Edward of March was even more laconic, when his message reached them. He reported nothing from Ludlow Castle, simply acknowledging that he was in position and passing on his mother's love. York had smiled to himself as he read the single line signed "E. March," imagining his son torn between the responsibility of leading an army, all the while enduring his mother's instructions. Nonetheless, York was satisfied. They were all out. Despite the rain and the dark and the cold, he had three armies in the field, ready to crush any forces Queen Margaret might have raised. He was almost ready to bless his enemies for gathering in one place, even in winter, where he could break them all at once. The year was ending and York felt the rightness of it. By the time spring came, he would have all England under his hand.

He thought then of a lonely young man in the bishop's palace, no doubt reading by his lamp. York shook his head to free it of the image.

Henry's fate was a knot untied and he knew he was not finished with the king. Yet for the moment, he would look only ahead.

Having scouts so far out meant it was impossible for York and Salisbury to be surprised. Neither man saw anything unusual in the galloping squire lashing his reins back and forth to drive his flagging horse back to their ranks. As they'd passed the town of Sheffield, seat of the Earl of Shrewsbury, York had entered lands he knew particularly well, from childhood on. The great city of York lay just two days to the north and he felt like he'd come home. His men allowed the scout through as they had done many times before. Most had nothing new to report and York greeted him with a smile as the young man dismounted and bowed. The scout was oddly pale and wet with perspiration, but York merely raised his eyebrows, waiting for him to settle himself.

"My lord, there is a great host by the city of York, ahead. An army such as I have never seen."

They were passing through a stretch of dark woodland, the road just a broken thread with half the stones missing. Trees encroached on both sides, sometimes growing right through the Roman slabs. York saw Salisbury turn his horse back, coming close enough to hear.

"It seems this young man has found our quarry," York said, forcing lightness into his voice. "Where are your companions?"

"My lord, I-I don't know. We saw they had their own scouts out and after that it was all fast riding. I lost sight of them." Without conscious thought, the young man patted the neck of his mount with a trembling hand, the animal lathered with long strings of spit flung back from the muzzle.

"How close did you come before you turned back?" York asked. To his surprise, the young man flushed, as if his courage had been questioned. "Just tell me what you saw." He and Salisbury had made a point of choosing only scouts who could count, or at least estimate large numbers. York watched impatiently as the young man twitched his fingers and muttered under his breath.

"They were in three battles, my lord. Three big squares, camped by the city. Each one was near s-six thousand men, if I'm any judge. A little less, perhaps, but I would say they had eighteen thousand, all told."

York swallowed, feeling a shudder run down his back. He had faced almost as many at Ludlow, but the king's nobles had lost thousands since then, as well as the leadership of men like Buckingham and Egremont. He felt a touch of despair at the thought of such a host. The queen and her noblemen seemed to raise armies like swarms of locusts wherever they went. York glanced at Salisbury and saw the older man glowering at him. The king's name was a powerful aid to recruitment, in his absence, or more likely because of it. York did not meet Salisbury's eyes, thinking hard as the scout stared.

"They'll know we are coming if the scouts crossed," Salisbury said suddenly. "How long ago was this?"

The young squire seemed relieved to look away from the pain on York's face.

"I saw them yesterday morning, my lord. I had to take a wide line to get past the riders coming after me, but it cannot be more than twenty, maybe thirty miles. I do not go out further."

"And they've had a full day to come south, if they marched as soon as our scouts were seen."

"No," York said. "We have other scouts at six and twelve miles. None of them have come back in with sightings. The queen's army has not moved, or at least not quickly."

"It is too many, Richard, even so," Salisbury said softly.

York glared at him, taking a moment to dismiss the panting scout and order another out in his path. He needed his dragonflies more than ever at that moment, with such a multitude out against him.

"No, it's not," York said firmly. "Even if winter stole the heart from half the Kentish men, Warwick will bring six thousand—or many more. My son has three thousand with him." York spoke dully, thinking through the odds.

If he called Edward back, there would be no one on the Welsh border to stand against the Tudors. Everything depended on how many marched with Warwick—and how far away they were. York cursed softly to himself, and Salisbury nodded.

"We need a stronghold," Salisbury said. "Somewhere safe while we wait. Middleham is too far and too small for eight thousand men."

"Sandal, then," York said. "It lies no more than four leagues from where we stand."

"And it may have been passed already, by the queen's army," Salisbury said. "I'd rather go west or north, perhaps back to Ludlow, even."

"They'd run us down before we reached it." York rubbed his face hard, as if to bring some life back to his flesh. "And I will not tempt fate to repeat itself. No. None of our other scouts have come in. We can reach Sandal Castle. It's an island almost, a fortress on a hill and simple to defend. It will do."

"I do not like the risk," Salisbury said firmly. "You'd have me head straight toward an enemy of twice our number."

He started in surprise when York laughed and breathed in sharply, filling his chest.

"I am *home*. They have made me march through storms and rain and I am only stronger for all of it. This year is ending—and this last, great hunt with it. Sandal is just a few miles away. I do not fear your 'risk,' or the movements of my enemies, no matter how many they have brought." York shook his head in saturnine amusement. "I will *not* run. Not today, or any day. Being forced to leave Ludlow was enough for one lifetime. I tell you, they will not see my back again."

His eyes were cold as he waited for a reply, wondering if Salisbury would continue to argue, while time they needed drained away.

"Four leagues to Sandal? You are certain? Twelve miles?" Salisbury said at last. York smiled at his friend.

"No more than that, I swear it. I used to ride from York to the market in Sheffield when I was a boy, traveling with your father. I *know* these lands. We'll be safe within Sandal's walls before the sun even begins to set."

"Then increase the pace," Salisbury replied. "We cannot make the sun stand still."

THE ARMY CAMPED outside the city of York was the largest Derry Brewer had ever seen, just about. Even so, he continued to fret, worrying at an infected scratch on a finger with his teeth, pressing against the hot flesh and spitting when bitterness seeped into his mouth. Storm clouds lay above the vast fields of tents and men, all suffering in the constant damp. They had dug trenches for their waste, only to see them flood on a single night of heavy rain, producing a stream of filth that ran through the camp, mingling with standing water. Sickness was spreading through them as well, so that at any moment, there would be a few hundred men groaning as they emptied their bowels with their hose or Gallic breeches down by their ankles. For some reason, the Scots were suffering worse than the other men, reduced to misery by the strange purge and as weak as children while it burned through them.

Derry dismounted at the edge of the queen's pavilion, the largest single structure on the plain. He passed the reins of Retribution to a servant, taking a moment to explain the horse's desperate desire for a wizened winter apple, if such a thing could be found. Derry showed the boy a silver penny as a promise and went in to the war council, hearing the voices of Margaret and her lords while he was still paces away.

Inside, the noise of rain was much louder. The tent leaked in a dozen places, dripping into pots in dull tones and making the air thick with moisture. Field braziers stood on soaked groundcloth, raising wisps of mist and adding the pungent smoke of charcoal and crackling green wood to the atmosphere. Derry draped his cloak along a bench, almost unnoticed as he left it to dry and came to listen.

Lord Clifford was in the middle of the discussion, a short, fine-boned man with a delicate mustache that would need trimming every single day to keep its shape. Though Clifford was only one of a dozen minor barons in that multitude, he had been brazen in using his father's death at St. Albans with men like Somerset and Percy. For that shared loss, they had granted Clifford a seat at their table and authority far beyond whatever was merited by his rank.

Derry didn't like the man, at all. The young baron had a tendency to talk over him, as if his opinion was utterly worthless. It would always have been hard to respect such a man but, as it happened, Derry had made no special effort to learn the trick of it.

Standing on the outskirts, Derry wondered if it was intentional that the group of noblemen all faced the queen, as if she were the fire that warmed them all. He noted the enormous red-bearded Scot standing by her shoulder as a guard. The man was impassive, but he was listening closely enough to those who would eventually order his companions into battle.

Derry took in every detail in a brief glance, settling himself and ignoring the smell of illness and weak bowels that hung in the air, along with damp wool and rotting leather. At least it was warm, he thought gratefully.

"If York has brought the king north, it will be as a prisoner," Clifford was saying. "I've instructed my captains to ignore any royal banners, if they see them. They know King Henry would never march against his wife and son, so I do not fear desertion. Such men are happier with simple instructions, as you know. Yet they are resolute, my lady. I think the sight of lions on the battlefield will raise their spirits, confirm to them that they are rescuing King Henry. Let us pray that York *has* brought him forth! It will give the men heart."

Margaret noticed Derry Brewer edging closer. She beckoned him in, ignoring Clifford's exasperated grunt as Somerset and Percy allowed him to the front of their group.

"What news, Master Brewer?"

"There is some sickness in the camp still, my lady, but fewer men affected today than yesterday. I've seen such things in France, but as yet we have lost only a few of the weakest men. I think it will burn out rather than spread further, God willing. I sent the worst sixty or so back to the city to rest, with orders for them to be given broth and ale. I had to insist on 'one in one out' after that, or we'd have the whole army resting up in the warm." He glanced up at the impassive stare of the Scotsman at her shoulder. "The Scottish lads refused to go, my lady. It seems they prefer to treat their own ailments."

Expressionless, the big man nodded to him, just a fraction, making Derry smile.

"Does this man have nothing more important to report?" Lord Clifford said suddenly, his voice too loud for the confined space. "We know there is sickness in the camp, Brewer. I imagine there are thieves as well, stealing the kit of their friends. What of it?" He looked around at the others, as if he expected them to throw Derry out into the rain.

Somerset shook his head, choosing to ignore the outburst for more pressing business.

"We await the order to march, my lady. Will it be today? It takes some time to pack up the camp and the light is already fading. I'd like the men to be ready to move."

Silence came in the tent, as every man there turned to catch Margaret's reply. Twin frown lines appeared between her eyes and Derry noted she picked at the skin of a thumbnail with the second finger of her right hand as she stood there. He understood her worry, with so many senior lords looking to her. She had *insisted* on their obedience, forcing her rank and right to do so down their throats. This was the price, that she had to give an order that might send them all to their deaths. Every man there had some personal reason for taking the field against York, but the responsibility was hers, for her husband and her son.

Margaret began to speak and then strangled the sound as it came out, turning it into a long breath. She had witnessed a terrible slaughter at Blore Heath and seen entire armies torn apart at Northampton by Warwick and March. She had traveled hundreds of miles to gather enough men to march on London and save the king. Long before they were ready, York had come into the north.

The decision had been forced by his presence. All Margaret had to do was risk everything. The finger picking at her thumbnail increased its urgency, so that Derry could hear the click as it snagged. His heart went out to her as the silence went on. She had brokered with Tudors and Scots to win their support. Her own son was promised, her own future wagered on a single throw. Derry could understand how she might fear to extend her arm and toss the dice once again. If York wrested another triumph from the men in that tent, she had nothing else to give.

"My lord Somerset tells me caution wins no wars," Margaret said at last. Something eased in her expression, some terrible tension vanishing from her frame. Her fingers stopped their feverish clicking and fell limp. She took in a sharp breath, almost a gasp. "Pass the order to break camp, my lords. We will take the field against York's army and whoever stands with him. Remember that you fight to save the King of England, held by foul traitors. You are on the side of right. God's blessing and my thanks go with you all."

Her head dipped as she finished, some of the brittle fierceness fading so that she once again looked tired and sad. The gathered lords bowed and thanked her in gruff chorus, released from the traps and already moving out to their men.

Derry was left almost alone with the queen, though the Scotsman too had remained, watching him closely. After the deal she had made beyond the border, they had clearly decided to protect her long enough to see it through. Derry winked at the big man, making him drop a hand to the hilt of a long knife in his belt in reply.

"I might have asked if you had any special instruction for me, my lady, though perhaps it is not yet *private* enough." He inclined his head theatrically at the dour warrior.

The man simply stared back.

Margaret twisted a thread of her hair around her fingers, tighter and tighter. Her tone was bleak as she replied.

"You always said your work ends when the fighting begins, Derry. You have been more help to me than I could ever say, but the fighting has come. I suppose it will be settled now by archers and knights and men-at-arms." She squeezed her eyes shut for an instant. "Derry, I have seen Salisbury command before. I saw him destroy an army three times the size of his own at Blore Heath. I do not know enough to fear York on the field, but I do fear Salisbury. Will you stay close to me?"

"Of *course* I will! As for the rest, you have good men in Somerset and Percy, my lady. You need not worry. Somerset is a fine commander. His father taught him well and the lads trust him. From what I can see, he has a gift for it—and he's not above taking advice. None of them love York, Margaret. They know the stakes and they won't falter, I promise you. Even the Scots, probably."

The big man at Margaret's shoulder gave a grunt of irritation, making her chuckle.

"Don't prod the man, Derry. He would tear you in half."

"Well, he's half my age and twice my height, almost," Derry said. "Though I think I could worry him a little first."

The Scot smiled slowly, showing what he thought of that suggestion.

"I should have my horse brought up, Derry," Margaret said. "Is yours nearby?"

"Retribution? I hardly need to tie him up, he loves me so. He is as loyal as a hound, my lady."

Margaret smiled, appreciating his efforts to bring her cheer.

"Let us hope his name is a good omen, then."

CHAPTER 31

Sandal Castle lay at the heart of a hundred and twenty thousand acres, almost two hundred square miles of land. As well as farms and forest, entire towns and a dozen parishes lay within the bounds of the estate, with every church, farm, or merchant business paying tithes to their liege lord. It was true that York preferred Ludlow Castle as his family home, but he still felt himself relax as he and Salisbury reached the edge of his holdings and rode the last few miles of road to the fortress.

As with all his outlying estates, Sandal was run in his absence by a trusted steward, the fortress kept ready for him. It had long been York's habit to visit each of his great houses at least twice every year, spending enough time there to count the incomes and assess all the costs of staff and supplies, anything from new blocks of stables to dredging a local river to prevent flooding. Almost as soon as the army with York and Salisbury had crossed the outer boundary, news went racing ahead and Sir William Peverill was disturbed in his private rooms within the castle, so that the steward came out and took charge. Peverill was far from a young man and yet the routines for the return of the duke were long established and caused him no especial worry. In the closest village of Sandal Magna, servants who had gone home for Christmas were summoned back at their best speed, rushing along the road to the castle in great panting groups to be there to welcome York.

Before the duke reached the foot of the long hill that led directly to Sandal, Peverill had revised his estimate of the meat required three times, shouting questions back at those who rushed in with news in a tone of growing disbelief. Butchers and their boys were sent out with cleavers to the barns well away from the main walls. Pigs in straw-covered pens, chickens and even drowsy geese were sheltered there from the winter cold. With talk of thousands of soldiers on the road, they would all have to be slaughtered for the spits. The twelve days of Christmas were still upon them and Sir William knew York would expect some sort of feast. The castle steward had the main kitchen fires stoked as well as two others in the undercroft basements that only saw use at celebrations. All over the fortress, boys and maids ran in all directions, dusting and cleaning, wiping windows and struggling into their best clothes.

York and Salisbury rode together at the head of the column, though they kept their scouts out for miles in all directions, even there. Salisbury had never visited Sandal before and he found himself impressed at the quiet order of the estate as it appeared from the outside. He could not see the frenzy of preparation going on within its walls. The paths and fields were well tended and dozens of charcoal-makers came from their winter huts in the forest to watch the column pass and raise their caps to their lord.

As the ranks marched slowly up the hill, the wind seemed to increase in speed with every step, biting at their hands and faces until they were all numb and shivering. Salisbury could see tiny figures on the highest level of the keep itself, far above the rest of the fortress.

He winced at the thought of spending a night up there to watch for enemies. The land had been cleared around Sandal for half a mile in every direction. Beyond those open fields, thick forest began that stretched across hills into the distance on all sides.

There was only one entrance to the actual fortress, over a deep moat designed to frustrate cavalry or marching men. York glanced into it with interest as they approached the gatehouse, seeing a few feet of water from the incessant winter rains. The drawbridge was down for his approach under banners and he and Salisbury stepped across the narrow gap together, passing beneath the gatehouse and through walls twelve feet thick at the base.

Salisbury guided his horse to one side with York, and the marching ranks came through the gate as if there would never be an end to them. The space beyond was a horseshoe of no more than two acres, surrounding another steep drop to a fist-like block of a barbican in dark gray stone, some thirty feet below the main yard. In time of war, it would have been a second obstacle, packed with soldiers and joined by its own drawbridge. The barbican guarded the only path up to the keep, rising above all the rest. That tower had been built on the crest of its own hill, the final defense if the castle was ever breached. Even to reach it, any attacking force would have had to fight their way across two moats and then uphill and over a third drawbridge. When that was pulled back, the keep was utterly isolated from the rest.

Sandal had none of the grace Salisbury had seen in Ludlow, or his own home of Middleham. It had been built for war, though never with the expectation of eight thousand men cramming inside its walls. Across the far end of the horseshoe, a line of wooden buildings lay close by the outer walls, with doors open and servants standing in ranks to welcome their liege lord. Soldiers streamed in past them, heading briskly out of the wind and cold, so that the latecomers found every room and corridor packed and had to struggle back to find a spot to rest in the yard. Still, they came in, until there was no space in the fortress that did not have a man sitting on it and looking around eagerly for food. Far above their heads, the banners of the house of York were raised on the keep, flung out by the gusting wind to show he was in residence once more. York watched his colors rise with a low curse and sent a man into the barbican and up to the highest point to have them taken down.

As night fell, lamps and candles were lit along every inner wall and a number of braziers brought out for shivering men to cluster around in the yard. As well as the joints carried back in by blood-stained butchers, every basement and winter store was ransacked for hams, ale, huge green joints of bacon with the knob of the bone showing, even pots of honey and preserved fruit—anything at all that might have a chance of satisfying the appetites of so many hungry soldiers.

Salisbury was one of those given a suite of rooms. York's son Edmund took it upon himself to show him the way, making polite and slightly awkward conversation down an endless track of corridors and halls. Two servants went with them, stopping on either side of a door and standing stiffly.

"This one is empty, my lord," Edmund said. "These two will wash or repair anything you might need."

"I needed only to know where I would sleep," Salisbury replied. "Give me just a moment and I will rejoin your father." He vanished inside and Edmund waited impatiently, held by the demands of courtesy to a guest, even in such unusual circumstances.

The baggage carts were still being unloaded outside the castle, so Salisbury had little with him. True to his word, he returned after a short time. He'd shed his sword and baldric, as well as his outer coat. He'd clearly found time to dip his hands in a bowl of water and he ran them through his hair as he and Edmund walked back along their route.

"You remind me of your father, when he was a young man," Salisbury said suddenly.

Edmund grinned.

"Though I am taller, I believe, my lord."

Both men considered Edward in that moment, and Salisbury was intrigued at the frown that flickered across the young man's face.

"Your brother Edward is the second tallest I have ever seen, after Sir John de Leon, when I served in France. Sir John was not so well made, however, not . . . um, handsome."

"Handsome, my lord?" Edmund said, smiling.

Salisbury shrugged, too old to be embarrassed.

"Yes, I'd say so. Sir John was both the tallest and the ugliest man I have ever encountered. An unfortunate fellow, all in all. He could throw a barrel, of his own weight, twice his height into the air. A fair test and not one I have ever seen beaten. Sadly, despite his great strength, he could not run. He shambled, Edmund, far too slowly as it turns out, at least when it came to French cannon fire."

"Ah. I'm sorry to hear that, my lord. I would have liked to see my brother meet a man who could make him look up." Edmund spoke with wry humor and Salisbury found himself liking the lad.

"I'm sure you have heard the phrase, but you know, it is not the size of the dog in the fight . . ."

". . . but the size of the fight in the dog," Edmund replied, delighted. "Yes, my lord. I have heard it."

"There's truth in those words, Edmund. Your father, for example, is no great giant of a man, but he does not give up, no matter the odds. It is a good thing he has old fellows like me to counsel him, eh?"

"He admires you greatly, my lord. That much I know."

They had reached the door of the main hall and Edmund pushed it open. It was more brightly lit than the corridor outside and he could hear his father's voice suddenly louder.

"I will leave you here, my lord. I must see to the kitchen staff, if there's to be food served."

Salisbury paused on the threshold.

"If you should . . . happen to come across a cold chicken, say, even a bit of bread or rice pudding, you'll remember where I am?"

Edmund chuckled, nodding.

"I'll see what I can find, my lord."

Salisbury went in, feeling the heat of the huge fire as well as the crowd of men inside. The chimney was not drawing particularly well and smoke lay thick in the room, so that those closest were coughing. Three small dogs were rushing about in wild excitement, one of them stopping to pee against a man's leg, so that a great shout went up from his companions while he roared and tried to kick it away. Salisbury was grateful for the warmth and swung close to the fire as he made his way to York.

"Your son is a good lad," Salisbury said.

York looked up from a table laid with maps.

"Who, Edmund? Yes, though I might wish his mother had not sent him to me. I'm tempted to order him back to Ludlow, until this is over."

"He, er . . . he wouldn't like that, I believe. He wants to impress you."

"All sons do," York said, a little more sharply than he intended. "Sorry. My mind is on a dozen other things. Let me pour wine for you." As soon as Salisbury had a full cup, York traced a line on the parchment with his finger. "There. I've sent a rider south to Warwick, on a fast horse."

"And west? Whatever the Tudors intend, we could use the three thousand with Edward."

York fiddled with the cups and jug again before shaking his head.

"No, not yet. Our second army will reach us in . . . three days, four at the most. If Warwick brings six thousand, yes, perhaps we'll need to strip Wales. Yet he could bring twelve or fifteen, even! Your boy is a popular man in Kent, Richard—and Scales gave them fresh scores to settle. They'll come against a king's army, I think. Even in winter."

York's eyes were wary and Salisbury wondered if the duke intended to keep his heir away from danger. With so many listening ears around them, Salisbury could not ask. Even as he tried to frame the question delicately, the doors opened and huge trays of food were carried in by sweating servants. A cheer went up from the gathered men, echoed all around the castle and its grounds as the kitchen staff found mouths to feed.

They had marched two hundred miles on poor rations and they fell on the dishes like the starving men they were, stripping them clean and then wiping fingers around the edges of the platters in search of the last traces of grease. Salisbury looked on in dismay until he felt a touch on his shoulder and saw Edmund had returned with a wooden trencher of cold meats and a half loaf.

"No rice pudding?" Salisbury said. "I'm joking. Bless you, lad, for remembering." His stomach was growling.

Edmund smiled and bowed, heading back to his own meal in the kitchens.

York had barely noticed the exchange as he pored over his maps. Salisbury joined him at his elbow, sharing the trencher as he and York ate and drank standing up. They could both hear rain spattering against the roof, increasing in force until it was a hissing roar.

"I don't envy the men outside," York said grimly, "but Sandal is too small for so many. Warwick will have to camp on the cleared land, when he comes. I don't think we could squeeze one more soldier inside these walls."

"It'll do the men of Kent good to see what a bit of real weather is like," Salisbury said cheerfully. "I only hope they are bringing food north with them." He gestured to the platters only to notice they had all been emptied. "My goodness, Richard. I hope you have stores for winter. These hounds will eat you out of house and home."

He turned back, expecting his friend to smile. To his surprise, York looked uncomfortable.

"I told the cooks to feed as many as they could, but eight thousand! Even a single meal has stripped every larder and storeroom. I'll send out hunting parties tomorrow, if this rain lets up a little."

Salisbury found himself yawning and smiled at the same time, so his jaw cracked.

"You should get some sleep yourself, Richard. Hungry or full, you must rest. You and I are not as young as we were."

"You have a few years on me, old man," York replied. "Anyway, I doubt I could sleep for worrying."

"Well, I cannot stay awake," Salisbury said, yawning mightily once again. The hand he raised to his mouth was copied across the room and many of the men began to settle down where they sat, shoving and cursing for the best places by the fire. The dogs had already curled up and the castle had quietened around them, so that the stillness of a winter night stole upon them all.

"I'm for bed, then," Salisbury said. "If my bones are not too sore tomorrow, I'll bring in a fine buck for you. We'll have a roast in the yard for all those who missed a full share tonight."

York looked up from his maps for just an instant, smiling as the older man winked and made his way across the crowded floor.

In the darkness, Derry Brewer cursed to himself, muttering under his breath as he trudged through leaf litter and felt his cloak snag on brambles for the thousandth time. He held up his lamp, but without opening the shutters it gave barely enough light for him to see his feet. The cloak tugged against his throat, choking him. In a temper, he pushed on like a horse in harness until the cloth tore free and sent him staggering. One of his boots sank into a pool of water up to his ankle.

The forest was a frightening place at night, especially for one city born and bred. Derry had never gone poaching, unless robbing a butcher's shop counted. The trees were not so much black as utterly invisible, with ferns and thorns clustered so deeply between them that he felt his skin was torn to ribbons already. He'd stopped to suck a wound on his hands a dozen times. More than once, he'd found small thorns embedded there for him to worry out with his teeth. The worst of it was when he'd startle some sleeping animal, so that it would explode against his legs, all terror and wet fur and wide eyes, barely glimpsed in his lamplight before whatever beast it was crashed through the undergrowth, hooting in warning. So far away from the haunts of man, Derry also failed to understand why any bird would roost on the ground, only to startle him with suddenly beating wings as he stepped past. Given a choice, he would have preferred the rookeries in London.

He looked left and right, checking once again that he was keeping up with the line of lamps. They stretched as far as he could see in both directions as the army made their way deeper and deeper into the forest. Somerset had ordered silence on the outskirts, but still men swore and cursed as branches slapped their faces, bent back by those going before. Those who had armor were the only ones who could stride through the thickest briars, though even they could snag a foot, and when they fell, it made enough noise to wake heaven. Derry raised his eyes in disgust as one of them did just that, not forty paces away, some knight shouting a curse at the top of his voice as he twisted his ankle. If their business hadn't been so serious, Derry would have seen the humor in it. As things were, he staggered grimly on with the rest, feeling as if every thorn or stinging branch, every plunging hole or drift of wet leaves, sucked away some of his strength. They were just past midwinter and the nights were at their longest, but this one seemed to have no end at all.

The line of lamps moved on. Trees dribbled fat drops above them, soaking them through. The rain had stopped for a time, but under the canopy the pattering went on for much longer, adding to their misery. The only glimmer of pleasure for Derry Brewer was that men like that pompous ass, Clifford, had been forced to dismount and trudge with the rest. He hoped the man fell into a badger sett, or better still, was bitten by something vicious.

It had not been luck that had placed scouts around Sandal Castle, watching for York's forces. Derry Brewer had sent those men out days before and yet, when he'd suggested it, Clifford had merely snorted at him and peered down his nose. By the time the scouts returned with news of York's army, the baron was nowhere to be seen and Derry had not been able to enjoy the man's embarrassment.

Thick clouds made any glimpse of the moon or stars impossible, even if they could have seen through a canopy that would have looked much the same before the Romans had come. As he grew weary, Derry worried that they would either miss the fortress completely in the dark, or worse, break out onto the cleared land as the sun came up. He had never actually seen Sandal Castle and it was hard to make plans without that detailed knowledge.

He took a moment to peer into his lamp, checking the candle

within was not about to burn out. He saw the wick was sitting in a pool of tallow and searched his pouches for a replacement stub. It was much easier to light a new one from the old rather than trying to strike a flint in the dark, or make his way over to the next man. Without stopping, Derry carefully opened the side of the pewter box, reaching in. He could see the men around him more clearly as he did so, glimpsing a line of striding Scots, all turning to see who was lighting them up. Then the wind gusted and his candle went out, making him swear.

"Keep that noise down!" someone said sharply, twenty paces or so behind.

Derry recognized Clifford's voice and, in the pitch darkness, he was tempted to fall back and land the man a good belt while he couldn't be seen. He clenched his jaw, moving across the line to the next swinging lamp instead. Hundreds of trudging men followed on his heels, needing his point of light to hold them on course. Without it, they'd wander off and vanish in the deep woods, never to be seen again.

CHAPTER 32

S alisbury awoke feeling old. His hips and lower back were just about locked solid, so that he had to sit and stretch out his legs while the sun rose, groaning softly as the aches became sharp pain and then dulled again, loosening. His packs had been unloaded the night before, the servants of Sandal working long after the rest of the castle had gone to sleep. He had no memory of anyone entering his room, but a fresh bowl of water and clean hose and undergarments had been laid out for him. He used a linen cloth to wipe himself down, cleaning away the old sweat and smell of horse from his skin. His questing hands found a thick earthenware pot under the bed and he placed it carefully on the dresser to empty his bladder, sighing to himself with closed eyes before dressing.

A soft knock sounded at the door and Salisbury called "Enter!" admitting two servants.

One carried a leather bundle of shaving materials and the other bore a bowl of steaming water, heated in the castle kitchens. He rubbed his chin, feeling the white bristles. Alice said they made him look like an old man when he let them grow. The fellow stropping a razor on a strip of leather seemed steady enough, but Salisbury was still sorry Rankin was not there. It took a certain level of trust to let another man near his throat with a knife. Salisbury grunted to himself, raising his eyes in amusement at his own caution while he took a seat. As the barber rubbed warm oil into his skin, Salisbury could hear his stomach creaking, close enough to a voice to make him chuckle. Eight thousand men would be waking with the same pangs of hunger and there was nothing for them.

The sun was still rising as Salisbury reached the main yard, stopping at the door and looking out on the packed ground, still in the shadow of the walls so that frost gleamed on every surface. Many of the men were up and about, swinging their arms, blowing and stamping, doing anything they could to bring some life back to numb limbs. Others lay curled up, groaning and snoring in tightly packed groups like sleeping dogs. One enterprising captain was bullying and cajoling out a stream of those who had slept inside, ignoring their drowsy curses and sending half-frozen lads in to warm up. Salisbury approved. Good officers looked after their men.

The earl shivered at the thought of spending the night outside. They were all young men, of course, but with December almost over, the cold was simply brutal. The thought made Salisbury raise his eyes to the keep, already lit gold. Three men stood up at the highest point, watching the cleared land all around the fortress and buffeted by a wind that must have chilled them to the marrow. They were not even allowed a brazier before the sun rose, for fear that the light would spoil their ability to watch for enemies. The men turned slowly as Salisbury watched them, sweeping their gaze back and forth with no sign of alarm.

The earl collared a passing captain and passed on the responsibility of putting a hunting party together. It was one of the perks of his rank that he only had to stand and wait, blowing long plumes of mist through his hands, while the man sent runners to the stables and called for volunteers who wanted first choice of whatever meat they could find. Around thirty men raised their hands at that, the number trebling quickly as news spread of the hunt.

Salisbury crossed the open ground as they began to gather at the gatehouse, fastening his cloak at his throat and wrapping himself in the thick folds. When he'd been young, he'd seen those who complained of the cold as somehow weaker than him. He just hadn't felt it the way they seemed to then, though the passing years had stolen away much of his immunity. The wind seemed to reach over the walls, tugging and blustering at the men so that they staggered with the force of it. At least the sky was clear, a small blessing. Before the sunlight had spread right across the yard, Salisbury had mounted with three knight-captains and two hundred men waiting on foot to flush game. He was pleased to see a dozen carried bows and quivers. They'd need anything they could find to feed so many in the castle, from birds and rabbits even to foxes or wolves unlucky enough to cross their path. The kitchen spits would take any living thing for roasting, though Salisbury hoped most of all to bring back a fine doe or stag.

The soldiers at the gatehouse whistled up to those in the keep. Those shivering men stared out one last time before calling "Clear!" down to them. The massive wooden door was pushed outwards and the portcullis raised. Six soldiers pushed the drawbridge out, dropping it into its ruts over the gap.

Salisbury looked out at a sodden field beyond the outer moat, with patches of water shining in the morning sun. He mounted as the first ranks of archers marched out, chatting and laughing with each other as they went. The forest lay ahead of them, at the end of half a mile of open land, an artificial line marked by the groundskeepers of centuries before and never allowed to grow too close to the castle.

With the gate open, every man within seemed to tense, made suddenly vulnerable, so that hands crept to sword hilts and hundreds stood who had been lying down. Salisbury rode out, feeling his heart beat faster with sheer joy as the exertion brought life to his limbs and blood coursing through him. His hips settled back into aching pain, but he ignored it, looking ahead for the best spot to enter the tree line. By his side and behind him, two hundred men broke into a trot, breathing harder as they strung bows and called out to friends. Behind them, the drawbridge was taken up, leaving a yawning gap down to the moat. The portcullis was winched back down to its slots in the stone and the castle gate was drawn in and barred once more. Salisbury looked back at the castle, seeing one of the guards on the keep raise his hand to them. He replied with the same gesture as his troop of hunters crossed the cleared land and approached the tree line, still in deep shadow.

York came awake suddenly, jerking up in his bed and wondering vaguely what had dragged him from sleep. He had stayed up very late, marking his maps and trying to plan for every possible combination of forces against him. For a moment, he turned over and began to drift back to sleep once again, then another horn sounded, high above his head.

The keep.

He threw himself out of bed, stripping off his bedshift and yanking on tunic and hose without conscious thought, swearing as he found one of his boots had somehow vanished under the bed in the night. His cloak hung over a chair and he grabbed it along with his sword and baldric, stumbling out into the corridor and strapping the weapon over his shoulder and around his waist as he went. The horn sounded again, over and over, the call to arms, to rouse the fortress against an enemy force. York began to run, shoving his loose hair back from where it fell over his face.

He skidded on icy stones as he came out into the yard. On the roof of the keep, the guards were pointing out over the walls. Soldiers were gathering already at the gatehouse, readying weapons and tugging mail shirts over their tunics. York crossed the second drawbridge over the inner moat, rushing through the barbican and hearing yelling voices pass on the threat. Earl Salisbury was outside Sandal, he understood that much. His mind was a fog, still struggling to understand what was going on.

He pounded up stone steps and entered the keep itself, taking internal stairs to the roof where he arrived, panting. York stared over the grassy field to the darker line of forest in the distance. It was a quiet scene and he turned in confusion to the guards watching him.

"What did you see?" he demanded.

The guard captain tensed his jaw, his gaze flickering to a younger man who would not look up from his boots.

"My lord, I was facing south. Young Tennen here said he saw some disturbance in the trees as the hunters went into the forest. It may have been no more than game flushed from hiding, but my orders . . ."

"No, he was right," York replied. "I would rather be dragged from sleep over nothing than surprised in my bed. Look at me, lad. Tell me what you saw."

The young man stumbled over his answer, his eyes glazed as he looked anywhere but at the Duke of York.

"The front ranks went in without a whisper, my lord. All quiet.

Then they gave a shout and I thought I heard fighting. The rest of them rushed forward all at once and then they were gone and I blew the horn. That's all I know, my lord. It were the noise, more than anything I saw. Hunters don't yell, my lord, not as I know it."

York turned away, staring out at deep woods that suddenly seemed to possess a gloomy menace as he peered into them.

"How many went out?"

The guard captain answered him.

"I saw them forming up at the gatehouse, my lord. Two hundred, at least. Some with bows."

"Not brigands, then. Two hundred soldiers would be too many for a few ragged thieves." York cracked his knuckles, his hands clenching.

"You've heard nothing since?" he said to the younger guard.

The man shook his head mutely.

"Stay here then, and keep watch. Call down anything you see at all. There is an army within a day's march of this fortress. If they are in my woods, I want to—"

He broke off as a small group of men came racing out of the trees, sprinting across the open ground. There could have been no more than forty of them, running like hares. York gaped, seeing that they had their eyes on the keep and were gesturing. Some of them pointed back into the shadowy trees behind.

"*Christ!*" York spat, running back down as fast as he could go. He managed to stay on his feet, though the stairs blurred under him and his steps thundered as he crossed the inner drawbridge to the main yard.

"Form on the gate!" he roared across the open ground. "Prepare for attack! My horse! To me."

It felt like the blink of an eye since he had been warm and asleep under the blankets. York shook his head, forcing calm where panic might destroy him. Salisbury was out there and he had come under attack. The only response was to overwhelm whoever was fighting in the trees, to throw every man in Sandal Castle at them.

York saw his son Edmund among those about to pass through the main gate. His heart pounded hard enough to make him feel faint and he reached out and pulled the young man close to him, bending his head to speak.

"Edmund, take the lover's door out, on the west side. You know where it is. Get far away from here and wait out the day." The tiny door was hidden high on the outer wall, invisible to any attacker. Yet York had shown it to his sons, parting thick ivy to show them where one man at a time might escape. Calling it the lover's door hid its true purpose, a secret way out when the fortress was about to fall.

His son looked shocked at the suggestion.

"Is it an attack, then? The queen's forces?"

"I don't know," York snapped. "Either way, you are not part of it, Edmund. Take two men with you and use the door. I can't be worrying about you today."

He reached out and kissed his son on the cheek, embracing him for an instant. "Go!"

Edmund might have spoken again, but his father turned his back as his horse and armor were brought. York sat on a tall stool placed under him, while servants bound and strapped thigh-plates and spurred boots onto his feet. He saw his son was still standing there, looking longingly through the main gate as it opened, revealing the desperate men trying to get back in.

"Go!" York roared at him, startling Edmund into movement.

York stepped away from the stool in a sudden motion as the hunters came rushing past. He grabbed one of them by the jerkin, almost taking him off his feet with the violent check to his speed.

"Who attacks us?" York demanded.

"I didn't see any colors, my lord. I thought I heard them call 'Percy,' but they were coming from all directions and I was—"

"How many? Where is Salisbury?" York shouted, making the man cringe in fear.

"I didn't see, my lord! There were many men, but the trees! I don't . . ."

With a growl, York shoved him aside. His men were pouring out across the drawbridge, forming ranks outside the fortress like grain spilling over the land, shuffling aside to let more and more come out into the light.

York went out to them as soon as he was encased in armor, walking his mount through and holding his helmet and sword in one hand. Outside the walls, he could feel the wind that blasted across the open ground, carrying the scent of ice with it. He shoved his helmet down, fastening the strap at his throat. He nodded to the soldier who offered his clasped hands, putting his metal boot onto them and mounting in one swift movement. He heard the man curse as a spur sliced the ball of his thumb, but York didn't look down. Instead, he raised and then sharply dropped his hand.

The captains roared the order to march while half their number were still inside the fortress. Sandal had not been designed for thousands trying to get out, but York was imagining Salisbury being brought down like dogs on a bear. He could feel every passing moment as a stab of fear and anger, and he would not wait. He walked his horse with the line, staring at the dark trees with something approaching dread. His head jerked up to listen as a horn sounded somewhere in that thicket of shadow and green shade, a thin weak sound, far away.

"With me!" York bellowed along the line. He dug in his spurs and his horse jerked into a trot, the reins held like bars of metal along its neck.

The men doubled their pace, jogging across the field with him, leaving the castle and safety behind.

SALISBURY CRIED OUT IN PAIN as something whirred past his eyes, striking his shoulder and vanishing into the bushes. His horse reared, kicking out at someone below as they grabbed for his reins. The forest had come alive with men, running in silently from every direction. Salisbury had turned and turned again, thanking God he had brought his sword and swinging it in great arcs that kept them away. The men with him were fighting savagely to keep themselves alive and the earl safe. He wasn't certain by then which way Sandal Castle even lay, but he knew he had to break free, if he was to have any chance at all.

They'd barely entered the deep wood when the assault had begun. Salisbury still had no idea if the enemy had been waiting for him, or if he'd sprung an ambush before they were ready. None of that would matter if he couldn't get back, yet the chances were vanishing before his eyes as the soldiers around him were cut down. Most of his hunting party wore mail shirts, garments so valuable that they would never be left behind. They had no shields though, and precious few heavy blades, just daggers and small axes that a man might carry on his belt. Those who sprang at them in the gloom between the trees swung war-axes and long swords and wore helmets and mail of their own.

On the far edge, some of Salisbury's men broke and ran, cursed by those they left behind. He could understand it, God knew he could understand it. Wherever he looked, men were creeping up on him and his sword arm was growing tired. They seemed to rise out of the thick bracken, faces scratched and torn and stained green, teeth bared as they grabbed his men and struck and struck until they breathed blood and fell.

One of his hunters had tried to blow a horn, the sound barely begun before an arrow slotted through his chest and he collapsed. Another snatched it up and tried to run and blow the note at the same time. He was stopped by a mailed arm held out like a bar, so that he crashed down to his back, and flung the horn to a third. That man blew a long note and somehow lost his nerve in doing so, sprinting away through the thick undergrowth with three enemy soldiers on his trail.

Salisbury looked around, feeling terror and a sense of helplessness. There was no end to them, and his men were being murdered all around. He dug in his heels and the horse lunged over a bush, snorting and screaming in thick panting breaths. The earl saw a man running between two trees and launching himself in a great leap at him. He swung his sword and felt the blade cut before he was sent tumbling onto his back. His horse bolted then and Salisbury could only watch it go, stirrups flying wild.

A bearded man dropped onto him, appearing from nowhere. Salisbury struggled, but he was much weaker. The man was snarling in Scots Gaelic as he brought an ax up over his head.

"Pax! Ransom!" Salisbury yelled, seeing every pore and scratch on the man's wild face.

To his relief, his attacker got off him and backed away, breathing hard and leaning on the long handle of the ax, watching him. As Salisbury sat up and tried to speak, the young Scot lunged with sudden speed and punched him into blackness.

York heard the horse before he saw it. His own mount was struggling through the trackless forest, forced away from the wandering threads of animal paths by the need to keep in line with his men. He reined in at the sound of pounding hooves and his heart sank when he recognized Salisbury's mount, running berserk and already battered by all the thorns and branches it had scraped through. The panicking animal saw no way through the line of men and they held shields up to it, forcing it to come to a skidding halt and spinning in place, kicking out.

"Let it through!" York cried out to them, pressing on. "They can't be far away now."

He could see some of the path the animal had made and he tried to follow it back, though it jinked and turned so many times it was almost impossible. He thought he could hear a noise ahead and he held his arm out straight until his captains saw it and repeated the gesture, halting the lines of men in silence.

The woods became still, all animals and birds long fled from their presence. York craned to catch the direction he needed and then made out the sounds of moving men, the calls and voices of enemies in his forest. On his land.

He pointed over to the source of the sounds and as his men marched forward once again, they saw the forest move ahead of them, a line of soldiers that seemed to stretch as far as they could see. The ranks with him were sighted at the same time and a great howl went up on both sides. York raised his shield and slammed his visor down, bringing his sword up for the first blow.

The armies crashed together and there was no room for maneuvers or formations. One line buckled against the other and every death was a sweating, grunting murder, close enough to breathe the same air and be spattered by the other man's blood when he went down. York struck and struck at anyone he could reach, using the height of his mount and his long sword to terrible effect. Yet in the moments between each blow, he could see a host of soldiers coming on the left and right. He was being flanked by a larger force. York gave a cry of grief for Salisbury, but he had no choice.

"Fall back in good order! Keep your faces to them, but fall back on the castle."

He roared the order again and heard his captains repeat it at the top of their voices, already stepping back. It was a hard business and some of them were just London lads, rough-trained and overwhelmed by a savagery they had not known to expect.

The enemy soldiers heard his order and pushed on. York set his jaw when he saw some of them wore blue and yellow. Percy men, come to take revenge for all the masters they had lost. He moved back in circles, wheeling his mount and trotting for a dozen paces before turning again and facing those who pressed in. He could not recall how far he had come from the castle, not with any certainty. Every step was hard, with ax-wielding, roaring men rushing against them, sweeping blades across as if they were scything barley. York's soldiers fell and scrambled up as they retreated, trying to present a wall of shields, but still watching their feet to avoid the roots and briars. They could not help crowding into the center, looking for support in numbers, though it left the men on the flanks to be thinned out and cut down.

York circled back once again and saw a brightening ahead. He prayed to God it was not a simple break in the foliage. He crossed himself and gave the order they wanted to hear.

"Now. Run and re-form in the open!" His men were pelting away while he still shouted and he had to canter to stay abreast of them, his horse leaping bushes and coming out into the winter sun and wind. He had not been wrong. Sandal Castle lay ahead and there were thousands of men rushing to stand in ranks on the clear ground, panting with their hands on their knees and anger in their faces.

The feeling of clean wind and space restored their confidence, making them want to meet the men who had terrified them in the gloomy forest. They raised their weapons and roared a great challenge as the trees vomited soldiers right across the length of the field.

The first ones were met with a clashing line of shields and stabbing swords, but more and more came out, flanking even the massed ranks gathered before Sandal and pouring around them. York turned his horse on the spot, seeing Scottish warriors racing across the ground, holding their swords low until they leaped up, crashing down onto the shields and mail of his men. His heart shrank as he spotted archers trotting out on the flanks, protected by hundreds more who stood with swords and shields before them, so that they could not be reached.

The arrows began to fly a moment later and the battle surged back and forth in front of the castle. All York's forces were committed, with no reserve, nor any way to break the flood of soldiers still coming through the trees in greater and greater numbers. Hundreds of the attackers were killed, but there were always more to hack at his lines, roaring and shoving. Arrows flew like flocks of birds, dropping men, or forcing them to raise their shields so they were vulnerable to a gutting blow beneath.

York was forced back and back with his men, until he sat his horse in the third rank, not fifty yards from the gatehouse of Sandal. He could not retreat over that small drawbridge. Just as it had slowed their leaving, the narrow entrance would be choked with bodies if they tried to gain the safety of the walls. He took a deep breath, closing his eyes and filling his chest with air he had known all his life. When he opened his eyes, he saw Margaret.

The queen rode a chestnut mare, with a dozen bearded Scots as her personal guard. They made a cluster at the very rear of the battlefield, barely out of the trees as she watched. York was no more than three hundred paces from her and he could see her smile. He thought he recognized Derry Brewer at her side and he shook his head.

For an age, York searched the battlefield with his gaze, looking for the slightest hope. The fighting went on around him and every moment brought his men closer to a complete rout. It was finished and he worked his tongue around his mouth, drawing spit enough to speak. Carefully, he sheathed his blade and raised his right hand.

"Peace! I surrender myself. In the name of York, put up your swords." He had to repeat the words at the top of his voice before he was heard.

His men stared up at him in shock, perhaps more in relief. They too could see the way the battle had been going. Those at the rear laid their blades on the ground and raised their hands to show they had done so. York could hear the same command echoed on the other side. The sounds of fighting faded slowly, to be replaced by the cries of the wounded and the dying, suddenly harsh and shocking in that greater silence.

CHAPTER 33

It was no small thing to disarm an army. Men who had borne swords and axes for years developed an affection for them. The owners were reluctant to give them up, just to be thrown onto a pile to rust or to be given to some unworthy sod. The wind pushed and flapped at them all, making them shiver and wrap their arms around themselves now that the heat of the fighting was over.

Lord Clifford took a group of horsemen right around the fortress of Sandal, seeking out any armed men of York who might still be waiting in ambush. On the frozen field, panting soldiers on both sides checked themselves and their equipment, looking for wounds they had not felt before. Many of them cursed to find cuts or even arrow-holes, staring at them in wonder as they hacked strips from their tabards to bind them.

All of York's men were searched for blades. When they had no weapons, Somerset sent his soldiers back to take their mail shirts. They grumbled and cursed, of course, though they knew better than to refuse. Under the trees, the piles of equipment grew: helmets and shields, mail, armor and axes all thrown together. The dead were stripped of anything of value, with even their boots tugged off and piled. After a time, all the corpses were barefoot and the grim soldiers came back among them once more, carrying away the dead to be laid out on the hard ground, folding their arms across their chests.

The work took hours and the sun was over the horizon by the time the first survivors were allowed to leave. In groups of a dozen at a time, those who could walk were pointed south and told to go. Some of them wore masks of frozen blood, or showed new pouting mouths where blades had cut their flesh. Others pressed their hands over seeping holes, or nursed stumps and rocked where they sat, pale and sick with the pain. The ones who would not walk were left to sit and die in the wind, staring at nothing.

Derry Brewer made a point of speaking to a few of York's captains as they turned to leave. Many of the battered, shivering men would walk all the way to their homes, stealing or starving until they were far from Sandal and all the memories of that loss. He did not doubt some of the survivors would be found dead on the road over the next month, while a few would be caught taking food and hanged. Derry merely mentioned that strong ones, unwounded ones, might choose to wait around Sheffield. He told them they might have a chance of joining the ranks of the queen's army as they came south. They laughed at him, but it was a long way home and they had no food. Derry knew some of them would remember and wait. He didn't like to see good men wasted, not with the armies of March and Warwick still unaccounted for.

The sun was heading down into the western hills, staining the sky. York's sword had been taken from him, though he had been left his armor. His horse had been led away and his hands were firmly tied behind his back. Two soldiers took up position near him, growling at those who might have come close to spit or land a blow. They said nothing to him and he waited, left alone while his enemies cleared away the detritus of the battle.

The sunset was deepening in gold and he looked into it until his eyes stung. All around him, the last of his army were slinking away to the southern road, a great stream of slumped figures that reminded him of refugees in France, a decade before. He kept his head up, standing pale and straight as they went past. Some of them muttered curses at him as they went, while many more whispered an apology. He did not respond to any of them, turning back from the sun to the queen and her lords.

When the field before Sandal was almost empty, Derry Brewer strolled across to him.

"There are some who want a word with you. Come on." He took York by the arm and tugged him over the field toward the queen.

York grimaced at his touch.

"I am of noble blood, Brewer. Have a care."

Derry chuckled, though it was not a pleasant sound. He pulled York to the very edge of the woods, where a dozen nobles and the queen herself turned to watch their approach. York raised his head a fraction further, refusing to be cowed by them. His eyes fell on a bound figure, kneeling and swaying on the ground. York smiled in relief at the sight of Salisbury alive, though the old man's head was bloody and his eyes dull.

Derry took the duke right up to Salisbury, tapping him on the shoulder to signal he should kneel. For a moment, York stood unbending, but he could feel rough twine on his wrists and he knew he had no choice but to endure.

He knelt on the muddy ground, cold water seeping into his armor. As he settled himself, Margaret came to stand close to him, her head tilted as she watched him with unnatural intensity. Somerset and

Henry Percy were at her side, looking almost as scratched and be-draggled as York felt himself.

"Should I congratulate you, my lady?" York said. "It seems I am your prisoner."

"I do not need you to tell me that," Margaret said. Her eyes glittered with malice for the man who had captured her husband and disinherited her son. "Where is the king, my lord? That is all I want to hear from you."

"Far away—and safe," York replied. He thought for a moment. "If your intention is to ransom us, perhaps King Henry can be the price."

Margaret closed her eyes, one hand clenching to a fist.

"No, my lord York. No. I have talked and *talked*, all this year. I will not make another deal now. It is over. If you will not tell me where my husband is kept, I have no more use for you." She turned to Somerset, standing in armor with his sword unsheathed. "Take Salisbury's head, my lord. I will find a place for it."

York stiffened in shock and fury.

"How would his death serve your cause? Stand back from him, Somerset!"

He turned in desperation to see Salisbury was watching him, the sinews on his neck standing out like wires. As their eyes met, Salisbury shrugged. His face was swollen and bruised. The earl looked up as Somerset drew his sword and stood at his side.

"God have mercy on my soul," Salisbury murmured. He closed his eyes and leaned his neck forward, shaking.

Somerset raised the sword as high as he could reach and then brought the blade down with huge force, cutting the earl's head free so that it dropped into the mud. The body slumped and leaned sideways as York gaped in horror and grief. He looked up at Margaret and saw his own death in her eyes.

A shout sounded nearby and the nobles around the queen reached for swords, then let their hands fall away as they saw it was Lord Clifford riding back in. The baron smiled as he caught sight of Salisbury's body and York bound and kneeling. He trotted his horse up to them and dismounted, walking the final few paces so that he could look down on York.

"It gives me joy to see you so reduced," Clifford said. "I thank God I came back in time. I caught a young man over by the walls, a couple of lads with him. He said he was your son before I killed him." York stared as Clifford held up his right hand, showing him a punch dagger with bright red blood on it.

The spiteful pleasure in Clifford seemed to sour the moment for Margaret.

"See to your men, baron," she said curtly to him.

Clifford looked wounded, but he obeyed, turning away.

Margaret shook her head, weary and sick.

"You have caused so *much* pain, Richard," she said. "So many fathers and sons have died and all because you would not accept Henry on the throne."

"It was too good a chair for him," York said. "You think you have won a victory?" His voice grew stronger with every word.

The death of Salisbury and the murder of poor Edmund had stunned him, for a time. Something about Clifford's petty, vicious hatred restored his pride like strong wine, making his heart pound. York straightened his back as the Duke of Somerset came to his side. He could sense the bloody sword rising over him and he saw the nod Margaret gave.

"All you have done is release our *sons!*" York shouted. "God save my soul!"

The sword came across and York's head rolled. Margaret let out a slow, shuddering breath.

"There is an end of it," she whispered. "There are good men avenged." She raised her voice to the lords around her. "Take the heads and spike them on the walls of York."

She watched in sick fascination as the grisly items were gathered up together, dripping blood down the arm of the man who held them. Margaret stepped very close, reaching out to touch the slack features of York. Her hand shook like she had palsy.

"Make a paper crown for this one, he who wished to wear a real one. Let the people of York know the price of his ambition."

The soldier nodded, bearing the heads away.

Earl Percy stepped up to Margaret's shoulder, pale at what he had witnessed.

"What now, my lady?"

"Now?" she said, turning to him. "Now to London, to take back my husband."

EPILOGUE

Edward of March brooded. His armor was spattered with blood and clotted dirt and he was weary, though his aching arms felt well used. Darkness was coming on and he could hear the cries of the wounded across the shadowed field, silenced as they were found and their throats cut. His men tramped in files and ranks, armor and mail jingling. There were no shouts of victory, no laughter. The grim mood of the earl had tainted them all. They kept silent as they passed the spot where he rested on a fallen tree, staring out, his great sword across his knees.

His father and brother Edmund were dead, brought down by dogs and lesser men. The news had come on the string of riders between them just days before, as a Welsh army came close enough to attack. March had lost himself for a time, then. He recalled ordering his men into ranks and the way they looked at him with fear on their faces. They had faced four thousand soldiers, with the best archers in the world, but he had ordered them in, even so. The result was all around him, a field of corpses sinking into the mud. He had thrown their lives away in his rage. He had struck and struck until his sword-edge was blunt and yet still crushed and broke with every blow. When his madness had been spent, the battle was won, the last of them running from the weeping giant in iron, who swept them away like leaves.

He did not know how many of his own men lay among the dead. He did not care if he had lost almost all of them. Owen Tudor had been killed, his army of Welshmen slaughtered, his sons forced to run. They had chosen to stand against him and they had failed. That was all that mattered.

Edward heaved himself to his feet, feeling a dozen aches and bruises he had not noticed before. Blood seeped from his side-plates and he winced as he pressed the spot and felt his ribs shift. The night would be long and he turned his face up to the dark sky, longing to feel the light of the sun once again. He lived, he thought in wonder. He had spent the dark passions that had consumed him, emptying himself until he was hollow. He had taken the blood price for his father.

He breathed deeply, recalling the strange vision that had come the morning before the battle. He had watched the sun begin to rise, though there had no longer been any joy in it. As it creased the horizon, two more suns had appeared, one on either side, gleaming eyes of gold that made strange and sickening shadows across the waiting ranks. His men had pointed and gasped, afraid. The darkness had still been coiling in him then. He had stared until he thought he would go blind, feeling the warmth on his bare face.

He did not know if that vision had been his father's last blessing to him. Edward felt as if he had been reborn under the light of that strange trinity. He had been made anew. He was eighteen years old. He was the Duke of York. He was the heir to the throne.

HISTORICAL NOTE

PART ONE: 1454–1455

THE AMBUSH by some seven hundred Percy retainers and servants on the Neville wedding party took place a little earlier than I have it here, in August 1453—around the same time King Henry VI fell into his senseless state. It was a key event among years of low-level fighting between the families as they struggled to control the north and widen their holdings.

That attack by Thomas Percy, Baron Egremont, was one of the most brutal actions in that private war, sparked by the marriage of Salisbury's son to the niece of Ralph Cromwell, a union which placed estates claimed by the Percy family into Neville hands.

The "Battle of Heworth Moor" failed in its main aim of slaughtering Richard Neville, Earl of Salisbury. I have not included a dozen minor skirmishes, but that feud played a key part in deciding where the Nevilles and the Percys stood in the first battle of St. Albans in 1455—and its outcome.

FOR FEAR of introducing too many major characters, I have made little of Exeter's role in the north, a strong and violent ally of the Percys, though he was married to York's eldest daughter. This was truly a civil war, with families torn between the sides. One of York's first acts as Protector was to have his son-in-law Exeter imprisoned in Pontefract Castle, the keys given to

Salisbury. When King Henry recovered in 1455, Exeter was released from Pontefract. Somerset was also released from the Tower and was quickly back at the king's side as his chief adviser.

There is no record of those present at the birth of Edward of Lancaster, only son to Margaret and King Henry. Until very recent times, however, it was common practice to have numerous witnesses to royal births. For example, Queen Victoria's son Albert was born in the presence of the Archbishop of Canterbury, two dukes, and seven other lords. For Edward of Lancaster (sometimes called Edward of Westminster, where he was born) there were indeed rumors that Somerset was the father, though it was likely to have been no more than a slander spread by Yorkist supporters. There is little doubt that Somerset and York hated each other with a bitter intensity.

When Henry VI woke from his stupor on Christmas Day 1454, he had been in a semiconscious state for almost eighteen months. He had no recollection of anything that had taken place over that time, though he was not in a coma, more a dissociative, listless waking dream. He did not remember having been shown his son, Edward, Prince of Wales. Though he had, in theory, been awake and present for the kiss of homage from a new Archbishop of Canterbury, he had no memory of that event either.

In reality, it was two more months into 1455 before King Henry was well enough to travel to London. There, he dismissed York and Salisbury from their posts and set about regaining his authority over the country with a massive Judicial Progress north from London. It was a unique period of energy for the king, completely different to his personality before the collapse. York and Salisbury traveled to Ludlow Castle.

York had ruled with sense and style for his period as Protector and Defender of the Realm. Though not above favoring his Neville allies, he had reduced the size of the king's household, cutting huge numbers of servants, knights, and even horses from the expenses. It is true he confirmed Edward of Lancaster as the royal heir, perhaps because the sympathies of the country were still with the damaged king. In the twenty-first century, it is perhaps a little difficult to comprehend the level of unthinking loyalty King Henry inspired simply by his bloodline and office. A king was anointed by God, with a divine right to rule over lesser houses. To challenge that was literally blasphemy and a path to tread very lightly indeed.

NOTE ON TITLES: While it is true that "Your Majesty" was not the common term for royalty in the reign of King Henry VI, and that "Your Highness" or "Your Grace" would have been more common, it *was* in use, as evidenced by York's letter in May 1455, where he complained to the king about the rumors spread about his "faith, lygeaunce and dewtee" (faith, allegiance and duty) by his enemies "under the whinge (wing) of your Magestee Royal."

NOTE ON THE EARL OF WARWICK, later known as the "Kingmaker": Nothing is known of his childhood, or the way he looked physically. The younger Richard Neville made an extraordinarily fortunate marriage to Anne Beauchamp, daughter of the Earl of Warwick. When the earl died, his son Henry became earl and then died at only twenty-three, leaving a three-year-old daughter who also died.

The rights to the title then passed to Anne—and to her husband, Richard Neville. At the age of barely twenty-one, he became Earl of Warwick, Newburgh, and Aumarle, Baron of Elmley and Hanslape, Lord of Glamorgan and Morgannoc. His new estates were these: land in South Wales and Herefordshire including the castles of Cardiff, Neath, Caerphilly, Llantrussant, Seyntweonard, Ewyas Lacy, Castle-Dinas, Snodhill, Whitchurch, and Maud's Castle. Caerphilly alone was a fortress to resist ten thousand men. In Gloucestershire, another seven wealthy manors. In Worcestershire, three great manors, the castle of Elmley, and twenty-four other manors. In Warwickshire, besides the incredible castle and town itself, nine more manors, including Tamworth. In Oxfordshire, five manors as well as lands in Kent, Hampshire, Sussex, Essex, Hertfordshire, Suffolk, Norfolk, Berkshire, Wiltshire, Somerset, Devon, Cornwall, Northampton, Stafford, Cambridge, Rutland, and Nottingham—another forty-eight manors in all. In the distant north, just one possession: Barnard's Castle on the Tees. So: twelve major castles, a hundred and forty-three manors, from the border of Scotland to Devon, making his union with Anne Beauchamp one of the most materially rewarding in English history. Perhaps it is not surprising that his father's will left him only two chargers (large dishes), twelve smaller dishes, a ewer and basin of silver, a bed, and four untrained horses.

The battle of St. Albans in 1455 was preceded by a number of letters sent to the king by Richard of York, at least two of which were received en route. Although York dared not name Queen Margaret, he pleaded with the king to resist the malign influence of "traitors about the king"—men like the Duke of Somerset. York was convinced King Henry was surrounded by those with ill intent. Again and again, he protested his loyal allegiance, to no avail.

With the forces of Salisbury and Warwick, some three thousand soldiers camped in Key Field, east of St. Albans, to await the king. King Henry's forces arrived around nine or ten in the morning and crossed Halywell stream to head uphill to the open market. Heralds were exchanged and Henry refused all York's demands. It is not known exactly when the fighting began, though the king's party clearly had time to block the three roads in from the east.

There are many examples in history when two forces facing each other will interact and begin a bloody conflict, regardless of the desires of their leaders. Alternatively, Salisbury may have given the order. He, at least, had a very clear desire for conflict, with both Henry Percy, Earl of Northumberland, and Thomas, Baron Egremont, within reach at last. For Salisbury, the moment to repay the attack on his son's wedding and settle old scores was at hand.

It was the twenty-six-year-old Earl of Warwick who broke through back gardens with a small force and ran uphill to the marketplace. Warwick's archers shot along St. Peter's Street and both King Henry and the Duke of Buckingham were struck and wounded in the first moments. It is true that Buckingham was struck in the face, though he survived.

With Warwick's breakthrough, the stalemate at the barricades was at an end. York and Salisbury made a quick entry into the town as soon as those defending the barricades left them to protect the king. In a very short time, the marketplace and surrounding roads were crammed with up to five thousand fighting men, crushed and panicking. Abbot Whethamstede's description of the scene, written after the battle, is especially vivid: ". . . one man with his brain struck out, another with his arm struck off, there a third with his throat cut, there a fourth with his chest pierced, and the whole place beyond filled with the corpses of the slain."

York himself gave the order for the wounded king to be taken to the abbey. The battle might have ended then if the only key players had been Lancaster and York. The exact sequence of events at this point is unknown. I have gone with what I consider to be the most likely scenario, that once the king was taken to the abbey, the real reason for the battle was pushed to its conclusion: the deaths of Somerset and Earl Percy.

It is true that Somerset died under the sign of The Castle pub, fulfilling a prophecy from years before that he would "die under the castle." For years, he had avoided Windsor Castle, to avoid fulfilling the prophecy. One account of the battle says that Somerset came out from The Castle inn and killed four men with an ax before he was brought down.

AS A SIDE NOTE, the Earl of Wiltshire, Henry's treasurer, decided to make his escape from the fray by casting off his armor, heading to the abbey, and disguising himself as a monk. I could not resist giving that part to Derry Brewer.

THE PROCESSION THROUGH LONDON, where York walked hand in hand with Queen Margaret behind the king and gave Henry his crown at St. Paul's Cathedral is a combination of two real events. Historically, the first procession took place just a few days after the battle of St. Albans in 1455 and involved Henry riding through London with York on his right, Salisbury on his left, and Warwick ahead, carrying the king's own sword. That "joyous occasion" ended at St. Paul's Cathedral, where the king apparently insisted on being handed his crown by York. Assuming he understood what was going on, that humiliation must have been exquisitely painful for Henry. The second procession was later, when York walked hand in hand through London with Margaret as a public display of healed rifts. The sad truth is that the king was a mere puppet of York at this point. His most powerful lords had been killed at St. Albans and four years would pass before the House of Lancaster was once again in a position to fight back.

PART TWO: 1459–1461

THE YEARS MISSING from this novel were not entirely without incident. King Henry suffered another collapse, allied to a fear of the sight of blood that he developed and never lost. York was appointed Protector for a second time—and for a second time, the king returned to London and removed him from his post. Repetition does not make a good tale, though admittedly the difference there was that Henry had not fully recovered his will and wits. Though York was dismissed, he was allowed to continue in various roles of government and authority. At one point, York was sent north to deal with Scots rebelling on his behalf as rightful king! His mere presence was enough to end it, as can be imagined.

King Henry spent a large part of those years either sleeping or at prayer and his health was always poor. It fell to Margaret to challenge the threat to her family, and it is from this period that she became known as an arch-manipulator—a charge and historical view that I have always considered harsh. It is true that she took her husband to Kenilworth and had the castle fortified with twenty-six serpentine cannon and a culverin. Those weapons had an extreme (and extremely inaccurate) range of around a mile, but they would have been devastating within four hundred yards, making the castle impregnable at that time. Yet what else could Margaret have done if not fight to protect her husband and her son?

Estimates of numbers recruited by Queen Margaret as "Queen's Gallants" vary. The army at Blore Heath was in the range of six to twelve thousand. Around the same number agreed indentures to fight for King Henry if he were threatened. The only difficulty then was to create the threat. The Bill of Attainder used to force the hand of York and Salisbury was employed for this purpose, an incredibly powerful and rarely used aspect of English law that could end a noble house and remove all protections and titles. Margaret's council of trusted men included Sir John Fortescue, the most senior judge in England. He would have been vital in the creation of the bill. The mere possibility of such a thing being used was enough to bring York, Salisbury, and Warwick back to the field, as Margaret desired.

NOTE ON BLORE HEATH: Sometimes described as the true opening of the Wars of the Roses, the Queen's Gallants were defeated by Salisbury's better use of tactics and terrain. His scouts spotted Lord Audley's ambush and he halted and secured his right flank with a laager of carts. Hempmill Brook lay between them and Salisbury staged a false withdrawal to bring the Gallant horsemen forward, then attacked, killing hundreds. Baron Audley led the counterattack, only to be killed in the fighting. It is said three thousand Lancastrian men lost their lives, to around a thousand of Salisbury's, though to have survived against such a host was no mean feat. Salisbury continued his march south to Ludlow, though he paid a local friar to fire a cannon on the heath all night to confuse potential Lancastrian reinforcements. There is a legend that Queen Margaret observed the battle and no real reason to doubt it, especially as it contains the interesting detail that she had a smith reshoe her horse with the shoes the wrong way round, to confuse any pursuers. The Gallants were her first army, pledged to her, after all. It makes sense that she would have wanted to see them in action against her enemies.

NOTE ON EDWARD, EARL OF MARCH: In modern times, a height of 6 foot 4 inches is not particularly rare and examples can be found in most gatherings of a hundred people and above. The average modern male height (inexplicably low to my eye) is around 5 foot 8. For the fifteenth century, when the best-guess average height of men was between 5 foot 3 and 5 foot 7, the eighteen–year-old Earl of March would have been a Goliath on the field of war. The equivalent today would be a warrior in iron who stood 6 foot 9 to10 inches (the height of the author Michael Crichton, by the way) and yet a man who could fight and move with enormous speed and strength. The effect of such a warrior on a hand-to-hand battle can hardly be overestimated.

It is socially interesting to note that diet is a key factor in height. Medieval noblemen ate fish and meat rather more often than commoners. As a group, they would have been taller than most other classes in the country, an advantage of strength and power that would have been increased by constant training from the earliest years.

EDWARD OF MARCH returned to England from Calais with Warwick in the late summer of 1459, responding to the threat of Attainder and marching quickly to meet up with the forces of York and Salisbury. They would return to complete disaster at Ludlow, with all hopes dashed and all the major players forced to flee. It is true that Captain Andrew Trollope refused to fight against an army apparently led by his king. His desertion with six hundred of the Calais garrison was the turning point of the battle and the cause of York's downfall. Trollope was later knighted for his service.

After that desertion, the "battle" of Ludford Bridge was practically bloodless. The king's army had surrounded a much smaller force and barely skirmished with the defenders. York, Salisbury, Warwick, and March made an extraordinary decision to leave. It is perhaps worth pointing out that the idea of slaughtering York's wife and children would not have seemed likely. York went to Ireland and Salisbury, Warwick, and March escaped back to Calais, arriving in November 1459. By any standards, it was a complete disaster and should have been the end of their cause. It must therefore be some testament to their energy and abilities that it was not.

WHEN RESEARCHING HISTORICAL FICTION, one of the joys is occasionally coming across scenes that are simply wonderful—and even better when they are not well known. In an action that could have graced any Hornblower story, Warwick stole a royal fleet from Kent, roping ships together and sailing them back to France, in January 1460.

On the second of July, he used that fleet to land an army on the English coast at Sandwich. With his father and Edward of March, they marched seventy miles through Kent, picking up around ten thousand Kentish men as they went. Some of them would certainly have walked that path before, with Jack Cade.

It is a matter of historical record that Lord Scales commanded the royal garrison at the Tower and that both cannon and wildfire were used against the London mob as they rioted. A royal arms depot across the river was raided and cannon were brought to bear on the Tower's outer wall, smashing it down. It is true that Scales managed to barricade the broken wall and survived long enough to surrender. He was then murdered in custody.

LEAVING A SMALL FORCE in London under Salisbury, Warwick and March raced north. Their speed paid off as they intercepted King Henry with only five thousand men, before the main royal forces could reinforce the king's position. The attack was aided by the sudden betrayal of Baron Gray of Ruthin. He changed sides at a vital moment, abandoning King Henry and supporting Warwick and March in exchange for a promise that he would be made Royal Treasurer.

Just eight days and a hundred and fifty miles after landing in Kent, Henry was captured and Margaret forced to run into Wales with her son, Edward of Lancaster. It was an extraordinary feat of tactics, arms, and endurance. It is true that Warwick and March found Henry alone in his tent.

IT WAS INTERESTING to include Owen Tudor in this story, mostly because of his more famous descendants. He had married Catherine de Valois, widow of Henry V. His two sons, Jasper and Edmund, would both play their part in the Wars of the Roses—and the Tudor period after it.

It is true that King James II of Scotland died in August 1460, when a cannon exploded during a siege. His son was ten years old and Queen Mary of Guelders would have had to meet and negotiate with Margaret without him, her grief still fresh. Margaret gained her support, perhaps because she was dealing with another foreign queen who had suffered great loss.

The exact number of Scots who returned south is unknown, though it must have been thousands to make it worth doing at all. The agreement was for Prince Edward to marry a princess of Scotland—and for Berwick-upon-Tweed to be handed over as payment. Margaret had her army and a huge force gathered that winter, by the city of York. It is true that the cold months usually made battles impossible. Only the extreme circumstance of Henry being captured could have brought so many to the field as the year ended.

In late December 1460, York and Salisbury found they were vastly outnumbered as they arrived in range of the Lancastrian forces. The best estimates are that they had around eight thousand men, compared to sixteen to eighteen thousand under Somerset, Northumberland, and Clifford. All three of those men had lost their fathers at St. Albans.

York and Salisbury holed up in Sandal Castle to await reinforcements, packing men into the small fortress. The reason they sallied out is not known. Given the small size of Sandal, it might have been because they were running out of food, or because they were drawn out by the sight of a small hostile force and then ambushed. However it happened, they left the castle and were defeated on December 30, 1460. York was killed in the battle. Salisbury was captured and beheaded, and York's son Edmund was killed by Lord Clifford as he tried to flee the field.

No one knows if Margaret was truly present at the Battle of Wakefield, but there is something very personal about York's head being made to wear a paper crown. Shakespeare chose to place her at the battle in *Henry VI, Part 3.*

MARGARET OF ANJOU had won her revenge. She had survived against the odds to see her two most powerful enemies beaten and beheaded. Yet I was struck by the tragedy of York. For all York's ambition, King Henry was helpless and in his power for months, held at Fulham Palace, the residence of the Bishop of London. We will never know York's most private reasons, but the fact remains that he did not make Henry disappear, when doing so would have won York the crown. He was a complex man and no clear villain. I could not escape the strong sense that neither York nor the house of Lancaster particularly wanted the struggle. Each house was forced into war, out of fear of the other.

With the deaths of York and Salisbury at Sandal Castle, Margaret seemed to have won. Yet in the end, what she had truly done was unleash their sons.

THE PHENOMENON WITNESSED by Edward of March, then Duke of York and heir to the throne, in February 1461, is known as "parhelion." It involves the reflection of the sun, so that three suns appear to rise. They are also known as "sundogs." At the time, Edward convinced his men it was a sign of the Holy Trinity and a good omen for the Battle of Mortimer's Cross, where Owen Tudor was killed. Edward would later take the symbol as his own, surrounding the white rose of York with the flames of the sun.

CONN IGGULDEN
London, 2014